THE FALLEN
CHARLIE HIGSON

Charlie Higson started writing when he was ten years old, but it was a long time before he got paid for doing it. On leaving university he was the singer in a pop group (The Higsons) before giving it up to become a painter and decorator. It was around this time that he started writing for television on *Saturday Night Live*. He went on to create the hugely successful comedy series *The Fast Show*, in which he also appeared. Other TV work includes *Randall and Hopkirk (Deceased)* and *Swiss Toni*.

He is the author of the bestselling Young Bond books, and *The Fallen* is the fifth book in his current horror series, The Enemy.

Charlie doesn't do Facebook, but you can tweet him @monstroso.

THE FALLEN

CHARLIE HIGSON

PENGUIN BOOKS

PENGUIN BOOKS

Published by the Penguin Group
Penguin Books Ltd, 80 Strand, London WC2R ORL, England
Penguin Group (USA) Inc., 375 Hudson Street, New York, New York 10014, USA
Penguin Group (Canada), 90 Eglinton Avenue East, Suite 700, Toronto, Ontario, Canada M4P 2Y3
(a division of Pearson Penguin Canada Inc.)
Penguin Ireland, 25 St Stephen's Green, Dublin 2, Ireland (a division of Penguin Books Ltd)
Penguin Group (Australia), 707 Collins Street, Melbourne, Victoria 3008, Australia
(a division of Pearson Australia Group Pty Ltd)
Penguin Books India Pvt Ltd, 11 Community Centre, Panchsheel Park, New Delhi – 110 017, India
Penguin Group (NZ), 67 Apollo Drive, Rosedale, Auckland 0632, New Zealand
(a division of Pearson New Zealand Ltd)
Penguin Books (South Africa) (Pty) Ltd, Block D, Rosebank Office Park, 181 Jan Smuts Avenue,
Parktown North, Gauteng 2193, South Africa

Penguin Books Ltd, Registered Offices: 80 Strand, London WC2R ORL, England

penguin.com

First published 2013
001

Text copyright © Charlie Higson, 2013
All rights reserved

The moral right of the author has been asserted

Set in 13/15.5 pt Bembo Book MT
Typeset by Palimpsest Book Production Ltd, Falkirk, Stirlingshire
Printed in Great Britain by Clays Ltd, St Ives plc

British Library Cataloguing in Publication Data
A CIP catalogue record for this book is available from the British Library

HARDBACK
ISBN: 978–0–141–33614–5

TRADE PAPERBACK
ISBN: 978–0–141–34841–4

www.greenpenguin.co.uk

For Billy and Charlie

28 SECONDS LATER ...

**THE EVENTS IN *THE FALLEN* HAPPEN AT
THE SAME TIME AS THE EVENTS IN
THE SACRIFICE AND JUST AFTER THE
END OF *THE ENEMY* ...**

1

Laughter filled the street. Laughter and singing. Maxie was laughing too, though she wasn't really sure why. She was filled with a wild, mindless joy. Here she was, out in the cool fresh air, marching through the streets of London with the surviving Holloway kids. It reminded her of Halloween when she'd been younger. That slightly hysterical feeling of escape, the normal rules broken, the streets being owned by children.

Only tonight the monsters were real.

No matter. They would destroy all monsters.

They'd just chased off a group of grown-ups. Sent them running. Maxie felt invincible. She was floating on air. There was a sort of magic about it. The energy of the other kids was combining into a powerful force. They were so much more than a gang. They were an army.

She'd escaped from the palace. Got away from that creepy loser David. After being shut away in the sick-bay for so long with Blue, the last half-hour had been mental, totally unreal, a mad film she'd watched on late-night TV while fighting to stay awake. There had been chaos in the palace. People running through the dark corridors, distant shouts, gunfire . . . At one point she'd seen one of David's captive royal family. The last surviving members from the old days.

An old woman wearing a tiara and a tattered silver dress, her face covered in boils.

The kids stomped down the middle of the road and their voices bounced off the high walls of the buildings, chasing away their nightmares. Taunting the grown-ups who hid in the darkness.

She turned to smile at the girl next to her. They'd rescued her from an attack near Green Park tube. She'd been badly cut up and had a bandage round her head. Maxie saw that she was crying.

'Are you all right?' Maxie put her arm round her.

'Yeah, yeah, I'm fine.'

'Only you're crying.'

'Am I?' The girl wiped her bruised and swollen face, sniffed and laughed through her tears. 'I'm only crying cos I'm happy.'

'Then we should all be crying.'

'Maybe.' The girl held on to her. 'Thank you, Maxie.'

'So have you got a name, bandage-head?'

'I'm Brooke.'

'Cool. Pleased to meet you, Brooke.'

It was Brooke who had told them about the Natural History Museum, how there was a group of kids living there. How it was safe and well organized.

And that was where they were headed in the middle of the night.

Maxie could feel Brooke's ribs through her clothing. She hadn't seen the girl eat anything in all the time they'd shared a room. She was running on adrenalin and guts. Maxie worried that if she squeezed her too tight she'd snap in two.

Brooke was about her own age and height. Hard to know what she might look like when her face healed. Right now it was a mess of scabs and yellow and purple bruising, and Maxie hated to think what might be under that bandage.

Just so long as Brooke led them safely to the museum the poor girl could rest up and get well, then Maxie could find out all about her, what she'd been doing when she was attacked, who she'd lost, why she'd lain so long in bed without moving or speaking.

Probably not a happy story, let's face it. There weren't too many happy stories in the world any more. Except maybe this one . . . *Escape from the Palace of Terror*, starring the Holloway Crew.

Maxie looked around. They hadn't all made it. They'd lost a few along the way since leaving north London, good friends, including the boy she'd loved, but there were still enough of them.

They were all around her, in a comforting knot.

Lewis, his Afro unmistakable in the darkness, was out on the left flank with his fighters; Big Mick was out on the other. Ollie was at the rear as usual, he and his skirmishers watching their backs. Clever Ollie with his red hair and his slingshot, the guy who had masterminded their escape plan.

Achilleus, the best fighter of them all, was walking stiffly just in front of Maxie and Brooke. Achilleus had been hurt pretty badly in the fight at the palace with Just John and one side of his head was taped up. He was leaning on someone for support. A stocky little kid with fuzzy hair who was new to Maxie. He was younger than Achilleus, and carried a golf-bag full of weapons. He looked like he was finding it hard work, but wasn't the complaining type. Wanted to show how hard he was. He and Brooke weren't the only newcomers; they'd also picked up a long-nosed guy called Andy, one of David's palace guards who'd defected and helped them escape.

In the centre of the group were the non-fighters – among them big, no-nonsense Whitney, Ben and Bernie the emo engineers, and Maeve, who acted as their doctor. They were looking after the younger kids – Blu-Tack Bill, Monkey-Boy and Ella – who were fussing over their little Alsatian puppy Godzilla.

It felt good to be with her friends. The world had turned cold and cruel, and friendship helped keep them warm. It was more important now than ever to help each other and work together.

But the best thing was Blue, the leader of the Morrisons gang, who had a lot more going for him than Maxie had ever imagined. He was walking on Maxie's left. Quiet and watchful. She'd been scared of Blue for ages. Had thought he was a typical tough guy. Cold and hard and stupid. The alpha male who had fought his way to the top and kept his place with violence. But she'd found, in the time they'd been locked up together at the palace, that it was all a front, and behind that front he was warm and funny and smart. Finding him had almost made it all worthwhile.

Almost . . .

'There it is.'

Maxie looked to where Brooke was pointing. She'd been a couple of times to the museum, once with her mum and dad a few years ago, and once with her school, but she didn't remember it being this big. Back then, though, she hadn't been thinking of living in it. It seemed to fill half the street, with tall, churchlike towers at both ends and another pair in the middle where the main entrance was. And then she shivered. There was something about this place. Something she didn't like.

A wide strip of garden, set behind iron railings, separated the museum from the road and a small gatehouse guarded the entrance. The gatehouse appeared deserted, the door hanging open.

'Something's not right,' said Brooke and Maxie felt her heart beat faster. It was late, probably well after midnight, and she hadn't thought about being tired before, but now weariness flooded her body and her bones felt suddenly heavy. She hadn't reckoned on having to deal with any more trouble tonight.

'What is it?'

'There should be someone at the gates,' said Brooke, looking around distractedly. 'There's always someone here. Guarding them. At least two kids. This ain't right.'

Blue rattled the gates. They were firmly locked. Maxie looked over at the museum building. There was candlelight flickering in the windows.

'How do we get in?' she asked, but before Brooke could reply Blue ran back along the pavement to where the railings were lower, climbed on to a bench and vaulted over to the other side. The rest of the kids followed him and they ran up a wide, curving ramp towards the two sets of big double doors at the entrance.

'They're open!' someone shouted and Maxie watched as a group of kids pushed one of the doors back.

She forced her way to the front and found Blue. They exchanged looks. She took a deep breath.

'What you waiting for?' Blue asked and Maxie went in.

2

The place was so big and so dimly lit it took Maxie a moment to get her bearings and work out what was going on, but when she focused she realized that a fight was taking place. A small group of kids were backed up against a huge diplodocus skeleton, surrounded by a much larger mob of grown-ups. Dead bodies lay all around them.

By the guttering light of several candles, Maxie could see that the grown-ups were a mangy bunch, skinny and feeble, with thin, bent arms and legs. Their grey flesh was eaten away by sores and open wounds. Many of them were covered in blood, whether their own or from the children they were attacking, it was impossible to tell. They had the advantage of numbers, but weren't like the street-hard grown-ups she was used to in Holloway.

'They ain't up to much,' said Lewis. 'Take 'em down!' And he and his fighters steamed into the pack, lashing out with spears and clubs. At the same time Big Mick and his crew circled round the dinosaur and hit them from the rear. The sight of reinforcements gave the defending kids fresh hope and it took them less than a minute to hack the grown-ups to the floor.

Maxie had noticed a kid who seemed to be leading the

9

locals. At first she'd thought it was a boy, but as she got closer she realized that she was mistaken.

'You in charge here?' Maxie asked her. The girl looked around at the other kids with her and shrugged.

'I suppose I am.'

'What's your name?'

'Jackson.'

'Well, Jackson, do you want to tell us what's going on?'

'Who are you?' Jackson said warily.

'It's all right, they're with me.' Brooke stepped forward. Jackson looked first shocked then delighted.

'Brooke . . . We thought you were dead.' Jackson gave her a quick hug. 'Are the others with you?'

Maxie remembered rescuing Brooke. The mangled bodies of her friends lying in the road.

Brooke didn't reply. She didn't have to. Her face said it all. Jackson swore and spat on one of the dead grown-ups.

'I don't get it,' said Brooke. 'What's happened here?'

'I don't really know, to tell you the truth,' said Jackson. 'It's been mad. No time to stop and think. Far as we can tell, the sickos have got in from downstairs; they somehow got past the locked doors. The museum's full of them. They're all over the place.'

'Where's everyone else?' said Brooke.

'It's OK. They're mostly safe. They're up in the minerals gallery.'

'Mostly?'

'I don't know.' Jackson peered into the darkness. She looked tired. 'I think we might have lost some. I can't keep up with what's happening.'

Maxie had a chilly feeling of unease. It wasn't just the grown-ups. There was something else. That shiver that had

10

run through her outside. She bent her neck back and craned up at the looming black skeleton of the diplodocus.

She remembered now what had happened when she'd come here the first time with her mum and dad – *the dinosaurs*. They'd totally freaked her out. She must only have been about four or five years old. There had been some kind of moving exhibit, with life-size animatronic dinosaurs, and she'd had nightmares for weeks. She still found dinosaurs a bit creepy. It was the teeth that did it. Maxie didn't like teeth.

She switched her attention to the dead bodies on the floor, crouching down to try and identify them. They'd been chopped up pretty badly.

'Any of this lot yours?' she asked Jackson.

'No. All sickos.'

Maxie gave her a questioning look.

'It's what we call grown-ups,' Brooke explained.

'Fair enough.' Maxie straightened and peered into the shadows. 'So how many *sickos* got in, d'you think?'

She was getting bad vibes from the place. Echoes of her childhood fears. This central hall was massive, the vaulted ceiling disappearing into darkness. It was full of giant fossils and weird stuffed things that threw eerie shadows on to the walls.

'No idea,' said Jackson, wiping blood from her face. 'I've seen at least ten others, but I reckon there's more.'

'And you think they got in downstairs somehow?'

'A guy called Robbie usually looks after security, but he's injured.' Jackson looked at Brooke. 'I guess things have slipped a little.'

'Do you have any more fighters, or is this it?' Maxie asked, checking out Jackson's crew.

11

'This is it.'

'All right,' said Maxie, raising her voice. 'Listen up. I know you're all knackered, but before we get to beddy-byes we got some work to do.' She pointed at Brooke. 'Take the smaller kids and put them with your people where they'll be safe.'

'In the minerals gallery?' said Brooke.

'If you say so.'

'It was designed to keep precious stones safe,' Brooke explained. 'It's built like a bank vault.'

'Sounds good. Round everyone up, Whitney.'

'You got it, girl.'

Maxie now turned to Jackson. 'We need to split up and search the museum, look for any surviving kids and any more grown-ups. How many groups do you think we'll need? I don't know the layout of the place.'

'We've closed down the red zone and the orange zone, so this part of the museum's sealed off from the rest, but it's still pretty big. There's the whole of the blue zone and the green zone. We'll need one group to go upstairs, two more to search this floor, taking one zone each, and another group to go down and lock the lower-level doors. That'll be the hardest bit. Don't know what to expect down there.'

Blue stepped forward.

'I'll go down,' he said, 'but someone's gonna have to show us the way.'

Jackson put her hand on the shoulder of the boy next to her.

'Boggle,' she said, 'you go with him. You know the lower level best.'

The boy they called Boggle nodded. Maxie did a quick check of who was left.

'Big Mick,' she said. 'You and me are going to take one squad and cover the left side of this floor.'

'That's the blue zone,' Jackson explained.

'OK.' Maxie was working now, all tiredness forgotten. 'Lewis,' she said, 'you take the other side, the green zone. Jackson, we'll need some of your guys to help us.'

'Take as many as you want.'

'What about me?' said Achilleus.

'Escort Brooke and Whitney and the rest to the safe area,' said Maxie. 'Then carry on up to the top, work your way down from there and join up with us when it's all clear.'

'Is gonna be bare quiet up there,' Achilleus protested.

'That's the point. You're hurt, Akkie.'

'It ain't so bad.'

'Even so. You've done enough fighting for one night.'

'I'll come with you,' Jackson said to Achilleus.

Achilleus looked her up and down, getting the measure of her, and then slowly nodded his head.

'Cool,' he said.

'We need to get the main doors shut,' said Ollie. 'Stop any more from getting in.'

'Let's chuck these bodies out first,' said Maxie. 'If you're sure none of them are yours, Jackson.'

'Get rid of them,' said Jackson.

'I'm on it,' said Ollie and his team immediately went to work dragging bodies across the black and white tiled floor towards the doors.

Blue came over to Maxie.

'So you in charge now, are you, girl?' he said, half smiling.

'You gotta keep up,' said Maxie. 'You're just too lazy. You keep slacking like this, we'll have to put you back to bed.'

'We'll see.' Blue shot her a look and walked over to Jackson.

'What's the name of this kid who's taking us down?' he asked.

'Boggle,' said Jackson, and when she clocked Blue's mystified expression she explained. 'He's got a Polish name, something unpronounceable with loads of consonants and no vowels. Justin nicknamed him Boggle, after the word game.'

'Don't know it,' said Blue. 'But he's OK, yeah?'

'Sure.'

Blue strode over and clapped Boggle on the shoulder. He was a big, chunky kid with stubbly hair so pale you couldn't tell where his skin ended and his hairline began. He was armed with a thin sword covered in fancy inlaid decoration. The end had snapped off.

'You do much damage with that toy of yours?' Blue asked.

'Is better than nothing.'

'Maybes. You ready for this?'

Boggle shrugged.

'Good. Let's go then, hench. Get this party over.'

3

Boggle led the way to the back of the hall, past the giant diplodocus, its immense long neck stretching out above them, and through an archway that supported one side of the main staircase. A smaller area here had served as one of the museum cafés; there were still tables and chairs laid out. Boggle went over to an ordinary-looking door that opened into an equally ordinary corridor, obviously part of the museum that had been closed to the public. He took a torch out of his pocket and switched it on. Blue did likewise.

'The lower level was for museum staff only,' Boggle explained as they walked down the corridor. 'It was used for storage and that. It's not all underground, there's windows in some walls.'

They reached another door. Boggle went to open it and stopped. His hand was shaking where it rested against the scratched paintwork. He was steeling himself to carry on.

'You see, when we first arrived here?' he said. 'The whole place was crawling with sickos. Reckon most of them were people who used to work here. We couldn't clean half of them out. The place is too big. Is like a maze of corridors and hidden rooms down there. So we left them to it. Made all the galleries safe and locked the doors so that they couldn't get up here where we were.'

15

'You've been living with them underneath you?'

'Yeah.'

'How'd they get in and out?' Blue asked.

'Through the windows mostly. We do what we can, try and block any holes from the outside during the day, but they still get in.'

'OK, open up,' said Blue. 'Let's see what you got down there.'

Boggle did as he was told and the kids nervously headed into the stairwell.

Jackson, meanwhile, was leading her party up the main stairs, past the white marble statue of Charles Darwin sitting happily in his stone chair, oblivious to what was going on around him. Achilleus stayed next to her. He had a round shield slung across his back and carried a sharpened metal spike for a spear. The end had been broken and the shaft was scraped and dented. It looked like he'd recently been in a fight. He was as bashed about as his spear. His chin was cut and bruised, one ear bandaged, and there were spots of blood across the front of the old T-shirt he was wearing. It had a logo on it for the Sarajevo Olympics. He moved with some difficulty and was obviously in some pain. Despite his injuries, he carried himself with a certain confident swagger. He had a razor-cut pattern in his hair and was pretty well a textbook bad boy, the sort Jackson's mother had always warned her about.

The sort she'd always liked.

They walked along the upper balcony, where the stuffed apes were. She expected some of the younger kids to say something, to make a joke, but she figured they were probably pretty spooked by the turn the night had taken. Only one of them spoke up, the little guy who was lugging the golf-bag full of weapons and who stuck close to Achilleus like a dog.

'I never been here before,' he said in a broad Irish accent. 'I like animals.'

'You come in here, they'd have to put you on show in a case, Paddy,' said Achilleus. 'With all the other monkeys.'

The little boy laughed.

'That's right. You said it.'

They soon reached the iron gates at the end of the balcony that closed off the minerals gallery. They were firmly closed and there were pale faces pressed up against the metalwork, fingers gripping the bars.

'What's going on?' said a voice.

'We come to rescue you,' said Achilleus. 'Open up.'

'We're not unlocking these gates,' said another voice.

'Do as he says,' said Jackson wearily. 'They're friends.'

She heard a rattle of keys, a clank, and the gates swung open. The big girl, Whitney, took most of the kids inside and Jackson was left with Achilleus, Paddy and seven of her team.

'We climbing,' said Achilleus, and he looked up towards the roof.

Maxie was helping Ollie's team drag the last of the dead grown-ups out through the front doors. There was a dark smear across the tiles. She took the body to the wide, shallow steps at the front and hauled it down, its head bumping as they went. She was too pumped up to feel frightened. She had a job to do and that was all. She knew she'd pay for it in the morning. She'd be exhausted and moody and short-tempered, but if they could clear the museum tonight then she could sleep all week if she wanted. Hell, she had no right to be tired. She'd spent most of the last day lying in bed. She supposed it was the stress that took it out of you, though.

She dumped the body with the others at the bottom of the steps and went back inside where she helped one of the museum kids secure the doors.

'So we've got the blue zone, yeah?' she said to him. 'Talk me through it.'

'It's about ten rooms. Half of them are locked, though, so we shouldn't need to check them.'

'OK. And the others?'

'Two main corridors. And the mammals gallery, human body and dinosaurs.'

Oh great. Just great . . .

Blue's party had already met two grown-ups halfway down the stairs to the lower level, wandering, confused. They didn't look too dangerous, more scared than anything, pale and thin and weak. They'd somehow got through the doors and now didn't really know what to do. Blue wasn't in the mood to show them any mercy, though. He wanted this night over. He wanted to sleep in peace.

'I'll do it,' he said, holding Boggle back, and clubbed the grown-ups to the floor. Then smashed their skulls against the steps.

'We'll collect the bodies later. Try and remember where they're lying.'

At the bottom of the stairs they found three more grown-ups, but these ones were already dead. There was the body of a young girl lying with them; they'd obviously dragged her down here before they killed her.

Blue shone his torch both ways down a long straight

corridor. Pipework, wiring and strip lighting ran along the ceiling; ancient filing cabinets, piles of boxes and junk lined the walls.

'How far to the doors we need to lock?' Blue asked.

'There's a sort of crossroads to the right,' said Boggle. 'A door there.'

'And the other way?'

'About the same distance that way. There's a T-junction. Another door.'

Boggle's voice sounded hoarse, and there was a catch in it. Blue shone his torch in his face. Boggle was crying.

'You all right?'

'Not really, no.' Boggle looked at the dead girl. 'She was called Emma. She was a friend of mine.'

'Sorry. You cool to carry on?'

'Yeah. Don't want anyone else to get hurt. We need to fix this up.'

'Good man.' Blue held out his hand and locked wrists with Boggle. Boggle took a deep breath and swallowed hard.

'I'm with you, mate,' said Blue and they crept down the corridor side by side, Blue's troops sticking close behind them. After about thirty metres they came to where another identical corridor branched off to the right.

They found two lads of about thirteen crouching there in the dark. They were staring off along the corridor towards an open door and nearly jumped as high as the ceiling when Blue's team stumbled on them.

Once they'd got over their shock they looked hugely relieved to see Boggle.

'What's happening?' Boggle asked.

'There's loads of them down there,' said one of the boys,

who was clutching a short ornamental sword like Boggle's. It was splashed with blood. 'We don't dare go any further.'

'We got to lock that door,' said Boggle.

'We ain't going no further. No way, Boggle.'

'Any idea what happened tonight?' Boggle asked the boys.

'Don't know. We checked all the doors earlier. They was fine. But maybe we made a mistake. Maybe we mucked up. Maybe it's our fault. That's why we came down here. And then our candle burned out and we were stuck in the dark.'

'We checked them all at nine o'clock,' said the other boy. 'Just like always. Even though Robbie's not around. They was all locked. We're sure of it.'

'We found Jason,' said the first boy.

'Who's Jason?' asked Blue.

'He's on one of the other security teams,' said the boy. 'He also checks the doors. We found his body, what was left of it, half eaten. God knows how, but all the doors are open . . .'

Blue looked at the frightened faces of the boys. Somebody here had either been careless or crazy, but finding out the answer to that would have to wait till later; right now they had to deal with the grown-ups.

'Looks like you got a war on your hands,' said Blue.

'Don't I know it,' said Boggle.

'So come on,' said Blue. 'Let's win it . . .'

Achilleus was staring at a cross section of a giant sequoia tree that was fixed to the wall at the very top of the museum. It must have been five or six metres wide. The sign next to it said it was thirteen hundred years old when it was cut down. Thirteen hundred years was a very long time. Like Paddy, Achilleus had never been to the museum before, would have sneered at the idea, but since the disease, since everything had changed, he'd found himself thinking about the world a lot more than he ever used to. Thinking about life and death and time and history. His dad had loved history. Was obsessed by the History channel. And here was this tree that had lived through it all. The Middle Ages, the discovery of America, the Napoleonic Wars, both world wars . . .

'There's nothing up here,' said Jackson.

''Cept this tree,' said Achilleus and Jackson laughed.

'Don't think that's going to attack us,' she said.

Achilleus turned to her and smiled. 'Could fall off the wall and merkolate us.'

'Could do.'

'We ought to check the opposite side from where we came up, I guess,' said Achilleus.

'OK. And then we'll stay at the bottom. Guard the main hall.' Jackson's voice wasn't what Achilleus had been expecting when he first saw her. She was posh. Like a private school kid. Didn't look like one, though. Looked like a bloke, to be honest.

She was staring at him, her lumpy potato face barely visible in the half-light. It was like she was waiting to say something, or for him to say something. He realized the two of them were alone; the others had moved down the stairs. All except for Paddy, who stood there, slowly drooping under the weight of the golf-bag.

Let him droop.

And let her wait. He had nothing to say to her. Except . . .

'So what are you waiting for?'

'Nothing.'
Jackson led them back down to the next level.
Bloody girls . . .

4

Dinosaurs . . . why did it have to be dinosaurs?

The gallery was stuffed with them, filling every space – fossils of complete dinosaurs, bits and pieces of others, heads, claws, teeth, models, toys, pictures. There were dinosaurs trapped in cases, leaning over them, hanging from the ceiling, up on platforms, peering round corners . . . The route through the gallery was on two levels: the ground floor and a raised steel walkway that snaked overhead. The route had been designed to weave past every exhibit, and in the near dark, lit by leaping candlelight and the jittery criss-crossing of torch beams, it had become a confusing maze, like some spooky fairground attraction, made all the more disconcerting by the jagged, skeletal shapes of the dinosaurs.

They weren't the worst part, though.

As far as Maxie could tell, there were about twenty-five mothers and fathers in there. She couldn't be sure, what with the kids running around and the busy jumble of exhibits, but there seemed to be adults everywhere. She could feel the sickly heat coming off their bodies. Smell that familiar sweet-and-sour stink. Hear them wheezing and shuffling and moaning. They weren't particularly aggressive, but they were scared and cornered and fought desperately when attacked. They'd split into little packs of three or four, and Maxie's team had split up as well, losing all their discipline in the labyrinth.

Maxie had Big Mick with her and two of his crew from Morrisons, as well as a boy and girl from the museum. She hadn't known Big Mick long, but it was long enough to know that, though he wasn't too clever, he was big and he was reliable. Knew how to handle himself in a fight.

The museum kids were a different story. They weren't a lot of use, except for holding the torches and lighting their way. Whenever they came across a knot of grown-ups trying to hide, the local kids would shrink back while Maxie and Mick and his boys cut into the adults with their weapons, hacking and jabbing them until they stopped moving. The museum kids seemed shocked by the violence, but Maxie just wanted it over, and the more aggressive and merciless they were, the better. She didn't like it in here with the dinosaurs. If she let them into her mind she'd be a little kid again, screaming to be let out.

She finished off a young mother with hair so fine it looked like candyfloss, driving the point of her spear right through her neck, but then slipped on her blood as it sprayed on to the floor. She tried to right herself and flailed with her free hand for something to hold on to. She felt a stab of panic. A burning sensation like acid rose up her gullet. It was silly mistakes like these that finished you. She grabbed hold of the cold, hard leg of some stupidly tall fossil and saw a movement, something coming fast round the corner towards her; she was still teetering, fighting to stay upright, and she lunged towards the movement, letting her momentum right her. At the same time she brought her spear arcing up.

24

Then pulled it back just in time.

It was a kid, one of the fighters from the museum, running the wrong way. Maxie swore at him, but saw that he was crying, his face wobbly with fear. Whether that was because he was running away from something or because he had nearly been impaled on Maxie's spear, she didn't know, and didn't much care.

'You idiot,' she snapped. 'I could have killed you.'

The boy didn't say anything. Just kept on moving, pushing past Maxie, who now saw what had spooked him.

Three big fathers wearing nothing but filthy underpants. They were fatter than the others, their skin studded all over with lumps and yellow-crusted spots, bulging where they shouldn't be bulging. One was missing both his ears; the other two had tongues so swollen they squeezed out of their mouths.

They were going too fast to stop and, as Maxie clumsily thrust her spear at the one in front, all three of them careened into her, knocking her painfully against the dinosaur skeleton.

She gasped and went down under the weight of them. Luckily Big Mick had seen what was happening and came at the fathers from the side, jabbing at them with short, hard movements, being careful not to hit Maxie, who was somewhere in the tangle of bodies that was writhing on the floor.

One father got up and reached out for a museum girl who was cowering by a glass cabinet, too startled to defend herself. Big Mick's focus was shifted from trying to rescue Maxie, and he aimed his spear at the father's kidneys, plunging it into the soft flesh of his lower back.

Maxie was struggling to get up. She was covered in bodily

fluids from the three fathers and the dead mother with the candyfloss hair and trying not to think about it. She'd been sick as well, so some of the filth was from her own stomach. She was furious. Furious with herself for having been caught so easily, and furious with the grown-ups for catching her. She'd dropped her spear, and the museum boy who'd been holding the torch was nowhere to be seen. In the dark Maxie didn't have a clue where her weapon might be. So she lashed out with her fists, battering at the fathers.

For a couple of minutes she was in the centre of a vicious hand-to-hand fight in the dark. Punching soft, stinking flesh, gouging with her fingernails, kicking, elbowing, butting, shouting her lungs out, her nostrils filled with the rancid stink of them. Sweating from the heat they were giving off, their skin slippery and greasy. And then there was a shout. A light shining in her face . . .

More kids were arriving. It was the rest of her team. Between them, they managed to deal with the fathers and it was quickly over. The kids stood in a circle, panting and heaving. The museum boy had disappeared. The girl was hurt, but not too badly.

Maxie was still furious, though.

'Where you all been?' she snapped at her crew, even though it wasn't their fault the local kids had run away.

'We was chasing a big pack of them,' said one of Mick's boys. 'They moved into another bit of the museum. We was after them when we heard you shouting.'

So it wasn't over yet. They had to regroup and press on.

Maxie groaned, feeling the pain in her back where she'd been rammed up against the fossil.

Bloody dinosaurs . . .

*

26

Down on the lower level Blue's squad were gradually driving a clump of grown-ups back along a dark corridor. Boggle and another museum kid stayed at the rear, shining their torches ahead. All Blue was aware of were white faces, gaping mouths, wide, frightened animal eyes, bony fingers held up for protection. And fingers didn't offer any protection at all. Blue drove steadily forward. Spears held the grown-ups at bay, clubs battered them down, knives finished them off. Gradually the kids were reclaiming the corridor, stepping over fallen bodies as they went, leaving a bloody carpet behind them. One of Blue's team stayed at the back, stabbing down with his spear at any grown-ups who still lived.

They reached a large door and Boggle cried out that that was enough.

Blue didn't want to stop. All his anger and fear and frustration had surged up from where he kept it nailed down deep in his guts. He wanted to press on, slaughtering the grown-ups, wanted to press on until every grown-up in the world was dead. He was filled with a burning blood fever. A sick drive to keep on killing. Boggle held him back.

'This is the door,' Boggle said. 'If we lock it then this corridor's sealed off. We're safe.'

'Safe?' Blue spat the word out.

'You don't have to kill any more,' said Boggle. Blue looked at him; even though Boggle hadn't been in the front rank his face was spotted with blood, and there was pus in his hair, probably from when Blue had smacked a grown-up in the face and his head had seemed to explode. There was blood and clumps of hair and bits of flesh stuck to the walls all down the way they had come. Blue fought the urge to be sick. His arms were sore. His head ached. He

27

had only just recovered from the concussion he'd got when a wooden shack had collapsed on him a couple of days ago. He had no idea what damage he might do if he pushed himself too hard.

He let it go. Felt his shoulders sag as the fight went out of him. Boggle and his friends were locking the door, shutting the remaining grown-ups in the darkness on the other side.

'Tomorrow we'll come back and finish what we started,' Blue said. 'Clear the whole place out. You can't live with these creeps down here.'

'It's too big,' said Boggle. 'We can't patrol the whole museum . . .'

'No. You listen.' Blue's voice was hoarse and croaky, his throat dry. 'We've got to do it properly. You hear me? Once and for all. We'll flush them out, then arrange regular patrols, inside and out. You got to be serious about it. You lost friends tonight. You don't want to lose any more. And you also got to find out how these doors got open.'

'OK. But that's enough for tonight. This is the last door. No more, yeah?'

'No more.'

'The lock doesn't look damaged,' said one of Boggle's boys. 'I reckon someone must have definitely unlocked it.'

'I don't get it,' said Boggle. 'Why would anyone do that?'

'Someone don't like you,' said Blue.

'But who?'

'Don't ask me. I'm new here myself.'

'Blue,' said Boggle, his voice wavering again. He lowered his torch so that nobody could see that he was crying.

'What?'

'Thanks.'

28

'Don't mention it. Seems all we do lately is other people's dirty work.'

'I hope you'll stay. We need people like you.'

'We'll stay. Least for a while. We ain't got no other home to go to.'

'This can be your home now.'

Yeah, thought Blue, *nice place*. There was a thump and a wail from the other side of the door. Blue kicked the door and swore loudly.

Bloody grown-ups . . .

Achilleus was sitting on the main stairs at the back of the central hall, Jackson on one side, Paddy the Caddie on the other, the rest of their team spread out behind him. They'd found no grown-ups anywhere on the upper levels and had checked that any connecting doors were securely locked. He was actually enjoying doing nothing. Letting others do the blood, sweat and tears for a change. His wounds hurt a whole lot more than he wanted to let on. He needed painkillers. And sleep.

He grinned as kids started to drift back from the green zone. Lewis strolled over, his spear slung over his shoulder, eyes half closed.

'Didn't find nothing,' he said, scratching his messy Afro. 'Just one crump old mother what couldn't hardly even stand up. Brap! She won't never stand no more. RIP mum. Apart from that, zeros, dude. We've went through all the galleries, shining our light into, like, every gap and behind every dead animal. All we've seen was bugs, birds and old bones. You?'

'Nothing,' said Achilleus. 'Looks like I'm having the night off.'

At that there was a shout and several museum kids came running through from the blue zone.

'They need help,' one of them yelled. 'There's too many of them!'

Lewis looked at Achilleus, who grunted and hauled himself to his feet. Tried not to wince as he set off at a slow jog.

The night wasn't over yet.

5

Maxie's team had got stuck. Weren't sure what to do. They'd chased some grown-ups through the corridors of the museum, past a load of stuffed bears and lions and bats. And then they'd run straight into a second, larger group that were coming the other way. In the chaos and near-panic, she'd ordered her kids through a big door into another gallery where they were now bottled up in the tight spaces between exhibits, unable to get back to the door.

Their madly slashing torch beams lit up a surreal fleet of creatures dangling from the ceiling: dolphins, sharks, killer whales, whale skeletons and, right in the middle, a gigantic life-sized model of a blue whale that dwarfed the stuffed elephants standing beneath it.

Her numbers were down. Most of the museum kids in her group had run off. She was left with Big Mick's fighting force and just two of the locals. She had no idea how many mothers and fathers were in here, scrambling and hissing among the exhibits. The kids were fighting on all sides and Maxie was too intent on trying not to get hurt to see what anyone else was up to. She knocked two fathers down and gave a little scream as she found herself face to face with a hippo, the teeth in its lower jaw as big as any tyrannosaurus's.

She swore and looked round. Big Mick was backed into a corner with no space to manoeuvre.

'We have to stick together,' she shouted. 'Don't get split up!' And she waded in to help Mick, spearing a mother in the back and twisting her weapon to free it. Big Mick swung at the mother's head as she went down and thanked Maxie.

'Listen!' he said and turned towards the door.

Maxie could just make out noise in the corridor. Commotion. Her mood lifted. Maybe help had arrived?

'Keep going!' she yelled, kicking another mother in the gut. 'They haven't forgotten us.'

Achilleus was going as fast as he could, but still lagging behind the rest of the group. He was right at the back with Paddy, his breath wheezing in his throat.

'You all right, Akkie?' Paddy asked and Achilleus slapped him round the back of the head.

'Course I'm all right,' he snarled. 'Keep moving. I just don't want to get ahead of you.'

'I can go faster.'

'Shut up, Paddy.'

But Achilleus couldn't go on. His vision was blurring, everything going dark around him. His legs felt loose and rubbery. He had to stop. He rested, leaning on a stuffed lion. He was sweating, his head pounding, his throat dry. He closed his eyes for a second, but that just made him more aware of the throbbing in his head. He forced them open again. Glared at Paddy.

'What you waiting for, caddie? There's work to do.'

He staggered on and they caught up with the rest of his group who had stopped by the entrance to another gallery.

'Whassup?' he asked Jackson.

'There's kids fighting in the whale room,' she said. 'And more sickos in the corridor.'

'Where's my mates?' Achilleus said. 'Where's Maxie?'

'In the gallery.'

'Get her out first,' said Achilleus. 'Then chase the sickos. I'll keep a team here and guard the door.'

Jackson took a fighting party into the gallery and Achilleus looked at Paddy. He was sagging under the weight of the golf-bag stuffed with weapons.

'Come on, Paddywhack,' he said. 'You can't rest now. There's work to be done.' Achilleus swayed on his feet and leant against the wall. A wave of freezing sickness passed over him. His head filled with fireflies and he felt himself losing consciousness.

'Bloody whales,' he said, and passed out.

6

Blue was coming out of the door that led back into the main part of the museum when Boggle, who was leading the way, froze.

'Now what?'

A horde of grown-ups was stumbling by, moving as fast as they could. They'd been forced round from the whale gallery and were now crossing the café and heading for the main hall.

'Too many of them.' Boggle held the kids back behind the door. Blue could sense the fear in him.

'We got to take them on,' said Blue, trying to push past him. 'You can't leave them running around the place.'

'OK, OK,' said Boggle. 'Let them pass and we'll go after them. Hit them from behind, yeah?'

'So long as we ain't hiding back here all night.'

They waited for the last of them to pass then crept out through the door and checked there were no more grown-ups around. It seemed to be all clear.

'We need to be careful,' said Boggle. 'There looked to be at least twenty of them.'

They moved slowly and cautiously through the café, trying not to make a sound, but then a long, high scream filled the night and Blue was running.

Sod that. No more being careful.

He raced between the scattered tables and chairs and back out into the main hall, glanced wildly around, looking for where the grown-ups had gone, where the scream had come from. At first the hall looked empty, but then he realized the pack had headed up the stairs towards the next floor.

And that was where the scream had come from. A kid who looked like he was dressed as Harry Potter, with glasses and everything, was being torn apart by the mob.

'Jesus,' Blue spat and he jumped up the stairs three at a time. There were too many grown-ups for him to get close to the boy, though. They were crowding round him where he had fallen on the steps. He didn't seem to be moving, and wasn't making any more noise.

Blue was desperate. As fast as he pulled one grown-up out of the way, another one filled the gap. They were ignoring him, intent on getting at their prey.

'Help me!' Blue roared, dragging another diseased body clear. And then he was aware of other kids running up the stairs behind him.

With the backup, Blue was able to batter his way to the heart of the pack where he managed to free some space around the boy. He knew instantly that he was too late, though. The kid was missing an eye and his throat had been torn out. They'd made a horrible mess of his stomach as well.

Blue cursed and started hammering the grown-ups, who were now turning their attention to him. He had to abandon the boy's body and back away down the steps with the others from his team who'd come to help.

All the other kids were now congregating in the hall below. Blue turned and saw Jackson, the girl who'd been in charge.

'Where'd Harry Potter come from?' he called down to her.

'Oh crap,' said Jackson. 'There was a group in the library. I'd forgotten all about them. God knows what's happening in there.'

'You need to take your lot and go get them,' Blue shouted. 'The rest of us will stay here and deal with these goons. Let's get this done.'

With the help of the reinforcements, Maxie had managed to clear the grown-ups out of the whale room, and as she led her gang outside she found Achilleus lying on the floor with a worried-looking Paddy kneeling over him. She grunted with shock. It was as if a cold, dark hand had gripped her throat.

Not Achilleus . . .

She hadn't always liked the boy – he was rude and a bully, a show-off, and he had a bad mouth on him – but he was the best fighter she'd ever seen, utterly fearless in battle and clever with it. To get this far without losing anyone only to have Akkie wind up dead was more than she could bear. Without Achilleus they were in big trouble.

And then she saw his chest rising and falling.

'What happened?' she said.

'He just fainted,' said Paddy. 'Just like that. I think he's all right, though.'

'Thank God.' Maxie sat down next to Achilleus and Paddy, leaning against the wall. Full of tiredness.

'We better get him back to the others,' said Big Mick, strolling over. 'It looks like we got rid of all the grown-ups from round here, but we don't know.'

'One second,' said Maxie. 'Give me one second of quiet.'

'Let's hope this is the last of it,' said Mick. 'I'm whacked.'

'Yeah. Help me up.' Maxie stuck out a hand and Mick pulled her to her feet. After a brief discussion they picked up Achilleus between them, got their shoulders under his armpits and dragged him down the corridor, his feet scraping along the floor.

They were the last. Following where the others had gone, they looped round to the back of the café and on through into the main hall where everyone else was regrouping.

It was a mess. Blue was hacking at something on the stairs; a steady stream of blood was dripping down to where fresh bodies lay at the bottom. The stink of it hung in the air, and worse.

A mutilated father was crawling across the floor towards the main doors, a trail of slime snaking out behind him. Big Mick let go of Achilleus, walked over to the father, put his foot on the back of his head and jabbed his spear down into his spine.

As Maxie lowered Achilleus down on a bench, he stirred and opened his eyes, disoriented and embarrassed. He shrugged Maxie off.

'Leave me alone, won't you?' he muttered. 'I'm all right.'

He rubbed his head, looking around at the scene of carnage.

'You got any water, caddie?'

Paddy fished out a half-empty plastic bottle from his golf-bag and gave it to Achilleus, who drained it in one long gulp.

'Did we win?' he said and tossed the bottle to one side.

'Think so,' said Blue from halfway up the stairs. There was a shout from above and they saw Jackson returning with another bunch of kids, younger for the most part and wearing a weird variety of fancy-dress outfits. Like characters in a cheesy school play.

'What's going on in this place?' said Achilleus. 'What they all dressed up like that for?'

'They were having a World Book Day event,' Boggle explained, and Achilleus burst out laughing.

'They was what?'

'Celebrating World Book Day. They're dressed as their favourite characters from books, I think.'

Achilleus' loud, mocking laughter almost distracted everyone from the fact that they had missed a grown-up. A big, ugly mother, wounded but not down, had been skulking at the top of the stairs, hidden among some display cabinets. As the last of the World Book Day kids came past her, she suddenly darted out and grabbed hold of a girl carrying a thick, leather-bound book.

Most of the kids were too surprised to do anything, but Ollie had never relaxed. He was always alert, always watching, always ready, and without thinking he had fitted a steel ball in his sling, pulled it back and loosed off a shot before anyone else had reacted.

With a meaty thwack, the ball hit the mother in the temple and she croaked and let go of the kid, reeling drunkenly. Blue bounded up the steps and finished her off with three quick blows. The little girl, meanwhile, was down the stairs like a startled hare and she ran straight into Ollie, who held on to her.

Jackson came down with the other kids.

'Are you OK, Lettis?' she said to the little girl and she nodded her head without saying anything. Jackson thanked Ollie, who simply shrugged.

'We've done enough for one night, I reckon,' said Jackson. 'I can't face any more dead meat. We'll sort the bodies out in the morning. We should all get up into the minerals gallery. We'll be safe there. But you'll have to move some more beds in.'

'Wrong,' said Achilleus. '*You* are gonna have to move some more beds in. We just saved your sorry arses. We want to be shown a little appreciation, yeah, a little respect.'

With that he stood up, tilted his face towards the distant ceiling and yelled, his voice echoing and unexpectedly loud in the vast, yawning space.

'Check me, Hogwarts, the SAS have just rode into town. My name is Achilleus. Don't you never forget it. *Achilleus.* And I expect to be treated like a king. You get me? I ain't taking no more crap from anyone. Ever!'

In the darkness of the balcony above, nobody had noticed Justin, the boy in charge at the museum, slip out from his rooms and come to look down at the new arrivals.

He leant on the balustrade and tapped his teeth with a fingernail.

He hoped this wasn't going to mean trouble.

7

Ella, Monkey-Boy and Blu-Tack Bill were sitting on a bed, huddled next to each other, their puppy, Godzilla, asleep in Ella's lap. He was warm and very still, only now and then twitching and shivering. They focused all their attention on him. As long as he was quiet, they could tell themselves that there was nothing to fear. They took turns stroking him, careful not to wake him up.

The local kids had set up a little camp for them inside the minerals gallery. The gallery was divided by two rows of square pillars and between the pillars were long display cabinets full of rocks and crystals and weird lumps of metal. The museum kids had made some of the spaces between the cabinets private by fixing up sheets and screens and walls of plywood and cardboard. A couple of oil lamps and some scattered tea lights gave off a warm orange glow, so that the gallery had the feeling of a sleeping shanty town at night.

Everyone else had settled down, but these three, the youngest of the new arrivals, were too disturbed to sleep and they sat in their makeshift cubicle, whispering in the dark like kids at a sleepover.

'I'm not sure I like this place,' said Monkey-Boy, who'd earned his name because of his love of climbing. 'I preferred

Buckingham Palace. I liked it there. It was where the queen lived. I liked that. This place is scary.'

'It'll be better in the morning,' said Ella, who didn't want any dark thoughts to creep in. Blu-Tack Bill didn't say anything. He never spoke, just listened, his fingers working away at the lump of Blu-tack he always carried with him.

'I don't like it. It's full of grown-ups,' Monkey-Boy complained.

'There were grown-ups at the palace,' said Ella. 'I saw them. Kings and queens. When we were leaving.'

'We should have stayed there.'

'If Maxie and Blue thought it was better to come here, then it's better,' said Ella. 'They know the best thing to do. They got us across London, didn't they?'

'There was nice food at the palace,' said Monkey-Boy.

'There'll be nice food here.'

'How d'you know?'

Blu-Tack Bill thought about food. He was hungry, but found it hard to eat and was getting very skinny. Before his mum and dad had died from the disease he'd always eaten the same meals every day. Sugar Puffs and toast with no butter for breakfast. A ham sandwich made with sliced white bread for lunch, and chicken in breadcrumbs with chips and beans for dinner. His mouth watered now that he thought about it. The past seemed an amazing place full of wonderful things. Food like that was only a memory now.

He looked to see what his hands had moulded. A dinosaur. Maybe it was meant to be a turkey dinosaur. They'd sometimes given him them to eat at school. They weren't too bad. He liked dinosaurs. This museum had been one of his favourite places to visit before the disaster. He never got bored of looking at the dinosaur fossils. They didn't change. They were always the same. You could see how they were made. He knew exactly how many bones were in each fossil. The stuffed animals he liked too. They never moved. You could look in their eyes and they didn't look back. Not like in the zoo where the animals were jumping and running all over the place, and they confused him and he didn't know what they were thinking in their weird animal brains. He wasn't like Monkey-Boy; he was happy to be here, looking forward to the morning, when he could properly explore. In fact, if you'd asked him before if he could choose anywhere to live in the whole world, he would have said here.

'Did you hear that?' Monkey-Boy looked up at the ceiling.

'What?' said Ella.

'I heard a scratching noise.'

Bill listened now, and he and Ella heard it at the same time, a rhythmical scraping sound.

'I don't like this place,' said Ella.

A boy wearing pyjamas stuck his head round the end of their space.

'Go to sleep, will you?' he said. 'You're keeping everyone awake.'

'We heard a noise,' said Monkey-Boy.

The boy listened. For a while there was silence, then the scraping started up again. The boy made a dismissive grunt.

'Could be anything,' he said. 'There's always noises here. It's a really big old building. You get used to it.'

'Could it be grown-ups?'

'Even if it was they can't get in here,' said the boy. 'This gallery's fortified. It was designed to keep the minerals safe.

42

Some of them are really valuable. There's a bit down the end that's built like a giant safe. No grown-up could ever get to us. Tomorrow I'll show you around. You can help us feed the chickens.'

'I'd like that,' said Ella. 'I like chickens.'

Bill smiled to himself. If they had chickens maybe they had chickens in breadcrumbs.

'Goodnight,' said the boy. 'That noise doesn't mean anything. Just go to sleep.'

'What's your name?' Ella asked.

'Everyone calls me Wiki.'

'Goodnight, Wiki. We're not scared of the noise now . . .'

8

Two floors above where the kids were sleeping, in a forgotten room inside the east tower, sat a boy. He wore a black roll-neck jumper and had very pale white skin. He was sitting cross-legged, sharpening a knife against a piece of stonework, the sound travelling through the walls of the building.

Scrape, scrape, scrape . . .

He'd taken the knife from the girl, Emma, after he'd strangled her down there on the lower level. Her last words had been, 'Why are you doing this, Paul?' He'd wanted to explain, but he hadn't been able to put it into words. All he knew was that he had to let the sickos through. The kids here, they hated him; they'd killed his sister, Olivia. He was sure of it. His memory wasn't so clear. He thought he must have been ill recently. A fever of some sort. It made you forget things. He wouldn't forget his sister, not Olivia. Never forget what they'd done to her . . .

What had they done . . .?

Had they really killed her?

He stopped sharpening the knife and stared at the wall, trying to remember. He was in some kind of abandoned storeroom, in a part of the museum that looked like it hadn't been used in years. A warren of poky rooms had

44

been constructed here with thin partitions. Like the cubicles the kids had made in the minerals gallery downstairs. Some were storage spaces; others were workrooms and tiny, box-like offices. There was a dusty, chaotic jumble of bits and pieces lying around the place. Old pieces of scientific apparatus, broken display cases, collapsing shelves, filing cabinets, and cupboard after cupboard stuffed full of rocks, crystals, lumps of metal, bits of meteorite, all neatly labelled. There was even a small kitchen up here, with a few cups and knives and forks sitting where they'd been left when the museum staff had deserted this part of the tower long ago.

He was safe up here. A narrow staircase led in a long, straight line down to where the other kids were sleeping, but the door at the bottom was firmly locked. He'd been busy shredding newspaper and pulling the stuffing out of an armchair to make a bed.

He could stay hidden for a long time.

He'd originally been intending to go back to see David at the palace . . .

That's right. That was how it had happened. It was coming back to him now.

David had shown him that the only way to fix everything was to open those doors, to let the sickos through and get revenge for what the kids had done to him. Which was . . .

Never mind. He'd remember that soon enough.

Soon enough.

He was still hoping to go back to the palace and live with David. But on his way out of the museum, after opening the doors, he'd had to hide, to avoid both the gangs of sickos who roamed the galleries and the kids who'd come out to try and stop them. Sneaking through the shadows, he'd found his way up on to the rooftops from the Darwin Centre and had enjoyed being up high, out in the open. His head had cleared and he'd stopped to stare in awe at the stars that were scattered across the night sky. For the first time it had struck him just how vast the universe was. Going on and on and on forever. He understood it now, what Buzz Lightyear meant by 'To infinity and beyond . . .'

What happened here, to him and all the other kids in the museum, meant nothing. Who would remember any of this in a billion years' time? Nobody. Down below were dinosaurs so old they'd become rocks; above him . . . *infinity and beyond*. Inside him – atoms, molecules, particles, circling like the stars of a nano-universe.

I am a star, he had thought. And laughed. A fallen star. And for a moment he had thought he could hear the stars calling to him, distant voices, like the voices you heard coming over the radio late at night.

He had no idea how long he'd stayed there on the roof staring at the stars and trying to understand what the voices were saying. Time had lost all meaning. Afterwards, though, he didn't want to go to the palace any more. He was going to stay up here on the top of the world for a while. He was a bat. He could fly out over the rooftops of London. He was God, sitting up there among the stars, looking down on Earth.

Exploring further, he'd found a way into the east tower, which stood at the corner of the museum, opposite the Victoria and Albert Museum. At the very top of the tower was a huge empty room, its roof supported by a complicated criss-cross of iron bars and struts. There were tall, thin windows looking out from each wall and from up here he could see everything that was going on.

It would be his own little world. He would go down into the museum when it was quiet and take his favourite exhibits, bring them up here and start his own collection, like . . .

Like.

Someone he had known. A *collector*.

The kids wouldn't miss anything, even if they did survive the night. One of them, the little know-it-all kid they called Wiki, had been very fond of telling everyone at any opportunity that the museum held seventy million specimens.

Seventy million specimens . . .

Seven billion-billion-billion atoms in the human body . . .

Seven thousand stars visible to the naked human eye . . .

He was better than the dozy kids below, because he was cleverer than them, stronger than them. Wiki might know useless facts and figures, but Paul *understood* things, how the world worked, how the universe worked, the stars, the planets.

I am a star . . .

He rubbed his forehead. It felt hot, throbbing. He pulled down the collar of his roll-neck jumper, found his neck slick with sweat. Tried to let some of the heat out. He ran his fingers over the half-healed wound where a sicko had bitten him two weeks ago. It itched horribly. He wanted to scratch it and scratch it, to tear his skin off with his fingernails, but he fought the urge. He had to let it get better. He hadn't told any of the other kids about it. Didn't know how they might react. They might want to do experiments on him, or maybe just throw him out to protect themselves. In case he turned into *one of them*. They could sense it in him, though. The sickness. That's why they hated him. Because he was different. He was bitten.

No. It was his secret and he had to fight it alone.

He pressed his hand to the wound, felt the heat coming off it, and closed his eyes, waiting for the throbbing in his head to die away.

And then he heard it.

A dry rustling sound, like an old man rubbing his hands together, and then a rattling of twigs.

Something was up here with him. Moving about. He opened his eyes and stared into the darkness below one of the windows, sure that that was where he'd heard the sound coming from.

Silence and stillness. Then the sound of claws scraping on wood. There was definitely something there. A patch of darkness that was blacker than the rest. It twitched, flickered, moving jerkily.

Paul held his breath and clutched his knife tighter, his eyes wide, trying to suck in any light.

A rustle and a leathery creak. The black shape grew bigger, rose up. It appeared to be forming itself out of the stuff of shadows, feeding on the darkness. What was it?

He heard a different noise now, rasping breath, almost like a laugh . . .

'Get away,' said Paul, his voice sounding feeble and weak. 'Get away from here.'

The shape continued to grow, continued to rise, up and up, until finally it showed against the deep blue of the window. A black silhouette. A nasty, bony head, with broken and skeletal wings poking up on either side, so that the head hung down in the middle, making an M shape.

A Boney-M.

Still Paul stared at it, willing it to come into focus, and slowly, slowly the thing emerged out of the darkness. It had a long beak, lined with vicious little teeth that clacked as it opened and closed. It looked like a fossil come to life, one of those weird part-lizard, part-bird, part-fish creatures he'd seen below, crushed and bent out of shape. Like a dead animal you might find squashed in the road. It was dark and greasy, its few feathers glinting in the moonlight. It hopped forward, one black eye fixed on Paul.

'Get away from me,' said Paul, sliding backwards on the seat of his trousers across the floor, the knife held out in front of him.

The creature made a sound like someone retching, but didn't stop. It hobbled on its shattered legs, using its wing tips like walking sticks. And all the while came the rustling and rattling of dry bones.

It opened its beak, an obscene little tongue waggling inside it, wider and wider and wider . . .

And then it screamed.

Paul put his hands over his ears, trying to block out the noise. It sounded like a hundred voices all shouting at once, a thousand, a million . . .

There were words in there, babbling, crazy; he tried to focus, to make sense of them, and slowly the voices merged together to become one voice.

'Don't be afraid of me,' it said, harsh and crow-like.

Paul was panting, his chest rising and falling. He stared at the creature.

'I'm your friend, Paul,' it said. 'Your only friend. And I'm going to help you, you miserable piece of dog dirt.'

'How do you know my name?'

'Don't be stupid. I've always known it, snot-for-brains. I know everything about you. We're the same, you and me. We're predators.'

'What do you want?'

The creature tilted its head, studying Paul. It laughed, the sound splashing inside Paul's head.

'Surely the question is *What do* you *want?*, my darling.'

'I don't know what I want. Leave me alone.'

'Don't you?'

'No.'

'You want to clean this museum, Paul. Get rid of the filthy kids. Now that you have a proper knife it'll be easier. Isn't that why you took it? Isn't it, you pussy maggot?'

'I suppose so.'

'You have to do it, Paul.'

'Yes.'

The bony thing was right in front of him now, the size of a dog. It reminded Paul of photographs he'd seen after the BP oil spill in the Gulf of Mexico, of rescued pelicans covered in black slime.

'I'm trying,' he said. 'I let the sickos out.'

'You have to try harder, you useless little tit. How many of the bloody kids do you think will be alive in the morning? Will the sickos get them all, or will they fight back?'

'I don't know.'

'*I don't know* . . . You don't know anything, do you? When it's light you need to go and take a look, finish off any of the brats who are wounded.'

'Yes. Yes, I will.'

'You can't go to the palace until your work here is done. You understand me? You have to make sure that all the kids are gone. Then the museum will go back to what it was meant to be – a place for dead things, like me . . . seventy million of them. And when you have finished there will be more. More dead things. You can lay the kids out on display. The dead kids. Your collection.'

50

'Yes . . .'

Paul swallowed. The bony thing, Boney-M, was almost upon him. He could smell it. It stank of death and decay. He fought off the urge to be sick. Closed his eyes as the obscene thing came right up to his face, probing with its tongue. He could feel its breath, on his mouth, his neck. Hear the creaking of its leathery joints. He flailed out with his free hand to push it away, but he felt only empty air.

His eyes snapped open.

It was gone.

He scurried over to where he had first seen it below the window, trying to find it. But there was nothing there except the half-decayed body of a dead pigeon.

He could hear Boney-M's voice in his head, though. Laughing . . .

'The ones in here are for laying eggs and the ones in the pen over there are for breeding. We always need more chickens.'

True to his word, Wiki was showing the new arrivals around. Ella, Monkey-Boy and Blu-Tack Bill were squatting down next to one of the chicken runs that had been built in a big central courtyard. The courtyard had once been used as a car park by museum staff. There were still a couple of cars parked there, and over on the far side was a big Tesco delivery lorry with flat tyres.

Godzilla was overexcited, crouching down, jumping up, bounding around in circles, barking like mad at the chickens and the children.

'They're all outside at the moment,' Wiki explained, 'because it's feeding time. They know when I come they'll get fed.'

'How many are there in there?' Ella asked, and before Wiki could reply Bill held up some stringy bits of Blu-tack he'd formed into numbers.

47.

Wiki looked at him. Confused.

'How did you know that?'

Bill said nothing, stared at his shoes and balled the Blu-tack up.

'He's a fast counter,' said Monkey-Boy.

'I can never count them,' said Wiki. 'They move around too much. Maybe you could be our official chicken counter, Bill!'

Bill carried on staring at his shoes. He didn't like the chickens. They were dirty and scruffy and disorganized. Feathers everywhere. And it hurt his brain the way they wouldn't keep still. Plastic dinosaurs you could put in a line and they wouldn't move. He'd had a box of them in his room at home. They were clean and smooth and every one of them was a different colour.

'Did you know that chickens are dinosaurs?' said Wiki.

Bill frowned. That couldn't be right.

'You're joking,' said Ella.

'No,' said Wiki. 'It's true. They reckon the dinosaurs didn't exactly die out, they evolved into birds. So, in a way, a chicken is a dinosaur.'

Bill frantically shaped his Blu-tack into a nice neat circle. He didn't want to think that those great prehistoric monsters had ended up as chickens. That wasn't fair.

Another kid came over to join them. He'd been talking to some older boys who were clustered round the lorry.

'What you doing?' he asked.

'Just showing them the chickens,' said Wiki, and he introduced everyone.

'This is Arthur,' he explained to them, 'but everyone just calls him Jibber-jabber. He's kind of like the opposite to you, Bill. You haven't said a word, but Jibber never stops gibbering.'

'That's not true actually,' said Jibber-jabber. 'I stop to eat.'

'Not always.'

'And anyway what's wrong with talking?' Jibber-jabber went on. 'It's what separates man from the animals, we're not like these chickens, they just cluck, yeah? Which is why we can take their eggs, you see that movie, *Chicken Run*, where the chickens gang up together and escape from the farm? I don't know, I think they were going to be made into this, like, super pie, or something, and they get together and make an escape plan like prisoners of war, and they all fly out of there, well, you see, that would never happen in real life, because chickens can't talk to each other, they just cluck, like I said, and without being able to talk you can't get organized, see this place, this museum? It would never have been built by chickens, the only way it could ever get done was by people talking to each other, I don't know exactly, but, you know, like, the architect and the builders and the labourers, the people who made the bricks and the scaffolders, that's why we'll beat the adults in the end, because they've lost the power to communicate with each other.'

'Will we?' said Ella. 'Beat them, I mean. Will we really?'

'Of course we will,' said Jibber-jabber. 'They're just dumb animals, like big stupid chickens.' And he strutted around, impersonating a chicken, which made Ella laugh.

'So they're dinosaurs?' said Monkey-Boy. 'That's pretty scary, like in *Jurassic Park*.'

'They're not chickens and they're not dinosaurs,' said Jibber-jabber. 'They're just sick, sickos, crazies, zomboids . . .'

'See what I mean?' Wiki interrupted before Jibber-jabber went off on another one. 'He never stops.'

'Well, you like to talk as well, Wiki,' Jibber-jabber protested.

'I talk sense,' said Wiki.

'Why do they call you Wiki?' asked Monkey-Boy.

'Cos he's like Wikipedia,' said Jibber-jabber. 'Ask him anything and he knows the answer, or thinks he does, it's quite annoying sometimes.'

'The difference between you and me,' said Wiki, 'is that I only speak when I'm sure I know something. You do all your thinking out loud.'

'Yeah, whatever.'

'So anyway,' said Wiki, turning to Ella, 'what are you lot good at? I know about him, old Blu-Tack Bill, he's good at counting.'

'Counting?' said Jibber-jabber. 'Oh yeah, I can see how that's going to be a *really* useful skill! I hope the rest of you can offer a little more.' He looked at Ella. 'What about you? What are you good at?'

'I don't know,' said Ella. 'Nothing really.'

'That can't be true,' said Jibber-jabber. 'You've lived more than a year since it all went opera-shaped, so you must have some skills, otherwise you'd be like most other kids, pushing up the daisies, knocking on heaven's door, sicko food . . .'

'No. I'm not really good at anything,' said Ella and she started to cry. She walked away from the group and stood at the end of the chicken run with her back to them.

'What's the matter with her?' asked Wiki.

'Her little brother got killed the other day,' said Monkey-Boy. 'Some grown-ups took him away in a sack.'

'Harsh,' said Jibber-jabber. 'Didn't mean to upset her.'

'I was going to say *staying alive*,' said Monkey-Boy.

'What do you mean?' Wiki asked.

'I was going to say that we were good at staying alive,' Monkey-Boy explained. 'But in the last few days quite a lot of us have got killed.'

'Some of our lot died last night as well,' said Wiki. 'Me and Jibber nearly did too; we were stuck in the library and some sickos got in. Best not to think about it really, so thanks, Jibber-jabber, for going on about being killed and eaten.'

'I'm sorry,' said Jibber-jabber, sounding more angry than sorry. 'I didn't know.'

'You see?' said Wiki. 'You talk and talk, but you don't think.'

Bill was concentrating on his Blu-tack. His mind was spinning, full of mixed-up dinosaurs and chickens and grown-ups. He hated it when people were sad, or angry, like Ella and Jibber-jabber. That's why he liked fossils. They were only ever one thing, one way. Stone.

He had moulded himself a chicken. A bald chicken. Smooth. It helped a little, made the chickens in the pen less frightening. He squashed it before any of the others saw it, though. He didn't want them saying how good it was and could they have a go at making something.

It wasn't a toy.

Sometimes he wanted to be completely alone, so he walked away from the others and got into one of the parked cars. Sat there, comforted by the dashboard, the gear lever, the steering wheel . . . Wished his own body was like a car and he could sit at the controls in his head.

He closed his eyes.

Everything was all right.

Wasn't it?

10

Justin and Jackson were looking in the back of the supermarket lorry with Boggle.

'No sicko could have unlocked it,' said Boggle, examining the padlock, which hadn't been forced. It was quite obvious that someone had used a key. 'It's definitely sabotage. No doubt about it, man. Someone's gone round letting all the sickos out, and letting them all in, if you take my meaning.'

'You know what I think?' said Justin.

'What?'

'I think David's behind it.'

'David?' Boggle looked amazed. 'How? He's all the way over at Buckingham Palace.'

'I don't know,' said Justin. 'But it's the sort of thing he'd do. Ever since that kid DogNut turned up the other day things have been weird.'

'You know he got killed?' said Jackson.

'What?' Now it was Justin's turn to look amazed.

'Brooke told me,' Jackson went on. 'After we were ambushed at Green Park I got back safely with Robbie and Ethan, but I had to leave DogNut, Courtney and Brooke behind. Brooke was the only one made it. She's been at Buckingham Palace apparently. She was quite badly hurt. It's where she met the others. These Holloway kids.'

'At the palace?'

'Yeah.'

Justin gave Boggle a 'told you so' look and fell silent.

'So what do we do about it then?' said Boggle once it was clear that Justin wasn't going to say anything else. 'If we *do* have a saboteur?'

'What *can* we do?' said Justin. 'Keep an eye on everyone. Listen to what they're saying, see if anyone's acting any different.'

'Why would anyone do it, though?' said Jackson, shaking her head in disbelief. 'Why would anyone want to hurt the rest of us? It's crazy, you calmly talking about a *saboteur*. It doesn't make any sense.'

'Crazy is right,' said Boggle.

'Who's missing exactly?' said Justin.

'You mean missing or dead?' said Jackson.

'I mean both,' said Justin.

'Five,' said Jackson. 'Two missing, three dead. Would have probably been a lot more if Brooke hadn't shown up with the new kids. I can't believe that somebody here just, basically, killed five of us.'

'Who's dead?' said Justin, trying to ignore Jackson.

'That we know of for sure?' said Jackson, her voice shaking with emotion. 'So far we've found the bodies of Jason Hickley, Emma Hudson and James Stornay.'

'We're going to take them up to Hyde Park and burn them,' said Boggle. 'If we bury 'em they'll just be dug up.'

'So who's missing then?'

'Paul Channing and Stacey Norman.'

'Five in one night,' said Justin, clenching and unclenching his fists over and over again. 'That's really not good.'

'None of this is good,' said Jackson. 'But it's not your fault, Justin.'

'It could have been a whole lot worse,' said Boggle.

'I know.' Justin was still clenching his fists. 'But it was bad timing, with Robbie out of action.'

'Bad timing or good timing?' said Jackson. 'Those new kids turning up made all the difference.'

'Don't you think perhaps it was a bit *too* lucky?' said Justin.

'What was?'

'Those kids arriving last night, just after the sickos got through. Saving us. Being heroes. They've come straight here from the palace and we've welcomed them in . . .'

'Come off it, Justin,' said Boggle. 'Now you're being paranoid. Just because they were at the palace . . .'

'Am I?' Justin interrupted. 'We can't trust them. We have to be very careful. First DogNut, and now this new lot, who we know nothing about . . .'

'Well, if DogNut *was* some kind of spy for David,' said Jackson, fighting the rising passion in her voice, 'you don't have to worry about him any more, do you? Unless you think his dying was some sort of clever plan.'

'I'm sorry, Jackson . . .'

'He saved my life,' said Jackson. 'Me and Robbie and Ethan. He held the sickos back so that we could get away. I've never run from a fight in my life, but I had to save Robbie. So don't you ever say anything about DogNut ever again. OK?'

'OK. OK. As I say, I'm sorry.'

'You better be.'

11

Achilleus was only just waking up. He'd slept long and deep, untroubled by dreams, but as soon as he woke his body told him it wasn't happy. He felt like he'd been run over by a steam-roller. He ached everywhere, his stiff muscles solid and creaky. The fight at the palace had taken more out of him than he'd realized at the time. His ear was the worst. Just John had cut it half off with his evil three-bladed spear, and that girl at the palace, Rose, the nurse, had clumsily stitched it back on. Now it burned and throbbed so intensely it made him feel sick.

He needed some heavy-duty painkillers, and he needed them fast. The bed was warm and soft, though. He could lie here forever. Wait for the pain to flow away. Maybe if he could go back to sleep . . .

'Hi there, how's it going?' Achilleus couldn't turn his head. His neck had seized up. He didn't recognize the voice. A girl's voice.

'Been better.'

'They thought it was best to let you kip.'

'They thought right.'

'Hurts, huh?' The girl leant over him, far enough for him to see who it was. A bandage covered half her head. What he could see of her face was bruised and swollen.

'You're the girl we rescued from the park, right?'

'Yeah. My name's Brooke.'

'Yo, Brooke. I'm Achilleus.'

'I know. Everyone knows. You made enough noise about it last night.'

'True that.' Achilleus sniggered.

'You like bigging yourself up?'

'Wasn't no bigging up. Just telling it like it is, yeah.'

'Well, Mister Big, you and me have got something in common.'

'Yeah? And what's that?'

'We both got pretty slapped about. Man, we are *flattened*. In my case it was sickos, but I hear you was swinging with another kid.'

'Yeah, the wiry tosser cut me up with his spear and put a few, like, dents in my skull with his shield.'

'I bet it hurts.'

'Like a bastard.'

'Me too.' Brooke sat on the edge of Achilleus' bed.

'Got bitten?' Achilleus asked.

'Nope. This one grimy mother had a knife.'

'She was carrying?'

'Yeah.'

Achilleus sucked his teeth noisily.

'Ain't heard of that before. If them zombies get tooled up, life is gonna get a whole lot harder.'

He looked at Brooke. Her eyes were black and blue. The rest of her face had a yellowish tint. There were spots of dark blood on the bandage and her lips were cracked and dry and flaking.

'Do I look as krutters as you?' he asked.

'You don't look too piff, to be honest, soldier, but then I don't know what you looked like before.'

'Never was no R-Patz.'

'That's a relief,' said Brooke. 'Not my type. You shoulda seen me before, though,' she added. 'I'd a broken your little heart.'

'Doubt it,' said Achilleus, sitting up and groaning with the effort. 'Take a lot to break this heart.'

'I can imagine.'

Achilleus closed his eyes and let out his breath in a long sigh.

'There's people here can help,' said Brooke. 'We got drugs, antiseptic, yeah, that kind of thing. Some antibiotics, but we got to be careful with them. I was going to go over and see about it. You want to roll with me?'

'Sure. If I can ever get out of this bed.'

'You want me to help you?'

'Yeah. Why not?'

Brooke took hold of one hand and hauled Achilleus hard. He swore and for a moment felt like he might faint again. He fought it, grunted and stood up. As he waited for his head to clear and the pain to subside, he spotted Paddy fast asleep on an inflatable mattress on the floor at the foot of his bed. Paddy's mouth was open and he was snoring loudly.

'Lazy little tyke,' Achilleus said and went over to give him a kick. 'Rise and shine, caddie. We've got some golf to play.'

'Wha . . .?' Paddy looked very confused. So Achilleus picked up the side of the mattress and rolled him on to the floor. Paddy swore at Achilleus, who laughed at him.

'If you want to be my slave you got to stick by me at all times, Paddywhack. Ready for anything. You're no use to me asleep.'

'Yeah, sorry, Achilleus, yeah, I'm on it.' The area around

Paddy's mattress was scattered with Halo action figures; he must have been playing with them before he went to sleep. Now he hurriedly packed them away into his backpack and pulled on his trousers.

'You want your weapons?' he asked, looking around for the golf-bag.

Achilleus looked at Brooke. Brooke shook her head.

'Nah,' said Achilleus and he booted Paddy up the back-side. 'But get your scrawny Irish arse in gear. My head hurts and I've got a doctor's appointment.'

As they went out on to the balcony outside the minerals gallery, Achilleus took in the view of the central hall. Light streamed in through two rows of windows on either side of the great arched roof and he could appreciate just how huge and ornate the place was, like a cathedral.

There were kids busy below, hauling bodies across the tiled floor towards the main doors.

'You find any more live ones?' Achilleus asked Brooke.

'I don't know. Don't think so. I ain't been involved in that.'

'I shoulda been,' said Achilleus.

'Maxie said to let you sleep. She said you'd be more use to us fit and well and rested up.'

'Yeah. But I sure do love to whack a grown-up in the morning.'

Halfway down the main stairs they met Maeve coming up. She was a serious-looking girl whose parents had both been doctors. She'd acted as a doctor herself for Achilleus and the other kids when they were living in Waitrose.

'I was just coming to find you,' she said when she saw Brooke. 'I wanted to have a look at the labs you've got here and somebody said you were heading off that way. I'm Maeve, by the way.' She smiled at Brooke, who smiled back.

'Yeah, we're off to see the docs,' said Brooke. 'Join the party.'

The two girls fell into conversation as they carried on. Achilleus and Paddy dropped back and sauntered along behind them.

'Can we do some training today?' Paddy asked.

'Nope.'

'Oh, come on, Achilleus. The deal was I'd carry your gear if you taught me how to fight.'

'You heard the girl, didn't you?' said Achilleus. 'She said I need to rest up. Right now I feel like someone's poured burning acid in my ear. I feel, like, dizzy and that. There was a guy, name of Arran, used to be our, like, leader sort of thing. Got a bite. Got infected. Went nuts. You don't want that to happen to me now, do you, caddie?'

'No.'

'We'll take our time, yeah. Ain't no hurry. I try to fight you now, you're liable to kill me.'

'Yeah, but you said . . .'

'Padawan!' Achilleus cut him off. 'Are you carrying any gear right now?'

'No.'

'OK. So I ain't doing any training then.'

They walked past the entrance to the dinosaur gallery and Achilleus caught a glimpse of Maxie organizing a work party.

He nodded to her.

She nodded back at him and gave him a look that said she could do without having to deal with this right now. She looked tired and harassed. Not a very nice job, getting rid of dead bodies. The smell was pretty chronic. Live grown-ups smelt bad enough; dead ones were another matter entirely.

They went off fast. The effects of the disease seemed to accelerate after death. Once they were out in the sunlight they'd probably bubble and split and pop. The Holloway kids called exploding corpses 'bursters'.

The passageway at the end of the blue zone opened out into a modern extension with a glass wall rising up five floors and supported by a grid of polished grey steel. That would have drawn all of Achilleus' attention if it hadn't been for the giant white concrete egg that stood next to the window, filling the space.

'What the bloody hell is that?' Achilleus asked.

'It's called the Cocoon,' said Brooke, who had stopped to let the boys catch up. 'We'll go up through it to get to the laboratories.'

'You really got laboratories here?'

'We got everything, soldier.'

As they made their way up the sloping ramps inside the Cocoon, Brooke explained how Justin had got a couple of the museum labs running under the supervision of a boy called Einstein. It was their hope to discover more about the disease that had so changed their world, maybe even find a cure.

Achilleus said nothing. He found the idea that a bunch of kids might cure anything ridiculous. But if they wanted to arse about playing doctors and nurses he wasn't going to stop them. That was their business. All he cared about right now was killing the pain in his head.

Paddy, on the other hand, seemed excited and delighted by everything, firing off a stream of questions at Brooke which she answered patiently.

The entrance to the labs was near the top and they emerged from the Cocoon to find several kids hard at work, studying books, squinting into microscopes, fiddling with dirty-looking liquid in test tubes. Some of the kids were even wearing white coats. Achilleus felt sick. He was right back at school.

He set his face into default mode, a lazy mocking grin that said, 'I am not impressed by you, and I never will be. You will never reach my level. So leave me alone, loser.'

Paddy was off and running, though, pestering the kids, asking them what they were doing, trying to look into their microscopes. Brooke left him with Maeve and took Achilleus through to a smaller room where a giant of a boy who looked about eighteen but couldn't be was being tended to. A fair-haired guy and a girl with a headscarf were dabbing a nasty-looking wound on his arm with some kind of white cream.

Achilleus raised his chin in greeting.

'This Holby City then, is it?'

'Something like that,' said the girl, and then she switched her attention to Brooke. 'We thought you might show up here this morning. How bad is that wound?'

'They looked after me pretty well at the palace,' said Brooke.

'Somebody going to take an interest in me?' Achilleus butted in. 'I didn't come over here to fix your computers.' He pointed to his bandaged head. 'See this? It's a clue.'

'You want to compare wounds?' asked Brooke. 'See whose is the grossest?'

'I'll beat you, no contest, girl.'

'You reckon.'

'I reckon.'

'OK,' said Brooke. 'I'll show you mine if you show me yours.'

Achilleus laughed.

'Deal.'

They each began to unwrap their bandages, the girl in the headscarf hovering nervously.

'Oh my God,' she said when she caught sight of Achilleus' ear. She had gone bone-white and her lower jaw had dropped about a metre. 'You look like Frankenstein.'

'Cheers.'

'That is the worst stitching job I have ever seen.'

'It was that or lose my ear,' said Achilleus.

'Did they even sew it back on the right way up?'

'Don't think you're going to get in there and try to make any improvements,' said Achilleus. 'Cos you ain't. What's done is done. If it gets infected, I'll need some of your pills. For now just keep it clean.'

Brooke had finished removing her own bandage, and when the girl saw what was underneath she was, if anything, even more freaked out. She put her hand to her mouth and couldn't say anything.

Achilleus took a look for himself and had to admit it was pretty rank. A ragged purple scab ran right across the girl's forehead. The skin around it was puffy and swollen and pulled out of shape. She'd been patched up like him. But none of the kids at Buckingham Palace had exactly been surgeons. Brooke would always carry a nasty scar there. She implied she'd been hot before. Hard to tell, the state she was in. She sure wasn't going to be hot any more.

And she knew it.

'Oh, Samira . . .' she said to the girl in the headscarf, and could say no more; her mouth quivered and she began to cry. Samira held her, waiting for her to stop.

Achilleus didn't have anything to contribute. He stood there awkwardly and nodded at the big guy with the wounded arm.

'You're back.' A kid with bad teeth and bad hair had come into the room. He was wearing a dirty lab coat and he looked at Brooke, Achilleus and the big guy as if they were specimens in a jar. He inspected Achilleus's ear, showing no reaction other than mild curiosity. He was the same with Brooke's ruined forehead.

'I heard about DogNut,' he said to Brooke when he was done. 'I'm sorry about that. He was no scientist, but I did quite like him.' He tilted his head to one side and gave Achilleus a proper once-over, noting his unimpressed manner, the pattern razor-cut into his stubbly hair, his scars and injuries.

And then he tutted.

'Looks like you've brought us another hoodie, Brooke. Chavs and hoodies are no use to us. We need scientists, doctors . . . clever people.'

Achilleus pushed the fair-haired guy to one side and stood up. Advanced on the kid in the lab coat, put an arm round his shoulder and held his neck just a little too tight.

'Ow,' said the boy. 'I was joking, OK? It was meant to be a joke.'

'You hear that sound?'

'What sound?'

'The sound of me not laughing.'

'I'm sorry, OK?'

'Yeah. Well, you listen up, funny man. If it wasn't for me and my friends, you wouldn't have no labs left here. You'd be fighting off zomboids, and you'd be losing. Badly. So let's have a little appreciation here, OK?'

'OK. OK. Ow. Let me go.'

Achilleus threw him away. 'Next time you tell a joke make sure it's a funny one, yeah?'

'Yeah . . .'

'Hello, Einstein,' said Brooke. 'You really know how to make friends, don't you?'

Einstein rubbed his neck and swallowed.

'I only came in to tell you that Justin's called a special meeting. He wants everyone there now, in the Hall of Gods.'

'We'll come when we're ready,' said Achilleus.

12

Maxie was sitting next to Blue in what the local kids had named the Hall of Gods, but which was actually only a side entrance area of the museum. There were star charts and images of the planets painted on the polished black walls that rose some thirty metres to the roof, where dim blue light washed down through tinted windows. At the back was a long escalator that led up through a rusty iron globe into the darkness of an upper floor.

Lined up along either side of the hall were six white statues lit by candles, and in the underwater glow from the high windows they looked weird and slightly sinister. There was a Cyclops, a gorgon with snakes for hair, a scientist, an astronaut, Atlas holding up the world, and the figure of a man that looked like it might be God. Maxie supposed they were meant to represent the advance of human knowledge about the world and how it worked. She wondered whether they ought to add another statue – of a diseased grown-up.

There were kids lined up on chairs as if ready for a show, but Justin was keeping them waiting. Maxie hoped they hadn't stumbled into the arms of another David. There was certainly a similar atmosphere here to the one at the palace. An attitude that said that the way these kids did things was the right way and the way everyone else did things was wrong.

She felt on edge, her eyes were sore and she kept seeing shapes and flickers in her peripheral vision caused by tiredness. After the adrenalin-fuelled events of last night, and a morning spent dragging bodies out into the sunlight, she felt drained and irritable. So she wasn't really enjoying the pantomime.

Well, they didn't get everything right, did they? Otherwise Maxie and her friends wouldn't have spent half the night dealing with grown-ups. They'd arrived here right in the middle of a bloody battle, for God's sake. And somebody had let those grown-ups in, which meant that at least one person in the museum was seriously twisted.

So she hoped there weren't going to be any speeches about how great life was here. She might just throw up. The best leader she'd ever known was Arran, and the best set-up was the one they'd had in Waitrose. She supposed they'd had no choice but to leave. Food was running low, the grown-ups' attacks were getting more frequent, and the two facts were probably related. Even so, Maxie looked back fondly on her time in the supermarket, and she missed Arran desperately. She'd been badly shaken up by his death and had had to take on the role of leading the Waitrose kids. She wasn't really ready for that, and was glad she'd made friends with Blue, who shared leadership duties with her. She didn't think she could carry everything by herself.

She wondered what this new bunch of kids had to offer. Would she make any friends here? She looked around at them, trying to read their faces. Brooke was sitting next to her, but otherwise the locals kept to themselves and didn't mix with the new arrivals.

She realized that quite a few of them were wearing weird costumes, as if they were extras from some old BBC drama series, or a Keira Knightley film. Nothing much surprised Maxie any more. In the last few days she'd seen a lot of weird behaviour. Left to themselves the kids of London were going nuts. For the last year the supermarket had been her whole world. She hadn't thought much about what existed outside. She'd been too busy getting on with the day-to-day business of staying alive. It was clear that there were far fewer grown-ups in this part of London than there had been in the north. The kids round here had it easy. They had too much time on their hands and so they were dressing up and playing at . . . Playing at what?

David at the palace had thought he was king. What did these kids think they were? Achilleus had told her about the laboratories in their white coats when he'd sauntered in late. Laughed about it. She didn't know how to take this information. Didn't know if it was a good or a bad thing.

But she did know that most of the kids here came across as nerds and misfits. The type of kids who'd been bullied and ostracized at school. Now they'd all clubbed together and had made this place into nerd-camp. Apart from the girl, Jackson, who was probably the toughest, scariest-looking girl she'd ever seen, they were soft. They had a soft lifestyle. And she resented it.

Maxie closed her eyes and rubbed them. She never used to think this way about people. It was a boy's way of thinking. Boys thought that fighting, spitting, swearing, front, respect and strength were all that mattered. She was becoming dangerously macho in her outlook.

She was turning into Achilleus.

She slowly let out her breath. Tried to de-stress. She was

just tired and grumpy, that was all. She'd look more kindly on them after resting up for a couple of days; for now, she'd see what they had to offer. See if she really wanted to stay here.

She sat back in her chair, arms folded, with a look that was meant to say 'go on then, impress me'. She wasn't too good at it, though. It didn't come naturally to her. Blue was a master at it. His take-no-crap vibe was awesome. She sneaked a look at him. His face was set like stone, giving nothing away. As still and hard as one of the statues, the blue light shining on his dark skin.

Maxie knew that underneath he was as vulnerable and confused as she was, but he'd learnt from an early age how to pull down the blinds and keep strangers out.

Achilleus was using a different technique right now. He lounged in his chair, grinning, laughing, making comments, shaking his head, like a disruptive boy at the back of class. He didn't need to bother with the stone face because he kept a level of violent menace bubbling just beneath the surface. He had the confidence to arse about because if anyone crossed him he would basically kill them.

It was different for her and Blue, though; as joint leaders they needed to pay attention. Maxie had to know what was going down. The smaller kids, and one or two of the older ones, like Achilleus, wouldn't be following everything, or even listening, and they'd be bound to ask her questions later.

At last Justin arrived. Wasn't much to look at. Serious expression, as nerdy as the rest of them, but confident with it.

He climbed a few steps up the escalator and then turned to address them.

'First of all I'd just like to welcome you all here,' he said, and Achilleus snorted. Maxie was giggling too. The boy sounded just like a headmaster and reminded her dangerously of David.

'I'm sorry I didn't welcome you all properly last night,' he went on. 'But, as you know, we were all rather busy. Running this place takes a lot of time and effort and brainpower. But, well, I don't suppose you want to hear too much about that.'

'No, we don't,' said Achilleus, and some of the Holloway crew laughed. 'We want to know what's for lunch.'

'Well, OK, that's understandable,' said Justin. 'A menu for the day is posted every morning in the canteen. Today I think it's baked potatoes and cabbage. To tell you the truth, it's potatoes and cabbage most days at the moment. We rely on what we grow, and that's rather limited.'

'We'll go shopping for you,' said Achilleus. 'It's what we're used to.'

'We'll get on to that,' said Justin. 'Now you've probably noticed that we're quite well organized, but we're only set up to cope with a certain number of people. Obviously having you lot here is going to make things harder. Um, well . . . everybody here has a job to do. We all pull our weight.'

'If we'd realized it was such a problem we'd have waited,' said Achilleus. 'Let them grown-ups take a few more of you out. Would have been less mouths to feed. Sorry we messed everything up for you.'

'Yes, point taken, but if you could let me speak . . .'

'Listen, mate. If it weren't for us you'd be speaking to an empty room. Either that or some greasy grown-up would be sinking his teeth into your fat butt.'

74

'As I say, I appreciate that. God, of course I do. We're very grateful for what you did.'

'Right. Spot on. You shoulda started with that, yeah? It ain't no afterthought. Instead of all that bullshit about cabbage and pulling your weight. We pulled our weight. We made this place safe. So say thank you.'

'Thank you.'

'And that's all you need to say.'

'Yes, sorry. It's just I wasn't prepared for this . . .'

'That's all you need to say.'

'. . . I didn't have a speech already written.'

'Nobody asked for no speech, just some thanks and a little bread and water for our troubles.'

'You'll be well looked after,' said Justin. 'But I need to know what you all do. I suppose you're in charge.'

'Me?' said Achilleus. 'Get lost. I ain't the leader. I'm a soldier not a politician, mate. They two back there – Maxie and Blue – they the bosses.'

Maxie smiled politely at Justin, even though she'd told herself she wasn't going to. Blue gave a barely noticeable nod.

'Well, maybe I could meet with you two in private afterwards,' said Justin. 'We could have a more detailed chat.'

'We'll do it now,' said Blue, standing up. 'This meeting is over.'

13

'You got a problem here, dude. You're looking at us like we're the problem. We ain't the problem. The problem is yours.'

Blue sat there, arms folded, giving Justin the stone face. They'd come to the museum library and were sitting round a big table in the middle of the room. Justin had thought it would be quieter here, but the place was a mess. It had been turned over pretty badly in the attack last night.

'I don't see a problem,' said Justin. 'We do all right here. We're almost self-sufficient and very well protected –'

Blue interrupted him with a harsh bark of laughter. 'Yeah, we noticed. Wake up and smell the zombies, bruv. Maybe you thought that was a party last night. Didn't look like no party to me, more like a massacre.'

'That was not normal,' said Justin, trying to keep his cool.

'Yeah,' said Blue. 'Which is what I'm saying – you got yourself a problem.'

Justin went quiet, struggling to find the right words. Maxie looked around the room. A group of kids wearing what looked like monks' robes were clearing up. There were books spilled on to the floor everywhere, broken shelves, some pieces of smashed up furniture and splashes of blood on the carpets.

Brooke noticed her looking.

'It's usually so peaceful in here.' Brooke nodded towards a tall boy with a wispy, underdeveloped moustache who appeared to be in charge of the clean-up operation.

'That's Chris Marker,' she explained. 'Our chief librarian. He was the one who organized the World Book Day celebration.'

'Looks more like they was celebrating World Wrestling Federation Day,' said Blue, and Maxie laughed through her nose and exchanged looks with him.

'Something went wrong last night,' said Justin quietly, almost to himself. 'Someone sabotaged us.'

'Seems that way,' said Blue. 'And that's your problem. Somebody here don't like you.'

'As I see it, there are two explanations for what happened,' said Justin.

'Go on.'

'It's possible that there's someone here who's, as you said, like a, you know, a traitor. And they might have unlocked the doors to let the sickos in.'

'That's all there is to it,' said Blue.

'But nothing like this has ever happened before,' said Justin. 'That's why I think there might be another reason.'

'What other reason could there be?'

'Don't take this the wrong way.'

'Try me.'

'That it's got something to do with you lot.'

'Us lot?'

'Yes. That you've come here to try to take over. You

somehow let the sickos in and then conveniently turned up to save us all and then we –'

Justin had been keeping his eyes on Blue, expecting any trouble to come from him, but it was Maxie who launched herself at him. She was up and out of her chair in a second and had latched her hands on to Justin's throat, forcing him back so that the two of them collapsed on to the floor, where Maxie sat on him, her fingers still locked round his neck.

'Don't you ever, EVER think that again,' she hissed. 'Or you'll have worse to deal with than a few manky grown-ups.'

'I'm sorry, I'm sorry.'

Maxie let him go. Stood up, embarrassed. She felt like a school bully. In a moment Justin had gone from being the main man here at the museum to a frightened nerd, slobbering on the carpet. She'd felt a brief thrilling surge of release, a rush of power to her head, and then a feeling of emptiness. And now she hated herself.

'No, I'm sorry,' she said. 'I overreacted. It's just – the last couple of weeks have been bare heavy. I lost a lot of mates. My boyfriend among them.'

She paused. Had Arran been her boyfriend? Nothing had ever happened between them. In her mind, though, he'd been that. Her soulmate. That's how she'd remember him.

She glanced at Blue. He was watching her. What were *they* now? The two of them.

Blue shrugged and turned to Justin who was sitting back down in his chair.

'Looks like we got us a situation, innit?'

'Please, you must understand,' said Brooke. 'We really, *really* can't thank you enough for what you've done for us.'

Blue didn't even look at her.

'You don't trust *us*,' he went on. 'And, to be honest, we

don't trust *you*. Makes sense not to give your trust too freely. So there's only one question really.'

'What's that?'

'How do we go about getting each other's trust?'

Justin stared down at the table, tapping his fingernails on the varnished wood surface. Thinking.

'There is *one* thing you can do for us.'

'Go on.'

'We need more medicine, chemicals, drugs.'

'You mean like vitamins and that? Makes sense.'

'Not only stuff to keep us healthy,' said Justin. 'We need materials for our labs. You might think we're crazy, but we're trying to figure out how the disease works. Maybe even find a cure.'

'You're right,' said Blue. 'We do think you're crazy.'

'Well, for a while we've been talking about setting up an expedition, but we've never had the manpower.'

'That's us,' said Blue. 'Manpower. Girl power too.'

'It would prove you were genuine.'

'So you want us to put a team together?'

'Maybe.'

'Fair enough. That's your side. What about our side? Why should we trust you? When one of you is a traitor? You get us out the doors, you might just lock them behind us.'

'I don't think –'

'Uh-uh, is my turn to talk,' said Blue. 'We didn't get here by being stupid. We'll send out a top squad, don't you worry yourself none about that. And you're sending some of your guys along with us.'

'Of course, we'll have to. I was going to say that, otherwise you won't know what to look for.'

'The rest of our people stay here. You feed them. You

keep them happy. The younger ones you look after, the older ones you put in charge of security.'

'We have our own security.'

'Listen, Mister Museum, you're not getting this. We are making a deal here. As I see it, your guy, Robbie, was supposed to be in charge of security, yeah, only he got himself whacked in a fight, am I right?'

'We've got Jackson,' said Justin.

'She's good,' said Blue. 'But she just one girl. You asked downstairs what we're good at. Well, this is it. We can properly clean out your lower level. Put some systems in place. Make sure there's no grown-ups within a hundred miles of this place. You show us some trust and we'll find your medicines for you.'

Justin thought about this for a while, tapping on the tabletop again.

Maxie stared out of one of the windows that ran down the side of the room. There was a view into the central courtyard and, above the buildings, clear blue sky.

'It's a deal,' Justin said at last and Brooke jumped out of her chair, delighted.

'Cool,' she said. 'We're all on the same side.'

Blue came over to Maxie as she got up from the table.

'What d'you reckon?' he said, walking away so as not to be overheard.

'So you're in charge now, are you, big man?' Maxie said, half smiling.

'You gotta keep up,' said Blue. 'Instead of sitting there saying nothing. Nice take-down, though.'

'Thanks. I felt a bit stupid, to tell you the truth.'

'He had it coming. Seriously, though, Max, you cool with all this?'

'I guess so. It's more of the same. Dirty work.' She headed over to the door where Justin and Brooke were waiting for them. 'Just more dirty work.'

14

Paul had given in to the itch in his neck. He was in an ecstasy of scratching. Eyes closed. Tearing at his skin. He stopped and looked at his fingers; they were covered in blood and pus. He licked them clean. He was very hungry. Separated from the other kids he was also separated from their food. He couldn't remember when he'd last eaten, it was at least twenty-four hours ago. Maybe later, when it grew dark, he could sneak down into the car park and take a chicken. For now all he could do was watch the kids eat.

His former friends.

They were in the staff canteen at the top of the museum, completely unaware that he was outside, hidden behind a stone buttress, spying on them through the big sloping windows.

'Look at them,' came a voice in his ear. A voice he recognized. Harsh and greasy. 'Like chicks feeding. Peck, peck, peck.'

'I don't understand it,' said Paul. 'Why are there so many of them? Why weren't more of them killed by the sickos?'

'I'll tell you why,' said Boney-M, and Paul looked round at the broken creature, as it flopped and twitched on the floor. 'Because you are a useless arse-wipe.'

Paul turned back to the canteen, trying to make sense of

it. How had his plan gone so badly wrong? And then he spotted someone he didn't recognize. A boy with bright red hair. Small, clever-looking, with quick eyes. He was sitting with three other kids Paul didn't recognize. And now more were coming in. Where had they all come from?

'It's not fair,' he said. 'There should have been less of them today, not more.'

'Useless,' said Boney-M and he nipped at Paul's leg with his beak. Paul kicked him away and sat down out of sight. He clutched his head, trying to hold it together. It felt as if his brain was expanding, growing too big for his skull. It didn't help that the sun was out, burning down on him, glancing sharp rays off the glass and metalwork and in through his eyes, making them water.

'Baby,' said Boney-M.

'Shut up!' Paul snapped. 'Leave me alone.'

All morning the creature had followed him around, sneering at him, whingeing and moaning and putting him down.

'I can't leave you alone,' said Boney-M, 'because you can't do anything by yourself. You need me.'

'No, I don't.'

'Yes, you do, yes, you do, yes, you do . . . because the brats are cleverer than you. Because you're a bottom feeder, a mouth breather. You'll have to work harder, move against them quicker, not let them breed and multiply, like chicks. Chick-chick-chick-chick-chick . . .'

'How can there be more of them?'

'They've made friends. They're good at making friends. Unlike you. Nobody likes you, pisswater.'

'Shut up!'

'Listen to me, little Pauly Pisswater. You have to watch

and wait. Choose your time. Get the measure of them. Pick your target. One of the smaller ones. They'll be easier to catch. Come down from the roof in the night, with your knife in your hand, and pluck one up. Pluckety-pluck, clucketty-cluck. Bring it back up here where they can't find you. Then you can start to collect their bones.'

'I don't know . . . have I made a mistake?'

'One of those ones would do. You know their names, don't you?'

'Yes. Wiki, Jibber-jabber, Zohra and Froggie. But they've got other kids with them I don't recognize.'

'The two little girls and the two little boys? Any one of them would do. Study them. Watch them. Pick your time. Soon.'

'Yes.'

Paul closed his eyes and licked his lips. He could already taste their warm, sharp blood.

15

Blu-Tack Bill had seen him – outside on the roof. A skinny boy all in black, with long, thin arms and legs, like a spider. He was out there talking to himself. Bill didn't like him. Wished he would go away. Nobody else seemed to have noticed him, and Bill took little glances out of the side of his eyes. At last the spider boy went away.

Bill looked down at his hands. They'd been making chips out of Blu-tack. He really loved chips, but he hadn't had any to eat in as long as he could remember. He'd eaten a little bit of the baked potato they'd given him. He had to. If he didn't eat he'd starve to death. He didn't like it, though, the potato. It was dry. And then Monkey-Boy had asked him if he was finished with it and he'd given him the rest. He'd eaten a tiny bit of cabbage too, even though it made him feel sick. They'd been promised some tinned fruit for afters. He was looking forward to that. He'd grown very thin over the last year. Not that he'd ever been fat. The bigger kids were always trying to make him eat. Whitney was like his mum – 'You must eat. You'll waste away. Eat something . . .'

If only he could eat Blu-tack. He couldn't. He'd tried it once. It was horrible. But just shaping it into chips made him feel a little less hungry.

The others were all filling their faces. Not holding back. As if this was the nicest feast in the whole world. Not even thinking about what they were eating as they chatted away, forks clattering on their plates.

Ella was busy telling the museum kids about her life back in Holloway, when she'd been living in Waitrose. It had been fine so far, like telling a great adventure, but he knew what was coming next and tried not to listen. He'd heard this story before. Many times. It didn't get any better the more he heard it. He hated sadness. He sang a song inside his head, trying to blot it out. At the same time his fingers quickly bundled his blue chips up into a ball and started making something else, something bigger and more complicated so that his attention wasn't on Ella.

The girl called Zohra was staring intently at Ella. She had long dark curly hair and big brown eyes. She was leaning forward, her fork forgotten in her hand.

'We used to call him Small Sam,' Ella was explaining, 'because there were two other Sams. *I* even think of him as Small Sam, even though he's my own brother and he was older than me.'

'How old is he?' Zohra asked.

'Nearly ten.'

'What happened to the other Sams? Are they still with you?'

'No. Big Sam died ages ago, and Curly Sam died on the way here. We were attacked by diseased monkeys in the park. They escaped from the zoo.'

'Diseased monkeys?' Zohra looked like she was trying not to laugh. 'You're joking.'

'No. It was horrible. They got Josh, and Joel died as well. Godzilla used to be his dog, Joel's dog. We look after him now.'

'So what happened to your brother then, what happened to Small Sam?'

'Grown-ups got him. They took him away in a sack. We were playing in the car park behind the shop.' Ella went quiet; tears welled in the corners of her eyes, then rolled down her cheeks as if racing each other.

Zohra put her arms round Froggie, who was sitting next to her.

'I couldn't bear for anything to happen to Froggie,' she said, holding him tight. 'Not my little brother.'

Froggie pushed her away.

'Oi, leave me alone,' he said, his mouth full of food. 'You're worse than Mum.'

This only made Ella cry more. 'It's not fair,' she said. 'Why did they have to take my brother? He looked after me. He was only small, but he looked after me.'

'Is he dead then?' said Froggie.

Ella looked at him and sniffed. Froggie reminded her a little of Sam. She nodded quickly.

'Are you sure?' Froggie pressed on.

'No,' said Ella. 'We never saw him get killed, but they took him, a load of mean grown-ups. How could he survive? Sometimes – sometimes I wish he *was* still alive, that somehow he escaped. That he's out there now looking for me. But I know it's just a dream. Lots of kids have died and they don't never come back. So why should Sam?'

'Maybe he will,' said Zohra, and she looked at her brother. 'I'd come back. If sickos took me. I'd escape and I'd find you again, Froggie.'

'I wouldn't,' said Froggie. 'I wouldn't bother. I'd stay with the sickos and have parties. You never let me do anything.'

Zohra gave Froggie a mock punch and he laughed.

'I wonder,' said Ella, watching a fat tear plop on to her plate. 'If he *was* out there, still alive, what he'd be doing right now. Would he be happy? Would he be sad? Would he be hungry? Would he be scared?'

She took a deep, shuddering breath and looked up into Zohra's eyes.

'And sometimes I think he's better off dead, because then he can't be cold or hungry or scared or lonely any more.'

16

'So we both gonna go on this bloody expedition? It's gonna be hairy out there. More fighting before it's done.'

'I don't know,' said Maxie. 'Do you think we can trust Justin? Maybe we should put someone else in charge of the expedition and both stay here.'

Blue grunted. He was straining to shift an ancient wooden cabinet.

'I wish I'd never agreed to it. I wish I'd never agreed to none of this.'

'As far as I can remember,' said Maxie, 'this was your great idea.'

They'd been working down in the lower level for two days now, moving from room to room, corridor to corridor, clearing out the grown-ups. It didn't seem so much of a maze now that they'd learnt their way around, but it was still dark and confusing enough to lose your bearings if you didn't concentrate.

And nobody wanted to get lost.

They'd eventually got their heads round the basic layout of two long, wide corridors that ran from one end to the other, linked in the middle by one main cross corridor. At the T-junction nearest the front of the museum was their chief navigation point – a sign on a pillar reading GIRAFFE

CORNER. There was a huge lifting platform here beneath a trap door. Boggle had explained that it had been where a herd of stuffed giraffes had once been kept.

If they ever got disoriented they only had to find Giraffe Corner and they could get their bearings.

The three big main corridors had cables, lighting and ducts running along the ceiling, and various cabinets, boxes and rubbish piled along the walls. Every now and then smaller passages broke off to either side and everywhere there were doors. Doors to countless rooms. More rooms than they could ever have imagined. Any that were locked they ignored, but if they were open they had to be investigated. The only windows down here were in the extreme outer walls. For the most part it was dark and airless.

As the kids cleared each section, they sealed it off to make sure no grown-ups could get back in. So far they'd found twelve living ones and had killed every one of them. It had been tense and often disgusting work. The grown-ups had been living down here like animals and had collected all kinds of filth – bits of rotting flesh and bone, faeces, ragged clothing.

They'd found no sign of the two missing museum kids yet – Stacey Norman and Paul Channing. They assumed that they must have either been torn apart and their remains mixed in with the foul piles of debris in the dark corners, or they'd been dragged away and disposed of somewhere else. Whatever the case, having got rid of the living, the kids didn't have the stomach to look too closely at the dead. As far as they were concerned, the quicker they could finish the job and make the place safe, the better.

Maxie and Blue were nearing the end of their shift. They had Big Mick and two more of Blue's crew with them.

They were all wearing face masks and rubber gloves and had spent the last half-hour scooping up the unidentifiable muck they'd found in one of the smaller rooms. The room had been lined with shelves containing fossils, but had obviously been used as a nest by the grown-ups. The kids had dumped everything they could into bin liners and were stacking them outside the door. The smell was appalling; it was so intense it was almost physical, as if someone was rubbing grubby hands over them, forcing the stench into their noses and eyes, their ears, their hair. The end was in sight, though, and they were working fast, sweat crawling across their skin beneath their clothes.

Mick and Blue were trying to shift a big, heavy cabinet. There was a crawl space behind it large enough for a person to just fit into and a hole in the wall behind leading to one of the locked rooms.

'I reckon one of you has to go on the expedition,' said Big Mick. 'Ain't no one else anyone'll listen to. Got to be someone in charge. You should split up. One stay here, the other go on the journey.'

'You're probably right,' said Blue, trying to get a grip on the chipped wood of the cabinet. 'So, next question. Who stays and who goes?'

'I dunno,' said Maxie. 'Mick seems to have all the answers. Maybe we should let him decide.'

'Cool,' said Mick. 'Nobody ever asked my opinion on nothing before.'

'That's cos you're a moron,' said Blue. He stopped trying to move the cabinet and wiped sweat from his forehead.

'You'd be nothing without me, Blue,' said Mick. 'You'd be lying in a dirt bed feeding the worms.'

'If you could think as well as you fight I'd put you in

charge of the expedition,' said Blue. 'And I could stay here and jam.'

Mick put his arm round Blue.

'You and me, darling,' he said. 'We're a team. Nobody splits us up.'

'Worse luck,' said Blue. 'You stink badder than a dead grown-up.'

Maxie tried to ignore the stab of jealousy that had slipped under her defences. She still felt slightly awkward around Blue, wished she could put her arm round him as easily as Mick had. The two boys were old friends, with a history. She'd only really got to know Blue in the last week or so. Sometimes she felt like an intruder.

'Come on,' she said. 'Let's get this done.' She picked up a bin bag; it was warm and squishy, and orange liquid dripped out of the bottom where it had split.

'Sir, yes, sir!' Blue put his shoulder to the cabinet and it shifted a couple of centimetres.

Maxie took the bag out to add to the pile in the corridor where the other two members of their party were keeping watch.

'Mick's made his choice,' said Blue as Maxie came back in.

Mick looked at Maxie. He had a big, bony head and sticking out ears.

'He goes and you stay,' he said. 'Sorry, Max.'

'It's a boy thing, innit?' said Maxie with a smile. 'Deep down you don't think I'm as good a fighter as Blue.'

'No, it's not that . . .' Mick looked embarrassed.

'Doesn't matter. It's fine with me,' said Maxie, actually quite relieved. 'The less fighting I have to do, the better. Now let's move that thing. I want to get out of here and get washed.'

All three of them put their backs into it. The cabinet creaked and groaned as it inched across the floor, revealing the hole behind.

'Right,' said Maxie bending down. 'Let's see what's back here.'

She shone her torch into the hole.

'Oh bloody hell . . .'

17

There were four grown-ups. Four that Maxie could see, at any rate. They'd made themselves a nest out of old newspaper, and were huddled in it, staring with wide eyes at the kids.

As Mick and Blue joined her, squatting at the entrance to the hole, Maxie flicked her torch round the rest of the room. It was very much like the one they were in, filled with shelves of fossils. She couldn't spot anyone else.

'We should just wall them in,' said Mick.

'The whole point of this is to make everywhere safe, and clean, you nunce,' said Blue. 'We don't want to be living above rotting corpses.'

'Fair point.'

The grown-ups looked almost like a family group. A mother and father and two teenage children – boy and girl. It would have made a weird family photo, though. Weird and pretty sick. They were all bald and the mother was naked. The father was missing his nose and top lip, exposing his top set of teeth. The boy was like a parody of a teenager: he had so many boils and spots and growths on his face it looked like a rotten cauliflower. The girl was shaking violently and had bitten the ends of her fingers down to the bone.

The hole into the room was maybe half a metre wide,

and the same distance tall. To get in would require crawling. None of the kids fancied that. It would mean going in one by one and being completely exposed until you were through. For now the grown-ups were quiet, but there was no saying how dangerous they might be.

'So what's the plan then?' said Mick. He was pretty fearless, and always up for a fight. Down here, though, in the cramped, dark and claustrophobic conditions, Maxie could tell that even he was uneasy.

'Can we lure them out, d'you think?' she asked.

'What with?' said Blue. 'You want to offer them a piece of you?' He shouted through the hole. 'Oi! Come and get it. Maxie's got a nice juicy arse on her.'

Maxie hit Blue, who sniggered.

'Very funny.'

'What then?'

Maxie took a deep breath. 'I'm gonna risk it.'

'You going in?'

'It's the only way.' Maxie knelt by the hole. 'You be ready to back me up. As soon as I'm in, I want one of you with me.'

'I'll be right behind you,' said Blue, and he picked up the short sword he'd been given by one of the museum kids.

'Me too,' said Mick.

Maxie poked her club through the hole and left it within reach on the other side. The four grown-ups were still just sitting there, watching.

'Hold up.' Blue grabbed Maxie's shoulder. 'Justin said he wanted us to try and take some of them alive, remember . . .'

'You must be joking, Blue. We kill them, and we kill them quick.'

'You're the boss.'

No, I'm an idiot, thought Maxie, *a stupid idiot*.

She didn't want to think about it any longer; she needed to get in before the 'family' knew what was happening and decided to get any more lively.

Here goes nothing . . .

She threw herself forward through the gap, scraping her back on the top, which knocked her flat. The wind went out of her and for a moment she saw stars.

This wasn't a good start.

She slithered forward on her front like a snake, groping for her club. And now at last the family came awake. With surprising speed, the naked mother came at her, her long fingernails raised like claws. Maxie floundered around, trying to keep away from her and get into a position from which she could stand up. The mother raked her fingernails down Maxie's arm, snapping two of them, but doing no damage. They were unable to penetrate Maxie's leather jacket.

Now the other three were moving too, making the familiar hissing noise of angry grown-ups.

'Hurry up!' Maxie screamed.

'Your feet are in the way,' Blue shouted back.

'Oh crap!'

Maxie drew her knees up, clearing the opening, and rolled on to her side towards where she thought her club was. She couldn't see it, and couldn't have picked it up anyway as she was having to use her hands to keep the family at bay. The daughter was scurrying around on all fours, snapping like a dog. The mother was trying to get her arms round Maxie. The son had stood up. He was tall. He swayed above the mother as if drunk. He had a long

96

bone in one hand that he swung at Maxie, smacking her in the side of the head.

Maxie howled in pain and managed to kick the legs out from under him before he did any more damage. Then she had to return her attention to the mother, whose skin felt slimy and hot as she wrestled with her.

Only the father remained unmoved. He just sat there, nodding his head like a novelty toy.

'Maxie!'

Blue was through. He stabbed the daughter in the back and put her out of action. She flopped to the floor and writhed around for a moment before going into an almighty spasm and freezing in a contorted shape like a startled kitten.

Blue used his boots to get the mother off Maxie, who was at last able to spring up and get sorted. She spotted the club where it had been shunted to one side in the scuffle.

She picked it up and, filled with a fury built from fear and frustration, she swung it with all her strength at the mother's head. It made a nasty, wet slapping sound followed by a crack as her forehead slammed into the floor. Blood and brains mingled with the squalid debris in the room.

Blue meanwhile had skewered the son, and only the father was left.

He appeared to be smiling. And stroking something in his lap.

Blue stepped closer.

'What is it?' said Maxie.

'Looks like we found Stacey.'

Maxie saw the girl's head in the father's hands.

'Bastard.' Blue stuck his sword into the father's mouth and twisted.

The fight was over.

Maxie put her back to the wall and slid down to the floor, sobbing.

'I hate this, Blue,' she said. 'I hate it, I hate it, I bloody hate it.'

Blue sat next to her and put his arm round her shoulders.

'I know, babe.'

'I pretend to be together.' Maxie's voice was wobbly, verging on hysteria. 'I pretend everything's all right. But it isn't. Nothing's right, and I sometimes think it never will be again.'

'Maybe the kids here ain't so crazy,' said Blue. 'We can't go on like this. Maybe we *should* be trying to cure them rather than kill them.'

'Yeah.' Maxie sniffed and dried her face. 'Something's got to give. Is gonna be dangerous, but this expedition of theirs has got to be a success.'

'You know it.'

Big Mick poked his head through the hole.

'You aren't half made a mess in there,' he said. 'I thought it was going home time. We gonna need bare more bin bags.'

'This is it for today,' said Maxie. 'I don't have the energy.'

'Yeah,' said Blue. 'I'm getting too old for this shit.'

18

'You gotta get yourself a better spear, Akkie. That one's good for poking and stabbing, but it's got no cutting edge on it. Anyone gets past the point and you're in trouble.'

'Nobody *does* get past the point.'

Achilleus tested the spear, spinning it around in the air, feinting at other kids, who swore and jumped out of the way. He simply laughed at them and accused them of being wimps when they complained. Finally he gripped the spear with two hands and thrust it at Paddy, the point just grazing his throat.

'That's not funny, Akkie,' said Paddy, backing away. 'You might of cut me.'

'I'll tattoo my name on your neck, bogtrotter.'

The expedition party was coming together under the diplodocus in the main hall. They were noisy and excited. Those who'd been working downstairs were looking forward to fresh air and open skies. The kids from the museum who were going were looking forward to seeing some more of the outside world. The hubbub of voices was making them sound like a much larger group than they actually were.

Achilleus was back to something like his old self. His ear was still heavily bandaged, but it didn't seem to have become infected. He was still sore from his various cuts and bruises, though, and he figured that the best way to shake off the stiffness and take his mind off the pain was to get out there and *do* stuff. He'd been the first to volunteer for the expedition and anywhere Achilleus went Paddy came too. He was standing patiently next to Achilleus with the golf-bag full of spare weapons and Achilleus' shield slung across his back. He'd polished it until it gleamed, and had sharpened Achilleus' spear to a new point, the old one having been snapped off in the fight with Just John at the palace.

'I made the mistake of over-sharpening it that time,' Achilleus had explained to Paddy when he'd handed the spear over. 'The tip wasn't strong enough. It don't got to be, like, needle-sharp, just enough to puncture skin without too much of a sweat.'

Achilleus had originally made the spear out of a steel pole, wrapping leather round the shaft to make a grip. It was short. Like Paddy said, it was good for stabbing, rather than slicing or throwing. Ollie had told him once that that was the way Roman legionaries used to fight, with a short spear called a pilum. And *they'd* conquered the world. He was very attached to his spear. As the whole thing was metal, he could theoretically keep sharpening it like a pencil whenever it got blunt. Although, of course, it would get shorter and shorter.

Ollie and three of his missile unit were coming with them. It was always useful to have fighters who could hit grown-ups from a distance. If you didn't have to engage with them face-to-ugly-face they weren't such a threat. Big Mick was in charge of another group of three fighters, and Blue was going to be their general. Lewis was staying behind with his squad, along with the rest of Blue's people.

Blue and Maxie wanted to make sure they didn't empty the museum of all their good fighters, or Justin might just be tempted to lock them out.

They'd finished cleaning out the lower level last night, carting away the last of the rubbish and the dead grown-ups. Justin had positively identified the severed girl's head as Stacey and they'd buried it that morning under a tree at the front of the museum. Of Paul Channing they'd found no sign and assumed he must have been eaten. It would be Maxie's job to organize all the remaining kids in the museum into work parties to block up broken windows, seal doors and board up any openings they found.

Right now Maxie was standing up on the first-floor balcony watching the group assemble. Wishing they didn't have to go.

'We'll be back tonight, tomorrow at the latest.'

Blue and Big Mick joined her at the balustrade.

'Don't do anything crazy, will you?' Maxie said and Blue looked at her like she was an idiot. Maxie apologized. 'I know you won't, but . . . Sometimes I wish we were still back in Holloway. Things seemed so much simpler there.'

'Life *is* better here, Max,' said Blue. 'I don't doubt it. We just got to prove to the nerds that we ain't the enemy.'

'I don't want anyone else to get hurt,' said Maxie. 'I don't want *you* to get hurt.'

'If it looks ugly out there I'm bringing everyone straight back, no chat.'

'Promise me. Don't be a hero, yeah?'

'I'll leave that to Achilleus,' said Blue and they looked down to where Achilleus was showing off to a group of the museum kids, working through his collection of weapons one by one, with Paddy looking on proudly.

'Idiot.' Blue chuckled and rolled his shoulders and picked up his backpack. It looked heavy with food and water. He gave Maxie a hug.

'Don't get fazed if it takes us longer, will you?' he said. 'We none of us know exactly what to expect out there. And it's possible this Einstein dude might want to do some more shopping.'

'Where exactly are you going then?'

'The nerds checked out the suppliers for the museum labs, where they used to get all their chemicals and equipment from. And they've found where the suppliers was based. The best bet seems to be a place called Promithios out near Heathrow Airport. There's some sort of science and technology park over there. Is only about ten miles away, straight down the M4. Should be a fairly safe route once we're on the motorway.'

Blue seemed so together, so confident. Maxie resisted the urge to kiss him. She wasn't sure if they were officially an item now. And none of the other Holloway kids knew that they'd got close during their time locked up together in the sick-bay at the palace.

Then, without warning, Blue suddenly kissed her. She must have looked surprised because he laughed.

'Whassup, girl?'

'Nothing. I just wasn't expecting it.'

'Well, you can expect a whole lot more where that came from.'

So that answered that one. She laughed now and threw her arms round him, giving him an over-the-top hug.

Big Mick made a rude comment and Blue swore at him, but before Maxie could say anything else Mick pointed down to where Einstein was marching along the corridor

102

that led from the orange zone with an entourage of kids in white coats. Justin was trotting along behind, trying to catch up.

Einstein had changed into a baggy tweed coat that flapped about him as he walked. He had an old leather bag slung over one shoulder, a tightly furled umbrella in one hand, and his untidy hair had been crammed into a wide-brimmed hat. He looked full of himself, happy and puffed up. This was his expedition after all.

'Don't let that guy screw things up,' said Maxie. 'Don't let him take you anywhere stupid. Don't let him take you away from me.'

19

Justin at last managed to draw level with Einstein and put a hand on his arm, holding him back from joining the main group. Einstein stopped and bared his green teeth at Justin in a horsey grin, wafting bad breath into his face.

'I've told you, Justin, there's no point in banging on and on about this. It's getting *bo-or-ring*.'

'All I'm saying is there's nobody else here as clever as you, Einstein. We won't get anywhere without you running the research department. You *are* the bloody research department.'

'That's why I have to lead the expedition,' said Einstein. 'It's my party. I'm the only one who knows what we need to pick up. I can't just send a shopping list out with these morons, it's not that simple.'

Justin snorted with embarrassed laughter and shushed Einstein.

'Don't let them hear you calling them that,' he said, keeping his voice low.

'Well, they *are* morons,' said Einstein. 'Look at them!'

Achilleus was now trying to swipe a tennis ball off Paddy's head with a lethal-looking sword. Justin sniggered.

'I want this to go well,' said Einstein. 'It's not every day we get this opportunity. And because it's important, *I'm* doing it.'

'What you mean is you want the glory, don't you?' said Justin. 'You want Chris Marker and his scribes to write you up in their history books.'

'Look around you, Justin. All the great men in this museum, the scientists and doctors, Darwin and the rest of them, they made their names by going out and *discovering* stuff. So yes, that's what I'm doing.'

'All right. But I doubt we'll get much done with you away.'

'I've left notes, clear instructions. Gordy's going to be in charge while I'm gone. You just carry on with what we've been doing, more of the same, and I'll be back by tomorrow.'

'There's not much to do really,' said Justin. 'Since our tame sickos got out we don't have any specimens to take samples from.'

'Then find some more,' said Einstein airily, waving his hand in the air as if all Justin had to do was go and pick some up at the local shops. 'I don't know why you didn't just get them to catch one on the lower level while they were down there.'

'I asked them to. They were too wild, though, apparently, too sick. It was too dangerous.'

'Tell you what then,' said Einstein. 'We'll bring you some back from our trip. OK?'

'Don't be funny, Einstein.'

'I'm not being funny. I'll pick you out some nice ripe ones and ship them back here. That way it'll be a proper expedition. Like capturing chimpanzees in the wild.'

'Einstein, you can't treat this as a big joke. It's going to be dangerous. You haven't left the museum in months. You missed what happened the other night when they broke in. And it's not just you. The other kids who are going with you – they could get hurt.'

'Isn't that what we want?'

'What?'

Einstein leant closer to Justin, his breath warm on his face.

'For our experiments. How are we ever going to know if the disease can be passed on from adults to children if one of us doesn't get bitten?'

'Christ's sake, Einstein. You can't want someone to be bitten!'

'That's exactly what I want. We could develop an antidote. Using infected blood. But for that we need a kid who's survived a bite. That's the thing we need most right now.'

'You're nuts, you know that? They don't just bite you, they bloody well eat you.'

'I may be nuts, but I'm not stupid, Justin. I know what sickos can do. But we've got the mighty morons to protect us now, haven't we! So, if you will excuse me, we need to get a move on.'

'Einstein . . .' Justin called out lamely after him.

'Everything's going to be all right!' Einstein shouted back without turning round.

20

Paul was leaning over the edge of one of the water-storage tanks in the roof of the museum. He could see himself and a patch of the ceiling reflected in the water's glassy surface. He looked bad. Too thin. Eyes red. Skin yellow. Lips cracked and dry.

He needed to look after himself better.

He'd climbed down from the roof in the night and taken a chicken from one of the coops. Had eaten it raw back in his den, leaving feathers and gizzards and crap everywhere. It had taken the edge off his hunger, but he still had a raging thirst. And the thirst was worse than the hunger. If he didn't keep drinking he would quickly start to feel faint and weak. Confused. He'd collected some old bottles, a discarded kettle. Was going to fill them all up and keep them close.

He wriggled further over the edge of the tank and leant down as far as he dared. The tank was huge and he didn't want to fall in. He got into a position from where he could reach down and scoop water up to his mouth with one hand, holding on to the tank with the other. As he reached out, his fingers broke the reflection and sent it shimmering off in all directions, the water no longer glassy but dancing, crazed. He brought his hand back up to his mouth, lapped water from his palm. It was cool, clean. Tasted of nothing.

It hurt to swallow. His throat felt like there were razor blades embedded in it. His whole head was bunged up and burning. Thick mucus filled his nose and ears and he was forever coughing up sticky green gobbets streaked with red.

The edge of the tank hurt where it cut into his belly. His guts were rumbling, churning. He dipped his hand in again, managed to scoop more water up this time. He drank it down greedily then belched and nearly threw up. That wouldn't do. He didn't want to poison his water supply. He held the puke down and splashed up more water, sucking it from his dirty fingers. He tried not to think about how sick he felt, how much his stomach hurt, tried to lose himself in the mechanical process of getting water to his mouth, his hand rising and falling like a machine. At last he had drunk enough and stopped, panting, his eyes closed. Listening to the water as it slopped about in the tank, the sounds echoing off the metal sides.

When he opened his eyes the world was settling down, the reflections slowing their mad dance, coming together again. He watched the hypnotic display. Gradually everything calmed and grew still and finally he could see into the dark depths of the tank.

He realized with a shock that there was something down there. Moving. Alive. A creature, rising slowly from the bottom, looming up at him. As he stared, he began to make out its shape.

Black flesh and grey bones, broken wings and a gaping chest, greasy feathers . . .

He wanted to be sick again.

It was Boney-M, swimming about down there, an oily trail following him through the water, spreading out like the filthy discharge from a ship's engine.

Paul clamped a hand to his mouth. He mustn't throw up. But the thought of drinking water polluted by this filthy beast made his stomach flip. Boney's beak opened like a shark's mouth and came up out of the water. It made a choking sound then closed with a clack.

One beady eye stared at him. The leathery eyelids closed slowly over it and then slid open.

'You shouldn't swim in my drinking water,' said Paul.

'You what? Who are you to tell me what I should and shouldn't do, puke boy? I can do what I sodding well like, you little sickie-puke-boy.'

'You'll poison me.'

'Don't make me laugh. You're already poisoned, you moron. Didn't your mother tell you?'

'I'm not poisoned. I'm just not feeling very well.'

'*I'm not poisoned. I'm just not feeling very well* . . . Listen to you. What a whiner. You know nothing, pus-for-brains. Look at you, drifting around up here like a wet fart. Why aren't you down there, sorting them out? The little bastards. You promised me you were going to do something about them.'

'I can't. Not yet. I don't feel strong enough.'

'Feeble excuse from a feeble specimen.'

'There's too many of them. More came. Didn't you know? I don't know where they're from. There's too many of them now. And they can fight. They're strong. I've seen them. I watched them, down in the lower level, killing sickos. What can I do?'

'Do what you always do, feeble-fairy-sicko-puking-chunks-and-chunder,' shrieked the horrible, broken bird thing. 'Nothing! You do NOTHING. You just watch and wait and watch and wait. Why don't you go and look and see what they're up to? Huh? Move your fat arse. Do it, do it, do it . . .'

Paul made his way out on to the roof and scuttled across it to the front of the museum, shielding his eyes from the glare of the sun.

Even before he got to the edge he could hear them, children talking, laughing, shouting, their feet scraping on the ground. And as he reached the low wall that ran round the building he shook with silent laughter.

'Look,' he said. 'Look! They're going! The new ones are leaving.'

Twenty-four children were trooping out through the gates and turning right on to Cromwell Road, heading west.

'What did I tell you?' said Boney-M. 'Now's your chance.'

21

The expedition moved slowly. They were wheeling two large trolleys that had once been used for shifting things around the museum. Their small, sturdy wheels were perfect for indoor use and for carrying heavy objects, but they rattled and bumped and had a tendency to get stuck on any uneven surfaces.

Ollie could see that the trolleys were going to be trouble. He was already nervous and the trolleys just made him more so. For the hundredth time he counted the heavy steel pellets he used as slingshot, transferring them from one leather pouch on his belt to another. Thirty-three, thirty-four, thirty-five . . . That should do it.

He really wasn't sure how he felt about leaving the museum so soon and putting himself back into the mouth of danger. Since leaving Holloway they'd been on a roller-coaster. He had to admit, though, that the most dangerous part of their journey had been through north London. It was noticeably quieter here in the centre of town, and the quality of the grown-ups was definitely inferior. They were weak and pathetic, and, luckily, pretty thin on the ground. Didn't stop him being scared, though. Something was nagging away at him, a dark thought; it had dug into his brain like a tick, its claws holding tight, and it infected him with a constant low-level anxiety. It made his heart beat faster every now and then for no apparent reason, and he was sleeping badly.

Even now, with the sun on his back, he felt kind of cold, and the day seemed dark. He knew what it was, the bad thought. It wasn't a threat from outside. It was from inside.

He made a decision.

He would go and talk to the geeky boy in the tweed coat. Einstein.

Ollie had taken his usual place at the rear of the group, regularly checking behind for any grown-ups. He'd chosen his three best shots to make up his team. He didn't have to worry about them, they knew the drill. He told them to keep their eyes open and sped up, working his way through the main group to where Einstein was strolling along with the other kids from the museum. Ollie spotted a younger girl who looked familiar. She was wearing what looked like old-fashioned monks' robes. The kids at the Natural History Museum all dressed weirdly, mostly in clothes they'd looted from the clothing and fashion galleries of the Victoria and Albert Museum next door. And this girl looked like she was auditioning for some *Lord of the Rings* style fantasy film.

'Why do I recognize you?' he said, drawing level with her.

The girl looked shyly down at the ground and mumbled something.

'Say again.'

'You saved me the other night.'

Now Ollie noticed that she was carrying a large leather notebook under her arm.

'You're the World Book Day kid.' What was her name? Something weird. Celery?

'Yes.'

'How you doing? You recovered all right?'

'I wasn't hurt. You shot that sicko just in time. You're a very good shot.'

'I do my best. So what's the book for? You got maps in there or something?'

'No. I'm going to make an accurate record of everything that happens.'

'Yeah? That really necessary?'

'Of course it is.' The girl sounded insulted. 'It's for the Chronicles of Survival.'

'Fair enough. I'll take your word for it. What's your name again?'

'Lettis. The same as lettuce, but it's spelled different.'

'Lettis. Right.' Ollie had already offended her once by questioning her book so he figured he'd better bite his tongue and not say anything about her name.

'Hi, Lettis. My name's Ollie.'

'I know. I've got it written down. I've already written down *all* your names. I wrote yours down first. It's the most important.'

'I dunno about that.'

'When I heard you were going on the expedition I volunteered,' said Lettis. 'Even though I was scared.'

'I'm honoured,' said Ollie. 'Though I'd have thought we'd be taking as many fighters as we could, rather than, like, writers.'

'The pen is mightier than the sword,' said Einstein, slightly sarcastically.

'Tell that to a hungry father,' said Ollie.

'We do need to keep an accurate record of what's happening, though,' said Einstein. 'You never know what's going

113

to be important. The boy who runs the library, Chris Marker, is making sure he keeps a proper history. When we're older it'll be a vital record.'

'If we ever *make it* that far,' said Ollie.

'Oh, I'm intending to grow old,' said Einstein.

Ollie moved closer to him. 'Can I ask you something, yeah?' he said. 'In private.'

Einstein looked him up and down and then moved slightly apart from his group. 'I suppose so.'

'You're like a what?' said Ollie. 'A scientist? Is that what you'd call yourself?'

'I suppose so.'

'And, apparently, you're, like, looking into what caused the disease; that's what Akkie told me anyway. You're trying to find out how it works, that kind of thing.'

'That kind of thing, yes,' said Einstein. 'As well as we can. I was outstanding at science at school. Did my GCSEs early. I was already studying A-level biology and chemistry. But I'm still just a teenage boy. So it's fairly basic stuff, quite limited really. Are you any good at science?'

'Not bad,' said Ollie. 'I'd certainly like to help out when we get back.'

'You're not *all* special needs then?'

'We've had to do what we can to get by,' said Ollie, ignoring Einstein's dig. 'Don't judge by appearances.'

'As if,' said Einstein.

Ollie wasn't sure how to take Einstein. He seemed unreasonably cheerful, considering how dangerous their situation was. He wondered just how cheerful he'd remain after the first attack.

Because there would be one.

That much Ollie knew. There was no way they were

going to get ten miles across London and back without coming across any grown-ups.

Not to mention what might be waiting for them when they got to the technology park.

'So have you found out anything yet about the disease?' Ollie pressed him. 'Anything useful?'

Einstein waved a hand in the air. 'We've made *some* progress,' he said. 'We're struggling, though, basically. In the end I probably know more about it than anyone else in London, but it wouldn't exactly fill a book. A small pamphlet maybe. Is that what you wanted to ask about? The disease?'

'In a way, yes. Well, actually, no . . . yes.'

'All right,' said Einstein. 'I'll tell you what I know, and I'll keep it simple.'

He quickly ran through the discoveries he'd made in the labs and what they might mean. Although he stressed that a lot of his ideas were just that – ideas, theories, guesswork. He was more than happy to share it all with Ollie, though, who asked the odd question here and there for clarity. Einstein obviously loved showing off his knowledge and Ollie needed to get to the root of what was bothering him. In the end, as Einstein didn't look like he was going to cover this area, Ollie came right out and asked him. Although he made sure that nobody else was listening first.

'What happens,' he asked, fumbling for the right words, 'when you, if you, you know, if *someone* got older?'

Einstein laughed through his nose. 'There's no "if" about it really, is there, Ollie? We all get older. Fact of life. Fact of death. No way round it.'

'Yeah, that's not what I meant, though. I meant – what happens when someone hits fifteen?'

'Ah, I get where you're coming from, ginger. The penny drops with a mighty clang. You want to know if you're going to get sick.'

'Not exactly, no, I don't mean me, I mean just in general.'

'No, *of course* you don't mean you. How ridiculous of me to think that. You were asking about a distant relative or a family friend no doubt. Maybe a favourite pet.'

'Seriously, I don't mean me. I just wanted to know. Out of interest.'

'I'm fifteen,' said Einstein. 'Does that answer your question?'

'Not really.'

'*Not really.*'

'Well . . . I don't know what you were like before, do I? So I can't tell if you've changed. I mean, were you always a sarcastic pain in the arse?'

'Oh, that wounds.'

'I mean, maybe your rude manner is simply a result of getting sick?'

'Afraid not,' said Einstein. 'I've always rubbed people up the wrong way. They can't cope with my superior intelligence. I've always had a very high IQ. I've always been very advanced for my age, and I've always been unnecessarily rude.'

'So what you're saying . . .'

'What I'm saying is that it's not like you'll get to fifteen and suddenly start frothing at the mouth and trying to eat people.'

'I won't – I wouldn't – get sick straight away?'

'Come on, Ollie, be a man. Oh no, wait a minute, that's what's scaring you . . . Listen, it doesn't make any difference to me. As I said, I'm already fifteen. We both know what you're talking about. You're nearly fifteen, you've got a birthday coming up and you're scared of what's going to happen to you.'

'No.'

'Oh *please* . . .'

'I've just *had* my birthday actually.'

'There you go. Well . . . Happy birthday. Do you *feel* any different?'

'No.'

'Exactly. The thing is, you need to look at it like this. We all talk about the disease only affecting people over the age of fourteen because, when it struck, that's what happened. But it wasn't a hard and fast rule, was it, if you think about it? It wasn't like an exact line was drawn through the calendar. It was just a rough divide. A convenient way of looking at what was happening. And, of course, since then we've all been growing older, and since then we've seen no evidence of kids getting the disease.'

'That's a relief.'

'It doesn't mean that kids definitely won't develop the disease in the future, though.'

'Great. You had me feeling good for about, oh, I don't know, three milliseconds.'

'Science can't give hard answers, only theories,' said Einstein. 'That's how it works. We observe what we can and make judgements based on that. And, as I say, so far we haven't *observed* anyone getting sick as they get older. Until we really understand the way the disease works we won't know what caused it and what might happen in the future. Are we immune? Are we incubating the disease? Did whatever was causing the disease stop doing what it was doing at a certain date? Did something happen fifteen years ago?'

'Or stop happening.'

'You got it. Exactly. And that's what I'm trying to find out. Are we immune? Or are we all carrying the disease, all slowly getting ill? We just don't know. That's the point of this expedition, to find what we need to carry on our research.'

'So we're fetching chemicals?'

'Chemicals, drugs, medicine, anything like that. I'm hoping the Promithios warehouse will have all we need. Unless it got burned down or cleaned out.'

'And that's what the trolleys are for?'

'Yeah. I know they'll slow us down, but we need to pick up a lot of gear.'

Ollie blew out his breath and rubbed the back of his neck. 'I never thought, when we were battling our way across London from Holloway, that it was to go on a shopping trip.'

'Weren't you all living in a supermarket?'

'Yeah.'

'Then maybe it's your destiny.'

22

This is the official report of day one of the expedition to the Promithios warehouse and supply depot near Heathrow Airport. Written by the scribe Lettis Slingsbury. It is as true as I can make it. Maybe someone else would see it differently. But I was there, and this is what I saw.

FIRST ENTRY: *We are stopped right now and this is my first chance to write anything in the journal. I don't know how much I can write before we have to start up again, but I will try my best.*

We set off in the morning when the sun was already high in the sky. There were twenty-four people. I have written the list of who they are at the end of the journal. We are bringing trolleys with us so that we can bring back all the supplies we are going to get. The trolleys are very slow. They have these very small wheels so they keep sticking in every hole and bump. The people pushing them don't like it. The trolleys rattle noisily and judder and every time they hit something they jerk suddenly and painfully. There was a lot of complaining and swearing and grumbling as we went along our way.

Einstein had calculated that we would be able to get to Heathrow in one day. Which is where the warehouse is. The distance is roughly about fourteen and a half miles. So it should take roughly about five hours' walking time, and a bit more for lunch and for resting. But he hadn't calculated how much the trolleys would slow us down. He also hadn't calculated what would happen if we met any sickos. Which is really stupid if you think about it, because there are lots of sickos out there, and London is a big place and nobody really knew what we might find. Einstein was confident and cocky because we had the new kids with us, the ones from Holloway, who are good fighters. He is not as clever as he thinks, I don't think.

Apart from the trolleys and the complaining and the swearing, the first hour went all right I suppose. We travelled west along the Cromwell Road to Hammersmith, past big old houses and along a wide road. We also passed many offices and buildings of that nature, and went over the Hammersmith flyover. It wasn't too hard to push the trolleys along this bit as the road was good, a four-lane highway, a bit like a motorway. It was good to be up high and look out over London.

This was the furthest I had been from the museum since we arrived a year ago. London is so big. There is so much of it. It all looked very still and quiet. There were some parts that had been burned down in fires, and there was some smoke in the distance. There was a mess still from the riots and battles that had taken place when the disease first came and there was no one to clear it all up. But it was a nice sunny day and actually London mostly looked quite nice. There was a big building that looked like a big glass bubble and Jasmine said it was called the Ark. Then there was a shopping centre on a roundabout and after that an old church, down below us. Nobody had damaged it. I felt it was quite comforting, seeing the church. I used to go to church before all this happened. I didn't always enjoy it, but we went every Sunday. This journal record is not about me, though, so I must write more about what I saw.

On the opposite side of the flyover was a big theatre sort of thing. Emily Winter said she had been to see a concert there once. A boy band I had never even heard of, but she said were really popular. I'm not really into pop music, but this is not about me. Then a group of boys got excited, they said they had seen some sickos down below, and everyone crowded over to the side. We couldn't see anything and thought they had made it up. We waited for a while, but nothing was moving and in the end Einstein said we should carry on.

Then there was an argument about who should push the trolleys – they really were a nuisance. A boy from Holloway settled the argument. His name is Achilleus. He is quite ugly. I know I shouldn't say that, but it is true. And I have to write the truth. He has lots of injuries and scars, and one side of his head is all bandaged up. The bandage is really quite dirty. Maybe if he wasn't so beaten up he would look OK, but I don't think so. I think he is quite scary. He has all swirly patterns carved into his hair and has another boy called Paddy to carry his weapons in a golf-bag. It looks very heavy and I could see that Paddy was tired, but the boy, the other boy, the big boy, Achilleus, didn't seem to notice, or at least be bothered by Paddy getting tired. Anyway, what happened was that Achilleus shouted at some children and threatened them and ordered them to push the trolleys. Einstein complained and said that it was his job to be in charge and tell people what to do and Achilleus just laughed at him.

Achilleus isn't even in charge of the Holloway people. A black boy called Blue is their leader. Blue didn't seem to mind that Achilleus was ordering people around. So we carried on. Nobody was very happy, but nobody would risk saying anything because, to be fair, it's not just me; they are all scared of Achilleus, even Einstein I think. Although he tries to pretend he isn't. The only one who isn't scared of him is Paddy, and he is all red-faced and sweating, puffing and panting along.

Achilleus has other tough boys around him from Holloway, including another ugly one called Big Mick. Who is not only ugly but also big. I suppose that's how he got his name. It's not a clever one like Little John. I will not be rude about Mick, because he is a very good fighter and also when I got a bit tired and said so he carried me for a bit, sort of like he was joking, but it was nice. Mick is not so scary as Achilleus. My favourite one is Ollie, though. He rescued me from a fearsome sicko on the night of the World Book Day attack. Ollie is not scary, he is quite friendly, but quite quiet. I think he is the cleverest of them. He was talking to Einstein for a long time. I thought that if there was trouble Ollie would be sure to look after me. I was not so sure about Achilleus.

My friends from the museum started to grumble and mutter about the new children, but I thought it would be another matter if we ever did meet any sickos. Which we did. But I will come to that in a minute. We carried on like that for roughly about another hour, maybe more, and everyone was cheering up because we were going faster, and the road was good and wide and safe all the way. It used to be the main road west out of London, so it is wide. We went quite easily and were not too fearful of attack. It was mostly raised up or had railings on the sides so there was no danger of sickos coming after us.

Our route was to go along the A4 to the motorway, the M4, and travel out to Heathrow on that. But when we got to the start of the motorway there was a big roundabout there that the road was supposed to cross over and we found that there had been a fire and maybe a bit of an explosion. There were burnt trees and buildings and the skeletons of cars and lorries and buses and other wreckage, and the upper bit of the flyover that crossed over the roundabout had fallen down. There was just a big pile of rubble and broken up concrete in our way. Einstein said we would have to go round it and find somewhere to get back up on to the motorway. That was easier said than done. It would have been quite easy if we didn't have the trolleys. But we did have the trolleys, we couldn't change that fact, and had to get them down over the rubble on to the roundabout.

The trolleys are quite heavy at the bottom and they had to be carried, so I don't need to tell you that now everyone was really grumbling and angry, and I suppose nobody was paying attention because the next thing we knew there were sickos there. I suppose they had come out from inside a nearby building. They were very diseased-looking and they threw everyone into a mad panic. There was all shouting and some people tried to run away back up on to the motorway. There were maybe about twenty-five of the grown-ups. It was Blue who took charge now, not Achilleus and certainly not Einstein. Blue was telling people what to do and the people from Holloway made themselves into a proper fighting squad.

Big Mick and three fighters took one side, Achilleus took Jackson and the museum fighters on the other side, Ollie stayed in the middle with his team. They had slings and javelins and even stones and other throwing stuff. Blue was moving all over, shouting out orders and bossing everyone around. I was scared and kept behind the fighters. There were others like me so I don't mind saying it.

Ollie's squad fired at the sickos, and they were very effective. The sickos fell back and one of them was knocked over. He looked dead. But the Holloway people didn't want to let them get away. Achilleus led a charge and Jackson was in the charge with them. It is hard to describe, but Achilleus' team came in from one side and Mick's team sort of came in from the other and they chopped and hacked at the sickos with their spears and clubs and swords.

To tell you the truth, I couldn't watch. I know I am

supposed to be a witness and write about everything,
I am supposed to be a neutral journalist, recording
what happens, but you see I was scared by the fight,
and there wasn't anything I could do about that, or
pretend it wasn't so. I didn't like to see the blood and
everything. Next time I will be more brave and try to
look properly. I promise. I did interview one of the
key players (Ollie) as they are called, afterwards, so
that I was sure I could make an accurate record. But
anyway what happened in the end was that seven of
those sickos were killed in all and the rest of them
got away. However, the bad thing was that as the fight
was going on another group of sickos came at us from
somewhere else. From the back actually. We weren't
ready for them. They got very close before one of the
museum people who was standing with me, Caspar
Leverson, spotted them and gave a great cry.

'More sickos,' he shouted. 'There are more of them.'
Or something like that. Certainly warning us there
were more sickos. Next Blue turned round and quickly
ordered everyone out of the way so that Ollie's team
could fire at them. The new sickos. They were just in
time. They were very accurate. I think Ollie is a bril-
liant fighter. Also Blue and Einstein, and some of the
museum people who weren't in the main fight, attacked
the new sickos after Ollie's team had shot at them.
Einstein boasted afterwards that he had fought them
off and won the battle, but actually it was Blue and
his fighters who really finished the sickos off.

Half of the new group were killed and the other
half was driven off under a hail of missiles. Then
everyone was loud and noisy and excited, all talking

125

about the battle. Showing off. Luckily nobody had been hurt apart from Daryl Painter who fell over when the second lot of sickos attacked and cut himself on the pile of rubble and concrete. It was not serious, though. Blue said that we should all get moving quickly in case any more sickos came. He said they would be attracted by the noise and the smell.

I suppose he meant the smell of blood and dead meat. It was very strong, but for me the smell of the sickos was stronger. They smell horrible. Worse when they are dead. I tried not to look at the bodies, but some of the children went over and started poking the corpses and saying things and making jokes. I suppose they did it to try and get rid of their fear. Caspar started to kick one of the bodies and it sort of burst. Everyone said 'eurgh', and he had all like sticky green gunge stuff on his trainer. One girl was sick. It was Jasmine.

So then we still had to get the trolleys over the roundabout and up the other side where there was a ramp back up to the motorway. It took a long time and everyone was getting crosser and crosser. The high spirits after the battle were turning bad. People were stressed and moody. Blue got in a big argument with Einstein, and Ollie had to calm them down. Ollie is calm and sensible. Without him I think the Holloway people would be much more difficult and moody and there would be more fights.

We did get the trolleys back up on to the motorway, but we found that the road here was badly damaged with all cracks and potholes. There were plants growing out of it and they made the surface even worse.

126

One of the trolleys got damaged when it went into a pothole; the wheel got sort of bent and wouldn't go straight and it made a horrid squealing, creaky sound and the trolley wouldn't roll straight. We tried to carry on, but it was too difficult, so Einstein said we had to stop and repair it. As you can imagine, this led to more arguments, but Einstein insisted.

That is where we are and why I can write this down while I have a moment. Jackson and Daryl worked on the wheel. Jackson had brought some tools with her. She is very organized like that, and very good with her hands. She has been working on the trolley for nearly an hour now and all the while everyone else has been getting grumpier and grumpier and more and more nervous. We haven't gone that far from where the dead bodies are still lying out in the sun. It would be easy for sickos to come up the ramps to where we are. Blue posted guards and look-outs everywhere, but everyone is well jumpy. There have been lots of false alarms.

I will stop writing now because I think Jackson has got the trolley sort of working. At least working well enough to push it along. I hope there are no more delays so I will write the next part when we get to the warehouse and stop. With the delay caused by mending the wheel, and the battle and the fact that we are going too slowly anyway because of the trol-leys, we are more than two hours over schedule. I heard Blue saying to Einstein that he was worried that we might not get to Heathrow before it got dark and whether we should go back and try again another day when we would be better prepared, but Einstein *said we should carry on or all that time and effort would have been wasted.*

I hope, really hope we are going to get there in time and be able to go home today, although I am already quite tired of walking and we haven't even come that far. Not very far, but the museum feels like a long way away, a million miles. I hope my friends there are all well and maybe they are wondering where we are and what we are doing and when they read this journal they will know.

23

At last it was growing dark. Shadows were creeping out of the corners in the museum, pooling like spilt oil. It had been a long day. Gripped by fever, his guts churning, Paul had sat in his den and waited, barely moving. Hot and cold at the same time, shivering, sweating, dribbling, burping — thick, caustic belches bubbling up his gullet like poison gas.

At least he hadn't been troubled by Boney-M for a few hours. The little monster gave him a headache with his constant shouting. He'd rattled around for a while in the morning, limping and moaning, picking up crap in his beak, shaking it and dropping it, claiming that it was him that had made the new dangerous kids leave the museum, the little liar, and then he'd disappeared. It had been quiet up here since then. Just the sound of the wind gently probing, trying to get in. And every now and then distant thin voices would drift in through the cracks. Like insect voices. They'd tickle Paul's mind then dissolve into silence. There had been a numb feel to the day, like nothing mattered. In the end even the wind had given up its nagging.

And Paul had waited, through the long, dull hours, and planned his move. Waited for when he could sneak down there and pick one of them off. A small one — a young one — too dangerous otherwise.

Couldn't risk a fight.

Couldn't go down there in the light either. Had to do it at night when he could think straight and there were more dark places to hide. If he left it too late, though, they'd all go into the minerals gallery and close the doors. He had maybe a half-hour window of opportunity. At dusk, when the light drained away and they all came strolling back from wherever they'd been working. They would gather in the main hall then move up to the gallery. He had to get one of them when they were on the move, defences down, looking forward to their beds.

Or in the toilet.

Yes. That was a possibility.

During the day the kids used some toilets Justin had had built outside. They'd been nicknamed the Dumper. Justin was very proud of his Dumper. The nerdy jerk. All their waste was collected in big stinky bins and emptied on to a midden, a great dunghill they'd started in some nearby gardens. They'd all sort of got used to the smell from the Dumper. But at night the kids couldn't risk going outside and used some toilets just off the main hall instead, flushing them with grey waste water from their cooking and washing.

Maybe that was the best place to ambush one of them?

Yes. Time to move. Time to show Boney-M that he wasn't useless.

Time to start his collection.

24

'I'm supposed to be the head of security,' said Robbie. 'I can't be stuck here. I'm useless. I could have helped the other night. But my leg . . .'

'It's all right,' said Maeve, 'we're gonna sort that out,' and she stuck a thermometer in his mouth.

'Can you really fix it?' Robbie asked, his words slightly muffled by the thermometer.

'I can try,' said Maeve. 'It's still sore, yeah?'

'You could say that.'

They were in a small meeting room at the front of the museum, close to the minerals gallery, that the kids had set up as a sick-bay. Robbie was lying on a bed, covered by a sheet. Maeve was trying not to think too much about what she might find when they lifted that sheet.

'I was helping Brooke,' said Robbie. 'Her and some friends of hers. Guy called DogNut, girl called Courtney and two other dudes, Felix and Marco . . .'

Robbie stopped and Maeve wiped some sweat off his forehead with a damp cloth. This was obviously a bad memory for him, but he needed to get it out, so Maeve let him talk.

'We were escorting them to the Tower of London,' he went on. 'But we were ambushed.'

'I know all about it,' said Maeve. 'I was there. Well, only after you'd got away. Brooke told me what happened.'

'Yeah,' said Robbie. 'All the rest of them were killed, along with two of my team. We underestimated the sickos. If it wasn't for Jackson and Ethan, who carried me back here, I'd be dead too.'

'I know,' said Maeve again, patiently. Robbie was slightly feverish, caught up in his own thoughts and nightmares.

There were kids in two of the other beds, sitting up, watching. A boy who'd been injured in the recent attack, and a girl who had some kind of stomach upset. Maeve had been brought here by Samira, who acted as one of the museum's doctors. She was sitting on the opposite side of Robbie's bed to Maeve, her hair tucked up inside a head-scarf. Ella and Jibber-jabber were on hospital duty and sat on an empty bed watching. For once Jibber-jabber was quiet. Robbie looked very unwell and there was a hushed atmosphere in the room.

Samira had explained on the way over that Robbie had escaped being bitten, but his injuries were still bad and were proving slow to heal. He had a badly wrenched arm and a nasty gash in his other arm, but worst of all, apparently, was a puncture wound in his groin, on the inside of his thigh where his leg met his abdomen. As far as Samira could tell, one of Robbie's friends had broken his sword in the fight and a sicko had got hold of a piece of blade that had snapped off. The pain as the sicko drove the metal into his body must have been awful and it had put Robbie completely out of action.

He was quiet now, tears rolling down his cheeks. Whether from the pain or the bad memories Maeve couldn't tell.

'The wound refuses to heal,' said Samira. 'It keeps oozing this mixture of very black blood and a thin, watery sort of gel and this horrible stinking yellow pus.'

'Nice.'

'I can't move my leg,' Robbie added. 'And the whole of the side of my body is burning up.'

'We just don't know what to do for him,' said Samira.

Maeve had learnt a bit about the set-up at the museum. As well as Samira, there were two other kids who acted as doctors. Alexander, whose father had been a surgeon, and Alexander's girlfriend, Cass, who'd picked up stuff from studying books she'd found in the museum. Samira had always wanted to be a doctor and had done several emergency first-aid courses at school. The three of them also worked with Einstein in the laboratories. Other kids helped out with general nursing duties and some of the younger ones also took it in turns to be general dogsbodies, cleaning up and running errands, mainly to keep from getting bored.

None of the three museum 'doctors' could work out what to do for Robbie, though. Their medical knowledge was still fairly limited. He lay there, sweating and groaning, and they could do little more than change his dressing, wipe his wound with antiseptic and give him painkillers. They'd been wondering whether to try him on antibiotics – they had a small supply of them at the museum – but weren't sure which ones to use, or how exactly to use them, and so hadn't risked it yet.

When Samira had found out from one of the other Holloway kids that Maeve was also a medic of sorts she'd asked her in to see if she had any ideas. Both of Maeve's parents had been doctors and it was a career she'd been set on before the world fell apart. Maeve had been intending to see Robbie in the morning, but he'd woken up half an hour ago shrieking in agony so she'd decided to take a look at him now.

The electronic thermometer beeped to show that it was ready and Maeve took it out of Robbie's mouth. It stuck for a moment to his parched lips. She checked the reading and frowned.

'It's pretty high,' she said. 'Nothing too dangerous yet, but if it keeps going up it's not good. I think I need to see the wound. Do you mind, Robbie?'

Robbie shook his head and tried to smile. He was a stocky kid with a broken nose and spiky hair.

'If you can stop the pain you can do what you like to me,' he said, his voice hoarse. Maeve offered him a glass of water and he gratefully took a sip.

Maeve called the two younger kids over.

'OK,' she said, 'can you carefully lift the sheet off him? Be as gentle as you can.'

Ella and Jibber-jabber took one side of the sheet each. Lifted it as if it was made of thin glass. Still Robbie winced.

He was wearing a T-shirt and some pyjama bottoms with one leg cut off. There was a big wad of cotton wool taped to the inside of his thigh. Maeve could see that it was stained with blood.

The whole area around the wound was purple.

'I've got to take the bandage off I'm afraid, Robbie,' she said, and then asked Samira to help. They did it quickly and Robbie cried out.

Maeve sucked in her breath. The wound looked horrible. It wasn't big, but it was dribbling and infected. If it wasn't

134

sorted out, the flesh around it would start to die and gangrene would set in. There was also the risk of blood poisoning. The bottom line was that even though the wound might not have been that impressive to look at, if it didn't heal Robbie might die.

'Sorry about this,' she said, 'but I'm going to have to touch it.'

Robbie gave a tight little nod.

Maeve had already washed her hands and put on some surgical gloves so she bent over to get a better look and put her fingers on either side of the wound. She gently pushed. Robbie gasped, thrashed his head from side to side, grinding his teeth.

'I haven't dared do that,' said Samira. 'I've been too scared of hurting him.'

'It helps that I don't know you,' Maeve said to Robbie, and he managed a smile.

'One way to get to know each other,' he said. 'But right now I think you're one sadistic bastard.'

'All doctors are,' said Maeve, peering more closely at the wound. 'They pretend to be doing it for the good of mankind, but actually they just like to hurt people.'

She gave another prod, pulling the wound wider. Blood bubbled out and Robbie gave a shout that was almost a scream.

'Who looked at the wound when he first came in?' Maeve asked Samira.

'Alexander and Cass,' she replied. 'There wasn't much to see. It didn't look too serious at the time; they were more worried about his shoulder and the cut on his arm.'

'OK.' Maeve sat down and took Robbie's hand. 'You know what I think?'

'What?'

'I think there's probably something still in there.'

'Really?'

'Yeah. You know what it's like when you get a splinter? It hurts a lot more than it should for such a small thing, and if you don't pull it out it can get all gummy and infected?'

'Yeah.'

'Well, I think you've got something like that in your wound. A bit of metal probably. What we've got to do is get it out. The only problem is that it's going to hurt like hell.'

'I don't know how it could hurt any worse than it does now,' Robbie croaked.

'Oh, believe me,' said Maeve, 'it can hurt a million times worse. But, like a splinter, once it's out the pain should go away pretty quick. As long as we make sure we fish everything out and nuke the infection.'

'OK. When shall we do it?'

'Now,' said Maeve, letting go of Robbie's hand and jumping to her feet. 'There's no point in waiting any longer. You'll only get worse.'

'What do you need?' said Samira. Her eyes were wide and shining. This was obviously all getting a little too real for her.

'The strongest painkillers you've got, antiseptic, disinfectant, more of these rubber gloves, some tweezers, a scalpel, a powerful torch and something to hold the wound open, you know, like some forceps? To be really safe, we're going to need to boil the scalpel and the tweezers. Oh, and we should grab three of the strongest guys we can find.'

While Maeve gave Robbie another painkiller, Samira, Ella and Jibber-jabber hurried off to get everything ready. Maeve was left to try to keep Robbie's spirits up. She chatted to him about his old life as a way of distracting him. Sometimes kids found it too distressing to remember the past, and all they'd lost, but Robbie was clearly relieved not to have to think about his present situation.

He told her how he'd grown up in Hammersmith, to the west of the museum, with one older sister and his mother. How they'd both got sick and died. It gave him some comfort to think that they hadn't become sickos. At least they'd found some peace. He'd been driven eastwards in the early days of the disaster, travelling with a group of friends to find somewhere safe.

'Hammersmith was mad back then,' he said. 'Battles in the streets. Not just sickos, but looters, criminals, gangs, rude boys. It was like a war. Bare dangerous. We had to get out. Only just made it too. Got me nose busted up by a gang who didn't like the look of us. Eventually we rocked up here. Met Justin and his crew, who'd arrived from south London in a big old supermarket lorry. We helped him break in and we been here ever since. What about you?'

'I grew up in the countryside,' said Maeve. 'I'm not a Londoner at all. We were visiting friends when it all kicked off. I've been wanting to get out of London ever since. Can't find anyone to go with me, though. Einstein's expedition, they've gone west, haven't they?'

'Yeah. Probably out through Hammersmith, then along the M4 to Heathrow somewhere.'

'Well, when they get back they can tell us what it's like,'

said Maeve. 'What the roads are like. If it's safe. I really, *really* don't want to stay in the city any longer. It's crazy. Out there, there are farms, animals, fields, proper places to grow food, space.'

'Yeah,' said Robbie. 'And sickos as well, most like.'

'Can't be any worse than here, can it?' said Maeve. 'We were persuaded to come into the centre of town by this weird guy who calls himself Jester.'

'I know him,' said Robbie. 'He's David's poodle at the palace.'

'Yeah, that's him. I tried to argue against it, said if we were going anywhere we should go to the countryside, not into the middle of town. I was shouted down. And here we are. And it's crap. No offence. Just more of the same. Getting from one day to another, slowly being killed by grown-ups.'

'Tell you what,' said Robbie. 'If you can fix me up, make the pain go away, give me back my leg, I'll personally escort you.'

Maeve gave him a twisted smile.

'Like you escorted that last lot?' Instantly she realized that she shouldn't have tried to make a joke about the attack. It was still too raw for Robbie.

'I'm sorry,' she said quietly. 'That was wrong.'

Robbie was silent for a while then he looked up at Maeve. 'I'll make a better job of it than that whole mess,' he said. 'Do it properly, get a decent crew together. Take you on a trip to the countryside.'

'I'll hold you to that.'

'Yeah, good. Good.' Robbie appeared to brighten up.

'You might never forgive me, though.' Maeve stared at the ugly hole in Robbie's leg.

'I'll forgive anything if it works . . .'

Maeve said nothing. *If it works.* She had no idea about that; she might just do more damage. There might not be anything in the wound.

After a while Jibber-jabber and Ella came back, carrying a steaming saucepan with surgical instruments rattling in the bottom. They were closely followed by Samira, who had found Lewis, Boggle and Whitney.

'OK,' said Maeve. 'Lewis, you take his feet. Hold them down, sit on them, whatever it takes, but I don't want him kicking about.'

'Cool,' said Lewis sleepily and he sauntered to the foot of the bed.

'You two lie across his body, so he can't move.'

Whitney giggled and raised her eyebrows at Robbie.

'Why don't we just take his arms?' asked Boggle.

'His arm's cut and his shoulder's been pulled about,' said Maeve. 'I don't want to make it worse.'

She handed Robbie a wad of rolled-up bandage. 'You better bite on this,' she said.

He swallowed hard then clamped the wad between his teeth. He had a glassy-eyed, anxious look about him. Poor bastard. It was about to get a whole lot worse.

Samira put on rubber gloves and soaked everything in disinfectant. Once she was ready Maeve picked up the scalpel.

'I'm going to open the wound up a bit,' she said to Samira. 'So we can get inside. Then you need to use the forceps to hold the edges apart so I can get the tweezers in. OK?'

'OK.' Samira looked as glassy-eyed and anxious as Robbie.

Maeve had read about this kind of surgery before, watched countless hospital programmes on the TV, but she'd never had to do anything like this in real life. She breathed out.

'Hold him still . . .'

Sniggering and making rude comments, Boggle and Whitney manoeuvred into position and lowered their bodies across Robbie, pinning him to the bed, while Lewis casually took hold of his legs.

'Ow,' said Robbie, and he gave Boggle a filthy look. 'I thought you was supposed to be my friend, Boggle.'

'Moist,' said Boggle, and he grinned at Whitney.

Maeve took a deep breath and stabbed the point of the scalpel into Robbie's skin about a centimetre away from the wound. His whole body jerked and he whimpered pathetically. Boggle and Whitney weren't grinning any more. Lewis was unmoved; he stayed his usual calm, cool self, watching Maeve, almost bored, like someone spectating at a game of chess. Maeve didn't stop. She quickly dragged the scalpel towards the wound, then repeated the process on the other side, making a long slit with the puncture at its centre. Robbie was struggling against the bodies that held him down, but this was nothing.

'OK, Samira,' said Maeve. 'Over to you. Get the tip of the forceps in and open them out. I need to see what I'm doing.' Samira nodded and moved in closer. Maeve turned to Jibber-jabber. 'You're on torch duty. Shine it directly at the wound.'

Jibber-jabber came over to join Samira, who forced the forceps into the slit and opened them out. The inside of the wound was pink and shiny, like raw chicken.

The torch beam was wavering all over the place. Maeve

looked at Jibber-jabber; his face was turned away and screwed tight.

'If you're too squeamish give the torch to Ella,' Maeve snapped. 'But you have to shine it in there or I can't see a thing.'

'Sorry.' JJ pulled himself together and aimed the torch directly at the gaping wound. It jiggled slightly in his trembling hand, but he kept his eyes fixed in place.

Maeve held her breath again and tried to still her own trembling hand. She leant closer, closer – Samira widened the opening – and then she saw it, deep inside Robbie's leg: a black tip.

'There's something there,' she murmured, and Robbie moaned into the gag.

'Here goes,' she said and poked the nose of the tweezers inside the opening. 'Wider,' she said to Samira, and closed the tweezers on the sliver of metal, pulled . . .

'Rrrrrrrrrrrrrgh,' Robbie growled, fighting the two bodies on top of him.

Maeve tugged harder and the shard of metal slowly slid free. There it was, dripping blood. About two centimetres long, with a nasty jagged edge. She dropped it into a saucer by the bed.

'Is that it?' said Samira. She was trembling, sweat running down her face.

'No. I need to check there's nothing else in there.' Maeve tried to give Robbie a reassuring smile. 'Nearly over.'

He glared at her through angry, pained eyes.

'Get the torch in closer, and Samira – wider still.'

'I can't . . .'

'Yes, you can.'

Samira managed to force the forceps a little wider and Maeve poked about with the tweezers in the hole.

141

'There!'

She dug deeper, causing Robbie to shudder down the entire length of his body. Then she extracted a small piece of mushy material.

'Part of his trousers,' she said triumphantly, tossing the scrap next to the shard of blade. 'You can take the forceps out now, and, JJ, you can stand down, dude.'

Jibber-jabber let out his breath and collapsed on to the next bed. Samira gratefully returned the forceps to the saucepan as Maeve sloshed antiseptic into the wound.

'Can you stitch?' she asked.

'Yes. We didn't think it was worth it before, it was such a small hole.'

'It's not so small any more.'

'I'm an idiot,' said Samira. 'I should have got the sewing stuff before. I'll need to go back to the labs. If I hurry, I can probably just make it over there before they close down for the night.'

'Go to it. And I think we'd better risk some antibiotics. I'll accept responsibility. And *you*, Robbie, can relax . . .'

But Robbie had passed out.

'If only he'd done that sooner,' said Maeve. 'Would have made it a whole lot easier for all of us.'

'That was well awesome,' said Lewis, nodding his head in approval.

'You guys can get back to whatever it was you were doing.'

Maeve stood over Robbie and wiped his forehead again with the damp cloth.

'Cool.' Lewis sauntered out.

Maeve waited for the older boys to leave, then sat down before her wobbly legs gave way. She was exhausted. Felt

142

like she'd run a marathon. She'd been incredibly tense and now her body was being flooded with endorphins that were turning her a little spacey.

She couldn't really believe what she'd just done.

25

Jibber-jabber couldn't believe what Maeve had just done either. He'd not only been holding in the words that usually poured out of him, he also badly needed the toilet. He'd forgotten about it while Maeve had been digging around in Robbie's leg. He'd been too transfixed by the operation, but now he was reminded, as a pain gripped his guts and he felt a dangerous rumbling and bubbling inside. If he didn't do something about it soon there was going to be an accident. The only thing was, he was nervous of going down to the toilets. He never went by himself if he could help it. He was subtle about it. He didn't want to be thought of as a wimp, even though – he had to admit – he was one. Usually he'd wait until a group of kids were going down and tag along with them. There was always a rush before lockdown, but he'd left it too late tonight.

It was getting dark outside and they'd be turning in soon, locking the doors of the minerals gallery. He had to go now and be quick about it. And who was he going to go with? The bigger boys had left before he could ask one of them. Maeve was busy looking after Robbie. Samira had gone off to the labs.

So that left Ella.

Jibber-jabber wasn't sure how much use Ella would be

in a fight. She was smaller than him, and younger, and would probably be even more scared than he was. She was better than nothing, though. He asked her quietly if she'd go with him and she looked doubtful for a moment.

'Come on,' he said. 'You don't have to come in and watch or anything, just stand guard outside the door.'

'But what would I do if a grown-up attacked?' she asked, and Jibber-jabber stopped himself from saying that that was exactly what he'd just been thinking.

'They won't attack, will they?' he said, trying to sound casual. 'There aren't any in the museum.'

'So what do you need me for?'

'I just need someone to, you know, like, keep me company. Come on, Ella, I'd do it for you.'

'All right then.'

They told Maeve where they were going and left the sick-bay.

'You won't take ages, will you?' Ella asked as they walked along the primates gallery that ran above the main hall down one side. 'Some boys spend hours on the loo.'

'Of course I'll be quick,' Jibber-jabber protested. 'I don't want to hang around down there any longer than I have to, do I? It's dark and it's smelly and you always think some-thing's going to be hiding in the shadows.'

'You said there weren't any grown-ups around.'

'There isn't anyone around,' said Jibber-jabber. He'd been hoping they might bump into someone else on the way. It didn't look like that was going to happen, though.

As they passed the stuffed monkeys in their glass cases, Jibber-jabber almost felt they were laughing at him.

'So what are you scared of then?' asked Ella.

'Well, just because you know there aren't any sickos

around, it doesn't stop you from thinking about them, does it? I think of all sorts of scary things, dinosaur skeletons coming to life, although they're not really skeletons, they're fossils, made of rock, so they never were alive, but that doesn't stop me thinking about them . . . Rats. I often think about rats, eating me while I'm asleep, I've seen six rats since we've been here, and apparently there were loads of them down in the lower level, then there's . . .'

'JJ!' Ella interrupted him. 'You're not helping one bit. Will you shut up about scary things?'

'Yeah, sorry.'

They came to the stairs at the end of the hall and went down past the seated statue of Charles Darwin. In front of them now was the fossilized diplodocus, stretching half the length of the big open space. Darkness clung to the walls. There were only a couple of small candles burning. They were precious and the museum kids didn't like to light them unless they absolutely had to. When it came to lockdown they'd be snuffed out. There was still some brightness showing at the tall, church-like windows at the front of the museum; it was slowly fading, though, the blue deepening.

'We'd better hurry,' said Jibber-jabber.

'Like you have to tell me that.'

Two thirteen-year-olds came out of the blue zone. They were chatting to each other and they laughed at something, the sound of it filling the hall. The thirteen-year-olds were the worst for teasing, so, while Jibber-jabber was comforted by their presence, he didn't want to risk asking them to escort him like a toddler.

He hurried over to the toilets at the back of the hall near the base of the stairs. Ella trotted beside him. She stopped when they came to the door of the gents.

'I'm not coming in there with you,' she said.

'I'll be in a cubicle.'

'Yeah, but you'll make noise and smells. I can't even go if I think someone can hear me.'

'All right,' said Jibber-jabber. 'But you won't run away, will you?'

'No.'

'Can I prop this outside door open so that I can, like, call out to you?'

'I won't go anywhere,' Ella snapped. 'I'm staying here until you come out. I don't want you shouting out to me as you do a poo.'

'I'll just prop it a little way.' There was a wooden wedge nearby and Jibber-jabber kicked it under the outer door so that it was held open just wide enough for him to slip inside.

'Will you come in with me to check it's all right?' he asked when he was done.

'If you want.'

The two of them went in and Jibber-jabber quickly shone his torch around.

'There's nothing,' said Ella, who seemed keen to get out as quickly as possible. Jibber-jabber walked over to the shelf by the sinks where there was always a tea light in a holder and some matches. You could light it when you were in there, but had to blow it out before you left.

By the time he'd got the candle going Ella had gone. He shouted out.

'Can you hear me, Ella?'

He heard her voice coming back from outside, sounding small and distant.

'Hurry up!'

He picked up a bucket of flushing water and went to the cubicle in the middle. He closed the door, undid his trousers and sat down. You weren't supposed to waste batteries and he knew he should turn his torch off. But he kept it in his hands, shining it at the gap under the door.

It was very quiet in here with all the noises of the museum shut out. He realized that his knees were shaking, and he was too frightened to do what he had come in to do.

'Come on,' he muttered to himself. 'Come on . . .'

Even before the disease, in the old days when the world had been normal, he'd been scared of going to the toilet alone. At home, if he woke up at night when everyone else was asleep and he needed a wee, he'd lie there for hours holding it in before it got too bad and he'd have to leap out of bed and run to the loo. The toilets at school were the worst, though. His school, Rowhurst, had been built a long time ago, and the toilets in his House were like something out of a museum. A museum of toilets. He giggled. Wondered if there was such a thing. Probably in America. In America they had museums of everything.

That was better. Have a laugh. Entertain himself.

It didn't last long. He couldn't stop thinking about those Rowhurst toilets. They'd been noisy, with big pipes everywhere, clanking and hissing. It was like being inside some enormous engine or something. He'd hated going by himself. Always made sure there was someone else in there with him. He had even gone through a stage when he was frightened that something would come up out of the bowl. A rat, or a squid's tentacle, maybe a giant spider, or someone's hand . . .

And they'd grab you and drag you under.

As he thought of it, he suddenly felt a slap of panic. He hadn't shone the torch into the bowl when he'd come in, had he? There could be anything in there.

He half got up and awkwardly aimed the torch down past his naked backside, but in his fumbling, the torch caught in his shirt and dropped into the bowl.

It hit the water with a splash and the light went out.

He swore. Stuck his hand in the murky water – thank God he hadn't done anything yet! – and lifted out the dripping torch. What was he going to tell Justin when he returned it like this? Or Ella? That he'd been frightened of toilet monsters? He dried it on some of the scraps of newspaper that hung from a hook and sat down again, miserable, in the darkness.

He really couldn't go now. His bowels had seized up, turned to cement.

He swore again. This was taking too long.

There was a long creaking sound. What was that?

'Hello . . . Hello . . .?'

26

Samira had only just made it to the labs in time. Gordy, Einstein's best friend and the second-best science student in the museum, had been about to lock up. Samira had explained what she needed and offered to lock up for him. Gordy had reluctantly given her the keys. He was obviously enjoying being in charge of the labs while Einstein was away, but he didn't want to hang around any longer than he had to. Especially now that it was growing dark. Everyone was still pretty freaked out after the sicko invasion the other night. Samira had hoped he'd be more of a man and stay with her, but the thought never seemed to cross his mind. All he wanted was to get back to the main museum building where the others were.

Samira had taken the keys and hurried into the labs as he trotted off. So now here she was searching through the drugs cabinets for needle, thread and antibiotics. The only problem was that the needle and thread weren't where they were supposed to be and there were too many different antibiotics to choose from.

To make matters worse, she really needed a pee. She was absolutely bursting. It had been a very busy afternoon and she hadn't had time to use the outside loos in the gardens. She was tempted to use one of the toilets in the lab. She could find some water to flush it away with tomorrow. Samira had always obeyed the rules, however. It was just the way she was. And no one was supposed to use these loos. Besides, what if someone saw her wee in the bowl before she'd had a chance to get rid of it? That would be just too embarrassing.

She swore out loud, safe in the knowledge that nobody else could hear her. Where the hell were the sewing things? Maybe she should just forget about the bloody needle and thread, grab a plaster and a selection of antibiotics and explain the situation to Maeve. She was no happier about the falling darkness than Gordy. There was more light in here than in the other buildings because there was so much glass in the walls and roof, but she was still having to use a torch to see what she was doing. Maeve would understand if she gave up the search. Samira could make it back to the toilets in the main hall in five minutes if she ran.

She imagined she was already there . . . Bliss.

She picked up three different bottles of antibiotics and stuffed them in her pocket. They'd just have to sew up Robbie's leg in the morning. She closed the cabinet and headed for the doors – one step nearer the loos. She was just locking up when she remembered that Alexander and Cass had rearranged everything the other day. They'd announced that they were moving stuff like needles and thread to a different area. Samira pushed her hair back off her face and let her breath out in a long sigh.

She could lie about it. Say she'd forgotten.

Who would know the difference?

No.

She knew she couldn't do it. She'd been brought up to be a good girl and always tell the truth. And, besides, it wasn't fair on Robbie. She turned and hurried back into the lab.

The toilet would have to wait.

Paul was moving in towards his prey. Slowly, slowly, carefully, carefully. Stay in the shadows. Try not to make any sound. When he was close enough he would show himself and that would be it.

End of.

He had to do this quickly and cleanly, and then get the body away as fast as he could. That would be the hardest part. The killing would be simple. The kid wouldn't put up much of a fight.

He licked his lips. They were cracked and bleeding. He tasted his own blood. Sharp. Metallic. Alive. It zinged in his mouth and a wave of dizziness came over him. He closed his eyes for a moment, calming down, slowing his breathing. When he opened them again he cursed inwardly. Boney-M was there, lolloping across the floor.

Not now, he wanted to say, *they'll see you.*

Boney-M turned and fixed one glinting black eye on Paul. Like a shark's eye. Cold and uncaring. It looked right through him.

'Do it!' the bird thing screamed. 'Do it now!'

27

Jibber-jabber had heard a noise. A shuffling sound. Something scraping along a wall.

He was shaking all over, the toilet seat rattling under him. He was too scared to move, to pull up his trousers, to call for help.

He didn't want to give himself away.

Where was Ella?

If only somebody would come. If only somebody else needed the loo. Then they'd come in. Rescue him. He'd never been a fighter. Had always relied on running away. He closed his eyes and felt tears squeeze out from under his eyelids.

This was a horrible way to die. Sitting on a stupid toilet. Horrible. Horrible.

Ella thought she heard something. Someone. Moving about in the dark places of the hall. She called out very quietly.

'Who is that . . .?' but there was no reply. She wanted to look, but had promised Jibber-jabber not to move. She wanted to hide. All his talk had made her scared. She'd been fine before. There had been too much happening to think about bad things. She wished Sam was here. They'd kept each other going through the bad times. Looked after each other. She sent a sort of silent prayer out to him, wherever he was. To watch over her.

She froze.

There was definitely someone there.

But where could she hide?

If she moved they'd hear her. If she called out again . . .

Who was it?

Why were they creeping about like that?

Jibber-jabber sat there, eyes clamped shut, knees knocking together, feeling cold and dumb and terrified. He was on the verge of throwing up. The shuffling noise was coming ever closer. They'd sussed him out. They knew he was in there. If only he'd locked the cubicle door. His heart was thumping so hard he was sure they could hear it.

But there was hope, wasn't there? Someone might still come. A bigger kid. Even one of the small kids. Anyone. It didn't matter.

There was hope, there was . . .

The toilet door suddenly banged as it was pushed open and Jibber-jabber screamed.

Samira had managed to make herself not think about going to the toilet by concentrating on what she was doing. Searching for the box of sewing things . . .

And there it was! Neatly stored away in the new cabinet. A plastic tub labelled 'needles and sewing stuff'. Alexander and Cass were mad keen on labelling things, organizing them. Why they couldn't leave everything together in one place, she didn't know. They didn't know that much about medicine, weren't particularly great at being doctors, and still had a lot to learn before they would even come close to her, or Maeve. Maeve was amazing.

So maybe they organized stuff as a way of showing they had some kind of control. To try and convince everyone that they knew what they were doing.

They didn't fool her. They were administrators. Management. They'd never be as good as her.

She picked up the box and elbowed the cabinet door shut.

Turned to go.

She made a sort of hiccoughing noise as she jumped in shock.

There was someone there.

She relaxed. It was a boy. He moved out of the shadows and she saw that it was Paul Channing.

He looked sick, red-eyed, his skin dry and peeling.

'Paul,' she said. 'What are you doing? I nearly wet myself. Don't ever do that again!' And then a thought struck her. 'Where have you been anyway? We looked everywhere for you. We thought the sickos had got you.'

He moved closer still, and his hand came up as if he was going to stroke her face. Samira frowned, and at the last moment Paul jerked his arm up quickly and punched her in the throat.

The stab was hard and deep. And then, with a sideways swipe, Paul's knife tore through Samira's windpipe and carotid artery. She choked and gurgled. Fell backwards, paralyzed by the shock. Her heart spasmed and froze and she crashed into a glass display case and then flopped to the floor.

As her heart stopped beating there was surprisingly little blood.

Paul leant over her, sniffed, checked she was dead.

He hadn't expected it to be quite this easy.

He'd come in through the door that led from the roof terrace next to the laboratory café. He'd been intending to make his way to the exhibition hall, but had spotted Samira and changed his plan. It would be easy to drag her back out on to the roof and across to his den from here.

Boney-M waddled and flopped over, poked at the unmoving body with his long, hard, pointy beak.

'I didn't know you had it in you. Thought you had piss-water running in your veins.'

Paul kicked the bird aside.

'Go away,' he snarled. 'This is my kill.'

Boney-M called him a string of dirty names and Paul booted him into the corner. Laughed as the bird fell apart in a jumble of bones and leathery bits of skin and oily feathers.

He'd show the bird who was boss. He'd show everyone.

He leant down and picked Samira up.

28

'Ella? What the hell are you doing?' Jibber-jabber was standing with his trousers round his ankles, shaking violently, anger and relief and embarrassment struggling to get the upper hand.

Ella burst into tears. 'I heard something,' she said. 'I wanted to hide. I didn't know where you were. I came in here. I didn't want to shout out in case it heard me.'

'What? In case *what* heard you?'

'The thing, the thing out there, it was following me. It's after me.'

Jibber-jabber pulled up his trousers.

'We're getting out of here.'

'But it's there. It's out there.'

'We're going to run,' said Jibber-jabber, his voice wobbly. 'Back to the stairs and up to the gallery, and we're going to yell and scream all the way and somebody's going to help us. I'm not staying in this bloody toilet a moment longer.'

They stumbled out of the cubicle, Ella clinging on to his arm. The guttering tea light sent wild shapes leaping and skittering about the toilet. They stopped by the sinks. They could see something moving outside, approaching the open door, throwing a big shadow across the floor. Crawling, sniffing, inhuman.

'Are you ready?' Jibber-jabber whispered. 'We're going to run.'

'I don't like it . . . It's coming towards us . . . It's coming in . . .'

'Get ready . . . we'll barge it out of the way . . .'

'No . . . I can't . . .'

'Now . . .!'

Godzilla stuck his furry face round the door and cocked his head to one side. He barked. In his relief Jibber-jabber relaxed his bowels and unclenched his buttocks and did what he had been unable to do for the last five minutes.

29

This is the official report of day one of the expedition to the Promithios warehouse and supply depot near Heathrow Airport. Written by the scribe Lettis Slingsbury.

SECOND ENTRY: Evening.

After the repairs were mended, and Jackson had fixed the trolley, we carried on. People were nicer about Achilleus now and didn't moan about him so much behind his back, as they had seen how well he could fight. It was the same with all the new children. My friends understood now that it was going to be dangerous, and without the new children we were going to be in trouble, so they had better just accept it and be grateful for the help. Of course it wasn't a surprise to Jackson and some others who had seen the new children in action when they had arrived at the museum and fought off the sickos from the lower level. I was also in a fight at the museum when some sickos got into the library, but Chris Marker is writing down that story so I won't write it down here as well, except I will say that it was *frightening and made me more scared of sickos than I was before.*

Sorry, this is getting long. The important thing that happened on the road was that everyone understood that without the people from Holloway we wouldn't have been able to make this journey at all. Jackson is a good fighter, and some of the other museum people, but we don't have enough good fighters who are experienced in fighting out on the streets. We all feel safer having Achilleus and Blue and Ollie and Big Mick and the others with us. And more than that. I have seen the way Jackson looks at Achilleus. It is my job to watch and notice things (which is why I am sorry I didn't watch the battle). Jackson is jealous of him and wants to be able to fight as well as him. Maybe she fancies him a bit as well. She might have a chance. He is ugly and probably doesn't have many girlfriends, and Jackson is not very pretty. I don't mean to be mean, but it is the truth and I have to write the truth.

I hope if Jackson ever reads this she will understand that I am only writing what I see. I am not saying anything about her. I like her, but she is not one of the pretty girls. Maybe she and Achilleus should get together. They are well suited, with the fighting and the not being good-looking and everything. She walks next to him all the time. With poor little Paddy struggling along behind them. They talk all the time. I think mostly about fighting.

We were going even slower than before, but the road got a bit better as we went. It was all up high, elevated is the proper word, so no sickos could get on it and be where we were. We went past tall buildings and offices with logos on them, still with more good views over London, and I started to really realize that we were actually going a very long way and I don't think I was the only one who was getting more nervous the further we went. We felt like a very small bunch of people in a very big place. We mostly stopped talking. As we got tireder and tireder, and the people pushing the trolleys got tireder, the journey got harder. The road seemed to stretch on forever in front of us.

I also realized that I think I must have driven along this motorway, the M4, before with my mum and dad because I have seen signs for the west. My Auntie Val used to live in Bath which I know is west, also there is a church group near Glastonbury we used to visit (also west), so we must have come this way I think. Also I know we have flown from Heathrow Airport. When we went to Corfu one time we flew from Heathrow. So I don't know how many times I must have been along this road in the car. In the car you could do it really quickly, unless there was traffic, and you don't really notice things in a car always. I probably never even looked out of the window to see where we were and what we were travelling past. When you walk you see everything and have time to study it. As I wrote before, it is a long way.

We passed a few cars abandoned on the motorway. But we knew that even if we got them started somehow they would have no petrol in them, that's why they were abandoned. When the illness came, the big disease, it was amazing how quickly things changed.

Ships couldn't arrive in the ports and lorries couldn't drive things around the country. The petrol ran out really quickly, then the food ran out, then everything ran out. So now we walk, and we push our trolleys.

As I am writing this, I know I have strayed from the history of the day, but I don't want to write about the next bit. I don't really want to remember it. I know I will have to, though, because it is the job given to me by Chris Marker. My job is to remember things in this journal for all time.

So I will force myself to remember what happened and tell you about it. We carried on, plodding along, for mile after mile, the road seeming to go nowhere. Then at last we came to some parkland and trees on either side of the motorway and it felt like we had finally got to the edge of London. We were getting worried that we might not be so safe now, though, because the motorway wasn't high up any more (not elevated). It was running along the ground like a normal motorway, and the trees and grass and weeds came right up to it, and in some places right on to it, so that the road was disappearing. It felt strange to be away from buildings. I'd been among buildings for so long I couldn't hardly remember what the countryside was like, especially having no TV to look at.

Instead of making me happy to be out among trees and bushes and twittering birds it made me fearful. It was all too unfamiliar and strange. I wasn't the only one. All the others were huddling together and they went even more quieter. We had come such a long way it seemed. We were walking along like that, all muddled and huddled together, eyes fearful, nobody laughing or joking, and nobody even complaining any more, when we heard a noise.

There was this one time we went on holiday to Dorset. A nice little cottage in some fields. This was obviously a long time before the illness came, when the world was normal and everything was all right. But the cottage was near a dog kennels where they bred Alsatians. There were big, scary signs everywhere saying 'KEEP OUT'. You wouldn't have gone near it, though, because of the noise of all the dogs. All day and night they seemed to keep it up, barking away like mad, and howling. It sounded horrible. I did get used to it, but sometimes I think the wind would change direction and we would hear them well loud and close and then I'd get scared. I was scared they might get out and come charging across the fields. All dogs together like that make a different sort of noise to one dog barking, they all mix into one big noise. A din it is called.

Well, I recognized it straight away this afternoon when I heard it. It was dogs, a big pack of them, all barking and yelping and howling one on top of the other, making a din. Blue and Einstein told us not to panic, but I could tell the noise was getting nearer, and there were a lot of dogs coming. We tried to hurry up and run along the road, but the trolleys were making it too difficult. Blue said we should leave them behind and Einstein got really cross. Next thing, instead of running, we were all standing in the middle of the motorway, yelling and screaming at each other in a big row. Blue was pushing Einstein and Einstein was pushing Blue, and Achilleus was just laughing, and they all seemed to have forgotten about the dogs. I hadn't. I could hear them getting nearer and nearer and nearer, and then I did the only thing I did in this story when I shouted that the dogs were coming. Only it wasn't dogs, not at first, it was these three sickos.

Suddenly they came crashing out of the trees on one side of the road and ran right into us. They were really crazy ones, badly diseased, their skin all hanging off, no hair, their clothes just rags. Achilleus and his team snapped to attention really quickly. They thought we were being attacked, and they cut the sickos down fast, Achilleus sticking his metal spear right through the neck of the first sicko, who was a mother, before I could turn away. As I have written, they thought that the sickos were attacking, but they weren't attacking, they were running away, which became quickly clear, because the next thing the dogs came, hundreds of them, pouring out of the trees.

I say hundreds, I don't mean hundreds, I am trying to be descriptive, to let you know what it felt like. At school they said we should write using descriptive language. And metaphors. The dogs were like a wave crashing on a beach. I want to be accurate, but I didn't count the dogs. There were loads of them, big ones mostly, but also dogs of all sizes, even some small ones, a huge hunting pack. They were all scabby with squinty eyes full of pus, some with red bleeding sores, some starving, with their bones showing through their skin. And they were crazed. Slobbering and hungry as hell.

They fell on the sickos that Achilleus had killed, to bite at them and eat them, but they also started snapping and snarling at us. There were so many of *them, they couldn't all get to the dead bodies so they started to attack us. Especially Caspar, who still had blood and stuff all over his trainer from where he had kicked the sicko's body earlier. I saw three dogs attack him and try to bite his foot. They dragged the trainer off him, and his foot was all cut up and bloody. They tore the trainer to pieces and then they went back to Caspar for more. I saw all this. I was there watching with my own eyes.*

There was other stuff going on as well, and the fighters were trying to kill the dogs. They moved so fast, though, and there were so many of them and they were in among us. Half the kids broke and ran away into the woods on the other side of the road. The others stayed to fight, and then some of us went into a tight bundle, trying to protect ourselves. Caspar's whole leg was badly cut, and Gabby, one of Einstein's scientists, was pulled down by the arm, and before anyone could help her some dogs had bitten her in the throat. I can still hear her screams and the way they were shut off.

Big Mick was nice. He came with his fighters to protect us, the ones who couldn't fight. They were good and brave and Mick killed lots of dogs. The fighters eventually managed to take control and regroup and start to defeat the dogs, fighting them back, and the bigger dogs started to drag the bodies of the sickos away. Blue shouted to let them take them. It was all very confusing, chaos even. Ollie's team now eventually managed to start getting some missiles fired off which scared the dogs. Big Mick told us we all had to wave our arms and shout really loud. Those with weapons hit them and eventually the dogs were defeated and they slinked away into the trees.

It was a bad mess. The road was filled with dead animals. As well as poor Gabby, who was dying, and Caspar, who was really badly wounded. Lots of the other kids had bites and scratches, and now Mick had to put a search party together to find the ones who had run off into the trees. I think there was a big park of some kind there or something (maybe a forest?). Mick was gone for a long time and we got worried that he might not come back. He did, though, in the end, with all the kids with him, and he was in a very grumpy mood. They had scattered far and wide, but he managed to find them all.

We had another meeting then. Sitting in the middle of the road while they tried to help Caspar. We had to decide what to do about poor Gabby as well. She lost so much blood from her neck she went very white and then went into a coma, and her heart slowed down and in the end she died, so we decided to wrap her up and bring her with us, so that she wouldn't be eaten. By sickos or by dogs, or another animal. We put her in one trolley. Caspar couldn't walk so he was put in the other trolley. Einstein said it was lucky we had brought the trolleys and Blue said that if we hadn't been slowed down by them we would have been at Heathrow a long time ago and wouldn't have been attacked in the first place. They would never agree. It was stalemate.

Half the people wanted to go straight back to the museum. Einstein spoke for the other half, who wanted to press on. He said that it would all have been a waste to go back, and that Gabby would have died in vain. She was a scientist, she knew the importance of the expedition. If we went home we would only have to come back later and that might be even more dangerous. We had come this far, we should carry on, surely the worst of it was over. Etc.

They argued and argued, but Einstein won. He is very stubborn and won't listen to other people. So we limped on. It was late now. The trolley with the wonky wheels was even slower with Gabby's body in it and it started to rain, which made everyone even more miserable. I don't mind admitting I was really scared now, crying all the time. I liked Gabby. What else might happen to us? It was hard to keep going. It felt like we were pushing a boulder up a mountain. Which is another metaphor. Strangely it was Einstein who kept our spirits up. He changed a bit, he wasn't so almighty and sarcastic. He encouraged us, he checked we were all right, he urged us on.

Roughly about an hour ago, as the sky grew heavy and dark, we got to a red church in among some trees near Heathrow and managed to break inside. It is dry and not too cold. The walls are thick and we can keep a look-out on the tower, or I should say steeple. I feel safe at last here. It is familiar. I feel safe enough to write these words, with sadness in my heart and a fear of tomorrow and what it might bring.

'Can't you get him to shut up?'

'He's hurt.'

'Yeah, that's pretty obvious.'

Achilleus looked over to where Caspar was lying on the floor of the church, on an inflatable mattress that the museum kids had brought along with them. He was yelling and screaming, lashing out angrily at his friends who were trying to help him. Swearing at them, telling them to leave him alone. He was delirious from pain and his growing fever.

'I got hurt,' said Achilleus. 'Didn't cry like a baby.'

'Leave it out, Achilleus,' said Ollie, who could see that the museum kids were all pretty freaked out by what had happened earlier in the day. 'He's really badly cut up. He could die.'

'Yeah . . . Well, he should still shut up about it.'

'We can't all be as tough as you, Akkie.' Ollie loaded this with edge, and wondered for a moment whether he'd gone too far and Achilleus might have a go at him. It wasn't beyond him to physically attack Ollie. Ollie tried to hold his cold stare as Achilleus turned it on him. Daring him to say something else. At last Achilleus smiled.

'You're right, ginge,' he said. 'You can't all be as tough as me.'

Now Achilleus turned on Einstein. The three of them were sitting at the back of the church on a hard wooden pew.

'You're a doctor, ain't you?' he said. 'Some kind of scientist, medical expert. So do something for him.'

'We've done all we can.' Einstein sounded tired, his voice slightly hoarse. It had been a long day. 'We've soaked him in antiseptic, and tried to bandage him up, but those dogs tore his leg to pieces.'

'He lost a lot of blood?'

'Quite a lot. But dog bites, they're not clean.'

'You got any alcohol? Something like that, to calm him down?'

'No. Just painkillers. We've given him all we can. We just have to wait.'

'Yeah,' said Achilleus. 'Wait for him to die so we can all get some sleep.'

He got up and walked away to where Paddy was waiting for him at the other end of the small church. Paddy had been making Achilleus a bed of sorts out of stuff he'd found in the church. Achilleus slapped him round the head when he got there, prodded at the bed with the toe of his boot.

Ollie found himself alone with Einstein.

'Not exactly soft-hearted, is he?' said Einstein.

'Nope. He's a dick.' Ollie rubbed a bruise on his arm. Wasn't even sure when he'd got it or who'd given it to him. Must have happened in one of the fights. But which one?

'I really have done all I can for Caspar,' said Einstein.

'Yeah, I know. It's bad news. But it happens.'

Ollie looked around the church. Everyone had broken up into their separate groups. Waitrose kids on one side, Blue and Big Mick and the other Morrisons kids on the other. The museum kids were in the middle, clustered round where Caspar was lying on the mattress. About half of them were holding on to each other and crying.

The dead body of the girl, Gabby, was wrapped tightly in some dust sheets they'd found and lying on the altar. Ollie could see that a reddish brown stain had seeped through the white material.

Lettis, in her funny robes, was sitting at the other end of the pew, scribbling away in her big book by the light of a candle. She was very dedicated, keeping up with her journal entries. She had a serious expression on her face and her tongue was sticking out between her teeth.

'Look at them all,' said Einstein. 'Children. That's all they are.'

As far as Ollie could see, he and Einstein were the only two kids who were mixing it up right now and he was going to take the opportunity to get some more stuff straightened out in his mind.

'Can I ask you something else?' he said, and Einstein grunted.

'You want to ask me some more about whether you're going to die?'

'Not really, no. Don't want to think about that too much.'

'What then? You've got a lot of questions. Why now? Why me?'

'Because you might have some answers. You think about stuff.'

'Don't you?'

'Yeah.' Ollie winced as he discovered another bruise, this time on his leg. 'You've seen what the others are like,' he said. 'Achilleus isn't exactly a deep thinker. And Blue . . . I don't know him well enough, to tell you the truth.'

'I thought you were all friends,' said Einstein. 'A gang.'

'No. I've only really known him for a couple of weeks. Before that we kept to ourselves. They had one camp. We had another. Didn't mix. We were all fighting over the same things, with food running out everywhere. Didn't trust each other.'

'No time to think,' said Einstein.

'No. So we had this guy in charge called Arran and he thought about things. I could talk to him. He was clever. That's why he was our leader.'

'What happened to him?'

'He died.'

'Stupid question really.'

'Yeah. Only, listening to Caspar shouting his head off, it made me think about Arran, about when he got injured. You see, he was bitten by a grown-up, got really sick and then got hit by an arrow in a fight. That's what finished him.'

'So what's the problem exactly? What do you want to know?'

'This weird thing happened when he got bitten. At the time I didn't think too much about it. There was too much other stuff going down.'

'And what happened then?'

'We were out on a scav hunt, looking for food, and we decided, well, some of us decided, I never thought it was a great idea . . . So the others wanted to look in this swimming pool. See if there was anything in the vending machines still.'

'And was there?'

'Yeah, there was; only it was a trap. All these grown-ups were, like, waiting for us, under the water. They ambushed us.'

'Great story and all that.' Einstein sounded bored and impatient. 'But what's the question?'

Ollie hesitated before going on. Was it all going to sound stupid when he came out with it?

'It's just *that* – an ambush. Like they'd worked it out. Like they were waiting for us.'

'And?'

'It's not like grown-ups to do that. I've never seen them that organized before. That clever.'

'You sure it wasn't just random?'

'No. And then there was the fact that they were under-water.'

'How do you mean?'

'Somehow they were under the surface of the water, waiting. How did they do that? How did they breathe under there?'

'They didn't,' said Einstein with a slightly snotty tone to his voice. 'Human beings can't breathe underwater. We're not fish.'

'I know. It was like they were a new breed of grown-up.'

'Not possible,' said Einstein.

Ollie wasn't going to give up, despite Einstein's negative vibe.

'You've studied grown-ups,' he said. 'You've studied the disease. Could it change people somehow?'

'No. A disease can't give people new skills. We can't suddenly grow gills or something. Illness doesn't add anything, it just takes things away.'

'So how did they do it then?' said Ollie. 'How did they survive underwater? How did they plan it all?'

'As I say.' Einstein sounded more dismissive than ever. 'They didn't. You must have imagined it.'

'I'll admit it was all a bit confused and way intense. I suppose they could of maybe, I don't know, had their noses sticking out or something.'

Einstein laughed. Ollie would have laughed himself if someone else had told him this story. Whichever way you looked at it, it didn't make a lot of sense.

'It was messed up,' he went on. 'It freaked us out, took us all by surprise. One boy, Deke, got killed there, and Arran was wounded, as I said. Died later. Because we weren't ready for it. We never expected grown-ups to behave like that. I mean, they can't get organized, can they? Not really. They can't get clever.'

'I've never seen any evidence of it,' said Einstein. 'The way I see it, you worry too much, Ollie.'

'I think too much.'

'Same thing.' Einstein stood up, signalling that the conversation was over.

'*You* think, though,' said Ollie. 'Does that mean you worry? You don't seem too cut up about what happened today.'

'I think I'm a bit like your Achilleus.'

Ollie snorted. He couldn't think of anyone less like Achilleus.

'What are you talking about?' he said.

'I don't think I really care about people.'

'That's nuts,' said Ollie.

'Oh, I long ago came to the conclusion that I'm nuts,' said Einstein and he chuckled and walked off.

Ollie shook his head. Einstein was one of those kids who couldn't help making snotty comments and had probably been badly bullied at school. Now he'd found a place for himself at the museum. He had some useful survival skills after all and he was making the most of it. It wasn't enough just to have good fighters; without clever kids there was no hope of getting through this.

He was aware of a movement and he turned round to find that Lettis had scooted along the pew and was sitting looking up at him.

'OK?' he said and she nodded, keeping her lips tightly pressed together. Looked like she'd been crying.

There was a shout from the other side of the church. Achilleus was giving little Paddy a hard time about something. Ollie could see Paddy rubbing his shoulder where the strap of the golf-bag had dug into him.

'That poor kid,' he said. 'He lugged that heavy bag full of weapons all this way without making a fuss. That's real hero worship.'

Lettis didn't say anything. Just sat there staring at him.

'Come on,' he said. 'Let's find you somewhere to sleep.'

31

A stripe of bright early-morning sunlight lay across the laboratory floor illuminating a small crimson spatter.

'It looks like blood.' Maxie was squatting down inspecting the tiles.

'Could be anything,' said Justin. 'Food, blood, something from an experiment.'

'Don't suppose you can do DNA testing?' said Maxie.

'Not really, no. It's a very complicated process and it's not like it is in films basically . . .'

'Justin.' Maxie straightened up. 'I was joking. I know you can't do DNA testing.'

'Oh, right. Yeah, OK.'

They'd waited ages for Samira to return last night. In the end Maxie, Maeve and Boggle had led a party over to the Darwin Centre laboratories. They took along some of Lewis's fighters and Gordy, the last person to have seen Samira. He talked all the way, trying to shift any blame.

'She didn't want me to stay . . . She was just picking something up . . . I thought things were safe now.'

In the end Maxie had snapped at him. 'Yeah, but even so, Gordy, with everything that's been going down here, you might have thought to wait.'

The lab doors were still unlocked and they could find

no sign of Samira in the darkness. So they abandoned the search and went back to the minerals gallery, left someone on guard at the entrance just in case she did show up.

She never did, and in the morning they'd organized a proper search. All that they'd found was this small patch – not much bigger than a 1p piece – and even then they couldn't be sure it had anything to do with Samira.

Maxie watched as Gordy went down on his hands and knees and started scraping whatever it was into a small plastic envelope. He was still feeling very guilty from last night and Justin had taken over from Maxie giving him a hard time about it.

'If you want to be in charge of the labs while Einstein's away,' he said, 'you've got to be more responsible.'

'It's not my bloody fault,' Gordy muttered. 'Anything could have happened to her.'

Now Gordy turned on Maxie.

'What do you think happened then?' he snapped. 'I thought you'd cleared all the sickos out of the museum. Or maybe you're not as great as you make out.'

For a brief moment Maxie considered laying into Gordy, really letting rip. But she held back. He was scared and turning his guilt on someone else. It took an effort, but she was going to be bigger than him and let it go. Instead she nodded to Justin to follow her and walked through to the lab next door, which was unoccupied.

She looked back through the glass wall at the lab they'd left. There were a few kids there, too distracted to work, standing in small groups, talking excitedly. She closed the door.

'What we talked about the other day. About one of your lot having a problem. A saboteur, a traitor – I don't know

what you want to call it . . . What have you done about it?'
she asked Justin.

Justin looked a little shifty and unsure of himself. 'I don't
want to start a panic,' he murmured.

'You don't think Samira disappearing is going to maybe
do that for you?'

Justin walked Maxie over to the windows, where they
could look down to the main floor of the Darwin Centre
eight storeys below. The great curving white wall of the
Cocoon that filled the huge space was shining in the
sunlight.

'I'm sorry,' he said. 'I should have done something. I was
just hoping, I don't know, that you'd find something in
your clean-up. I don't want it to be one of us. I want it to
be safe here again.'

'We can sort it,' said Maxie. 'But you have to tell people
that someone can't be trusted. No one should be going
anywhere alone at the moment.'

'Will you help me set up a committee?' he asked.

Maxie tried not to laugh. She wasn't quite used to Justin's
adult way of speaking. 'A committee?'

'Yes, to investigate what happened. We'll have to inter-
rogate everyone here, try to build up a picture of who was
doing what and where on the night of the attack.'

Maxie had to admit that out on the street life had a
certain simplicity to it. All you had to do was stay alive. To
kill grown-ups. This was different. This was complicated.
This was old school.

'OK,' she said. 'But we have to go about it the right way.
You've got a killer among you, remember.'

'We don't know Samira's dead. Is she dead?'

Gordy came in, wiping his hands on his white lab coat.

It was several sizes too big for him and he'd had to roll the sleeves up.

'I took a look at that sample under the microscope,' he said. 'As far as I can tell, it's blood.'

'Even if it is blood,' said Justin, 'we don't know it's hers. And if it is . . . She must still *be* somewhere. She can't have just disappeared.'

32

So much blood. He'd never expected so much blood, especially as when he'd killed her she'd hardly bled at all. Once her heart stopped beating it couldn't pump anything out of the wound. But when he'd opened her up it was like sticking a knife into a ripe peach. He'd had to quickly find some sheets of newspaper and had then rolled her on to them. Even so the blood had spread and spread and spread, a great dark pool of it, dripping down through the floorboards.

He had to hurry. He quickly hacked off a piece of fatty flesh from her side. It was somehow soft and chewy at the same time, and the raw skin was too tough to get his teeth through.

Suddenly he had an image of himself, crouching over Samira's body, and he spat the grey, mashed-up gobbet out on to the floor.

What was he doing?

He retched. Held his mouth, trembling. And mercifully his mind flipped again. One second he was a boy, alone, sick, appalled at what he'd done, and the next Boney-M was screaming in his ears and he was a stone-cold killer, a sicko, hungry and ruthless, and then it flipped once more and threw him into a strange place. He was a half-naked, brown-skinned tribesman living in the jungle, butchering a monkey to feed his family.

He knelt there, slipping in and out of madness, and then he fell so deep into the pit, he imagined he was an insect, a flea or a tick, sucking the blood from Samira's veins. The smell of her blood excited him and nauseated him and soothed him all at the same time. He tipped forward and stuck his face into the cavity he'd opened up in her body, and sucked.

And with a flip, reality came back to him, slapped him round the face. He rolled on the floor, clutching his stomach, trying not to throw up, while Boney-M danced about him, screeching with laughter, his bones rattling.

'Oh, that's a good one, that's rich, that's juicy, look at the boy, wants to be Count Dracula, but hasn't the *guts* for it . . . Oh, that's a picture. That's priceless. I'll post this one on YouTube. Oh, look at him! ROFL . . . Or should I say ROFP? Rolling on the floor puking, puking like the little baby bunting he is . . . Oh, what a day!'

It was hunger that pulled Paul back up, drove him on, took him back over to the body on the newspaper and put the knife back in his hand. His need to eat. He'd known Samira. He'd even liked her. She'd given him some medicine one time when he'd had terrible headaches. She'd been kind and thoughtful and . . .

'No!' Boney-M yelled at him, setting his teeth on edge. 'Not kind. Not thoughtful. She was a pig. They all hated you, remember? They killed Olivia. They killed your sister. They ate her. And laughed about it.'

'Did they?' Paul stopped what he was doing and closed his eyes. 'Did they really? Are you sure I didn't imagine it? I don't know any more.'

'Oh, look at him. One light snack and he's sitting back

on his fat arse, all bloated and thankful and full of the milk of human kindness. Hello, birds; hello, flowers; hello, sky; oh, isn't it a lovely day? No more cares in the world, little pissypants. One small meal and you feel good about things, do you? Think all the bad stuff's going to go away? What makes you think you can just pretend that things aren't how you know they are? Nothing's changed. You're still going to have to kill them all. To eat them all, and shit them out and add their bones to your collection.'

'Who says?'

'Ooh, listen to him, getting all uppity. *I* SAY! You hear me? *I* DO! We all do. All of us.'

'And who are you? You don't even exist!'

'You've hurt me now,' Boney whined. 'You've hurt your old friend, the only one who cares about you. You'll make me cry.'

'Go on then, cry. You're not real.'

'Oh, aren't I? Then who's this pecking your hand?'

Paul yelped as Boney-M jabbed his hard beak into the back of his hand. He looked down. There was a gash in it, his own blood spilling out, bright red. His knife was clutched in his other hand, the one he'd been using to cut Samira up with. There was no sign of the evil bird thing. But he'd pecked him, hadn't he? Made him bleed.

Hadn't he?

What if he'd done it himself? Stabbed his own hand with the knife.

He looked down at the awful mess he'd made of the girl. Started to cry. Threw the knife down and ran out of the room. Up the stairs, out through the window and on to the roof outside. Leant out over the wall, looking down at the road far below.

'Now look what you've made me do,' he sobbed, but who was he accusing? Boney-M? The kid downstairs? God? Those other voices that drifted in on the wind like fog?

For a moment he thought of climbing over, throwing himself off. Ending it all. It would be so easy. He wouldn't have to deal with all of this any more.

He belched, felt acid rise in his throat. He wished he hadn't eaten now; the girl's flesh had stopped the aches in his belly, but it had woken him up, brought awful clarity. He turned his face up to the sky and howled.

He knew he wouldn't jump, though.

Not this time.

Not yet.

33

'Shut up and listen. I'm changing up the way we're doing this. Here on in, only the best fighters and any other kids who definitely need to be there are going on.'

Ollie had been up on the church steeple and had walked in on Blue making his announcement. He'd hoped it would all have been sorted, but it obviously hadn't. For a few minutes he'd almost been able to forget about their problems. Forget about all the frightened kids down below. The body on the altar . . .

He'd climbed up to get away from them and to get a proper idea of where they were and what they could expect when they left the church. It had been dark when they'd arrived last night and, in the confusion, strung out and desperate for shelter, nobody had had much time to take in the view.

The church was ancient, built from red brick sometime in the Middle Ages probably. The motorway must have only been about a hundred metres to the north, but it was screened by trees, so that now, without the noise of traffic, you wouldn't know it was there. The church was almost completely surrounded by trees. Past them to the south he could see parkland and to the west there was a narrow road going over an old stone bridge. They might have been deep in the heart of the countryside. Somewhere out there, though, was Heathrow Airport, which had once been the fourth busiest airport in the world. What a crowded, bustling place England had been before all this.

It was sunny outside. The world looked green and fresh. Ollie had taken a moment to soak it all up and enjoy the solitude. Pretend it was the old days, before the fear set in. He had plenty of time. They'd been held up for ages trying to sort out Caspar, the kid whose foot had been half bitten off by dogs. He'd made it through the night and was now finally asleep. Asleep or in a coma. Who knew? Drenched in sweat, his eyes flicking about under his lids. His breathing was very shallow and fluttery and he was pretty weak. It was obvious they couldn't move him just yet, which was why the arguments had started downstairs.

So Ollie had left them to it, climbed the stone steps to the top of the steeple and leant on the parapet, watching the birds flapping about in the trees. So many of them. This was their world now. Not exactly quiet – they were making a right old racket – but peaceful.

Once he went back downstairs, however, he was right back in it, the arguing and the fighting and the tension, the wailing and the panic. It was business as usual. The day-to-day grind of making battle plans and hoping to survive till the next meal.

And shouting. Always shouting.

He could see that the museum kids weren't too happy about Blue's announcement. Some of them were clustered round him, having a go.

Shouting.

Blue stared them down until they fell quiet again. Then he pointed at Caspar lying on a pew.

'All right then,' he said. 'You pick him up and dump him in one of your stupid trolleys and we'll wheel him out there, yeah? How long do you think he'll last? As I get it from talking to Einstein last night, where we're headed ain't so far away. So I'm going to take a small group of experienced fighters rather than dragging all you museum noobs along. You'll only get in the way and slow us down. You are gonna stay here and barricade yourselves in, yeah? No way any grown-ups can get in.' Blue showed no emotions at all, neither happy nor sad. He was just stating how things were.

'You'll be a lot safer than out there on the streets with us. You can look after Caspar. Make sure he's all right. If any of you got a better idea let's have it.'

Nobody said anything.

'OK. For now, we're leaving behind the trolleys too.'

Einstein made to protest, but Blue cut him dead with a look.

'Once you've found what you're looking for we'll carry it here if we can. Otherwise we leave it, come back for the trolleys and everyone else. By then we'll know what it's like out there. No one got any problem with that . . .? Good.'

Blue looked at Einstein. 'I guess you need to come with us. Who else?'

'Only really Emily.'

'Who's Emily?'

'I am.' A blonde girl who looked to be about fourteen stepped forward. 'I'm Einstein's assistant. Emily Winter.'

'Emily can help me choose what we need to pick up,' said Einstein.

'Anyone else?'

'Jackson, I suppose, if we're taking the best fighters.'

'Good. It's decided then.'

A small voice piped up. 'What about me?'

It was Lettis. She went up to Blue, carrying her big book. Ollie smiled. She was a plucky kid.

'I'll need to be there,' she said.

'No way, babe,' said Blue, and he shook his head.

'But I have to come with you. I have to write about it. I have to be there and witness it with my own eyes.' Lettis was red-faced, almost crying.

'Who says?' Blue asked.

'Chris Marker. The librarian. He told me I have to bear witness to events.'

'You've witnessed enough,' said Ollie, walking over to her. 'We'll tell you all about it later on.' He put a hand on her shoulder and gave it a squeeze. 'As Blue says, we won't be long. We'll probably be back by lunchtime.'

'But finding the stuff, the drugs and chemicals and things, that's the most important part of the story,' said Lettis. 'I can't miss that.'

'I'll write everything down, OK?' said Ollie. 'I know how important it is to you.'

'No . . .'

'Uh-uh.'

Ollie cut her off. Squatted down to her level and looked into her face.

'It's too dangerous, Lettis. We don't want any more of you to get hurt. Don't argue. OK? You do what I say.'

'OK.'

'Good girl. Now I want you to promise me something, Lettis.'

'What?'

'That when we go you don't open these doors. OK? Not for anything. Nobody goes outside. You understand?'

'All right.'

'You only open them for us. When we get back. Will you promise me that?'

'I promise.'

Twenty minutes later a smaller war party left the church: Ollie with his missile team, Big Mick and Blue and the rest of the Morrisons crew, as well as Achilleus and Paddy. Of the museum kids only Einstein, Emily and Jackson were coming along on this leg. They'd left behind nine kids.

Ollie felt much happier with this set-up. They could go faster and he wouldn't have to worry about protecting anyone else – except maybe Einstein and Emily. That was manageable. He fell in beside Jackson, who was loping along, her spear over her shoulder.

'Can you make it your job to look after those two,' he said, nodding at the 'scientists'.

'If you like,' said Jackson.

'Any fighting and I don't want to be worrying about them.'

'No problem. Emily can look after herself pretty well. Einstein – who knows?'

She smiled at Ollie, which softened her severe-looking face a little.

Ollie smiled back. With any luck, today was going to be easier than yesterday. It was only two, maybe three miles to the Promithios site. It should take them less than an hour to get there.

They walked through the trees and into the park. The

grass had grown long and was filled with tall weeds. Ollie ran his hand across the top of the lush growth, stroking the seeds at the ends of the stalks. It tickled in a pleasant way. Reminded him that he was alive. And then he remembered coming through Regent's Park in the night, how the diseased apes had hidden in the long grass, waiting to ambush them.

He tensed as a startled brown bird flapped noisily up in front of him and hauled itself away, its wings rattling, flying low over the grass. Ollie laughed.

No bad things. Not today. Not in the bright sun.

A few metres away, sheltering under the trees, three sickos were lying on the ground. They were so filthy and encrusted with dirt that they blended perfectly with their surroundings. Only their eyes showed white. One of them rolled and managed to struggle up into a seated position, looking out over the top of some bracken. It had taken a great deal of effort as he had no arms. They had both rotted away. It made his head look unnaturally large.

He looked at his two companions. They were his hands and arms. The three of them worked together, their minds melded into one. They exchanged looks. Should they follow the walkers?

No. Stay here.

They were hungry, but they would wait. Not go crawling out into the burning sun. Not go chasing after the group of fighters who were steadily walking away from them. Not when there was other prey. Closer. Weaker. They'd smelt the fresh blood and sent out the call. Others of their kind were nearby, coming closer, ready to help. They were singing to each other. Their song of death.

34

Big Mick didn't like the countryside. Never had. He liked houses and wide roads, cars, offices, shops. They were familiar to him. Home. Not trees and grass and dirt. It didn't look right and it didn't smell right. He'd grown up in London. Felt safe among houses. He understood buildings. They had a use. Even if they were full of grown-ups these days.

This was different. He didn't know what to expect. There was no order to it. Things just growing everywhere. A mess. Confusing. He'd spent all his life in the streets around Holloway, apart from occasional trips down Oxford Street to look at the shops, and one disastrous holiday in Suffolk. He'd never forgotten that. He'd made a new friend at primary school, a boy called Charlie Piper, and when Mick was ten Charlie's family had asked him if he wanted to go on holiday with them to their caravan park in the countryside. Mick hadn't been sure, but his parents said he should go.

Worst week of his life.

All right, perhaps not as bad as the week when his mum got sick and killed his dad, but up until then it had been the worst, and he still felt wobbly when he thought about it. It had been wet and uncomfortable and there was mud everywhere. He'd been terrified of the noises at night, owls and foxes and probably wolves by the sound of it. And worst of all was the boredom. There'd been nothing to do. No TV, no games console, no shops to look at, no corners to hang out on. That was the worst thing about the countryside – no corners.

They'd had picnics on the beach in the rain and the sand had got in his food. They'd gone for walks in the woods and Mick had walked into a tree and poked his eye. He still had a little scar.

Yeah. It had been well bad. Mick had been bored and scared and had missed his mum and dad and his proper, normal food.

He'd stopped being friends with Charlie Piper after that. And it was the first and last time he'd been to the countryside.

Until today.

Although, now he thought about it, he could see they weren't really in the country, just a big park. There were houses up ahead and streets. He chilled. They were getting back to civilization.

'Are we still in London?' he asked Blue, who was walking just ahead of him.

'Dunno.' Blue looked around. 'It's London airport, innit, Heathrow? And the tube goes there, so I suppose we're in London. Or right on the edge.'

'I wish we were back in Holloway.'

'You homesick, big man?'

'Yeah, a bit.'

'That is *moist*, man. You're our top fighter, Mick. Don't want you wimping out on me.'

'I ain't wimping out, Blue. I'm just saying we was doing all right back in Holloway.'

'Maybe yes, maybe no,' said Blue. 'Was getting harder and harder to find food. In some ways they got a good thing going down at the museum.'

'We gonna stay there?'

'Dunno, mate. We'll see, we'll see. I'll tell you, though, Mick, whatever happens, when we get back to the museum we ain't going anywhere for a bare long time. We are staying put and resting up.'

'Sounds like a plan.'

'I'm glad you like it, blood, cos it's the only one I got.'

They were approaching the edge of the park and Mick could see houses through the trees.

'You reckon there's gonna be grown-ups out this way?' he asked.

'What do you think?'

'I think we've had an easy start today, but it's gonna get worse.'

'It always gets worse,' said Blue.

'Yeah. That's the one thing you can be sure of.' Mick laughed.

It was quiet when they broke through the line of trees and got out on to the road. There was a row of old-fashioned-looking houses, those ones with fake wooden beams in the walls. They were dark, the windows broken, some of the doors hanging open. Dead and deserted. Cars covered in dirt and dust and bird shit stood on flat tyres.

Soon they came to a good wide road and Mick felt happier. This was an ugly part of town, made for cars rather than people, with lots of small businesses and offices. Didn't bother Mick, though. It was familiar. The Holloway Road had been pretty butters, with its crappy shops and takeaway food joints.

192

They'd been walking for about fifteen minutes when they saw their first grown-up. A mother. Standing in an overgrown front garden, staring up at the sky, her arms straight out in front of her, as if reaching for something. They almost walked right past her. It was Mick who spotted her and he swore. The others stopped, made ready for a fight.

'Leave it,' said Blue. 'She ain't going nowhere. Look at her, she's like one of them stupid living statues you used to get down Covent Garden.'

'Are you saying we just ignore it?' said Einstein. He obviously wanted to get a closer look, but was too scared. 'Why's it out in the sunlight like that? You can see her face is burnt.'

He was right. As well as being deformed by the usual growths and swellings, the mother's skin was blistered and peeling. In fact, as Mick looked at her, he thought he could see her face sort of seething and boiling and twitching. He took a step closer. Maybe her brain had been completely eaten away? Maybe she was like a shell. Nothing inside. If you hit her head it might just crumple . . .

'Leave it,' Blue repeated and carried on walking. The others could do nothing but follow, glancing back over their shoulders at the mother just standing there. Even when they had left her well behind Mick felt a sort of prickle in the back of his neck. He knew she was still there behind him and one thing he'd learnt in the last year was that you never turned your back on a grown-up. It just felt wrong, to leave her there. It was bad luck.

They saw two more grown-ups in the same poses and each time Blue made them hurry past.

'If they ain't attacking us we ain't attacking them. Waste of time.'

Mick was itching, though. He wanted to lash out at something. Wanted to hit something. He carried a big wooden club and had a long knife at his belt. Sometimes the only thing that made him feel OK was to break something. Shake things up.

And then, when they arrived at the Promithios site, he realized he was going to get the chance.

The place was crawling with grown-ups.

35

Their route had taken them to the east of the airport into an area of small businesses, warehouses and factories. There were several car repairers mixed up with companies that had made all sorts of things – windows, swimming-pool pumps, kitchen cabinets, cardboard boxes – as well as places that had serviced the airport and airlines, like caterers and cleaners. Promithios Biomedical was on a slightly grander and more modern complex called a 'Corporate Park', which seemed to be mostly made up of big, ugly, windowless buildings clad in metal and concrete. It sat behind a black metal fence, with a gatehouse and big sliding gates, and that's where the grown-ups were clustered. Maybe twenty of them, out in the sun, scrabbling like mad dogs to get past the fence and inside.

As soon as he saw them, Blue ordered the war party to stop, and they hunkered down behind some parked cars.

'We could find another way in,' said Einstein. 'I mean, we're going to have to climb over the fence, whatever.'

'Yeah,' said Blue. 'But if we're going to shift the gear out we'll need to get rid of that lot. I don't want to be worrying about them all the time we're inside.'

'You're sure it's safe to attack them?' asked Einstein.

'Course it's not safe,' Blue scoffed. 'But it's still the best bet. I'd feel bare happy if we could kick them off the bus. Then we could try and get the gates open; gonna be easier all round if we do that.'

'They don't look too handy,' said Mick. 'They're a pretty sick bunch.'

Ollie looked at the grown-ups. They were on the young side. None of them looked much older than thirty. But the disease hadn't been kind to them. Most of them were missing body parts. One or two had lost so much of their flesh and skin that they looked like living skeletons. Others were fat and bloated, swollen, lumpy and mushy-looking.

'We need to kill them all,' said Blue matter-of-factly.

'All right, all right.' Einstein was going weirdly hyper, like he couldn't wait to lay into the grown-ups. Ollie hoped he wouldn't try to get to the front of the attack. He sidled over to Blue and spoke quietly to him.

'We got to keep the noobs out of the fight,' he said.

'Yeah.' Blue nodded and sucked his teeth. Then he made a decision.

'Einstein, you and Emily and Jackson stay back here with Ollie's team. Keep watch for any other grown-ups who might come up on us from behind.'

'We can fight,' said Einstein.

'Jackson, maybe, but you other two we need unharmed, or else this whole mission has been one big waste of time. And don't go getting in the way of Ollie.'

'I'm telling you, we can fight,' said Einstein.

'No, you can't,' said Blue in a way that told Einstein it was the end of the conversation.

Achilleus pulled his best spear out of the golf-bag and gave Paddy a little shove, sending him stumbling into Einstein.

'Look after this one as well,' he said to Ollie, and Paddy knew better than to argue.

'I don't want to have to carry me own weapons back,' Achilleus added, weighing the spear in his hand.

'Ollie, you know the beef,' said Blue. 'Keep spamming them pus-bags and once you've softened them up watch our backs.'

'Sure.' Ollie wasn't too happy about babysitting Einstein. His whole idea had been to be responsible only for his small missile unit, but he could see the sense in Blue's plan.

The kids quickly formed up into a battle line: Achilleus on the right with Blue; Mick on the left; Ollie in the centre; Einstein, Jackson, Emily and Paddy safely behind them.

When Ollie's team was ready they let fly. Two slingshots and two javelins flew through the air and whacked into the backs of the grown-ups clustered by the gates, and, as four of them went down, the others turned to see what was happening. Ollie had time to fire off another shot, but then had to pull his squad back as the grown-ups advanced surprisingly quickly, teeth bared, claw-like fingers groping the air. They were desperate for food, sent crazy by the sunlight, unafraid of any danger.

Ollie dropped in behind the advancing fighters and checked that Einstein and the others were holding their position.

'I should be up front,' said Jackson.

'You'll get your chance,' said Ollie. 'Don't worry.'

'I want to show Achilleus what I can do.'

'Save it,' said Ollie.

The rest of the kids slammed into the grown-ups, knocking down the front rank and forcing them back against the fence. Those who carried longer spears used them to keep the grown-ups at bay while the rest darted in with clubs and knives and shorter spears.

Ollie spotted a father breaking away and trying to escape. He quickly fitted a steel ball to his sling, pulled it back and felt the satisfying snap and twang as he let go. The steel shot smacked into the back of the fleeing father's neck and knocked him flat.

'Nice shot,' said Jackson, and she whistled. The last of the grown-ups tried to run now, but they were hunted down and Jackson couldn't resist steaming over and taking one down with her own spear, expertly pinning him in the side. She grinned at Achilleus, looking for his approval, but he hadn't even noticed. He walked straight over to Paddy, checked he was all right, and then handed over his spear to be cleaned.

All of the grown-ups lay dead or dying, the road covered with their blood. Blue and Mick were walking among them, finishing them off.

None of the kids were even scratched. They high-fived and whooped and jeered at the dead bodies.

Einstein approached Blue as he was kneeling down and wiping the blade of his short spear on a fallen mother's dress.

'You could have let us help.' Einstein's voice was shaking slightly. 'It wasn't dangerous.'

'It wasn't dangerous because we knew what we were doing,' said Blue. 'It only gets dangerous when we mix it up with kids who don't know how to handle theirself.' He looked up and stared into Einstein's face. 'Like yesterday – you remember, Iron Man? You ended up with one girl killed and one boy badly cut up.'

'I haven't forgotten,' said Einstein.

'Well, don't. Ever.'

'Yeah,' said Big Mick. 'This here was easy – but it's gonna get worse.'

'The smell of blood might attract more of them,' said Ollie. 'So the quicker we get inside, the better. We'll have to work out a way to get the gates open.'

He, Mick and Blue climbed over the fence, being careful not to get skewered on the sharp spikes along the top. They investigated the mechanism that opened and closed the gates, and after a short discussion Big Mick set to work with his club, hammering away at the machinery until he'd separated it from the gates, which could now be hauled apart by hand. Once all the kids got hold of them they were able to slide them open, and, with a cheer, they were through.

The Promithios complex had an office building at the front with walls made of green reflective glass. Behind it was a big, windowless warehouse covered in what appeared to be grey plastic panelling. It looked like a giant box, with no way in or out.

The only obvious entrance was at the front of the office building. The kids clustered round the thick glass doors and started arguing about the best way to get them open. Ollie left them to it. Took a step back to check the place out.

The building was about five storeys high, a couple of metres taller than the warehouse behind it. There was white lettering across the glass wall spelling out PROMITHIOS MEDICAL SOLUTIONS. Underneath was a list in smaller lettering: PROMITHIOS BIOTECHNOLOGY, PROMITHIOS BIOMEDICAL, PROMITHIOS MEDICAL SUPPLIES and, even smaller, PBC – PROMITHIOS BIOMEDICAL CONSULTING.

He was pretty sure that Promithios was a reference to Prometheus, the Titan from Greek mythology who created man and gave him the secret of fire. He wasn't exactly sure what all the other terms meant, though. He had an idea that biotech was something to do with using living things to make new products – cloning, genetic engineering, growing tissues, altering cells, that sort of thing. Science-fiction stuff, a lot of it. He was just wondering about all this when he saw a sudden movement, a streak of white and a scream.

It all happened very fast.

A half-naked father had darted out of some bushes and charged at the kids clustered round the doors. He initially made for Emily, but Jackson yanked her out of the way and the father came on, deeper into the group. He was small and wiry, more like an animal than a man. His nose was missing and in its place was a cluster of growths and boils. He headed for Mick, who knocked him in the teeth with his forearm. The father skittered sideways out of control and collided with Paddy, who fell over, tangled in his golf-bag. Ollie dived in to protect Paddy and felt a sudden hot flash of pain across his cheek as the father slashed him with his dirty fingernails and then tried to bite him. Ollie was aware of his teeth scraping the fresh wound in his face. He grunted and tried to throw him off.

The next thing the father hissed and dropped to the ground, twisting and writhing. Achilleus and Jackson had both stabbed him at the same time. Ollie was furious at being wounded and lashed out at the father, kicking him in the head.

'Go on, ginge!' Mick shouted. 'Give the bastard one from me.'

The father had stopped moving. Ollie stood there panting, blood dripping down his face. Emily came over and put a hand to his cheek.

'It doesn't look too bad,' she said. 'I'll get some antiseptic and stick a plaster on it.'

'I'm cut too,' said Mick. 'Should never have whacked him in the gob.'

'OK,' said Emily, who was already rummaging in her bag. 'I'll see to you in a minute.'

'Yeah . . . OK . . .' Big Mick was very pale; all the blood had drained from his face. Ollie had never seen him like this.

'Where did he come from?' Einstein asked, staring at the dead father. 'Did he get through the gate?'

'Don't know,' said Blue and he flipped the father on to his back with his foot. 'But the sooner we get inside, the better.'

Blue looked tense and worried; his hard expression had slipped a little. They were all a little rattled.

'I'll smash the doors in,' said Mick, who was trying to shake off the shivers.

'No chance,' said Blue. 'They're reinforced. We'd need a bulldozer.'

'What then?' Mick looked frustrated. Like he wanted to hit something.

Einstein jabbed a finger at Blue. 'You must have some kind of plan,' he said, almost shouting.

'How about we use your head as a battering ram,' said Achilleus with a smirk.

'How about we just walk in?' Jackson was by the doors and now she casually swung one of them open. 'They weren't even locked,' she explained.

A ripple of relieved laughter passed through the kids and Blue led them inside. Achilleus stopped by Einstein.

'Lucky,' he said, rapping his knuckles on the top of Einstein's skull.

Ollie gave the dead father one last kick. His head felt kind of mushy. Soft. Ollie pressed down on it with his trainer and something oozed out of one ear. Something grey and jelly-like. Was it the father's brain? What was left of it. The body started to bubble and twitch. If he was going to burst Ollie didn't want to hang around and watch the show. Always made him feel sick. He spat and hurried after the others before the doors shut on him.

36

There was a large reception area inside, going up to the full height of the building. It was lit by the cool green light that washed in through the wall of windows.

It was all very clean and orderly. No dust, no rubbish, no sign at all of the chaos that had ripped through London when everything started to fall apart.

Untouched chrome and leather furniture was artfully arranged; a clock on the wall had stopped at half past one; there were clusters of video screens with benches around them, even some carousels that still had magazines in them. At the back was a long reception desk with more screens on it, and the words PROMITHIOS MEDICAL SOLUTIONS spelled out on the wall behind.

It was easy to imagine that all the people who had once worked here had just stepped out for a cigarette and at any moment would return to work and the world would be as it had always been.

Ollie sat in a chair while Emily sorted him out. She was a quiet girl with a permanent half-smile on her face.

'So you work with Einstein then, do you?' Ollie asked her.

Emily just said, 'Mmm,' and carried on cleaning his wound.

'And you know what you're doing?' Ollie flinched as she wiped the cut.

'Let's face it,' said Emily softly. 'None of us really know what we're doing, do we?'

'Guess not.'

'Whoever stitched up Achilleus' ear certainly didn't. Made a right pig's arse out of it.'

'It's an improvement,' said Ollie.

'I helped him clean it last night,' Emily went on, 'and gave him some fresh bandages. It's a mess. He's going to look well rough when it heals.'

Ollie winced as Emily rubbed something stingy into his cut.

'I told you I didn't know what I was doing,' she said.

Ollie looked around. The kids were unwinding. There was something peaceful and relaxing about this place. Surely if there had been any sickos in here there would have been some signs of them.

He didn't allow himself to completely loosen up like the others. He could sense the relief all round at being inside and at least temporarily safe from attack. Achilleus was sitting chatting to Jackson and Paddy. Blue was talking to Einstein. Mick's fighters were casually searching the place, going through the drawers behind reception and studying bits of paper. Ollie's guys were slumped like him, lost in their own thoughts.

The only one of them who appeared uptight was Big Mick, who was pacing up and down muttering to himself. Eventually Emily finished what she was doing and went over to him. Made him sit down and roll up his sleeve. Ollie watched as Mick turned away, not wanting to look at his bleeding arm. The big man obviously wasn't as macho as he made out.

There was a shout from the kids behind reception and they started to lay some plans out on the desk. Blue and Einstein joined them and they all started nodding and pointing. After a while Blue jumped up on to the counter.

'OK, listen up,' he shouted. 'We got a plan. Looks like there's some big loading doors at the back of the warehouse where the supplies are kept, but we don't reckon we'd be able to get them open from the outside.'

'We could try,' said Achilleus.

'No,' said Blue. 'The less time we spend outside, the better. Ain't safe out there.'

'So what we gonna do then?' Achilleus asked. 'Sit around on our arses in here?'

'Why don't you just listen?' Blue was trying not to lose his temper. 'We think we found a way through from the inside. We got to go through the offices and down to the next level, then there's this sort of underground tunnel that will take us into the warehouse.'

Ollie's mouth went dry. He didn't like the sound of that. Tunnels, in his experience, were bad news. He gave the reception area another once-over, trying to reassure himself. Surely, surely if there was anything dangerous in here there'd be some evidence; it wouldn't look so clean and neat and tidy.

And there was no smell.

Usually you could smell grown-ups if they were nearby. He met Emily's gaze. She'd finished with Big Mick and was standing next to him.

'What do you think?' he asked, moving closer. 'Are we going to be all right in here?'

'Don't ask me,' said Emily. 'You're supposed to be the ones who know about that sort of thing.'

205

'Yeah, but as you said, Emily, none of us really know what we're doing, do we? I mean, I know sickos, as you call them, but what if there's something else? Something worse?'

37

*Closer, closer, they're coming closer. I'll wait for them. They'll
come to me. They have to. There's no other way. So I'll just wait.
I'm good at waiting. All my life. Stay hidden, stay still, stay quiet.
Alone. Stay quiet. Lie still. Wait. Listen to the buzzing in the air.
The hum and twitter of the creeps out there.*

The fallen.

Some had gone away just now. Something had shut them
up and they'd disappeared. Including one who'd been
bugging him for some time. Like he'd been switched off.

Bang-bang. Sing no more.

There were more of them, though, plenty more. They
kept him in touch with what was going on outside. Once
he'd learnt to understand their babble. Like tuning a radio.
Some days he heard them clearer than others. Some days
he understood more. And lately it had been getting clearer
and clearer. Was he getting cleverer or were they?

He wriggled deeper into the space between the walls.
Settled down to wait. Feeling the comforting toughness
of the concrete against his skin.

Maybe the new kids would give him some answers?

They'd be here soon.

They were coming closer and closer . . .

38

'Shall we get the next one in then?'

Ooh, yes please, let's . . .

Maxie was having a well boring morning interviewing the museum kids, one after the other. An endless succession of worried faces.

She was sitting in a stuffy little office at the front of the museum above the main doors, next to where Justin lived. She and Maeve were representing the Holloway kids, and Brooke, Justin and Robbie were representing the museum kids. Robbie was meant to be in charge of security, but with his wounded leg he was next-to-useless. It had been him Samira had been trying to help last night when she'd gone missing. That's why he was here, rather than lying down, resting his leg. Maxie guessed he felt responsible. He also obviously felt bad that he hadn't been able to help on the night of the attack on the museum. He kept saying he should have been there, and that he shouldn't have let Samira go to the Darwin Centre alone. He was a little bit feverish still, repeating himself.

All Maxie thought was that he shouldn't be up and about like this, even if they had found him a wheelchair to get about in. He looked grey and his skin was greasy with sweat.

The five of them had been sitting here for what felt like

hours while the museum kids trooped in and took it in turns to sit on the other side of the table and answer their questions. The idea was that they were going to find out who the traitor was. That's what they were calling him or her – *the traitor*.

Only they hadn't got anywhere, had they? Big surprise. It was the same every time. Nobody knew anything, they'd all been together the evening of the big attack, nobody liked to go anywhere alone, they were too scared . . . 'I was with so-and-so, we went there together, I helped such and such a person when the sickos came . . .'

Maxie supposed it was quite a good way to get to know people, but after a while, as she got tireder and hungrier, the kids all began to merge into each other and become the same person.

One single frightened child.

Unless they were the greatest actors in the world, not one of them seemed capable of opening those doors, letting the sickos in, watching their friends get attacked and killed. Not one of them had a motive.

She wished Blue was there. He had a good bullshit detector. Maxie had grown up trusting people, believing them when they told her things, thinking the best of people. Blue was the opposite. He didn't believe anyone, didn't trust anyone, thought the worst of people. You had to prove it to Blue when you said something. He'd have surely worked out by now who the traitor was.

If there even was a traitor.

All Maxie had to look forward to was a long afternoon interrogating the rest of the kids.

'Can we have a break?' Maeve asked. 'Robbie looks knackered.'

She was looking at the boy. Wasn't too happy about him being here either.

'I'm fine,' Robbie said and took a sip of water, his hand trembling slightly.

'I wouldn't mind getting out of here and grabbing some fresh air as well, actually,' said Maxie.

'All right,' said Justin. 'Don't be too long.'

Maeve and Maxie walked downstairs and out into the sunshine.

'It's like doing exams or something,' said Maxie.

'Oh, don't,' said Maeve as they settled down on the steps. 'There are some things about the old life I don't miss one bit.'

The main road on the other side of the fence was empty. In fact, since clearing out the lower level, Maxie hadn't seen a single grown-up. If it wasn't for the weirdness of Samira disappearing it would have felt pretty safe and secure in the museum.

A group of kids was working on the vegetable patches, checking for weeds and pests. Maxie recognized some of them from the interviews.

'But this new life,' said Maeve, 'it's killing me, Maxie.'

'We just have to make the museum safe.' Maxie leant back and turned her face up to the sun.

'It'll never be safe,' said Maeve. 'It'll never be safe as long as we stay in the city. We'll never be anything more than scavengers, fighting among ourselves because there's not enough to go round, scared and hiding from the grown-ups. We need to get out of town and into the countryside.'

'It's not that bad,' said Maxie, who'd heard Maeve's arguments about leaving town before. 'There's everything the dead left behind. We've done all right scavenging.'

'We can't just live like parasites,' said Maeve. 'In the countryside we could properly grow our own food. And there'll be a lot less grown-ups around. We should have gone months ago.'

'Yeah,' said Maxie. 'It'll be paradise.'

'Nowhere's going to be paradise,' said Maeve. 'I'm not saying that. But we'll never properly start to rebuild things if we stay here. It's like when the Romans left Britain. The British people didn't know what to do with the towns and cities. They were like us, like kids. They returned to the countryside, left the buildings to rot and went back to their farms.'

'What do we know about being farmers?' said Maxie. 'It's not like Farmville, you can't just click on a few keys and have a load of cute cows filling up your fields.'

'There'll be other kids out there. They've had a year to set up farms.'

'Oh yeah, and they'll be well pleased when we tip up and want half their food.'

'Anything's better than this,' said Maeve.

'It's gonna be all right,' said Maxie.

Just then something rattled next to her and she saw some bits of stone falling to the ground. She twisted round and looked up, squinting against the bright sky. Thought she maybe saw a movement high up on the roof, a dark silhouette. It was quickly gone.

Just a pigeon probably.

Everything was going to be all right.

39

Loser. Noob. Useless twat.

Big Mick wanted to kick himself in the arse. He'd always been like this. Scared of the sight of blood. Not other people's blood. He didn't mind that.

His own blood.

Just the thought of it made his head shrink in on itself and he'd go all dizzy and nauseous and pathetic. One time he'd had to give a blood sample. He'd made the mistake of watching the nurse stick the needle in his arm, saw the little plastic tube fill up with dark blood. It was like all the air had been sucked out of him. The next thing he knew he was waking up in the chair with his mum and the nurse staring at him. His mum looking worried. The nurse was smiling, virtually laughing at him.

Didn't like hospitals. Didn't like nurses. Didn't like doctors.

He'd grabbed Blue as they were getting ready to head deeper into the building. His heart had been thumping and he'd hoped he could talk without tripping over his words. He had to stay on top of things.

'Don't you think we need someone to stay here and keep a look-out?' he'd said, pleased that his voice hadn't let him down. Blue had shrugged.

'Maybe. Dunno.'

'What if more grown-ups rock up?' Mick pressed on. 'Try to get in behind?'

'Could happen.'

'I'll stay if you want.'

'Yeah? You sure?'

'Yeah. I'll keep my three guys. We'll watch your back.'

'Cool. Don't reckon we'll be long.'

Blue had clapped him on the shoulder then turned and joined the rest of the group. Soon they'd gone. Disappeared down a corridor next to the reception desk. It felt very still and quiet without them.

Now Mick was sweating in a chair. If he'd had to stand up any longer his legs would have given out, they were trembling so much.

Why was he such a loser?

He could mash grown-ups into the ground and knock their eyes out, slit their poxy bellies open, didn't bother him one bit. But his own blood. I mean, it wasn't as if the cut on his arm he'd got from whacking the grown-up in the mouth was even that bad, but there was this little waggling flap of skin, and a smear of blood up his arm and . . .

He closed his eyes, feeling faint again. Felt acid rising in his throat and choked it down.

Useless loser.

He'd got away with it, though, hadn't he? Made it look like he was being a hero. Guarding their rear. That was good thinking. And he'd be all right in a few minutes. The tingling sensation in his head would pass. Maybe he could go out and scope the area, walk the perimeter, do something useful. They really did need someone to watch their backs . . .

What if he'd got an infection, though?

He couldn't stop himself. Pictured germs inside him. Little tendrils spreading out from the wound, worming their way through his body. Down his arm to his fingers, then going all round his body, carried in his blood, carried to his heart, his lungs, his brain.

Didn't want that. Didn't want to go nuts.

Nobody really knew if a grown-up's bite could infect you with their sickness, like in zombie films. Most kids died pretty quickly if they got bitten, but there was no way of knowing if they died from some random infection or from the grown-up's disease itself.

Funny how nobody had given it a proper name. It was just the sickness.

The disease.

Mick knew all about diseases. The one thing he didn't want was to die of blood poisoning. His little brother, Ant, had got it and it had nearly killed him. Septicaemia, the doctors had called it. Sepsis. Mick would never forget those words. What happened was Ant had got the flu, and then he'd got a toothache. Silly sod never cleaned his teeth properly, drove Mum mad. He got some kind of abscess under the tooth, down in the gum. A nasty rotten hole full of pus. The doctors said the bacteria had got out of the abscess and into Ant's blood, and he was too weak from the flu to fight it off. They only worked all this out afterwards.

At the time they thought his symptoms were all just from the flu. He started shivering, his temperature went through the roof, he started panting like a dog, and then he went crazy. Spouting all this mixed-up babble. Mick had thought it was funny at first, before he'd got seriously freaked out by it.

It was only when Ant started fainting that Mick's mum thought to take him back to the doctor. Then it was all go. They rushed him to the hospital and stuffed him full of tubes and drips, pumped antibiotics into him.

Nope. Didn't like hospitals. Didn't like nurses. Didn't like doctors.

Ant nearly died. The whole family was there, round his bed in the Whittington Hospital, watching him as he took little tiny quick breaths, his whole body shaking and shivering. Sweat pouring off him. Occasionally he'd come round and look frightened and shout some nonsense. Mum had wanted to get a priest in. In the end, though, it hadn't come to that. Ant had fought the sepsis for three days and then it passed, the fever broke, the drugs kicked in, killed the bacteria and settled him down. Mum hugged the doctor. Mick had never really known what bacteria were before. But he'd hung around the hospital long enough to learn all about it. He'd even looked it up on Wikipedia. He wanted to know all about it so that *he* didn't get septicaemia, or any of the other illnesses bacteria could give you.

He found out that bacteria are tiny living organisms, and they're everywhere. They live in your gut, and on your skin, and in the ground. Forty million of them in a single gram of soil. A thousand million of them in a litre of fresh water. They were so small you couldn't see them, but they were in everything, and if you piled them all up in one place they'd weigh more than all the other plants and animals on the planet put together.

When it came to the ones in Ant's blood, the doctors had settled their hash, though. Wiped them out. Napalmed them with antibiotics. Saved poor Ant. Well, there were no doctors now, no one to fix you if the bad bacteria got inside you. If you got the sepsis you were dead meat.

What if Mick had septicaemia now? What if there were tiny little creatures infecting him? His arm felt suddenly itchy and he manically scratched away at it, being careful not to scrape his bandage off. Was he hot? Feverish? Or was it just warm in here? His feet felt cold. He was shaking a bit.

Sod it. It couldn't happen this quickly. He was all right. Just imagining his worst nightmares. It wasn't bacteria that had got in him – it was fear.

How do you tell your stupid brain to shut up? It was just a scratch. Don't be such a baby.

He took a long, slow breath. Tried to calm down. If he was still feeling jittery in a while he'd take the other three outside. Much better to be doing something rather than just sitting on his arse worrying about shit.

40

Jackson was sticking close to Achilleus. It had felt like something real when they'd both attacked that father together, hadn't it? A moment. They hadn't said anything to each other, just moved fast. One mind. Got the sucker from both sides. Surely Achilleus had noticed? The way they'd worked together. Surely he'd seen that she was more than just some museum nerd? Surely he could tell? But he was hard to get through to, with his gnarly head all chewed up, his manner like nothing mattered. His swagger. Like he could deal with anything and was laughing at you the whole time. She'd never known how to be with boys. Always said the wrong things, did the wrong things. Tried to impress them by doing something extreme, dangerous, wild, something she thought was cool or funny but they always thought was stupid and weird. It was OK when she was just hanging out, being their mate. She'd always had lots of friends who were boys, just no boyfriends. She wished it wasn't important to her, wished she didn't care. Why did it matter whether she had a boyfriend, whether boys even liked her?

Hormones probably. In the end it all came down to hormones. Those pesky little chemicals that made you act like an idiot. Turned you into a nutter or some swooning girly girl in a pink dress. Her dad had once had a long talk to her about being gay, just because she had short hair and preferred boys' clothes to frilly skirts and lace. She knew she wasn't gay. She was always thinking about boys. If anything she thought about them too much and wished with all her heart that she didn't.

She remembered when life had been easier. At primary school, when you could hang out with other kids and that's all they were – kids. Boy, girl, black, white, brown, tall, short, clever, stupid, straight, gay – none of that meant anything, they were all the same. Kids. But as she'd got older it got harder. And now here she was, heading deeper into the darkness of this unknown building, with God knows what waiting for them inside, and instead of being alert and thinking about what she'd do if something attacked, she was thinking about Achilleus. An ugly bully who hardly even knew she existed.

'I was ahead of you,' she blurted out, without really meaning to. Achilleus didn't even turn. Just grunted.

'Huh?'

'Back there, when the father attacked, yeah? I got him just before you did.'

'You reckon?'

'I know.'

'Paddy?' Achilleus booted the little Irish kid up the backside to get his attention.

'Who d'you reckon was quicker? Me or the girl?'

'You,' said Paddy. 'For sure.'

'He's biased,' said Jackson.

'Are you biased, Paddy?' Achilleus asked.

'No way. You was quicker. She was just copying you.'

'I was not!' Jackson protested as Achilleus laughed.

218

They were walking down a long corridor that seemed to run the length of the building, with other corridors off to the sides and windows into open-plan offices. There were glossy framed photographs on the walls, of brightly coloured pills, and smiling, happy, healthy families, nurses and doctors in impossibly clean hospital wards. Smiling. Attractive scientists peering into microscopes. Smiling, smiling, smiling. There were also some slightly random photos of nice landscapes and sunsets. It was clear what message they'd been trying to put across – everything is all right in the world, we will look after you. You're safe in our hands.

Yeah. Right. Good one.

When it had come down to it the doctors and scientists had been taken just as much by surprise as everyone else. They'd been no help at all. They'd been struck down by the disease along with all the rest of the adults. Died before they could find a cure, or even find out what the disease was, where it had come from.

It had all happened so fast. One day it was all sunsets and smiles, the next . . .

Night of the living sickos.

At the end of the corridor was a lobby, with lifts on either side and thick glass doors at the back. A sign above the doors read UNIT B. ENTRY TO AUTHORIZED PERSONNEL ONLY. To the right of the door was a flat electronic card reader and a small numeric keypad.

Blue shone his torch at the flat black panel of the card reader.

'Now what?' Emily asked.

'Simple,' said Einstein. 'We press our access card to the pad then punch in the secret code and – ta-dah – the door will magically swing open.'

Blue gave Einstein a look that said he was just holding back from punching his teeth out. Achilleus went to the doors and studied them up close by the light of Paddy's torch beam.

Jackson had a thought and pushed past him, gave the doors a gentle nudge. They swung open.

'You guys never learn, do you?' she said, walking through.

On the other side of the doors was a stairway that split in two and went down either side of a square central column. There was less decoration in this area. Nobody had bothered to stick up any inspiring pictures. Jackson sniffed the air. Often when you went into a building that had been empty for a long while the air was stale and nasty. Here it didn't smell of anything. It was as if the sterile, air-conditioned atmosphere the building must have had in the old days was somehow still lingering.

Blue pushed to the front and led them down the stairs, going noticeably more slowly now. At the bottom was another corridor leading straight ahead into darkness.

'It's gonna be a pain getting the supplies back up them stairs,' said Blue, looking back.

'There must be a way of getting the main warehouse doors open from the inside,' said Einstein. 'For when lorries made deliveries or picked stuff up. There must be some proper warehouse doors.'

Blue started walking and the others fell in behind him, still keeping bunched up, the torch beams probing ahead. They didn't have to go far before the corridor widened out into a storage area with rows of metal shelving stacked with packing materials: flat-pack cardboard boxes, empty plastic crates, rolls of bubble wrap and plastic binding material. Rolls of sticker labels.

Blue shone his torch into every corner and under every shelf.

Nothing.

'What would a grown-up want to be hiding out down here for?' said Achilleus. 'They can't get in and out, there's nothing to eat. Unless they wanted to send some parcels to their aunties they wouldn't have no interest in all this junk.'

'They make their nests underground,' said Blue.

'I know it,' said Achilleus. 'This just don't feel like the sort of place they'd choose.'

'What about all those sickos outside?' said Jackson. 'What were they trying to get in for? What were they after?'

'They only ever after but one thing,' said Achilleus. 'Fresh meat.'

'You think there might be kids down here?'

'No way. We'd have seen some signs.'

'Yeah, well, let's push on,' said Blue.

The door out of the storeroom through into the next part of the warehouse complex was also unlocked. It led to a short corridor that ran a little way then turned a corner. Its walls were bare concrete. Bundles of cable and bits of pipework ran along either side and there were various shelves and cabinets spaced out along its length. The further they went into the building the plainer it was and the more nervous the kids became. There was no joking now. No talking.

Halfway to the bend they heard a noise. A shuffling, rustling sound. It went as quickly as it came.

They all froze.

'What was that?' said Emily.

'We don't know, Emily, OK?' said Jackson, trying not

to lose her cool. 'How could we know? It came from round the corner. We've never been here before. So just shut up and listen.'

'Does someone want to go and take a look then?' said Einstein.

Jackson stepped forward. Said nothing. Just carried on walking slowly towards the corner where the corridor turned.

Well, this was dumb. Weirdo Jackson. Showing off again. Doing something stupid and dangerous to impress the boys. Only this time she had no idea what she was getting into. For the first time today she was actually scared. She heard a scuff behind her and turned round to find Achilleus catching up with her.

'Can't let you have all the fun,' he said.

'Thanks,' said Jackson. And she meant it. She was marginally less frightened now.

When they reached the corner they stopped and flattened themselves against the wall. Jackson wiped her face. Dried her hand on her jeans. Felt a droplet of sweat scurry down her back under her sweatshirt.

'When I say so we both look round,' she whispered. 'I'll keep close to the edge and shine the torch. You go wide and be ready with your spear.'

She wasn't sure if Achilleus would accept being told what to do by a girl, but he just nodded and said, 'OK.'

'OK.' Jackson swallowed, her mouth painfully dry. 'Ready ... one ... two ... three.'

On three they both moved, together, Achilleus going quickly to the centre of the corridor, spear up, tensed and ready for a fight, Jackson keeping tight to the wall.

She had no idea what to expect. All she saw, though, was

222

a rack of shelves fixed to the wall, with thin sheets of metal on them, piled high so that there was only a very narrow space between the shelves. Five, maybe ten centimetres at the most. Not big enough for a human to hide in. She took this all in fast, peering along a gap at head height, her torch beam bouncing off the metal and making strange dancing shapes. She sidestepped, keeping her eyes fixed ahead, and as she did so she caught a glimpse of something on a lower shelf. Out of the corner of her eye. A hint of a hint. She swung the torch beam back. Gone.

But she'd definitely seen something. Something pale. Something alive. She was sure of it. It had been such a brief flash though, that she couldn't make sense of it. She crouched down and threw more light along the shelf. There was a hurried movement. A quick whip and a wriggle.

'What are you doing?' said Achilleus.

'There was something on the shelves.'

'What something?'

'Don't know. A creature. A face. I definitely felt it was looking at me.'

'You mean like a rat or something?'

'No. It was hairless, naked, I don't know. I didn't really see it clearly.'

'A creature?'

'I'm sure of it. Almost white, with black eyes, set wide apart. Looking at me.'

'So what was it then?'

'Like I say, I don't know, it was like a . . . It reminded me of something.'

Achilleus came over and looked where she was aiming the beam.

'There's nothing there.'

'There was. It went to the back of the shelves. Look, can you see? There's an opening there, a hole of some sort.'

'What's going on?'

It was Blue. The other kids were coming round the corner to join them now, in ones and twos.

'Jackson reckons she saw something,' said Achilleus, poking the point of his spear into the hole. 'But I reckon she's imagining it.'

'I didn't imagine it. It was alive. It was long and flat, pale skin, dark eyes. It looked at me. I'm sure of it. Its eyes were on me. Very dark. Black, like a snake.'

'You saw a snake?' Einstein sounded dubious.

'Not necessarily a snake, but that's what it reminded me of, a snake.'

'What would a snake be doing down here?' Achilleus scoffed. 'You're seeing things, girl.'

'It was there.' Jackson tried to move some of the sheets of metal so that she could get to the hole. They were heavy. It would take ages to shift enough of them.

She swore. Maybe Achilleus was right. Maybe she *had* imagined it. Snakes couldn't survive in places like this. They needed sun and heat. And those eyes. Not really a snake's eyes. Too intelligent.

She shook her head to clear it, grabbed a water bottle from her pack and glugged half of it down. She remembered being in bed, when she was little, seeing things in the darkness, making monsters out of dressing gowns and toys, curtains.

'OK,' Blue shouted. 'It's pretty clear there's nothing down here. We got to stop getting all jumpy over every little thing. We need to get on quick, find the gear and get gone.'

'I think you'd better look at this.'

Everyone turned to Ollie. He'd been to the end of the corridor to check out what lay ahead.

'What is it?' said Blue.

'Come see.'

There was another set of doors, with words scrawled on them, painted with what looked like blood. Dark red, sloppy and dripping.

The kids read the words, their torch beams crawling over them. Not knowing what to think.

Wev'e got what your after. If you really want it you have to porve it. So come and gettit if you think you can. We are waiting 4 you.

41

Why were they taking so long down there? How far could it be to the warehouse? Why weren't they back yet?

The truth was Mick had no idea how long they'd been gone. He didn't have a watch. Hardly anyone wore a watch these days, because there was no way of setting them to the real time. Pick any three clocks at random and you could bet they'd all be showing different times. Or, most likely, stopped. In fact Mick had never worn a watch. Not even in the old days. His uncle had given him one for his birthday once, but he'd never even tried it on. What was the point when you had a phone? But now, without any electricity, the phones didn't work any more, and the clocks all showed different times, or sat frozen at the point when the juice had dried up.

So he could only guess at how long the others had been gone. It could have been five minutes; it could have been half an hour. He was getting twitchy. Couldn't stop thinking about the cut on his arm. About germs and bacteria and Ant, nearly dying in his hospital bed . . .

He looked at his three friends, Brandon, Jake and Kamahl. Boys he'd known for years, had fought alongside, his *team*. Boys who looked up to him. Trusted him to be there for them. They were sitting on a cluster of benches chatting casually to each other. He called over to them.

'Is it hot in here?'

Jake shrugged.

'You're not hot?'

'I'm all right,' said Kamahl.

'Yeah,' said Mick. 'It's not hot, is it?'

'Nah.'

He started to drum a rhythm on his thighs, slapping them. He'd show he wasn't scared of any stupid bacteria. He'd drum them out of there.

Slappity-slap-bang, slappity-slap-bang.

The funny thing was . . . No, not funny, the opposite of funny, not at all funny. Ironic really. A real kick in the teeth from God, to be fair. It was while they were in hospital, sat round Ant's bed, with the bedside TV on, that the first report came on the news about some weird new illness that had broken out in the East End, over Hackney way. The whole family watched it, because it was about illness, and they were obsessed with illness right then. The newsreader said the symptoms were similar to bubonic plague – fever and swellings. Not so different to what Ant was going through. Though he didn't have any swellings.

God, it happened quick after that.

Ant never made it out of hospital. Poor little bastard. All that work the doctors had done. All those drugs. All that worry. All for nothing. By the time Ant was well enough to get up and walk about, the disease was slicing through London. The hospital was locked down, to try and stop the spread. Nobody allowed in or out. Mick was stuck at home trying to cope. His mum got it early. Killed his dad. The police took her away. Mick hadn't known what to do. It all went crazy. He tried to get back to the hospital and rescue Ant.

That was the worst part.

He'd got in OK. The security guards were all sick. And then inside. Like something out of a horror film. Sick people, dead people, blood and pus and excrement everywhere. He'd worked his way back to the ward, trying to find Ant. It was hell. The doctors and the nurses all had the sickness, the patients, everyone. They were killing each other. Mick knew Ant couldn't have survived, but he never found his body. He was glad of that in a way.

It was in the Whittington, scared and angry and desperate, that he'd killed his first grown-up. A fat nurse. He pushed her down some stairs. Didn't mind that at all. It had been a release for him. Didn't get scared in a fight. But he didn't like hospitals. Didn't like nurses. Didn't like doctors.

A movement caught his eye and he turned to see a dark, squirming shape outside. The others had spotted it too. Brandon stood up.

'Look at that.'

Big Mick couldn't work out what it was. He'd spooked himself so badly he was getting confused. The tinted windows didn't help, all crusted with dirt and dust. It looked like there was one big shapeless thing out there, writhing against the glass. Forming, breaking and reforming, like something under a microscope. Liquid. Shape-shifting. Then he saw that it had eyes, and teeth, and legs, legs all over the place. Hundreds of legs.

Not possible.

Not freaking possible.

42

'How many kids did we see this morning?'

Justin looked at his notes. 'Thirty-two.'

Maxie sighed. It had felt like a lot more than that. A whole lot more. And still no closer to figuring out who the traitor was. A weird word that, like something out of a history book.

She was up in the staff canteen at the museum with Maeve and Justin and Brooke. Robbie had gone to lie down in the sick-bay. Worn out. Maxie felt tired too, almost more tired than when she was out on the streets doing stuff. She hadn't had to think this hard, really concentrate, in a long time. She could do with a lie-down.

She stared at her food. Tiny portions, but she was used to that.

'Who have we got left?'

'It's mostly smaller kids now,' said Justin. 'Made sense to start with the older ones, the ones more likely to be able to do something like that.'

'Unless it was a little kid mucking about,' said Maxie, 'and they opened a door by mistake, you know, like they were playing a game or something.'

'It's possible, I suppose,' said Justin. 'But they'd have had to have got the keys off one of the older kids.'

'And we've spoken to all the kids who had keys?'

'Yep, all except for Jamie, who was killed, and Paul Channing.'

'Who's missing?'

'Yep.'

'So it's most likely that whoever got the keys got them off one of those two?'

'I suppose so, yeah. That makes sense.'

Maxie thought about this for a bit. She was pushing the last forkful of rice around her plate, making it last, holding off eating it, as it would mean there was nothing more.

'And so far nobody really remembers seeing this Paul guy all evening?' she asked, looking up at Justin.

'No. But he'd been keeping pretty much to himself since his sister got killed. He was pretty depressed.'

'He went a bit nuts actually,' said Brooke.

'How do you mean?'

'He, like, totally flipped out,' said Brooke. 'Big time. Started cussing everyone about his sister, saying we didn't, like, care. He had a knife. Waving it about. Don't think he'd have shanked anyone, though.'

Maxie put her fork down with a clatter and gave a hard stare, first to Brooke then to Justin.

'Why are you only just now telling me this?'

'Only just remembered about it,' said Brooke. 'With all else that's been going on.'

'I'd forgotten about that as well,' said Justin. 'Do you think it means something?'

'Of course it means something, you idiots,' said Maxie. 'It means that he had a motive.'

'Edge up, girl,' said Brooke. 'It was all just breeze. We never had nothing to do with his sister getting killed.'

'In his mind we did,' said Justin. 'He blamed us somehow.'

'He had keys, yeah?' said Maxie. 'To the lower-level doors?'

'Yes.'

'And now he's disappeared?'

'We assumed the sickos had got him.'

'Well, there's your bloody traitor,' said Maxie. 'It's obvious.'

'Maybe.' Justin wouldn't catch Maxie's eye.

'Oh, come on,' said Maxie, trying not to lose her temper. 'He let them out and then ran off.'

'I suppose it's possible,' said Justin. 'He'd been ill. Was definitely a little screwed up. But I still think we should keep interviewing everyone.'

'We ask them all about Paul, though,' said Maxie. 'Maybe someone saw him, one of the little ones.'

'OK . . .'

Maxie scooped up the rice, shoved it in her mouth. Wondered what Blue was doing right now. Wanted him to be here. This was too deep for her; she couldn't carry it alone. She wished she'd gone with him. Would have preferred to take her chances on the streets than sit it out here.

She swallowed the rice without tasting it.

43

Blue wasn't going to show it, but he was all churned up. His stomach was gurgling, bubbling with acid. It was nervousness more than fear. Wouldn't take much to tip him over, though. He was only just holding it together. He had a feeling of being off balance, not sure what to do.

Mustn't let anyone see that.

He needed them all to believe in him.

It had taken a year to get sorted back home in Holloway. People forgot just how crazy it had been back in the day, when it had all kicked off. How nobody had been in charge, but eventually some leaders had stood up, taken over, and one by one they'd all been killed, till there was only Blue left. Last man standing. It was luck more than anything. He knew that. By then he'd learnt to walk the walk. To put on his armour. Not let the mask slip. Stone cold.

Nobody remembered that at the beginning he'd been as scared as all the rest, how he'd taken over the crew because no one else wanted the job. He'd been a good leader, though. Had grown into it. He knew his territory, his ends. Knew where was safe, where not to go, where to find food, where there were places of safety. Knew how to survive. Leaving Morrisons and the old familiarity of Holloway had been tough. And ever since then he'd been making it up as he went along. Trying to give the impression he was on top of things. Trying to pretend he had some idea what he was doing.

And now this. Down here in the dark in this strange place. He had no previous experience of anything like this. Didn't know how to go ahead. Hated the unknown. They'd blundered into a whole heap of weird voodoo.

But there was something else.

He felt alone in a way he hadn't known for a long while. He'd got used to Big Mick being right next to him, whatever happened, wherever they were. Why had he let Mick stay up top? Should have been one of the others. He felt naked and unprotected.

And then there was Maxie.

God, he wished she was here. She had a cool head on her. He needed that support. Mad to think she'd been so close to him all that time. Just down the road, but they'd never spoken. Never even met. And now it had all happened so quickly. He'd found her and, next thing he knew, here he was, alone and missing her. If he could only get this done he could get back to her.

But without her here he had to do it all by himself.

None of this lot were much use. Einstein didn't have a clue about this sort of thing. OK, so Achilleus knew how to handle himself all right, but he kept well clear when it came to making decisions. That left Ollie. He was smart. Not a leader, but reliable. And Blue was going to need all the help he could get. He just had to ask for it in a way that didn't show his hand.

The door through to the warehouse was padlocked shut. A combination lock. You had to put in a code. The door was solid. Couldn't be forced. They had to figure out the code or go back and find another way in.

And did they even want to get in? What was in there? Who had left that crazy-arsed message on the wall?

'There's another one here,' said Ollie, who'd been studying the lock, and he pointed out some more lettering, low down on the door. Much smaller writing to the other message. Neat, spidery, spelled properly. It had obviously been written by someone else.

'What's it say?' Blue asked.

'It's a quotation of some sort,' said Ollie. 'But some of it's worn off. I can't read it all.'

'Try.'

Ollie began to read. '*Then I saw another beast, coming out of the earth. He had two horns like a lamb, but he spoke like a dragon* – can't read this bit, um – *he performed great and miraculous signs, even causing fire to come down from heaven to earth* – next bit's gone – *He deceived the inhabitants of the earth. He ordered them to set up an image in honour of the beast who was wounded by the sword and yet lived* – I can't read any of this next bit, except – *He also forced everyone, small and great, rich and poor, free and slave, to receive a mark on his right hand or on his forehead, so that no one could buy or sell unless he had the mark, which is the name of the beast or the number of his name. This calls for wisdom. If anyone has insight let him calculate the number of the beast, for it is man's number.*'

'Yeah, great,' said Blue. 'That's a real help.'

44

'Cats,' said Kamahl.

Big Mick grinned. Cats. Of course. It was pretty bloody obvious when you came to look at it properly. It wasn't one creature at the doors, it was about thirty of them. Feral cats. Tangled, writhing, up on their back legs scratching at the glass. Mick had never liked cats, and these ones were horrible. They were scabby, chewed up, half bald, with chunks of fur missing, runny eyes, snotty noses, desperately thin, their bones showing through stretched skin.

He felt suddenly sick. He wanted to get out there and smash them to pieces. Needed to take out his frustration on something.

'First dogs, now cats,' said Kamahl. 'What next? Mutant killer mice?'

No one laughed.

'What are they after?' Jake asked.

'Who cares?' Mick replied. 'Let's get rid of them.'

'What for?'

'For fun.'

'Fun?'

'I don't like them.'

'If we don't have to go outside let's not go, yeah?' said

Brandon. 'We're supposed to keep watch and wait here for the others to get back.'

Brandon was a bit nervous, careful, but you could always rely on him in a fight. Jake had a habit of being a bit crazy and rushing into things. Brandon and Kamahl used their brains a bit more.

'We'll check outside,' said Mick. 'See if any more grown-ups have got through the fence.'

'Mick – if we don't have to . . .'

'We *do* have to, Brandon. We have to guard the rear, and that means we might have to walk the perimeter.'

'Mick . . . They're cats.'

But Mick wasn't listening. They could stay here if they wanted. He couldn't stand it any longer, being cooped up in here, like the waiting room for something horrible. He had to *do* something. Get out there. Kill a cat if that was what it took. And while he was out there it wouldn't do any harm to check what was going on. If there was an army of grown-ups waiting for them, Blue would want to be warned. Jake, Kamahl and Brandon might look up to Mick, but Mick looked up to Blue. Blue had got them through everything. He was a good leader. He was Mick's best friend.

Mick grabbed a spear and tugged the doors open, scattering the cats that were clawing at it. They squealed and screeched, regrouped and foamed about his ankles like a living carpet. He swiped at them and they parted, dodging out of the way, and then joining up into a solid mass again.

He cursed and started to chase them. Threw his spear at a big, one-eyed, mangy freak and missed by a mile. Went to pick his spear up. He turned back. Jake, Brandon and Kamahl were staring at him through the windows. Laughing and

236

shouting. Though he couldn't hear anything. That made him even angrier. He was determined to catch the big cat now. He ran after it, trying to separate it from the others. Swiping with his spear, kicking, yelling a string of harsh swear words.

Every time he looked back his three friends were still laughing and enjoying the show.

He chased the pack of cats along the building to where the floor-to-ceiling glass wall curved round the corner, Brandon, Kamahl and Jake following him all the way.

Mick yelped and hopped as a hot, sharp pain stabbed into his Achilles tendon. He looked down – one of the cats had bitten him. Others were scratching at his trouser legs.

Bastards. He swung his spear. Connected with a cat and sent it flying, only for it to land on its feet and come back at him. And there was One-Eye, hissing at him, jaws wide.

He chucked the spear, saw it embed itself in the ground, went into a crouch, arms flailing, hands grasping. The cats were mewling and screaming at him, like little children.

He had One-Eye cornered.

'Here, pussy, pussy . . . Bastard pussy . . .'

Threw out his hands. Lunged . . .

Got it! He had One-Eye by the loose skin on the back of its neck. He held it up like a trophy as it wriggled in his grasp, paws scrabbling at the air, legs kicking. He showed it to his three spectators, a look of triumph on his face. They were still laughing, but cheering now as well, clapping.

And then One-Eye wrenched its head round and bit deep into his hand. Mick roared, hurling the cat to one side where it landed harmlessly. He swore, shaking his hand.

Why had he been so stupid? All he'd done was get himself cut again. Now he'd be full of cat germs, bastard cat bacteria. He couldn't let it go. Couldn't let it live now. He ran after it. Tripped and fell.

Didn't want to see what the other boys' reaction would be to that. Could imagine it, though. This was turning into a comedy. Something off YouTube. Epic fails. He looked over to them. Ready to jeer.

They weren't laughing any more, though. They looked scared, eyes wide, mouths shouting something at him.

What?

Jake was waving his arms frantically. Trying to get Mick's attention.

What?

45

'It's from the bible.' A kid stepped forward and knelt down by the door. One of Ollie's missile crew, an African guy called Ebenezer, or some mad name like that.

'Thought it might be,' said Blue. 'So what's it mean?'

'It's from the Book of Revelations,' said Ebenezer. 'Nobody really knows what any of it means.'

'*If anyone has insight let him calculate the number of the beast,*' Ollie repeated. 'Is it asking for a number to put in the lock?'

'The number of the beast?' said Achilleus. 'Everyone knows the number of the beast, man.' And he stuck his hand up in a heavy metal horn sign.

'Six-six-six.' He stuck his tongue out and went, 'Blaaaaah!'

A couple of the kids tittered, and Paddy joined Achilleus, putting both hands up in a stiff-armed rock gesture.

'We who are about to rock salute you!' he said in a bad American accent.

'So what do we do then?' said Blue, ignoring him. 'There are five numbers on the lock.'

'Let's try all sixes,' said Ollie. 'It's the best guess we've got.'

'Wait.' Blue held him back.

'What for?'

What for? If only he knew. It was like playing a new video game for the first time. You never knew what to expect when you opened a door. Usually died the first time you tried it.

Couldn't stop playing now, though.

'Nothing. You're right. Go for it . . .'

46

Was it the smell that made him turn? The rank stink of rotting grown-ups? Or was it the sudden surge of fleeing cats, belting past him, over him, round him, and disappearing?

They'd come up on him from the gap between the office block and the warehouse building. Almost as many of them as there were cats. Moving quickly for grown-ups, despite being out in the sun. Older ones, knotted and hairless, deformed by swollen flesh, like they'd been pumped full of jelly. One mother had a head so eaten away there was virtually nothing left of it. Mick wondered how she was still walking around. He scrambled to his feet, ignoring the pain in his ankle. Desperate to get to his spear. Even as he went for it, though, he was thinking that maybe he should've just run.

Too late for that now.

He got to the spear and pulled it out of the ground. Looked back along the front of the building towards the doors. There were more of them there, coming from the other direction. If he wasn't fast they'd cut off his route back to safety.

Then he saw Jake come charging out of the doors like the idiot he was.

'No!' Mick shouted. 'Stay back. I'm all right!'

Brandon and Kamahl had waited inside, waving and pointing through the windows. Smart. That's what he'd have done. No need to risk getting hurt when all he had to do was get to the doors . . .

He was still taking all this in when the world gave a sort of jolt and he went staggering sideways, head spinning. He struggled to make sense of what had happened and then realized something had hit him in the temple.

One of the grown-ups was carrying a half-brick. Mick put a hand to his throbbing scalp. More blood.

Jesus.

'Mick!' Jake was haring towards him.

Distracted by Jake and still dizzy from the first blow, Mick lost sight of the father with the brick, who hit him again. Mick staggered drunkenly, swinging the spear, and then Jake was there, pulling his arm.

'Come on, Mick, get away from them.'

'Bloody cats,' said Mick, confused and disoriented.

'Come on.'

Mick groaned as the pain pulsed in his head, shaking him back to reality. 'You shouldn't have come out,' he said. 'I can handle this.'

'We have to get back inside!'

'I'll show them.'

Mick took a deep breath, getting it all back together, head clearing, drove his spear right through the chest bone of the father with the brick, twisted and yanked it free. Laughed. Stooped down to pick up the brick.

'You want some?' he shouted and the bulk of the grown-ups were on him. 'You want to see what I can do with this?'

A mother came at him; he could only tell it was a mother

from the remains of the clothes she was wearing. Her face wasn't a face any more, it was just one huge swollen boil, a featureless blister. He smashed the brick into the part where her nose should have been, cursed as he was sprayed with hot liquid. Saw that there was nothing left of her face; it had burst, exposing the skeletal bones beneath it. Somehow the mother kept upright, though, and her eyes were still intact, staring at him.

'Go down,' he screamed and hit her in the mouth with the brick, shattering her teeth. Kept going. Threw the brick at a father. Stuck another in the thigh with his spear.

'There's too many to fight.' Jake was struggling in a clump of adults, working hard with his own spear.

'Not for me, Jake. This is payback time.' Like he was in some dumb action movie.

Mick went hard into the mob of grown-ups around Jake, keeping two hands on the shaft of his spear, wide apart, stabbing, butting with the blunt end, smashing the shaft into their stupid, bloated faces.

This was what he was good at.

Someone was by his side, fighting alongside him. He turned to smile, assuming it was Jake. It wasn't. It was a short father with a bright red face.

'Get lost,' Mick snorted and shoved him aside. There was Jake, over by the wall of the warehouse, fighting off the pack of grown-ups, and now Mick saw that they all seemed to be carrying weapons of some sort, stones and sticks, bits of rusted metal.

'Watch out!'

His fault if Jake got hurt. Had to help him. Shouldn't be here. What was he doing? Shouldn't have started this fight.

Jake went down with a small cry of pain, the grown-ups

243

on him, slashing and gouging. Mick kicked into them, pushing with his spear, careful not to stab Jake, who was in this mass of bodies somewhere.

No. Gone.

Where was he?

Jake?

Mick looked around, trying to find some sign of where his friend was. Gasped as something hit him in the neck. Felt a warm flow of blood down under his shirt.

Who did that?

A big father with one eye . . . Like the cat . . . Sharp teeth . . . Bits of jagged glass in each hand. Blood pouring down his forearms. Cutting himself as badly as he'd cut Mick.

Not allowed to stand. Not this one. A spear thrust to the belly. Out and back again and, as the father bent forward, a third jab into the back of the neck. Go down. Die.

So much blood.

Where was Jake?

Just grown-ups, everywhere, backing away from him, defeated, retreating. Cowards. Useless sick morons. Run.

Where was Jake?

Find Jake.

So much blood. He looked down. His clothes were wet. Couldn't bear to touch the wound on his neck. Scared of what he'd find.

How come they were armed? They'd changed up. That wasn't fair. Grown-ups didn't use weapons. Too stupid. Stayed in the dark. Used teeth and fingernails, like animals. No better than cats.

Find Jake.

Still a press of grown-ups by the doors keeping Brandon

and Kamahl inside. Good, they were safe. Stay that way.
Mick's job was to keep everyone safe.

So where was Jake?

47

'I did see Paul, yeah, in the afternoon. I was with Wiki.'

'Who's Wiki?'

'Thomas Rutherford, that's his real name, not Thomas Hopgood, he's another Thomas who we're friends with, we were at school together, me and Wiki, that's Thomas Rutherford, not Thomas Hopgood, I met Thomas Hopgood here, in the library, I met Wiki at Rowhurst School in Kent, we call him Wiki because he knows everything, like Wikipedia, he's from northern England, that's why he has a different accent, we've been friends since . . .'

'Yeah, yeah, all right. I don't need his life story.' Maxie put up her hands to stop the little boy rattling on. She understood now why the other kids called him Jibber-jabber.

'So you and this Wiki saw Paul in the afternoon?'

'Yeah, we did, yeah, we were going round trying to get kids to sign up for our event.'

'What event?' Maxie interrupted him before he went off on another one.

'World Book Day,' said Jibber-jabber with a very serious expression. 'We were having this all-night book-reading session where we dressed up as our favourite characters from books, I was Bilbo Baggins, from *The Hobbit* . . .'

'Yeah, all right, I know who Bilbo Baggins is.'

'My costume wasn't that good really.'

'So that was you lot in the library the other night?'

'Yes.'

'The boy that died, the one they got on the stairs, was he with you?'

'Sort of,' said Jibber-jabber. 'That was James, he only really came along to the event to muck it up, I'm sorry he died, though, he was with Paul when we saw him earlier, the two of them worked with the sickos on the lorry.'

Again Maxie put her hands in the air.

'Hold up, not so fast. I need to get this straight. Is Wiki around?'

'He's waiting outside, he's next up, we didn't know who was going to be next, we flipped a coin, I won, so I came in first, that's all coins are really good for now, isn't it, I suppose, flipping . . . and doing magic tricks, of course, I can do a good trick.'

'Shut up for a second and get him in, will you?'

In a minute Wiki was sitting alongside his friend, two small, serious-looking boys, thin, like most kids were these days, and a little pale.

'OK,' said Maxie, fixing on Wiki. 'Tell us exactly when and where you last saw Paul.'

'It was on the afternoon of the attack,' said Wiki. 'We were signing up names for the event.'

'We didn't get many,' Jibber-jabber butted in.

'One at a time.'

'OK,' said Wiki. 'We went to the car park, that's where the lorry was. Einstein kept three sickos on the lorry for his experiments. They were named after the X-Factor judges. James made us go on the lorry to see the sickos. We had to go to show we weren't scared.'

'We were scared, though,' said Jibber-jabber. 'We didn't want to go on the lorry, and the sickos were quite horrible, and later on they got out and attacked the library.'

'We'll get to that in a bit,' said Maxie. 'Tell me about Paul.'

'Paul was on the lorry,' said Wiki. 'He looked after the sickos. He was quite angry about something, and looked ill. He shouted at us, saying books were stupid and the real world was too harsh to be in books. He said we didn't know about things and that he did. Like he was going to prove it to us.'

'And the three sickos escaped?'

'Yes,' said Wiki. 'When we were having our event in the library the sickos got in and attacked us. We beat them off, but James ran away and got killed.'

'And you didn't see any more of Paul after you were on the lorry?'

'No.'

Maxie looked round at Justin, who was sitting on her left.

'I presume these sickos were kept locked up?'

'Yes, of course. They were chained to the side of the lorry and there were bars and padlocks; the whole thing was really secure. It had to be. We couldn't risk them getting out. I mean, they *couldn't* get out.'

'Well, they did.'

Justin shrugged. There was no arguing with that.

'Someone must have opened all those locks,' said Wiki.

'Yes.' Brooke turned to Justin. 'Paul had keys presumably. Who else?'

'Keys to the lorry? I'm not sure. James, I think. Einstein must have, but he wouldn't have let the sickos out, they were too valuable to him.'

'And James is dead.' Maxie turned back to the two little boys. 'You say James was with you in the library when the sickos attacked?'

'Yes.'

'Did he look to you like he knew anything about what was going on?'

'No way,' said Jibber-jabber. 'He was more scared than the rest of us, acting all tough when all along he was just scared and a wimp basically . . .'

'OK, thanks.' Maxie smiled at the two small boys, sitting there with dirty faces, scruffy hair, eager to please. 'I think you two might as well go. But if you think of anything else you'll come and tell us, yeah?'

'Anything else about what?' asked Jibber-jabber.

'We're trying to find out how the sickos got out.'

'Oh, right. Yeah. It wasn't us.'

Maxie smiled. 'I know it wasn't you.'

'Do you think it was Paul Channing?' asked Wiki.

'I don't know,' said Maxie. 'What do you think? You saw him last. Do you think he could do something like that?'

Wiki thought about this for a long time, chewing his lip. Then he had a whispered and muttered conversation with Jibber-jabber that turned into a bit of an argument.

'I know lots of things,' said Wiki in the end. 'I know the answers to almost any questions you can ask me about science and facts, and the world, and the *Guinness Book of Records*, things like that. But I can't answer your question.'

'Neither can I,' said Jibber-jabber.

48

Why was he carrying a shoe? He looked at his feet. He had his own trainers on. So whose shoe was this? It was important. He remembered that. It was important he didn't drop the shoe.

Where was Jake?

He looked around. Somehow he'd left his home and was on another planet. A huge, empty, alien space. Never known anything like it. The emptiness went on forever. He couldn't really remember how he'd got here. He'd been trying to get back. Back to his friends at the big glass building. He'd got lost. Way lost. And now he was here.

He flopped down to his knees. God, he was tired. Way off in the distance he could see some white birds. They were huge, gleaming in the sun. Must be the biggest birds he'd ever seen. The rest was emptiness. The sky over him. No end to it.

Find Jake.

His clothes were caked with blood. It was drying, but there was more running down his neck where . . .

Yes. Where that grown-up had cut him with the broken glass. He must have lost a lot of blood. He was very thirsty. It hurt to swallow.

And they'd taken Jake. *Where?* He'd lost them.

They'd dragged Jake away and he'd tried to follow. Found he couldn't walk very well. His balance was shot. He'd stumbled after the grown-ups, but they were quicker. Got out through a big hole in the fence.

So that's how the bastards had got in.

He remembered them pulling Jake through it. How he'd tried to resist. Still alive. Good boy. Good old Jake. And his foot caught in the wire. They yanked hard and his trainer came off. Mick almost caught up. Then paused to pick up the trainer. Jake would need it, wouldn't he? To get back.

After that.

He remembered crossing a road, going through trees and bushes into fields, a lake; one moment he'd been among buildings and then . . . somehow he was in the countryside again. Countryside. He'd wandered around in circles. Couldn't find the grown-ups, couldn't find Jake, couldn't find his way back.

There had been birds circling above the lake. Different ones. Normal birds, not the giants he could see now. Then he'd spotted a grown-up, standing stiff and still, like it was pointing the way. He'd gone over, followed where the grown-up wanted him to go, crawled up a bank on to another road. Walked on for a bit. How long? No idea. No watch. No idea. *Where was Jake?* Lost him. Lost everyone. Another grown-up, pointing. Keep plodding on. Shirt wet. So much blood. Watched his feet as they moved in front of him, like they were in a film. And in the end everything had disappeared, he'd left his world and ended up here. Walked right into another dimension. Maybe it was heaven. Or hell?

A big nothing.

251

Just him and this shoe and the sky.

How could this be? How could anywhere be so big and empty? Apart from the giant white birds. So gigantic they looked like aeroplanes.

He laughed. They *were* aeroplanes. It all made sense now. He must have got on to the runway at the airport. This wasn't hell, it was Heathrow Airport. He'd lost his spear. His shirt was red, soaked, sticking to him. Blood pumping down from his neck. Thirstier than he had ever been before.

He should get up. Go over and get on one of those aeroplanes. Fly away from all this. Yeah. One of those planes could fly him somewhere nice. Somewhere hot where there weren't any sick grown-ups. Just him and his family. Mum and Dad and Ant. Sitting on a beach in Spain, like when they'd stayed in his uncle's flat. That had been well good. With all them tall buildings, hotels, apartment blocks, shops, all along the back of the beach, keeping him safe. Just like home.

Yeah. It was going to be a cool holiday. He smiled. Showed his ticket to the air hostess. She was nice. Said hello. Beamed at him. He held his mum's hand. Everything was all right. Mum was there, and Dad, and Ant. Ant hadn't died. Why had he thought that? Ant was fine. Funny little kid. He said sorry to Ant for thinking he was dead and Ant just smiled at him. They found their seats. Settled down. There were headphones, a TV screen. He looked out of the window. Already they were taking off. Up in the sky. Up where no one could get to you.

He turned to his mum.

'I'm really looking forward to this holiday. It's going to be the best.'

'Yes. Yes, it is. But you won't need that shoe, love. Let go . . .'

Oh, right.

He was still holding on to that stupid shoe.

He let go.

Watched as the shoe dropped out of his hand. Slowly, slowly, down out of the sky, slowly turning, through the clouds, disappearing . . .

. . . the blood stopped running down his neck and he fell very still.

'It would explain what happened the other night.' Maxie was coming down the stairs past the statue of Darwin with Brooke and Maeve. 'But what about Samira?'

'What if Paul never ran off?' said Brooke. 'What if he was still around . . .?'

She left the sentence hanging as they thought about what that would mean.

'What was he like?' Maxie asked when they reached the bottom of the stairs.

'Just, like, normal really,' said Brooke. 'Never really stood out, until that day he went off on one. Never seen him like that before.'

'I've seen plenty of kids crack up,' said Maxie. 'And I guess if his sister died . . .'

They stopped by the diplodocus. They'd finished the last of the interviews and Maxie was keen to catch what was left of the daylight outside. It could get really gloomy in the museum with no lights on.

'What do we do now?' Maeve asked.

'I guess that's down to Justin,' said Brooke. 'He's in charge. Only we've never had anything like this before.'

'I was gonna say we should search the place,' said Maxie.

'See where he might be hiding. But that would take ages, wouldn't it?'

'Yeah. It's bare massive,' said Brooke. 'Took you long enough just to clear out the lower level. Up here . . . It goes on forever. I never even been in half the rooms. If he was hiding, and he knew we was looking for him, he could easily just move about, and change up his hiding places.'

'It's all whack,' said Maxie.

'True that.'

Maxie saw that Ella had come over to join them. She hadn't noticed her arrive. She just appeared out of the shadows and stood there in silence, her eyes shining.

'You all right, babe?' Maxie asked. Ella shrugged. It was obvious she wanted to say something, but was holding back.

'What's up?'

'You're looking for a boy, aren't you?'

So far nothing had been said to the kids. Justin didn't want to make any kind of official announcement until he was sure of what was happening. He didn't want to panic anyone, but they'd obviously been talking among themselves.

'We don't know yet,' said Maxie.

'You think a boy did something to Samira?'

'As I say, Ella, we're not sure.'

'It wasn't a boy.' Ella shook her head.

'What do you mean?' Ella had Maxie's attention now.

'We've seen him,' said Ella. 'In the dark. At night. We've seen the monster.'

Maxie was going to say that there were no such things as monsters when she stopped herself. That might have been true before, but now? The disease had created a whole world of monsters.

'It isn't a boy,' Ella went on. There was no stopping her now. 'It's the bogeyman. A spider man with long arms and legs, all stretched and black, like a spider. It's the slenderman.'

Maxie laughed, trying to reassure Ella.

'Well, which is it, babe? A spider? A bogeyman? The slenderman?'

'All of them maybe.' Ella didn't sound too sure of herself any more.

'Have you actually seen him? This monster? I mean, *you yourself*, with your own eyes?'

Ella looked at the floor and gave another little shrug with a tiny shake of the head.

'I haven't,' she said very quietly. 'But other people have.'

'I bet they haven't. I bet they all say it was someone else who saw the monster. It's all just hype. You're all just getting panicky and making stuff up.'

'But there's something . . .'

'And whatever it is we'll find it,' said Maxie. 'I don't want you to get scared. Trust me, OK?'

'I don't like it here,' said Ella. 'I want to leave.'

'You can't leave,' said Maxie. 'There's nowhere to go, OK? So you just hang in there. As I say – you trust me now.'

Ella didn't respond straight away. She stood there for half a minute chewing her lip, then said, 'OK,' and abruptly turned, walked over to the stairs and sat down, resting her head in her hands.

'She gonna be all right?' Brooke asked.

'I hope so. She's done all right so far. Funny how some kids are cool and some just give up. She lost her brother.

He was a good kid. Small Sam we called him, because at one time we had, like, three Sams I think, maybe four. Small Sam, Big Sam, Curly Sam, who had curly hair, and there was another. I forget what he was called.'

'Fat Sam?' Brooke suggested and Maxie smiled.

'I can't remember,' she said.

'Me either,' said Maeve. 'You put them out of your mind when they get killed. Otherwise . . .'

'So what happened to Small Sam?' said Brooke.

'He got taken just before we came away,' Maxie explained. 'One of the reasons we left. It was getting too dangerous there. It was a real shame about Sam. They'd been good together, him and Ella. He looked out for her, even though he was only young himself. Not even ten I don't think. I was worried she might lose it when he was taken, but so far she's done good.'

'It's like you and me,' said Brooke.

'How so?'

'When I was lying there in the palace I was only pretending to be asleep a lot of the time. I was listening to what you were saying. You and Blue. I learnt quite a lot about you both.'

'We kind of forgot you were there.'

'Yeah. So the thing is . . . I know about Arran. You were kind of in love with him, I think, weren't you?'

Maxie was embarrassed, felt her face flushing. She'd never really talked about any of this with anyone. Not even Maeve.

'Kind of,' she said. 'Maybe.'

'I lost some good friends along the way as well,' said Brooke quietly, staring off into infinity. 'And more when you rescued me.'

'At Green Park?' said Maxie. 'Those other kids with you? The ones who'd been . . .'

'Yeah. There was a sweet, crazy guy called DogNut and a girl called Courtney. My two bests. DogNut wanted to be more than that. I knew he wanted to, like, link up and that. Who knows? Maybe with enough time he'd have got what he wanted. He used to make me laugh. I try not to think about all that, though. Is bare harsh. What we had, what we lost, what might have been. You got to harden yourself. Make, like, a shell around you. But not everyone can do it. If they got nothing to hang on to some of them screw up. They're not in the game no more.'

'Like Paul?' said Maxie.

'Yeah, like Paul.'

Brooke spotted something and her mood changed. She smiled. A girl with a secret. 'Listen, Maxie,' she said. 'I figured you might need some stuff.'

'Stuff?'

'Clothes and that. I seen that minuscule backpack you tipped up with. You can't have been able to fit too much gear into it.'

'I'm OK.'

'You need more clothes, girl.'

Maxie looked at Brooke, who was wearing a floor-length grey dress that looked like something out of a history book. If more clothes meant dressing up like her she wasn't interested. She'd never been that bothered about clothes. Never been confident enough to carry off anything too funky. Was happy in jeans and T-shirts. Loved the new leather jacket she'd picked up in Selfridges on the way down here.

'You can't be busting the same look twenty-four seven,

girl,' said Brooke. 'You need to rest them garmz, let the stink out.'

'I'm fine,' said Maxie. 'I can pick some more stuff up when we got more time.'

'We got time now,' said Brooke, and then Maxie spotted a group of kids approaching. Lewis was among them and at their head was a tall, elegant guy wearing brightly coloured robes that made him look like some kind of African prince. She tried to remember his name from the interviews that morning. Luckily Brooke reminded her.

'Kwanele's gonna take us shopping,' she said. 'I arranged it all earlier.'

'I don't want to go shopping,' Maxie protested.

'This ain't any old shopping, girl. We gonna take you to the Victoria and Albert Museum. It's nang!'

50

'They look like insects from up here.' Boney-M was standing on top of the wall, keeping very still so that he looked like some black stone gargoyle. Paul risked leaning out to look down, careful not to knock anything off like he'd done earlier. Watched a group of kids way below going towards the gates, Kwanele leading them in one of his stupid outfits.

'I could swoop down and snatch one up in my beak,' said Boney.

'No, you couldn't,' Paul scoffed. 'You can't fly, your wings are broken, you've got no feathers. You're just . . .' He paused. What was he? A fossil? An exhibit? A living corpse? A joke.

When he turned to look at Boney he wasn't there any more.

'You're just a bad dream,' said Paul.

He'd been talking to thin air. He had a sudden stab of sadness. He wanted to be down there, with his friends, talking to real people. Not up here talking to himself. But he couldn't ever go back, could he? Not after what he'd done. He could never undo it. Never travel back in time and take a different route. He'd ruined everything.

He realized his cheeks were wet. He pictured Samira's mutilated body, lying in the corner, starting to rot.

No going back.

51

This is the journal of Lettis Slingsbury. Date unknown.
Place unknown. Almost unknown. It's a church somewhere near Heathrow Airport. Which is to the west
of London.

In the morning, after we all woke up, I wanted to go
with the fighters to the medical place, because that's
what this story is all about, but they wouldn't let me.
I did think it was unfair and I didn't think that Chris
Marker would be very happy about how things were
when I got back, but in the end he is just a librarian,
just a writer, and Justin is in charge of us and Einstein
is a scientist who does amazing things and will cure
the disease and Blue is a fighter, he is in charge of
the search party, so I cannot argue with them, and
Chris is not at the top of the table, if you take my
meaning, which means that the others are more
important than him. And I am even less important
than Chris.

I have never been important. I dreamt that one day
I might be, that I might do great things and maybe
be a great writer or a journalist or help people somehow. I don't think that will happen now. I don't know

what will happen, but I don't think it will be good. I'm sorry, I'm doing it again. I am not supposed to write about myself. Chris told me that. This book should be like a newspaper like we used to have, with just news in it. Though I think they sometimes used to put in bits by famous people talking about themselves. They were called columns. As I say, I am not famous so nobody will want to read about me and what I have to say. I will never have a column.

This is what happened next. The search party left the church to go to the medical place to get the things we need. I had to do what I was told and stay here at the church. I thought I would spend my time writing something, but nothing had happened and so there was nothing really to write that wasn't just thoughts and feelings and I was cross and a bit depressed about being left behind and couldn't face any writing. My heart wasn't in it. Caspar is hurt very badly and is quite unwell. He is sort of moaning and shivering a lot. It is distracting. And then there is the body of Gabby, a corpse, wrapped in a sheet, lying there for all to see. It isn't nice and it was upsetting everyone. I was upset too. Stuck here in the church we were all left alone with our worst thoughts. There was nothing to do but think and think and think and worry and worry and worry.

I couldn't concentrate enough to even pick up a pen, which sounds pathetic, I know, but that is the truth as it happened. I mainly couldn't stop thinking about the night when the sickos got into the museum. We had all been in the library. Me and Chris Marker and some other children. It was our World Book Night.

It wasn't really World Book Night, but we were trying to do things like in the old days before the illness. As we are all book lovers, we wanted to stay up all night in the library to share our thoughts and read bits out and we all dressed up as our favourite characters from books. I dressed up as Clarice Bean. At first it was fun, but then a boy called James came in and was laughing at us and spoiling things and calling us nerds and geeks and bookworms and then it got even worse as some sickos got in. Nobody knows how they got in, but they did. They were all over the museum. There was an awful fight. James was killed. He was not the only victim of the invasion, though. Many children were killed that night and it is still in my nightmares.

So I had to try and not think about it. I was in this church now, not back in the library, so I joined in with the other children who had got talking about things. There was Jasmine. She is quite religious. Much more religious than me. I used to go to church, but I didn't really believe in any of it. Jasmine is always praying. She was very upset about the corpse lying there, the sheets all brown and red from blood and things. Flies buzzing round it and crawling everywhere. I didn't like to think of them laying their eggs and the body having maggots in it.

Jasmine said eventually, after some thought, that we should bury the body. It would give us something to do and we were in a church with a graveyard so it was only right. After all, I mean to say, we all knew that we could take the body with us, but where would we take it? It would rot and start to smell and all the time it was reminding us of the horrible thing that had happened on the way here. And reminding us that poor Gabby was dead. There she was inside that sheet. Wrapped up like an old parcel. It was making me sick. People were getting hysterical. We didn't think we would be there that long, but the search party wasn't back yet even though Blue had sort of promised that they wouldn't be away for long, and the hours were passing by, like the steady ticking hands of a clock ticking round. Jasmine was getting more and more stressed about it, saying, 'We must bury her, we must bury her.' It was making us all quite edgy.

Reece said that Blue had ordered us not to go outside, and I said that I had promised Ollie, but nobody was listening to me and Daryl Painter said he had been up on to the top of the steeple (the church tower) to have a look and there was nothing out there, it was just trees and grass and birds singing, things of that nature.

'The body will smell more and more,' said Jasmine, 'and it will attract sickos from all around. They will come and try and get in. We should bury the body while it is quiet.'

Then Reece made a practical point. 'How are we going to dig a grave?' he asked. Jasmine didn't know how we were going to do that. I think she really just mainly wants to get the corpse out of the church so that she doesn't have to look at it all day long. Then Demi said something. She had been exploring the church a bit and had found a little room with a sort of office in it, and some keys on hooks. And she went and fetched one of the keys and it had a paper label *fixed on by a bit of old string and the label said 'tool shed'.*

So she said there must be a tool shed and they might have spades in there, and other gardening things for looking after the grounds of the church. Daryl, who had been up on the steeple, said he had seen some sheds and things all among the trees and bushes behind the church and Reece said we should go and have a look.

I said it was a very bad idea and that we were not to open the door for anything. Jasmine said I was being stupid and babyish, so I didn't say anything else. I kept my thoughts to myself. So the next question on everyone's lips was who should go outside and do it.

As you can imagine, nobody put their hand up. Nobody wanted to volunteer to be the first to go outside.

'But it's perfectly safe,' said Jasmine. 'The others went off all right, didn't they? I watched them go, there were no sickos around. If there were they would have followed them or attacked them.'

'I still don't want to go out there alone,' said Reece. And there was an argument.

The argument is still going. I can hear them as I am writing this. I got bored of it, and didn't want any more of it. Nobody would listen to me. So as an excuse I said I had to write the journal, which wasn't really an excuse and is certainly not a lie. I do need to write the journal. And finally I had something to write about. The argument obviously and whether we will open the doors and go outside.

I don't want to go outside. I wish nobody would have to go. What I really want is for the others to come back. They must be back soon. Hopefully the argument will go on and on for a long time and before anyone decides anything there will be a big knock on the church doors and there will be Blue and Ollie and the others and we will all cheer and be safe again.

They will know what to do about the body as well.

That's what I want. But, as I say, I am only small and unimportant, so who cares what I want?

52

Blue wouldn't have been able to say just exactly what he was expecting on the other side of the door. But it wasn't this. This was way outside his comfort zone. A weird day had just got a whole lot weirder.

The door opened into a large room. He'd seen from the plans that the warehouse was divided into two, with this smaller area at the rear, connected to the rest of the warehouse by a big roll-down door. There was a sort of steel cage built around the door, with wire-mesh walls and roof.

To get to the door they'd have to go through the cage.

And inside the cage were four fathers.

They didn't look like the usual skanky sickbags you saw on the streets. They were thin and pale, with greyish skin, their dark eyes sunk in their cheeks, but showed no obvious signs of the disease. On top of that they were reasonably well dressed, in clean clothes, and they were armed. Two of them had spears and the other two had butcher's knives and what looked like truncheons. They were like no grownups Blue had seen in over a year.

They were still human.

They were sitting on the floor of the cage, staring at the kids as they filed in through the door from the utility room. The cage was bolted to the floor, but Blue could see where it had been battered and bashed. The mesh was bowed out in one section. The grown-ups had obviously been trying to get out. Now they just sat there. Blue felt slightly awkward, embarrassed, not sure what to do or say. He'd got out of the habit of talking to grown-ups. Hell, they *couldn't* talk.

It was Achilleus who broke the spell. He walked over to the cage and rattled his spear against it.

'Yo. Sick dudes. Whassup?' The fathers slowly turned to look at them. Blue now saw that they had water bottles. He was still trying to figure it all out when one of the fathers spoke, making him jump.

'You come to get us out of here?' He was maybe forty, with very black hair, wearing jeans and boots, a denim shirt and a heavy canvas jacket. He had a bandage covering one eye.

'You can talk?' said Achilleus, standing back from the cage.

'So can you,' said the man.

'That ain't a thing,' said Achilleus. 'I'm a kid. You're a gonk. You ain't supposed to talk.'

'Yeah,' Paddy sneered. 'You ain't supposed to talk, you're supposed to die.'

'Shut it, Paddy,' said Achilleus and he slapped him round the head. 'This ain't a film.'

'Sorry.'

Slowly the father who had spoken did up the top button of his shirt and got to his feet. He was stiff and tired-looking, groaned as he straightened his legs. Sighing with the effort, he hobbled over to the mesh and Achilleus dropped further back, not sure about any of this. The father was carrying a short spear with a wide leaf-shaped head on it. He rested it against the mesh and looked into the faces of the kids who were standing there gawping.

'I asked if you'd come to let us out of here,' he said, his visible eye glinting. His voice was dry and croaky, with a mild Irish accent. Blue wondered how long he'd been in the cage.

'Maybe we have,' he said and the man turned his glare full on him.

'You in charge?' he asked.

'Yeah.' Blue settled his face. Took control. Turned down the temperature. Set his features in stone. Didn't want to let this stranger read anything in him. The man held his stare for a few seconds then softened. Smiled.

'I'm sorry,' he said. 'Got off on the wrong foot there. I expect you've got a lot of questions.'

'I expect we have,' said Blue. 'Like how come you can talk for a start? How come you ain't diseased? Still got your marbles.'

'You know what this place is?' the man asked.

'Course we do.'

'Then you know what's through those doors.' The man jerked his thumb over his shoulder.

'We got a pretty good idea,' said Blue. 'At least we know what we hope's in there.'

'Medicine,' said the man. 'Drugs. Equipment.'

'Are you saying you been using drugs from here to fight the disease?' said Einstein, stepping forward and gripping the mesh. He was almost shaking with excitement.

'Something like that,' said the man.

'So what you doing in that cage, soldier?' Achilleus asked.

The man sighed again and ran his fingers through his hair.

'We were doing fine,' he said. 'We were surviving. There were more of us. But then the monsters came.'

'Monsters?' said Achilleus. 'Get out of here.'

53

'Yeah.' The man stared at each kid in turn with his good eye, daring anyone to challenge him. '*Monsters*. That's the best word for them. That's the only word. They're in there right now. They took over, kicked us out. We've been trying to get back in, but we're stuck here. With your help, though, we can do it, we can open this bloody door and we can kill the monsters.'

'What do you mean, monsters?' Ollie asked, but before the man could reply Einstein butted in.

'Are you saying there's a cure?' he asked.

'What does it look like to you?' The man came right up to Einstein and stood in front of him, separated only by the thin steel mesh.

'How did you know what to do?' Einstein went on. 'Are you doctors? Scientists? What drugs did you use?'

'Too many questions,' said the man wearily. 'Can't you just get us out of here?'

'What sort of monsters?' Ollie repeated. He was holding back, keeping to the rear of the group in the shadows.

'Freaks, mutants, horrible things, deformed . . . Clever, though.'

'What? Like some kind of animals? What are you saying?'

'Not animals. People.'

'With the disease?'

'No, something else. They're not human any more. As I say – they're monsters.' The man seemed to come alive, filled with a sudden flush of energy. He picked up his spear and paced up and down. 'But together we could beat them,' he said. 'Kill them all. If we can get the door open we all go in together. You guys look pretty handy. Must be to have come this far. We can defeat them. Then all the stuff in there – it's ours.'

Blue thought back to when they'd been in the corridor. Jackson saying she'd seen something. Something she couldn't explain, hiding on the shelves. A snake thing, she'd said.

At the time nobody had believed her.

'So how do we get in?' he asked.

'The keys are over there.' The man jabbed his spear towards the wall behind the kids. Blue swung round and shone his torch over the breeze-block wall until it fell on a set of keys hanging from a hook.

'I don't get this,' he said. 'How did you end up in there?'

'We came through the door from the main warehouse. We were beaten back, the freaks had been attacking us, we weren't enough, they killed all the rest. We had a good thing going in there.'

'They chased you into the cage?'

'Yeah, and pulled the door down on us. There's keys there that'll let you in. And other keys that will get us all through into the warehouse proper.'

For the first time Blue noticed that there was a door into the cage with a heavy-duty lock on it.

'We go in hard,' said the man. 'And kill them before they know what's happening. We got to be quick, though, cos,' as I say, they're clever. They'll fool you. Twisting every-thing around. They're more dangerous than I can get across.'

'So to open the door to the warehouse,' said Ollie, 'we have to open your cage and come in there with another set of keys?'

'What's the matter? Don't you trust us?'

'No,' said Ollie flatly.

'It's the only way in,' said the man.

'We can go back outside, force the main loading doors.'

'Hah! You'll never break your way in through them, pal. Believe me, we've tried. And while you were knocking politely on the doors they'd take you down one by one. It's like a fortress, this place.' The man paused, then offered the kids a smile. 'I'm Seamus, by the way. I'd shake your hands and give you the old how d'you do, but until you open this door I can only wave.'

'I can't say as I like grown-ups so much,' said Achilleus. 'What's stopping us coming in there and killing you?'

'Well, there's this for starters,' said Seamus, holding up his spear. 'But why would you want to go and do some-thing nasty like that? Hmm? Can't you see we don't have the sickness in us? We're the good guys.'

'Who wrote that stuff on the door through there?' Ollie asked.

Seamus hesitated, thinking this over.

'Why do you want to know?' he said.

'Did you?'

'Who else is going to do something like that?'

'Who were you trying to warn off?' said Achilleus and Blue heard Ollie swear under his breath. Blue wondered what had made him angry, and then realized that Achilleus had told Seamus something about what the writing said. Blue was learning that, while Achilleus was a fearsome fighter, he was something less than clever.

'We wrote it there to try and warn off anybody who might want to come and get hold of what we had here,' said Seamus. 'It worked for a long time. Until the monsters came.'

'But grown-ups can't read any more,' said Ollie. 'Normal grown-ups. The only people who could read it would be kids. Why warn off kids?'

'Do you know everything that's going on in the world? Huh? Do you, Mister Clever-sticks? Do you know every threat? Every twist in the tale? You never knew there were any like us, did you? No. Now get the bloody keys and open up. We're hungry and thirsty and knackered and we want to smash those stinking monsters to pieces for what they done to us.'

'Why can't we check them out before we go hammering in there?' Blue asked and the man responded with a harsh bark of laughter.

'Would you try and chat to a shark if you fell in his tank?'

'No, but . . .'

'You can't talk to them, sunshine. You can't argue with them or reason with them. They're stone-cold killers. They don't ask questions first. They're clever. An animal kind of cleverness. If you hesitate for just one moment they'll be on you and you'll either be dead or in one of their cages. You got to go in quick before they even know you're there. You understand?'

'The quote on the door?' Ollie asked. 'Where's it from?'

'No more questions.'

'Where's it from?'

'Yeah,' said Achilleus, 'where'd you get the old six-six-six bollocks from?'

Once more Blue heard Ollie curse.

'The holy sodding bible,' said Seamus. 'Where d'you think? Any more questions?'

Blue had had enough. Enough talk. Enough brain strain trying to work out if these goons could be trusted. All he wanted was to get away from here and back to Maxie. And the quickest way he could see of doing that was going straight through the cage. Straight through the four fathers if necessary. The kids outnumbered them, so unless they had some traps in there, or some friends hidden, they could be taken down. Harder than normal grown-ups, true, but Blue's squad knew what they were about. One wrong move and he would bang Seamus out.

He'd make sure he was first through the door as well, in case of any surprises. That was his job. His responsibility. Get Achilleus to back him up. God, he missed having Big Mick here; he was a useful hulk to have at your side in a bundle. Blue felt naked and unprotected without him.

He walked over and scooped the keys off the hook. Walked back to the cage with them jangling at his side. Had a quiet word with Achilleus, who nodded that he was cool with Blue's plan.

It took Blue a couple of goes to find the right key for the lock, and the others watched him in tense silence as he fiddled with them. There was a loud *clunk* as the lock turned.

He swung the door open, caught Achilleus' eye and stepped into the cage.

54

Blue looked at one of the other three fathers, who was still sitting on the floor, tapping his butcher's knife on the concrete.

'Easy.' Blue jerked his chin in greeting. The father just stared back at him with a cold expression on his face and then stood up. Blue tensed, ready for the worst, but the cage was filling with kids, who fell in around him, and the father did nothing more than just stand there giving him the dead-eye.

'See,' said Seamus. 'We don't bite. Now get the gate unlocked.'

The roll-down gate was about ten metres wide, made of jointed strips of metal. There was a chain system by the side of it connected to clutches and gears to move it up and down. The only lock Blue could find was by a crank handle. He selected the one key that looked big enough to fit and slotted it in. It freed the handle, which he began to turn. There was a loud rattling, ratcheting sound as the various gears turned and the chains moved. Slowly the door began to rise.

'Wait!' Seamus shouted. He was licking his lips, his eye glittering, turning his spear shaft in his hands, like a dog straining on a lead. Blue stopped winding and waited.

'You got to be ready,' Seamus said, his voice thick with fear and aggression. 'If you even open that thing a little way they can get under. We have to be ready. Anything that moves – stab it.'

'Do you want me to open it or not?' Blue asked.

'Yeah, yeah, in a minute,' said Seamus and he swallowed, his Adam's apple bobbing in his throat. 'When I say so try to get the door up quickly and as soon as the gap's wide enough we all go through in a rush. But ready, yeah? Ready to kill? I know you lot can kill or you wouldn't have survived as long as you have.'

Yeah, thought Blue, *we can kill, but the reason we've lived so long is we're careful*. This was all tipping out of his control. It was in situations like this that people got hurt.

He grabbed Einstein.

'Take over here,' he said. 'When I say, turn it as hard and as fast as you can. Don't stop till we're all through.'

'OK. OK.' Einstein was still excited, shaking and jittery.

Blue marched to the centre of the door. A dull orange light showed under it where it had opened a crack. He could hear something echoing and distant. It sounded almost like music. He gripped his own spear tight. Realized he was scared. Out of his depth.

Monsters, Seamus had said. Could they be worse than a bunch of diseased adults? If only he knew what to expect. He hated Einstein for bringing him here. Hated Seamus for putting him in this situation. Hated himself for not knowing what to do.

'How many of them are there?'

'Not sure,' said Seamus. 'Ten at least.'

'Ten? Is that all?'

'You don't know them, Rambo. Don't know how

dangerous they are. They're not human, remember, they're freaks, they're deadly. We go in hard and fast and kill anything that moves. Don't give them a chance.'

Blue looked at one of the other fathers. He didn't speak, but bared his teeth in a doglike grin. Licked his lips.

'Wind her up!' Blue shouted, and he took up a defensive stance, ready for anything that might come under the door. What if it was a snake thing? Like Jackson had seen. How fast did they move?

He looked along the line. There was Seamus and his three friends, then Achilleus with Jackson, Ollie staying back in the second rank with his missile crew, Ebenezer looking like he was praying. Emily was over with Einstein. Good. They were out of the way there.

God, but the door was taking an eternity to go up. It was agonizingly slow, and *loud*. Any monsters on the other side would know they were coming for sure. Blue kept his eyes on the widening gap, looking for any signs of movement – shifting shadows, dark, skittering things . . . A drop of sweat dropped from his chin and hit the floor with a soft *pat*.

Then he mouthed the word 'Maxie' and Seamus was ducking under the door, yelling at the others to follow.

Blue had no choice now. He too shouted, a meaningless yell of battle fury, and rolled in after Seamus, aware of bodies coming with him.

The place was too big to take in in one go. A huge warehouse filled with white cardboard boxes, skylights in the roof letting in some light. Lamps and candles dotted about, giving off the orange glow. Far off that sound, a beat, definitely music.

But no movement.

No sign of any monsters. No sign of anything living. Nothing to fear.

No. *There*. Behind some boxes. A white face. Watching. Black eyes. And then it was gone. Too quick to see if it was human. And then another. Higher up. Peering down at them. Perhaps a reptile, with wide-set eyes, fishlike. But twisted. Unbalanced.

What were they?

He was looking around frantically now. Trying to spot if there were any more of them. Ten, Seamus had said, but he hadn't been sure.

'There's one!' It was Seamus who had shouted. He was striding down towards a corner where two aisles met. The kids went with him, but holding back, letting him take the lead.

When they reached the corner they saw what he'd been following. It was scurrying away from them, but none of them could have said what it was. Human. Animal. Insect . . .

It moved surprisingly fast for such a weirdly shaped creature. Pulling itself along by its arms, which were long and spiderlike, the elbows pushed forward, the backs of its hands flat on the floor, palms upwards, long, thin fingers waving in the air, so that it was 'walking' on the bones at the back of its wrists. Its body was fat and bloated, its belly scraping along the concrete with a dry rustling sound, and there were two tiny shrivelled legs dragging along behind. The vertebrae that ran down its back stuck out like the plates along the back of a dinosaur. It was hairless, and on the sides of its neck were two big bulges, like inflated air sacs.

'Got the bastard!' Seamus yelled, raising his spear.

Now Blue saw that the thing was wearing some sort of clothing around its waist, a skirt or a kilt, made of leather. He felt as if he was in a strange dream, trying, and failing, to make sense of what he was seeing.

Then several things happened at once. When it heard Seamus's shout the creature stopped and turned, just as Blue caught sight, on the edge of his vision, of another one, hiding in the shadows. A female. Impossibly thin with a head like a ball, very big eyes and a tiny mouth. Her head was so large and her body so stretched and skinny she looked like a matchstick drawing, a child's picture of a person.

Seamus twisted, one arm forward, the other pulled back ready to throw his spear.

Blue saw the first creature's frightened face.

It was the face of a fourteen-year-old boy.

Ollie leapt forward.

'No!' he shouted.

He grabbed hold of Seamus's spear. Seamus was so surprised he let go of it, and whipped round, off balance, snarling in fury, to see who had ruined his attack, and then, before Blue could stop him, or even take on-board what was happening, Ollie rammed the point of the spear into Seamus's good eye.

Maxie was standing stock-still, mouth hanging open. The massive room was stuffed with huge statues, bits of buildings, tombs, gigantic columns reaching many metres up towards the roof . . . It was like being inside the ogre's castle in *Jack and the Beanstalk* or something. Everything was way too big, crammed together like it had been looted from the treasure houses and palaces of kings.

'What are they?' she said.

'They're all, like, plaster casts of amazing things from around the world,' said Brooke. 'These columns are from Rome. They're, like, thousands of years old, I think.'

They were in the Victoria and Albert Museum, which was right next door to the Natural History Museum across a side road. In the centre of the museum was a large courtyard that the local kids were using as an area to grow food. Some of them had been busy working away as Maxie and the others had come in off the street. But Brooke had hurried past them and on through to here, her favourite part of the museum, the cast court.

'Isn't it cool?' she said, flinging her arms wide and spinning on the spot like a little girl. 'This is all just here, and we can come and muck about whenever we want. This is all ours now!'

'Boring,' said Lewis. 'Is just old shit.'

'No,' said Maxie. 'It's beautiful.' She didn't say anything more, didn't want the others to tease her, but what she thought was that people were extraordinary creatures. To build a place like this, and fill it with these amazing objects. To *make* those objects. The work that had gone into it. She fought back tears. Was this the end of civilization? Would humankind ever be able to make anything as awesome as this again? How many centuries would it take before they could relearn these skills? For now they'd have to live in the ruins of the old world, build mud huts when everything else crumbled and fell down, use burning wood to heat themselves, dress in the cast-offs of the dead, stare in wonder at stuff like this.

In a way the whole world had become a museum.

Too much to take in.

'Come on,' said Lewis. 'This is stale. I thought we was going shopping.'

'Yeah,' said Brooke, 'better push on before it gets dark.'

And the spell was broken.

'I'm telling you I don't need any new clothes,' Maxie protested for what felt like the hundredth time. 'I'm fine. I picked up this leather jacket just the other day. It's all I need.'

Brooke looked Maxie up and down and sucked her teeth.

'You can make a lot more of yourself, sister,' she said.

'More of myself?' Maxie shook her head. 'I don't want any more of myself. I'm happy with what there is.'

Brooke laughed. 'You know your mind, don't you?'

'I do now. Didn't always.'

'Is it safe in here?' asked Ella, whom Maeve had brought along to try to cheer up. She had latched on to the older girl and wouldn't let go of her hand.

'Sickos never learnt how to get in,' said Brooke. 'Why would they bother? There's nothing for them here. It's full of, like, statues and old furniture, jewellery, paintings, pottery. It's mad.'

'Jewellery?' said Ella, her eyes lighting up.

'Yeah. There's some sick stuff in here. You want some?'

Ella nodded, her lips pressed tightly together.

'We'll see what we can do,' said Brooke and she led them out of the gallery and deeper into the cold, quiet museum.

'This is stupid,' said Maxie. 'What do we want with jewellery?'

'Ain't there nothing you need in the world?' said Brooke. 'Nothing you want?'

'Oh, I want a lot of things, Brooke, believe me,' said Maxie. 'I want a hot bath and a pepperoni pizza with extra mushrooms; I want a chocolate cake with whipped cream; I want my mum's shepherd's pie; I want my mum, and my dad, like they were before this all happened . . . I want Facebook, and music, and TV and the Internet. I want my friends back, all the ones who died. I want to be in the park with them, laughing, not scared of anything. I want to watch *South Park* again, and see them make jokes about the sickos. I want them to take the piss out of them and laugh at them, so that they're not so scary any more. I want to rewind time. I want to be a little girl again.'

'Well, I can't help you there, girl. No way. But what about a new sword? I can swing that.'

'What type of sword?'

'Howzabout a katana? Would that do it?'

'A katana? What's a katana?'

'Samurai sword.'

'Now you're talking.'

'Right on.' Brooke walked over to Kwanele, who was sauntering along, tapping a silver-topped cane on the floor. 'Let's head to the Japanese section, yeah?' she said. 'Then we'll take Ella up to get some jewellery.'

'Fine,' said Kwanele and he turned to grin at Lewis. 'We can get you some lovely Japanese robes while we're there.'

Lewis made a dismissive noise and raised his eyebrows.

'I ain't wearing no dead Japanese swag,' he said.

'Maybe you'll change your mind when you see what there is.'

'Yeah, an' maybe that statue over there will come to life and kiss your ass.'

Lewis was pointing to a statue of two men wrestling.

'I'm wasting my time giving fashion advice to you ragged hoodies,' said Kwanele.

Maxie laughed. She'd always liked Lewis and was glad that he'd come along with them. Despite what Brooke had said, she didn't feel completely safe here. She never did when she went somewhere new. Lewis might look half asleep most of the time, but she knew that was a front and he was always ready. And lethal in a fight.

'Japanese robes,' he said to her. 'What the guy thinking of?'

'Smartening you up,' said Brooke.

'I've got my style,' said Lewis. 'I rock this look.'

'You sure look funky with that Afro,' said Brooke.

'You don't look so bad yourself,' he replied, casting an eye over her. 'Even if you do have that shonky bandage round your head and you're, like, done out in some kind of weird, old woman's nightie.'

'This is a nineteenth-century English noblewoman's dress,' said Brooke. 'For your information.'

'Yeah? Well, it says something about you that even in that blunder you look piff.'

'Are you trying to chirps me, Afro?'

'Maybes.'

'Well, save your horny breath for later. Believe me, you are *not* my type.'

'Yeah? Who *is* your type then?'

'When I see him I'll let you know.'

Lewis turned to Maxie, who laughed at his hopeful expression. 'Forget it, Lewis,' she said. 'I'm with Blue.'

'I knew it.'

When Lewis tried Maeve she blew him off simply by raising her eyebrows and finally he turned to Kwanele. 'Looks like you and me, gayboy,' he said with a sleepy grin.

'Sorry to disappoint,' said Kwanele. 'But you're not *my* type either.'

'This just ain't my day, is it?' They came to the statue of a naked woman and Lewis slapped her on the buttocks. 'You wouldn't turn me down, would you, princess?' he said.

Soon they were standing in front of a glass cabinet in the Japanese section of the museum. There were two display stands of samurai weapons inside it, though the glass had been broken and most of the swords and daggers removed. There were a couple left, though, and Maxie looked them over. In the end she chose a long katana in a bamboo-covered scabbard and a shorter knife in a sheath covered in white ray fish skin. She stuffed the knife into her belt and drew the katana from its scabbard. The blade was still shiny and unrusted. Sharp. Shimmering. She moved it through the air, feeling its perfect balance, and allowed herself a small smile. Lewis helped himself to what was left, whistling as he studied the blades.

And then he spotted two suits of samurai armour in a nearby cabinet.

'Now *that* is what *I* call beautiful,' he said, and turned to Kwanele. 'These the robes you meant?'

'What? No. The robes are much nicer. You know, like silk kimonos, and . . .'

'Not in my world,' said Lewis and he smashed the glass with the hilt of his sword and hauled one of the samurai suits out.

'This is bare cool,' he said, beaming like a little kid at Christmas. 'This is *treasure*, dude.'

'Come on,' said Kwanele with a sigh. 'Let's go up and look at the jewellery.'

As they walked on, Brooke put an arm round Maxie.

'You happy now?'

'Happi*er*,' said Maxie. 'I'm never *really* happy. Don't remember the last time I was. There's always a tense feeling in the bottom of my stomach.'

'I know what you mean,' said Brooke. 'We need to have a laugh. Scare them tense snakes out of your bottom. I miss *South Park* too, but we can still make jokes of our own, can't we? We can show them sickos we ain't scared of them, yeah?'

'Yeah.'

'OK then,' said Brooke. 'Why did the sicko cross the road?'

'I don't know,' said Maxie. 'Why *did* the sicko cross the road?'

'*Braaaiiins!*' said Brooke.

Maxie laughed and Brooke pressed on.

'How many sickos does it take to change a light bulb?'

'*Braaaiiins!*' said Maxie.

'Oh, you've heard it!'

'What's the difference between a sicko and a washing machine?'

'*BRAAAAINSSSS!*'

Now Lewis joined in. 'A sicko walks into a bar,' he said. 'WHAM! And then I hit him with the bar again, an iron bar, and knock him flat, then I hit him again, and again and again until his brains are, like, smashed all over the pavement. And then I slice him up with my new katana!'

'Yeah, Lewis,' said Brooke. 'Funny joke. Way to lighten the mood, bruv.'

56

Blue watched, stunned, as Seamus gurgled in fright and pain then fell away, hitting the shelves and crumpling to the ground, dead as you can get.

Everyone froze. Shocked. Except for Blue, who turned on Ollie.

'What the hell you doing, you idiot?'

'What's it look like?'

'It looks like you just killed that guy for no reason.'

'I killed him because he's a grown-up. Isn't that a good enough reason?'

'No. He was helping us.'

'Since when did grown-ups help kids?' Ollie stalked over to where the other three fathers were crouching by the shelves, weapons ready. The weird spiderlike creature and the matchstick girl had disappeared. In the distance Blue could hear old jazz music, scratchy and echoing.

'Don't attack them three!' he yelled, and pulled Ollie back.

'Don't you get it?' Ollie said, shrugging him off. 'Everything Seamus said about the monsters was bollocks. It was really all about him. We had to hit *him* hard, not talk to him. He was clever, twisting things. Kids aren't the enemy. Adults are the enemy. We mustn't ever forget that.'

'But he's not diseased.' Blue flung a hand out towards the lifeless body on the ground.

'Isn't he?' said Ollie. 'How do you know? Because he told you? We shouldn't have listened. I saw that crawling thing. It was a boy.'

'It was a freak,' said Achilleus.

'This is a bad place,' said Ebenezer.

'Seamus had the sickness,' said Ollie. 'They all do.'

'Yeah? And how can you be so sure of that?' said Blue.

'Makes no odds now,' said Achilleus, nudging Seamus's body with his foot. 'He's dead.'

'He's dead and we're stuck in here with these monsters.' Blue looked around for any signs of the creatures they'd glimpsed before. Still the other three fathers cowered by the shelves, like cornered animals, not sure what to do. Outnumbered by the kids.

'We shouldn't be here,' said Ebenezer. 'We should not have killed this man.'

'He's right,' said Blue. 'There was nothing wrong with him.'

'*Blue*,' said Ollie. 'We all know it. There *is* no cure. They're all sick. Seamus was sick, just not as bad.'

'You don't know that!'

'Ask them.' Ollie pointed to the three fathers.

'Ask them what?'

'If there's a cure.'

Blue looked at the three fathers. Hesitated.

'Ask them!' Ollie said more forcefully. 'See what they've got to say for themselves.'

'Did you really find a cure?' Blue asked quietly. 'Some medicine that worked?' The fathers stared at him. He might as well have been speaking Swahili to them. There was no

289

understanding in their eyes, just dumb animal fear and rage. They looked ready to attack.

Ollie shifted the spear in his hands.

'What's the capital of France?' he said. 'Who wrote *Oliver Twist*? What colour is the sky?'

The fathers switched their attention to Ollie; one of them bared his teeth. Not a smile.

'All right,' said Ollie. 'Here's an easier one. Can you even talk? Simple answer, either say yes or just grunt for no. Hmm? Can you? Say something!'

One of the fathers suddenly broke and ran. Ollie raised Seamus's spear and hurled it at the man, taking him in the middle of the back. He went down with a gasp. The other two came at Ollie, but Blue knocked one down without hesitating and Achilleus had the other. He'd been waiting for this. The grown-ups sprawled on to the concrete floor next to Seamus, blood spreading like spilt oil.

'You believe me now then?' said Ollie.

'Not necessarily, but they *were* attacking you.'

'While I was at the museum,' said Ollie, walking over to Seamus, 'I talked to some of the kids there. They told me about a guy called Greg. He picked some of them up in a coach way back when it was all starting to go crazy. He claimed not to be infected. Claimed he'd beaten the disease. They believed him. But he hadn't. He'd just slowed it down. That's all they can do. Seamus must have found a way to slow it.

'But I was listening to what he was saying and I realized it was all about him. None of that stuff in there made any sense. Them being in that cage, the way the door opened, the business with the keys. It was all too much like a video game. You know – solve the puzzles to get out of the room.

It was designed by kids. That's what it felt like to me. The message on the door, the warning, all designed like a game. And Seamus – he was part of the game, part of the puzzle we were supposed to solve. He didn't write those warnings, they were really old, they'd been there for ages, but Seamus can't have been in that cage too long. And then the candles as we came through, and the music. It was Duke Ellington. My big brother was a jazz fan. Monsters don't light candles and play jazz. And those three . . .' Ollie pointed at the dead fathers. 'They didn't say a word the whole time. Why so quiet? Because they couldn't speak. That's why. They were too far gone . . . No. You can't beat the disease.'

'You don't know that for sure, Ollie,' said Blue. 'You've got no proof. And now they're dead and we're still clueless about the monsters.'

'You want proof? All right. I'll give you proof!'

57

Ollie knelt down by Seamus's body, put his hand to the collar of his shirt.

'I saw him, when we went in there; the first thing he did was do up his top button. Why?'

'I haven't got a freaking clue. Maybe he was cold.'

'Only one reason you'd do a thing like that.' Ollie yanked the front of the shirt down and the buttons popped off and clattered on to the floor. There was a circle of lumps around Seamus's neck, sores and boils. A couple of them had burst and were oozing pus.

Blue swore.

'You still didn't know for sure, though, Ollie. When you topped him.'

Ollie shrugged. Wouldn't catch Blue's eye.

'Let's look at this.' Einstein had joined Ollie and was studying Seamus's face. He peeled back the bandage that covered his bad eye. The eye was missing and the socket was filled with more growths and boils. Einstein prodded a growth with a biro and then shrank back as it burst and some sort of grey jelly bubbled out.

'Nice,' said Achilleus. 'That's dinner sorted.'

Einstein leant closer.

'It's moving,' he said.

'You're joking.'

'No, no . . .' Einstein was furiously scrabbling in his backpack for something. Finally he pulled out a plastic box with a peel-off lid. He wrenched it open and poked some of the jelly into it with his biro.

'Sorry to interrupt your picnic,' said Jackson, backing towards them. 'But aren't we forgetting about the monsters?'

'We don't know they're monsters,' said Ollie. 'That's just what Seamus told us, and he obviously wanted us to kill them before we found out what they really were.'

'Doesn't mean they're not still monsters,' said Jackson. 'I mean, did you see that thing?'

Blue walked to the edge of the group and shouted into the shadowy depths of the warehouse.

'Hey! Come on. Whoever you are. Show yourselves.'

For a moment nothing happened.

'We passed your test!' Ollie shouted. 'We're here and you're going to have to deal with us.'

Achilleus wandered over to a shelf and put the sharp point of his spear against a box.

'Come out or the box gets it!'

Paddy laughed.

'Can you understand us?' Blue shouted.

'We're kids like you,' said Ollie. 'Didn't you want us to come in here?'

'Come out, come out, wherever you are!' Achilleus called out in a sing-song voice. 'I warned you – the box dies in five!'

At last they had a reply. A voice from out of the darkness, a boy's voice, starting to break so that it was a little croaky.

'How do we know you won't attack us?'

'We killed the grown-ups, didn't we?' said Blue. 'Isn't that what you wanted?'

The boy's voice came back out of the shadows.

'I'll warn you. We're watching you. Anything weird, anything we don't like, and we'll attack. We haven't lived this long by taking risks. We're hidden all around you.'

Blue sighed and quickly glanced up and down the aisles of shelving. He could see nothing. There were a thousand places to hide. The shelves were high, going right up to the ceiling. It would be easy to have people perched above them, armed with God knows what.

'Do you want us to drop our weapons?' Einstein shouted and Blue hissed at him.

'Don't be a dick. We ain't dropping our weapons. You heard what the man said. We ain't lived this long by taking risks either.'

'We don't want to hurt you,' said Jackson.

'Much,' Achilleus muttered under his breath.

'Then what are you doing here?' came the voice.

'Good question,' Achilleus replied, quiet enough so that only the kids nearest to him could hear. 'If this goes on much longer it's no more mister nice guy. I am going postal on these noobs.'

'We've come to get drugs,' shouted Einstein. 'Medicine. We've been trying to find out about the disease, maybe find a cure. We thought there might be, like, useful stuff here.'

'Oh, there's useful stuff here all right,' came the voice. 'But it's not yours. It belongs to us.'

'To be fair,' said Blue, 'it belongs to Promithios, but I take your point. Salvage rights. We get it. But maybe we can just talk?'

'Come and find us then.'

'OK . . .'

Silence. One by one the candles went out. Jackson edged closer to Blue.

'We don't know what they are,' she whispered. 'We don't know what any of this is.'

'If you're telling me to be careful,' said Blue, 'save your breath. I'm always careful.'

'I mean, like, did you see that thing?'

'Yeah. It didn't make much sense, but . . . Did it look dangerous to you?'

'There were others. He might have been, like, a trap or something, a decoy, you know, like a lure, like hunters use.'

'Torches on,' said Blue. There was still a pale haze coming in through the skylights, high up in the roof, but they were dirty and didn't let a lot of light in. Without the glow from the candles the place became even murkier. Blue fished out his torch and snapped it on. He heard Achilleus and Ollie and the other Waitrose kids winding theirs up.

'Where do we go then?' asked Einstein.

'Towards the music, I guess,' said Blue. 'Stick close together. Ollie, watch our backs. Achilleus, take the right. Jackson, you can have the left. Let's move.'

58

Mick, where are you when I need you? Blue felt horribly exposed without his friend by his side. At least he was guarding their way out. That was comforting if they needed to make a speedy exit. But Blue hadn't gone it alone like this for a long time. It was like blundering into a fight without a familiar weapon in your hand. He sent out a silent prayer for Mick to give him some of his strength.

The kids crept forward, eyes scanning the gloom. Trying to see if anything was hiding among the stacks of boxes.

Blue became aware of a movement, something shuffling on the other side of a row of shelves.

What was it . . .? Impossible to tell.

Somewhere he heard laughter, sounded like a girl; it seemed to skitter away and get lost in the huge space, and then there was a scraping sound off to their left.

'Anything behind us, Ollie?' he asked.

'Nothing.'

It was hard in the half-light to pinpoint exactly where the music was coming from, too many hard surfaces for the sound to reflect off, and as they wove among the shelves it seemed to sometimes get quieter and sometimes louder. Blue listened hard until he was fairly sure he had pinpointed the direction they should be heading. Of course that didn't mean the things, whatever they were – *monsters*? – would be there. But it was all he could think of at the moment. He kept expecting that croaky voice to come floating out of the darkness again, shouting 'Warmer' and 'Colder' like in a child's game. At last they cleared the end of a row and he saw an open metal staircase leading to a raised platform. There was a lit candle on every step. At the top was what looked like some kind of an office, some four or five metres above the warehouse floor.

'Do we go up?' Einstein asked.

'It's what they want,' said Blue.

'Is it what we want?'

'Do we have a choice?'

'Guess not,' said Einstein.

'Achilleus, you take point,' said Blue, almost whispering. 'We'll follow on behind.'

'Sure.' Achilleus shoved Paddy out of the way. 'Paddy, dress back, yeah?'

'I need to stick close to you, I'm your helper. I can fight.'

'No to all three, soldier. Not right now. I want a proper fighter at my back, not a caddie. We don't know what's up there and I don't want to be worrying about you.'

'But Achilleus.'

'Shut it and do what you're told, you little rat.'

Scowling and muttering, Paddy dropped back and Jackson took his place. Achilleus looked her up and down and nodded his acceptance. The stairs would only take two people safely side by side, and even then they'd be getting in each other's way if they had to fight. So Achilleus made sure he was in front with clear space around him. He gripped his spear with both hands widely spaced. It wasn't

297

the best weapon to use in cramped conditions, but it was the best he had.

He started to climb. The stairway had one return halfway up, where it switched back on itself. Achilleus reached that point safely and waited for the others to join him before proceeding. He wasn't taking any chances.

They clattered on up to the top. The sound of the jazz was much louder here, though it was slightly tinny and distorted. It was a long time since Blue had heard any recorded music. A couple of his mates had played guitars back in Morrisons, but this was different. He'd almost forgotten what proper music sounded like. This was all brass and drums and piano, a driving beat, but something from ancient history. Old and weird to Blue's ears.

The noise of their feet on the stairs partly drowned the music out and when they got to the top Blue realized it had finished; there was just a weird, repetitive clicking noise. At least nothing had attacked them. There was another candle burning in the office; he could see its flickering glow through the window.

'A game,' Ollie had said. And that's what it felt like. The things, the monsters, the creatures . . . whatever they were, were playing with them. Blue wanted this over now. Wanted his questions answered. He'd had enough. If there was something nasty waiting for them in the office then he was ready for it. He'd smash it to pieces. He shouldered his way to the front of the group where Achilleus had halted again, pushed past and went on through, three of the others coming in behind him.

There was nothing waiting for them in the office except an old-fashioned record player standing on a desk. It was a wind-up one with a big, shiny brass trumpet thing where the music came out. The sort of record player you saw in old movies. There was a black plastic record turning on it, the heavy needle clicking over and over at the end of the track. Blue went over to it, lifted the needle off and pulled a lever that acted like a brake, stopping the turntable from rotating.

'They got us where they want us,' said Jackson. 'Now what?'

'It's up to them now,' said Blue. 'I ain't playing their games no more.'

Ollie came in and lifted the record off the turntable. Read the label.

'"Take the 'A' Train."'

'You take it,' said Blue wearily and Ollie laughed.

'It's what the track's called. Duke Ellington.'

'If you say so.' Blue was too strung out to try and get his head round this piece of information. Was the track important? Was it a message? Or was it just . . .

'In here.' A voice called to them from somewhere behind the office, through an open doorway. Blue glanced at Ollie and Jackson. Shrugged. He was the leader. It was up to him to lead. He wasn't sending Achilleus ahead this time. The 'monsters' had had plenty of opportunities to lay traps for them. He set his face hard, raised his spear and started to walk, brushing the door frame with his shoulder as he went past it. Ollie and Jackson followed him.

There was a large raised area back there, a platform with a floor made of wooden boards. It extended out above some lower shelving units and had protective railings around the edges. It had something of the feel of a secret den, or a kids' tree house. A selection of furniture had been dragged up there: armchairs, sofas, rugs, tables, some beds, a sideboard with an empty goldfish bowl on it, a fat, old-fashioned TV set with no workings inside it.

And monsters.

That was the word that had lodged in Blue's mind. Planted there so firmly by Seamus that he couldn't get rid of it, even though he could see that the three people up here weren't technically monsters. They were kids. Like him. Only not like him.

Blue's team were filtering out on to the deck. Achilleus appeared, eyes wide, mouth open in a sloppy grin.

'Freak of the week,' he said.

'Shut up,' said Ollie. 'That's not funny.'

'Freak lives.'

'I said shut up. Can't you see they're kids?'

'Nope.'

It was hard. They obviously *were* just children. But something had changed them.

There were two boys and a girl. The girl sat in a big, high-backed chair that looked a bit like a throne, and indeed she was wrapped in some sort of robes and had a crown on her head. Although, as Blue looked more closely, he saw that it wasn't a crown; she had a ring of bony growths on the top of her bald skull, jutting up and stretching the skin. And he saw, too, that she was sitting in a wheelchair, and the 'throne' part of it was just painted cardboard, or maybe thin sheets of wood, that had been fixed to the back of it. Her face was slack and expressionless, but her eyes were glittering and intelligent, watchful. The boy standing next to her was only wearing a pair of ragged jeans. His body was huge and bulging with muscle, like something out of a comic book. His muscles, however, had grown in an unbalanced, misshapen way, giving him a lumpy look.

A badly drawn comic book.

Blue used to read a lot of comics. One of his favourites was about an ancient Celtic warrior called Sláine, who went into a warp spasm in battle, so that his whole body distorted. Well, here was the living Sláine, in permanent warp spasm. The boy's head appeared small in relation to his body, and one eye was unnaturally large, maybe five times the size of his other eye.

The second boy's head was completely normal, but the rest of him was twisted, as if his skeleton had been broken and remade. His back was in an S shape and his arms and legs were bent. He was sitting on the floor, his knees up round his ears, taking his weight on his arms. He was smiling.

'You found us then,' he said.

Found what exactly? Blue didn't know what to say. He didn't want to stare, but it was hard not to. He fixed on the boy's eyes – he was a human being after all. But what the hell had happened to him?

'I hope you're not planning on attacking us,' said the boy. 'But I'll just warn you.' He jerked his head at the tall, muscular kid. 'Him there. The big golem. He's stronger than Arnie in his prime. He'll rip you apart. He won't be scared of your weapons.'

'That's tough talk, tiger,' said Achilleus. 'Seeing as how you is bare outnumbered.'

'Oh, there are more of us,' said the boy on the floor. 'Hidden about the place. Watching. So . . . maybe we'll accept your offer.'

'What offer?' said Blue.

'To put your weapons down.'

'Wasn't *my* offer.'

'Don't care whose offer it was,' said the boy. 'Why don't you be nice and show that you *come in peace*, eh?'

Ollie nudged Blue. 'Come on,' he said. 'We don't want a fight.'

Blue didn't like being told by Ollie what they did and didn't want. He was still trying to make sense of this weird situation. Maybe they *would* need to fight. What did Ollie know about these kids? Nothing. Blue stayed rock solid. Weapon in hand.

'Blue . . .?'

'Shut up, Ollie, I'm thinking.'

Ollie backed off. Apart from the Incredible Hulk, these kids didn't look dangerous. They'd lived this long through the bad times, so they must know what they were doing, though. They must have some sharpened survival skills. The kid on the floor certainly seemed smart. Ollie kept coming back to that one thought. If they'd wanted to attack Blue's team they could have done it before now. But Blue had lived this long as well, hadn't he? And he'd done that by making sure he didn't take any chances.

'OK, here's what we're gonna do,' he said at last. 'Ollie, you take everyone else back downstairs and make sure nobody does nothing stupid. Hang on to your weapons, and keep a look-out. I don't want no more surprises. Jackson, Einstein and Emily, you stay with me. Any weapons you got, lay them down.'

There was some muttering and complaining, but Blue didn't budge and in a minute it was quiet. There was still tension in the air, wariness from both sides, and Blue could sense the rest of his team were as confused as he was, but the situation was less likely to kick off now. They settled down in armchairs, embarrassed, not knowing where to look. The boy on the floor walked closer to them in a crouch, using his hands. His limbs were loose and awkward; they moved in odd ways almost as if they had extra joints. His head wobbled. His back snaked from side to side.

'My name's TV Boy,' he said, and held out a dirty hand for Blue to shake, the fingers long and bent. Blue didn't hesitate; he gripped the hand, squeezed it and then gave him the full homie handshake. TV Boy kept up with him and gave it back, finishing with a thumb press.

Blue smiled, introduced his team, and then it was TV Boy's turn.

'That's the Warehouse Queen,' he said, nodding at the girl, who remained expressionless but watchful. 'She's kind of in charge,' TV Boy went on, 'but she don't say much. The boy wonder is Monstar. Half monster, all star. And he will kick your ass inside out if you step out of line.'

'We ain't stepping out of line if we can help it,' said Blue. 'But I have to tell you I don't know where the line is right now. No offence and all, but this is bare strange. You gonna have to tell us just what the hell is going down here.'

'OK,' said TV Boy. 'You want to know? We'll show you.'

59

This is the journal of Lettis Slingsbury. It is quiet now and I can write. Some things have been happening that I need to set down in the record.

My last entry was about the argument we were having about going outside to bury Gabby. I had to stop writing before because the others were distracting me and I never got to the end of the story. The story is still not over, but there is more to tell and while it is quiet again I can carry on with my writing.

I have read my last entry. I am sorry if it is not really good proper writing and too much of it is about me. I liked writing at school, but I'm not a professional obviously.

I was telling how the others were arguing and arguing about who would volunteer to be the first to go outside.

In the end I think it was Daryl who said it (I am trying to remember all this, and the words I am writing that people were saying are not necessarily the actual words they said, they are as close as I can remember and sometimes the right person might not have said the words I said they said, but

*it's the best I can do under these difficult circum-
stances).*

*So someone, I'll say it was Daryl because I'm pretty
sure it was him – it was his idea at least – said it didn't
need to be just one person going outside, that was
stupid. Lots of us should go, then it would be safer.
If anyone was definitely going to go, outside, which
I still didn't think was a good idea, then at least it
was sensible if they didn't go alone. We talked about
it and thought that maybe half of us should all go out
together and see what was in the sheds and find tools
and quickly dig the hole, all working together to do
it quickly. The other half would stay behind and make
it safe in the church, and sort of guard the doors from
attack and look after Caspar.*

*So they asked for volunteers. But still nobody said
they would go outside and there was another long
argument. And in the end Jasmine lost it big time and
started sort of screaming that it was horrible being
in here with a dead body and that even if they didn't
find any tools or even look in the sheds they should
take the body outside. It didn't seem like a very Chris-
tian thing to say, but she was just scared and freaked
out I suppose. I thought this was maybe a stupid idea,
to leave a body outside, because sickos might not be
able to smell it if we kept the corpse inside, but if
we took it outside they would definitely smell it and
come from miles around, like a pack of hungry wolves.
But I didn't say anything because I could see that
Jasmine was very upset and all crying and everything.*

*'Will you go outside then?' said Reece. 'As it was
your idea.'*

Jasmine said she would, and she said come on, are none of you as brave as me? Come on, we spent all day yesterday outside! I'll go outside by myself if that's what you want. And more of that sort of thing.

I've always liked Jasmine, she is one of my friends, but she has always been quite moody and when she gets cross she gets really cross, and goes red in the face, all shouting and crying, and it can be a bit scary, but it had the desired effect. Lots of children now said they would go outside and didn't want to be thought of as cowards.

In fact it was almost quite funny, because there were too many now. We didn't want everyone outside and risk being attacked out there with no one to guard the church, so there was more arguing. The thing was, all the tougher kids who usually stop the arguments and tell people to shut up and what to do were all on the search party, so nobody was really in charge. It was like trying to organize a game when everyone's arguing about the rules and what teams you're on. And it was quite boring. I went away and sat on a pew (a church bench) with two of my friends who joined me (this was Aiyshah and Scott). I didn't think I needed to watch the argument and observe what they were all saying because they were just going round and round in circles like a dog chasing its tail. After a while, luckily, the others sorted it out to their satisfaction and got ready to go outside.

I am not brave. I've never said I was. I'm not exactly a coward, but I am not one to volunteer for dangerous missions. So I was one of the ones to stay inside the church. I thought I should be there because I could write about things and observe, rather than be part of the things that were happening. Scott and Aiyshah were the same.

I am writing now and Daryl went back up to the top of the tower to be a look-out and the others are outside. That is Jasmine and Reece and Bradley and Demi. They were all singing and shouting to make themselves braver as they went, calling out things like 'hey, you sickos, we're not scared of you' and other much ruder things that I won't write down. They put the body on one of the trolleys and pushed it out, bumping and jolting on the uneven floor. They had to lift the body up by the sheet to get it on. Nobody wanted to touch it. They said it was cold and hard and heavy. So they went and for a little while there was heavenly peace and I thought it would be a good time to start my entry, not sure when I would be able to write again.

It is easier for me to bury my head in a book and not think about the bad things happening. If I can write about it maybe I will be safe. But I will have to stop writing soon. Something has gone wrong you see.

It happened like this. For a while we heard nothing from the steeple or from outside. Aiyshah and Scott had been waiting at the church doors, peeping out, ready to open them wide when the children were ready to come back in. They were by the church doors and guarding them. I'm sorry, I think I already wrote that - I don't have time to check and make corrections.

At first the two door guards were giggling and laughing a bit, sort of overexcited like primary school children, turning their scaredness into laughter as if

307

it might protect them. They were joking, saying they had seen something, and making each other jump and then cursing like mad. And then after a while one of them, Aiyshah, said no, she really had seen something and Scott mocked her and carried on messing about and teasing, but she got quite agitated and kept saying it over and over and saying 'no, look!' and pointing, and in the end Scott saw it too and they screamed and slammed the doors shut.

Caspar asked them what they had seen and they weren't completely sure, but they were fairly sure it was sickos, three of them, in a pack, all dirty and muddy and brown, coming out of the trees. Now the children inside the church really were scared and they were running around, and Daryl came down from the tower and asked what was going on. 'Didn't you see it?' said Aiyshah. 'There were three sickos coming.' Daryl said he hadn't seen anything, he had been too busy watching the children who were trying to dig a hole for the grave. They were still talking about it when we all heard a sort of rattling and a scratching and banging at the door. Aiyshah shouted out to see if it was other children. We heard no voices back only the rattling and scratching.

We told Daryl to go back up on to the steeple and see what was happening and warn the others, and then we did hear voices outside, and shouting.

'We have to open the doors,' said Aiyshah, 'to let them back in. We can't leave them out there with sickos.'

'But if we open the doors the sickos will get in,' said Caspar, who is more frightened than the rest of us because he is already wounded, and can't walk easily.

There were voices all talking over each other now, Caspar saying things like, 'We need to be ready for them.' And Scott saying, 'Are you sure there were only three?' Nobody really wanting to know the truth.

It is very difficult. It is a difficult decision and we don't know what to do. I will stop writing now because I need to help. I can't hide in this book after all. My hand is shaking too much to write and real things are going on. We are in a desperate situation and I hope the search party comes back soon. Surely they can't be much longer? Unless something has happened to them as well. I do not want to think about that. I will stop writing because it is making me think too much.

I have to help. I have to do something.

60

Ollie and the other kids were still waiting down below, clustered round the foot of the metal staircase, hyped up, excited and nervous. There was some grumbling going on, from those fighters who wanted to be up where the action was and didn't like being left out. Mostly, though, they were in huddles, talking in brief, urgent, hushed bursts, trying to make sense of what they'd seen. They all had their theories. Only Ollie was keeping his thoughts to himself, staying quiet, his eyes moving ceaselessly over the rows and rows of shelves.

Ebenezer approached him. He was carrying Seamus's spear.

'You want this?' he asked. 'Looks like a good one.'

'Don't you want it?' Ollie looked at the spear. The head was covered in dark blood that was still sticky.

Ebenezer shrugged. 'Don't like to use a spear.'

'Me either,' said Ollie, 'but I know who does.' He took the spear off Ebenezer and walked to where Achilleus was sitting on the bottom of the steps. He looked tired and there was a thin film of sweat on his skin. The wounds he'd got at the palace were still healing and now that he'd stopped moving the pain was obviously getting to him.

'You want this for your collection?' Ollie said.

'Dunno,' said Achilleus. 'I already got three spears. I'm not sure Paddywhack can carry any more.'

'I'm all right, Akkie,' said Paddy eagerly. He was sitting next to Achilleus, the golf-bag leaning against the steps. 'I can carry another one.'

'Yeah, but do we need another one, though?'

'That's a good spear,' said Paddy. 'It's really cool. It's got a good wide head on it, with a sharp cutting edge, good for close-up fighting. Your main spear's a stabber, a good stabber mind, like a needle, but it doesn't have an edge on it. It doesn't cut so well, so it's no good for slashing.' Paddy jumped up and took the spear off Ollie. He tested the balance and nodded appreciatively, as if he was some kind of weapons expert. He then took out a rag from his golf-bag and started to clean the blood off it. 'Now this spear,' he said, 'this one's a beauty. With this big fat blade on it you can use it like a sword to hack. It's a proper spear, made for fighting not for show. You know what this is? It's the *Gáe Bolg*.'

'The gay what?'

'The *Gáe Bolg*. It's Irish. It means the death spear or the belly spear, for cutting open bellies. My da used to love to tell me the old stories about the Irish heroes and all the old legends. Da used to play the fiddle, in pubs and that. He was from a traveller family before he married my ma. He knew all the old folk songs and the stories, used to be a storyteller too. We went to all the festivals. Gaah, it was a crack, man, he knew some grand tales. Of Finn MacCool, and the greatest hero of them all, Cúchulainn. You remind me of Cúchulainn, Akkie. The *Gáe Bolg* was his spear. He was the only one who knew how to use it. This famous warrior woman called Scáthach taught him how. It was made from the bone of a sea monster.'

'Yeah,' said Achilleus, taking the spear off Paddy and weighing it in his hand without bothering to stand up. 'Ova happs. That's a cool story.'

'You like the spear?'

'It's sick. The belly spear, the death spear, the Gay Bulge.'

'Cúchulainn was like an Irish superhero,' said Paddy. 'He was well strong, and brave, scared of no one, he was. He killed the hound of Cullen with his bare hands when he was still just a boy, like you. And his strength, all his power, like, was in his middle finger.'

'You mean like this?' Achilleus grinned and gave Paddy the finger.

'I didn't mean like that, no.' But Paddy was giggling. 'I never thought of that before. His middle finger.'

'I have the power!' said Achilleus, sticking his finger up at everyone in the group. 'The power to give you the finger!'

Ebenezer shook his head and tutted. He didn't like crude stuff, as Achilleus well knew. It only made Achilleus worse, though. He passed the spear back to Paddy and gave Ebenezer the finger with both hands.

Ebenezer turned away from him, made a face at Ollie.

'That was clever back there,' he said. 'Working out what Seamus was up to. Knowing he had them lumps round his neck.'

'It was a guess,' said Ollie. 'A lucky one.'

'What would you've done if you were wrong?'

'I'd have thought of something.'

'Yeah. You always think of something.' Ebenezer slapped palms with Ollie and glanced up towards the top of the stairs.

'What are they doing up there?' he asked.

'We'll find out soon enough, don't worry,' said Ollie.

'We got to get back to the church,' said Ebenezer. 'We left all them other kids there.'

'Yeah,' said Ollie. 'I'd almost forgotten about them. They'll be all right, though. That place was pretty secure.'

'I wonder what they're doing.'

'Not our problem right now, Ebenezer. We just got to find out who these weird kids are and then grab what we need and go.'

'I wish I was there in the church with them. A church is a good place. This place . . . It's all wrong, Ollie.'

Ollie smiled at Ebenezer, trying to reassure him. Ebenezer had a strong faith. Prayed every night. Ollie sometimes wished he had someone to pray to. He pictured the kids back at the church. Wondered if they were praying right now.

Wondered if God would bother to listen.

A voice called down to them from up on the platform. 'They're ready.' It was Emily. 'You can come up now.'

61

Blue still felt like he was in some weird dream. Not the first time he'd felt this way over the last year. He'd lost track of how many times he'd woken from some twisted nightmare only to find that he was deep in a worse nightmare – what the world had become – and wishing he was back in his bad dream, not having to cope with reality. *Reality*. You kind of got used to things when they went on around you all the time, so that he'd almost forgotten what the world had been like before the disease came creeping into it.

What was going down now, though, was something else entirely, something new. Something deeply strange. Einstein had had a million questions, but TV Boy had told him to keep them. Told him he was going to make everything clear. That it was going to be 'show-and-tell' time. This was shaping up to be one wigged-out show-and-tell, though.

The rest of the warehouse kids had gathered on the platform now, and Blue didn't know what to think, where to look. To say they were all different shapes was the understatement of the century. And the thing was, they weren't all *human* shaped. How they were alive he didn't know, because the way they looked was . . . *impossible*. Alien.

His mum had been a nurse, working in a home for

disabled children. Blue used to go in and help her out sometimes in the school holidays. At first he'd been nervous and
shy, uneasy, but he'd soon realized that, apart from those
one or two kids with really severe learning difficulties, they
were just like any other kids. They had the same thoughts
and interests as him. Just like in any other group of kids
there were show-offs, jokers, quiet ones, clever ones, thick
ones, cool ones and arseholes. It made no difference what
they looked like, or how they spoke, whether they were
in wheelchairs or had neck braces or whatever – kids were
kids. In the end he'd made a couple of good friends there.
He'd got used to their disabilities, stopped noticing them
in most cases.

This was way different. He'd never seen kids like these
before. There were the girl and boy they'd spotted downstairs, him with tiny legs and a huge round spider body,
her with an impossibly thin frame and a head that looked
like a huge round ball. Then there was another girl with
legs that looked to be over a metre long and a tiny body on
the top. Another boy had a lower leg and foot that had
grown into what looked like a long, wide blob. Another
girl, who Blue was very careful not to stare at, seemed to
have her guts growing on the outside of her body, covered
by a thin, almost transparent membrane. One girl had what
appeared to be a normal body but a strange, fishlike head,
with the eyes pushed round to the sides and a wide, wet
mouth.

Perhaps the strangest of all were what he'd at first thought
were a normal boy and girl. When he'd realized that they
were actually fused together, and that there was a third
body growing out of their backs that looked lifeless and
shrivelled, he had actually gasped. He knew they couldn't

be conjoined twins, because you couldn't have conjoined twins of different sexes, and he'd certainly never heard of conjoined triplets.

No. This was impossible. It was too much to take in. These kids weren't disabled. It was more like they were a different species. *Monsters*, Seamus had called them, but they were human, weren't they?

They were children.

They all had made-up names, as if they were comic book characters rather than real people – Spider Boy, Betty Bubble, Legs, the Pink Surfer, Flubberguts, Fish-Face, Trinity. They'd come up by another staircase and had erected what looked like very basic scenery from a school play. There was some shredded green and brown paper hanging down like curtains or leaves in a forest of some sort. One or two of them had gone behind the 'curtain'; the rest were sitting around on the platform, some on the floor, others on the various chairs and sofas. A couple of them looked excited, pumped up and ready for the show, but most were quiet, watchful and wary. As were Blue's lot, who were sitting where they could, waiting for the show to begin. A few of his party, however, including Achilleus, had stayed downstairs. Maybe they hadn't been comfortable, were worried that they wouldn't be able to stop themselves from sniggering with embarrassment.

Blue had no idea what this was going to be all about, but he'd watched TV Boy climb awkwardly under the table where the old television sat. Like a long-legged crab crawling into a hidey-hole. And now silence slowly settled over the platform.

TV Boy had lit some candles around the table and they illuminated the TV with a soft yellow glow. It was getting dark in here. It was later in the day than Blue had realized. He had a stab of guilt when he thought of Big Mick stuck out in the reception area and the kids they'd left behind in the church. He had wanted to get back there by nightfall, but they hadn't picked up any supplies yet and they needed to know who these kids were and what their story was.

Someone put a record on the ancient wind-up gramophone, a jolly number, bouncy and crackly, sounding like an old children's song from years ago.

And then the kids started to sing over the top of it . . .

'*We are the Twisted Kids. Tit-fed gits, the gifted twits!*
We are the screwed-up, twisted kids.

Our backs are bent, our knees bend back,
Our heads have tails, our bones are whack.
We're freaks and that is plain for all to see!

Our guts hang out, we scare good folk,
We're God's bad joke, the moulds got broke,
With arses where our elbows ought to be . . .'

Blue caught Einstein's eye. *WTF?* The day was getting weirder and weirder. Now TV Boy popped up, inside the set, looking out at them all, with only his head and shoulders visible. When he appeared the warehouse kids clapped and whooped and cheered. TV Boy stayed like that, staring out at them, waiting for everyone to settle down, and then finally he began to speak, making his voice deeper, serious, posh. A TV announcer's voice.

'And now here is the news . . .' He added a day and a date

from fifteen years ago. The record was changed, the children's song being replaced by a scratchy old military march. TV Boy nodded in time to it for a few seconds before putting on a pair of glasses and carrying on. His voice had changed again, so that he sounded like a newsreader. It was unreal. Blue couldn't help smiling. He'd got hung up on the idea that these kids were comic book superheroes, and he reckoned TV Boy's superpower was being able to impersonate people.

'Good evening. The headlines at six o'clock. Flooding in south-west England, earthquakes in the Middle East, tornadoes in the American Midwest, starvation in Africa and twenty million people watch a cat playing the piano on YouTube.'

A couple of the warehouse kids laughed. Blue's lot just sat there open-mouthed. The needle was lifted off the record and TV Boy carried on.

'But first, loggers in the Amazonian rainforest have discovered a "lost" tribe who speak their own unique language and have a culture that appears unchanged for thousands of years.'

Some of the kids came through the curtain, the fish-faced girl, the one called Flubberguts and the boy with the elongated foot – the Pink Surfer. They crouched low, looking around, scared and amazed, acting out the South American tribe emerging from the forest.

TV Boy carried on.

'We talked to one of the international medical team who have flown out to study the Stone Age tribe. So called because they have had no previous contact with the outside world and live a life very similar to how we believe our distant ancestors lived at the time of the last ice age.'

318

TV Boy whipped off his glasses and quickly put on a battered old sun hat. His voice changed, to something accented and European. His whole face seemed to change too, so that Blue could imagine he really was watching a scientist on a news broadcast.

'We are still working to decipher their language, which bears no relation to any other language we know of in the area. This is not unusual. At least a thousand different indigenous languages are spoken in the Americas . . .'

The three actors started making a peculiar insect-like clicking, whirring noise.

'. . . So far all we have been able to discover for certain is that they call themselves the Inmathger. They are small people, and many display genetic birth defects, indicative of centuries of inbreeding. It is quite clear from their reactions, however, that they consider us to be the ones who are deformed.'

The actors now pointed at Blue and his friends and started miming laughing and jeering. Meanwhile, with the skilful speed of a magician, TV Boy replaced the hat with a blonde wig, and his voice morphed into that of an English-woman.

'We've been working with the Inmathger for several weeks now, and we've taken DNA samples so that we can establish if they are related to any of the other tribes in the Amazon Basin. As this is their first contact with the outside world, the Inmathger are being quarantined to safeguard them from catching any diseases to which they will obviously have no immunity. Even something we think of as completely harmless, like the common cold, might prove fatal to them.'

The actors now started coughing and sneezing.

319

'It is our hope that the tribe will remain undisturbed and be able to continue living where they are, isolated and protected from intrusion. It's very important that their unique culture is not changed in any way.'

TV Boy suddenly started moving his head in a very jerky way and speaking in a crazy, speeded up, high-pitched gibberish, giving the effect of a TV programme on fast forward. At the same time he lost the blonde wig and went back to his original TV announcer voice and the three actors scurried to find some seats to watch the rest of the show.

'We go now to the Royal Society, where Professor Ian Livingstone is giving the annual Richard Dimbleby lecture . . .' A new pair of glasses, thin and wire-framed, and a new voice, older and posher. Slightly frail.

'Genetically, culturally and linguistically, the Inmathger have no immediate connections to any other tribes in the area. This has made it extremely difficult to decipher their language, which sounds to the untrained ear more like animal and insect noises, or even birdsong, than a human language. It consists of clicks and whistles and grunts and strange guttural sounds. There aren't direct translations of all their words, and in fact they view the world very differently to how we do. To them, colour and light and sound are very important, and they see themselves as part of the animal kingdom, little removed from the wild creatures whose sounds their language so closely resembles. The closest translation I can offer of their name, Inmathger, is "*the Fallen*".

'They believe that they were once shapeless and formless spirits who lived in the sky, among the stars, and fell to earth many centuries ago. Their spirits inhabited first the insects, then the lower animals, and finally took on the human form they now possess. They consider their birth defects to be evidence that they are trying to evolve into a new, higher form. They believe that somewhere in the forest there is a great tree that they will one day climb and return to their homeland in the stars. Until the loggers discovered them they thought that the forest was the entire world and they were the only people in it. Interestingly their word for it is the same as their word for the colour green. And they refer to the world as the green. They believe existence is divided into two realms, the green and the blue. The earth and the sky . . . Any questions?'

TV Boy snapped a large pair of black plastic-framed glasses over the wire ones and plopped a baseball cap on top of his head. The cap was studded with badges. Blue spotted a pyramid with an eye hovering above it, and a standard 'grey' alien with bulging black eyes. There was a small cheer from the local kids; it was clear that this next character was a favourite of theirs.

'Ah, huh, yes, hi, my name's Buddy Dumpster and I have a question, sir . . .' TV Boy was using a nerdy American voice. 'Ahm, it is indubitably clear from your, ahm, talk, that the Ingathmer, sorry, Ignumther, in the forest there, the Ingumper, the Forest Gumper, the Nerdy Dumpster, the, ahm, I'll get it . . . In-math-ger! There. I got it. It is indubitably clear that they are space aliens from outer space. Indubitably so. Or at least, if they're not, ahm, extra-terrestrials, they are indubitably descended from the same extraterrestrials who built the pyramids of the Incas as well as the ones in Egypt and the ruins of Angkor Wat in Cambodia, Stonehenge and quite possibly Westfield shopping centre. Indubitably so.'

Off came the plastic glasses and the cap and TV Boy was back to being Professor Ian Livingstone.

'That's a lovely notion, Mister Dumpster, but sadly untrue. The Inmathger are the same as you and me. They're human beings.'

A voice came from the back of the platform. Blue couldn't see who it was, but thought it might be one of Trinity.

'Gabba gabba, we accept you, we accept you, one of us.'

It was joined by another voice. 'Ain't nobody here but us chickens.'

And soon there was a hubbub as all the local kids joined in.

'We're beans, I tell you, human beans.'

'What is the law?'

'Are we not men? If you cut us, do we not bleed?'

'Take your stinking paws off me, you damned dirty ape.'

'What is the law?'

'Not to go on all fours, that is the law.'

'Those poor things out there in the jungle. Those animals. They talk!'

'You made us in the house of pain . . .'

62

'What are they shouting about up there?'

Jackson shrugged. She didn't know any better than Achilleus what was going on. They were downstairs with Paddy and Ebenezer. Ebenezer was quiet and edgy. He hadn't seemed scared when faced with the sickos outside, but in here, with these weird kids, he wasn't so sure of himself. Achilleus was winding him up, teasing and joking, Paddy laughing with him. Jackson had wanted to know what the kids upstairs had to say, but she also wanted to stay close to Achilleus and this gave her a very good opportunity to be almost alone with him. Only Achilleus was ignoring her – as usual. She tried to act casual. Just hanging. As if it was no big deal.

Achilleus was needling Ebenezer.

'You scared you gonna catch something then, Ebenezer? Become like them?'

'I am not scared, Akkie. I just did not want to be up there.'

'With the freaks and weirdos.'

'You shouldn't call them that,' said Jackson without thinking. She hadn't wanted to get on the wrong side of Achilleus. He could be a right dick sometimes, though.

'I can call them what I like,' he said, without even looking at her. 'What would you call them?'

Jackson shrugged. 'They're just kids, like us.'

'Like you maybe,' said Achilleus. 'Not me, girl.'

'Have you seen yourself lately?' Jackson had given up trying to be nice; maybe she should treat Achilleus the way he treated everyone else. Maybe he'd respect that.

'You got a problem with how I look?' Finally Achilleus made eye contact, challenging her.

'It's only that you look like something a dog chewed up and spat out.'

'And what about you?' Achilleus was staring hard at her now, daring her to look away, and Jackson tried not to blush.

'What *about* me?' she said.

'You look like a boy.'

'So?'

'What's it take to get you riled?'

'What you want to rile me for?'

'For fun.'

They heard shouting from upstairs and what sounded like chanting. They looked up, wondering what was going on, and then a boy's voice floated out of the darkness surrounding them.

'The natives are restless tonight.'

Ebenezer jumped. Achilleus simply picked up his new spear, his eyes flicking around. Paddy inched closer to him.

'There somebody there?' said Achilleus.

'Only a freak, a weirdo, a spazzmoid,' the boy's voice came back, slightly muffled, as if he was covering his mouth. Jackson peered into the shadows, trying to see where he was.

'You been spying on us?' said Achilleus. 'Listening in?'

'All the time,' said the boy. 'If I'd wanted to I could of taken the lot of you.'

'You could've tried. You gonna come out now?'

'Not yet.'

'Too embarrassed to show us what you look like?'

'I don't want to scare you.'

'Oh, my knees are shaking,' said Achilleus and he laughed dismissively.

Jackson could see, though, that Ebenezer and Paddy were nervous and unsure.

'Why you not upstairs with the rest of your dogs?' Achilleus asked.

'Why aren't you?' came the reply.

'I guess I'm sort of keeping guard,' said Achilleus. 'Don't trust no one. How about you?'

'I've seen the show too many times. It's boring. TV Boy just likes to show off. Doing all the voices. He's a pain in the arse sometimes. Acts like he's in charge. He's not in charge. The Warehouse Queen – she's in charge.' The boy paused. There was a silence and then he went on, his voice still muffled. 'It was TV Boy who wrote those messages in the corridors.'

'What was that all about?'

'He said if anybody was going to come in here they had to earn it, show they were clever enough, brave enough, I guess. Tough enough.'

'Why was that important?'

'It's dangerous around here. Lots of sickbags. We can't stay in here forever, though, and just rot. TV Boy said that if anyone was going to help us they had to prove how good they were. He's always making traps and tricks and crap.'

'You saying you were waiting for someone to ride in to your rescue?'

'Something like that.'

Jackson had worked out that the boy was hiding behind a nearby stack of boxes; he'd been moving about at first to confuse them, but he'd stopped still now and she could just make out a shape crouching in the dark. The light was fading fast outside, the skylights only showing a soft blue glow against the black of the roof.

'Come out,' she said. 'We can't talk to you lurking about behind there.'

'Achilleus was right,' said the boy, who must have been listening for some time. 'I'm embarrassed. I'd forgotten what normal children looked like. I've been here too long. Got used to it. Forgotten what creeps we are.'

'It's all right,' said Jackson. 'We won't laugh or anything.'

'I might,' said Achilleus and he grinned.

'Shut up, Akkie,' said Jackson and he made a face at her. Jackson turned back towards where the boy was hiding. 'Are you going to come out?'

'I don't know.'

'What's your name?' Jackson asked.

'Skinner.'

'Is that your surname or a nickname?'

'It's my name. My only name.'

'What's your real name?'

'We don't deserve real names. We were unwanted. Ugly. Shut away. We were a dirty secret.'

'Yeah, but you had names, right?'

'I told you. I'm called Skinner.'

'Are you not going to tell me?'

'It's Skinner.'

'What?' said Achilleus. 'You skinny then, are you?'

'Something like that.'

'Let's see it.'

'You can laugh if you want.'

'Thanks. I might.'

There was a movement and Ebenezer stretched the elastic on his slingshot, although Jackson didn't think the boy in the shadows had any intention of attacking them. There was a shuffling and scraping as he moved along behind the shelves and then a very thin cat appeared, smoky grey and short-haired. It looked at Jackson and the others and then sat down and began to clean itself.

A moment later a boy rounded the end of the shelves.

63

The cat got up and started to rub against the legs of the
boy. He was only about five foot tall, slightly hunched.
Jackson tried not to show in her face what she was feeling.
The boy looked awful, as if he'd once been much bigger
and had suddenly shrunk leaving his stretched skin hanging
in loose sheets. There were great folds and ridges of it
around his eyes and mouth and it was rucked up around
his neck, and piled on his shoulders. More folds hung out
of the bottom of his sleeves, half covering his hands. He
was walking with some difficulty, and his eyes, where she
could see them, looked sad and ashamed.

'That is so *cool*!' said Achilleus. 'Let me look at you, Skin-
boy. How the hell did you end up looking like that?'

'I didn't end up like this,' said the boy, 'I started out like
this.'

'You were born that way?'

'Yeah.'

'Does it hurt?'

'No.'

'So is there, like, a proper medical term for it?'

'Nope. Nobody else has ever been like this. All of us,
we're all different.'

'Are you, like, experiments, or something?'

'In a way, but not the way you mean. No person made us like this. It wasn't a mad scientist, or an evil Nazi doctor. A disease did it.'

'*The* disease? I thought kids couldn't catch it.'

'Sort of. It's connected. Hard to explain. Our parents all worked for Promithios.' Jackson could see that the boy had some trouble speaking as the folds of skin hung down over and around his mouth, giving it the muffled sound she'd noticed before. She also saw that he had no teeth.

'Our mums all got sick, though they didn't know it until a long time later. They went to the rainforest to work with this lost tribe. And they were really careful not to pass on any germs and diseases to the natives there. They knew they'd have no immunity. The tribe was fine. They didn't get sick. But instead they passed on a disease to our parents. Our parents had no idea. It wasn't any disease they knew about. It showed no symptoms. Except one. *Us*. We were the first symptom.'

'You?' Jackson was trying to make sense of this information.

'Yes,' said Skinner, forcing the folds of his skin into a sort of smile. 'We got the disease in the womb. We were born like this.'

'That's harsh,' said Achilleus.

'It's all we're used to.'

'You're like the X-Men,' said Paddy. 'You're mutants who've teamed up. Do you have any special powers?'

'Yeah,' said Achilleus. 'He has the power to frighten kids at Halloween without wearing a mask . . .'

Paddy started to laugh, but then stopped suddenly as Skinner opened his mouth wide. Jackson clamped her hands to her ears and screamed. Skinner was shrieking, a terrible high-pitched siren sound. Jackson didn't so much hear it as feel it, right inside her brain like a dentist's drill tearing into her head. She fell to her knees. Saw that the others were also collapsing in pain. And then Skinner closed his mouth and the sound stopped. The cat, seemingly not bothered by the noise, jumped into his arms.

'We do have some talents,' Skinner said quietly, stroking the cat. 'We haven't lived this long by being defenceless.'

Jackson stood up, rubbing her temples. She looked at Skinner with a new respect. The others looked shaken and wary.

'You shouldn't have done that, man,' said Achilleus, and Skinner shrugged.

'We've been too long alone together, here in our warped little world, living on top of each other,' he said. 'We don't really have any perspective. Life's become a sick joke. We talk and we talk and we tease each other and play tricks and we shuffle about the place, living off drugs and medicine. We make up jokes and songs, and TV Boy does his shows, and we laugh at what's going on out there. We laugh at ordinary kids like you. We need to get out of here. We need to get some fresh air. We need to mix with other people. I don't know if we can, if it's too late, if it's been too long, though. I'm scared it's going to be too hard, too painful. There's a lot of hurt out there. We've gone sour, shut away here with our games and our stories. We've got snotty and arrogant and turned in on ourselves.'

'Do you really want to risk it?' said Jackson, getting shakily back up on to her feet.

'Yes,' said Skinner. 'All I want, all I really want . . . is for you to take me away from here. I've had enough of this place. We all know, though, that we couldn't make it on our own. Not out there. I'm not scared any more. Whatever happens. Just as long as I get out.'

'It's cool,' said Achilleus, massaging his jaw, as if he'd been punched. 'We can do that. You are one ugly little bastard, Skinner, and I don't know what you just did to us, but you're on my team now.'

64

There was a mob of grown-ups outside the reception area now, growing bigger by the minute. Pressing themselves against the glass walls, pawing at the doors, smearing the windows with their pus and snot and dribble and blood. The dirty bastards. It was disgusting what could come out of a human body. This was one badly diseased bunch of meat-bags. Some looked barely human, just a mess of growths and swellings and open, gaping wounds, like extra mouths. And they were falling apart. There wasn't one of them that didn't have some part missing – eyes, ears, noses, lips, arms, legs. One mother's arm was hanging half off and she was holding it with her other arm. The father next to her looked like he'd been skinned alive. Something from a medical exhibition. Just raw muscle and flesh. Wet. Dripping. Sick . . .

'They're gonna get in,' said Kamahl. 'I know it, they're gonna get in and there's nothing we can do about it.'

He was sitting on one of the benches, side on to the doors. Not wanting to look. Holding his spear between his knees, his head hanging down.

'Well, they're not in yet.' Brandon was standing near the doors, looking at the stinking wall of flesh outside. He had Kyle's club in his hands. Ready and waiting. If the grown-ups did manage to burst in he was going to take down as many of them as he could.

Yeah, right.

He knew full well that if the adults did get in then he and Kamahl were dead meat. He'd seen what had happened to Mick and Jake outside. Jake dragged off, Mick wounded, limping after him. Brandon had to accept that they'd probably seen the last of them. Seemed impossible. Not Jake – that had always been on the cards. He'd always been a bit reckless, wading into fights he couldn't win. Brandon was amazed he'd got this far, coasting on luck, scraping by. But Mick – Mick was different. Mick had been so big, so tough, so unafraid. He'd been such a good fighter. The best in their crew. And now he was gone. While Brandon had stayed inside. Done nothing. Told himself they were trapped. No way of helping Mick with all the grown-ups round the door . . .

'Maybe we should go and find Blue,' said Kamahl quietly, sounding miserable, his voice small.

'And tell him what?' said Brandon, unable to keep the bitterness out of his voice.

'Tell him what happened.'

'That we sat here and let them get killed?'

'There was nothing we could do.'

'Yeah, we stick to that story.'

'Shall we go then?' Kamahl sounded a little brighter, perking up with the thought of getting away.

'I don't know,' said Brandon. 'We're supposed to be guarding this entrance. So we've got a way to get out of here.'

'Hah!' Kamahl finally looked round at the horde of grown-ups. 'Does that look like a way out to you?'

'Why isn't he back?' Brandon swung the club uselessly at thin air. 'All they had to do was get the stuff and come back. An hour maybe. Two hours tops. How long have they been gone? I mean, what if it's just us? What if we're the only ones left?'

'Shut up. Shut up, Brandon. Don't say that. Let's just go and find him.'

Brandon looked towards the back of the reception area, in the direction that the others had gone. 'In the dark?' he said. 'Down under the building? Not sure of the way? You want to do that or do you want to wait?'

'I don't know.' Kamahl's brief spark of optimism had died out. 'I don't know, Brandon. I wish we'd never come. I wish we'd stayed in Morrisons. We knew where we were.'

'Yeah, we knew where we were. Up the bloody creek.'

'And this?' said Kamahl. 'What's this? Disneyland? What's that out there? The Disney parade? Snow White and the seven hundred zombies . . .?'

Brandon laughed at that, hysterical, couldn't stop himself. He laughed until he was crying. Looked at Kamahl, who was crying too. They sat down together on the bench and Kamahl put his arm round him and they held on to each other, waiting for the grown-ups to smash their way in, as the light slowly faded from their world.

65

I can't write much. It is getting too dark. I can hardly see the paper in this journal. Sorry if my writing is not very clear and neat. I don't know where they are. I don't know why they're not back. I don't know why they have just left us here. Please come back. We really need you now. Please come back.

66

Maxie was standing by the main entrance at the Natural History Museum looking out as Boggle and another local kid called Cameron got ready to close the great heavy doors for the night. With Robbie still out of action, and Jackson off on the expedition, Boggle was temporarily in charge of security.

'You'll need to move so we can shut these,' he said.

'Wait a minute longer,' said Maxie, scanning the darkness.

'They should be closed already,' said Cameron.

'I know,' said Maxie. 'I'll take responsibility.' Boggle and Cameron waited there, anxious and unsure, keen to be secure. Brooke appeared, stood next to Maxie. She had a fresh bandage on her forehead, but still looked like death. She was worst around the eyes, puffy and bruised. Maxie wondered what she might have looked like before.

'Still no sign?' said Brooke.

'No,' said Maxie. 'Where are they?'

'It must have taken them longer than they thought,' said Brooke, staring out through the doors. 'They're probably holed up somewhere for the night; it's too dangerous to travel in the dark. You worried about them?'

'Blue can look after himself,' said Maxie. 'Only we don't know what's out there where they've gone.'

Brooke put a hand on Maxie's arm. 'They'll be back. Don't stress, yeah. We need to close up, though. We'll make sure the night watch don't go to sleep, just in case Blue rocks up in the middle of the night. But my guess is they'll be back when it's light. Is a bare long haul to Heathrow Airport.'

Maxie gave Brooke a quick hug. Hoped she was right. She couldn't stand the thought of losing Blue so soon after finding him. Just her luck, she thought, to have the only two boys she'd ever really liked die on her within days of each other. She tried to be strong, but there was a limit to how much she could take. She'd seen people crack before. People who had coped great for months, lost friends, killed grown-ups, survived . . . and then it was usually something little that did it. One of her old girlfriends, a girl called Lila, had found a cat with a kitten. She'd taken them in and fed them, made them a cosy sleeping place. But the mother had got some kind of cat flu. She died and the kitten couldn't look after herself. Lila tried everything but couldn't get her to eat and slowly the kitten starved to death.

Lila had been heartbroken, couldn't stop crying and saying how unfair the world was, how mucked up it all was, how there wasn't any God.

One day she threw herself off the roof. Didn't die straight away, but had terrible internal injuries. In the end she drowned in her own blood.

Maxie didn't want it to end like that.

'We can close the doors,' she said, 'but I'm going to wait up. Stay down here. I can sleep in a chair if I need to.'

'You sure, girl?'

'Yeah. You go, Brooke. I'll be fine.'

★

337

From way up on the roof, pressing his face to the dirty windows, Paul could just make out the silhouette of two figures in the open doorway far below. A dry voice croaked in his ear.

'One?' it said. 'You've only got *one* in your pathetic collection?'

Paul's stomach rumbled. He hadn't been able to face eating any more of Samira and now he was hungry again. And when he was hungry Boney-M came back to him and his thoughts clouded over.

'It won't be done until you kill all of them,' said the bird thing. 'The night-time is your time and it'll be dark enough soon to go hunting.'

It had started to rain; a light drizzle fell on Paul's back. He watched as the doors were closed, and he couldn't see the two figures any more. They were down there, though, and all he had to do was slip into the building and keep his knife handy.

Boney-M poked him in the ribs and Paul swore at him, turned to swat him away . . . and all he saw was a jutting piece of stonework.

He turned his face up to the sky and let the rain fall on his face, opening his mouth wide to try to get some precious water inside him. His blood fizzed and simmered in his veins, carrying the itch around his body. The maddening itch that made it hard to think straight. He put his hand to the wound in his neck and scratched it. It was hot and sore, but felt slightly better than it had done. Maybe he was healing at last.

He remembered when it had happened. That had been a bad day. When he'd got too close to one of the captive sickos on the lorry in the yard, the ones that Einstein kept for his experiments. The sicko they called Simon Foul. That had been their joke – James, the guy who used to help him look after them, had named them after the original X-Factor judges. Simon Foul, Louis Corpse and Cheryl Ghoul. Simon had been a biter. Not too bad at first, but over the weeks he'd got worse and worse.

Paul was usually OK around them. They were used to him and he was used to them. They never tried to attack him, but he'd relaxed too much, forgotten just how dangerous they were, got careless, and one afternoon . . . He remembered very clearly the tearing pain as Simon dug his teeth into his neck. The feeling of warmth as the blood poured down his neck. Paul had managed to pull away before any real damage was done. He'd kicked Simon and swore and spat at him and after that he'd kept him muzzled like a vicious dog, but it was too late. His skin had been broken. Simon's germs had been injected into his blood. He didn't tell anyone, he'd been too embarrassed, ashamed. Didn't want anyone to know how stupid he'd been.

Besides, what could anyone do? They played at being doctors, and scientists, when they were just kids, clueless. About as much use as doctors in the Middle Ages with their leeches and poultices and bleedings.

He'd stolen some antibiotics and some painkillers from the labs. Far as he could tell they hadn't made much difference. The wound had still got infected. Still hurt like hell.

But maybe, just maybe, it was getting better at last. He took his hand away from the wound and looked at it: his fingers were smeared with pus. He held them out in the rain till it washed the filth away. Maybe it wasn't the drugs that helped. Maybe it was meat. Maybe eating Samira had been what had changed things. But she was rotting now, starting to stink the place out.

He needed fresh meat.

He smiled, felt a shiver of excitement.

Yes, he thought, Boney-M was right. *Soon it would be dark enough to hunt.*

67

Blue was struggling to stay awake. He wasn't sure how much more he could take of this. Was it ever going to end? He'd lost track of how long they'd been here. It seemed that once TV Boy got started it was hard to stop him and he was making the most of having a whole new audience for his performance. As far as Blue could tell, scientists working for Promithios Biomedical had brought samples of Inmathger DNA back here to the UK for analysis and had somehow become infected. What with, he wasn't really sure, and now Blue had lost track of who exactly TV Boy was supposed to be. It was the guy with the nasal, nerdy voice. Buddy someone.

'Ah, but, Professor, isn't it indubitably true that the logging story is a cover-up? It wasn't loggers who found the Inmathger, it was scientists, who were studying what they believed to be a giant crater caused by a meteorite strike many thousands, indeed millions of years ago, in the exact spot where the Inmathger live. Indubitably so.'

A quick change and TV Boy was someone else again.

'I must say you have a lot of fanciful notions, Mister Dumpster, and finally, here's a joke for you.'

The Twisted Kids cheered. Blue perked up. Maybe this was the end at last.

'How many flies does it take to screw in a light bulb? Two, but how the hell do they get in there? Ha, ha, it's the way I tell them. What's the last thing that goes through a fly's mind when it hits your windscreen? Its arse! What do you get if you cross a motorway with a flock of sheep? A flock of dead sheep. What do you get if you cross a praying mantis with a flea? A bug that says grace before drinking your blood. What do you get if you cross a flea with a donkey? An itchy ass. And finally what do you get if you cross a flea with a human being . . .?'

He waited a moment before all the other kids shouted out together.

'A bloody mess!'

TV Boy whipped his wig off.

'That's right, that's what we are, folks! The Twisted Kids. A bloody mess. A mistake. Thank you and goodnight.' So saying, he blew the candles out and the platform was immediately plunged into darkness. Blue saw that it was now night outside. It took a minute for his eyes to adjust as all around him the warehouse kids started making an eerie noise, whooping and chirping and clicking, humming and buzzing, mimicking the sounds of a jungle at night. It was spookily realistic and sounded completely inhuman.

Blue's own crew sat there in confused silence. Not sure how much of what they'd just seen they could believe, and totally freaked out by the insect and animal sounds.

Suddenly Einstein switched on his torch and stood up, calling out over the din as his beam fell on the faces of the warehouse kids, mouths wide, chirping and hollering.

'Wait!' he shouted. 'You have to tell us more. Are you saying the disease originated in the Amazon rainforest and was carried to England by people working for Promithios?'

There was no response. 'Wait!' he shouted again. 'Listen! You have to tell us more!'

Blue jumped as TV Boy popped up by his side and half whispered into his ear.

'There isn't any more. That's the end of the show. That's all we know. When it comes down to it we're just like the rest of you. We're only children.'

68

Downstairs Jackson and the others were listening to the strange noises coming from the platform.

'Now what's happening?' said Achilleus. 'Sounds like we're missing a party.'

'That's the jungle lullaby,' said Skinner. 'Memories of the big green.'

'Yeah,' said Achilleus. 'Now say it again in English.'

'It's one of the things we're good at,' said Skinner. 'Making animal noises.' He joined in for a few seconds, grunting and croaking like a howler monkey, and then he laughed. 'We can keep it up for hours.'

'I saw an animal of some sort in the corridors,' said Jackson. 'What was it? At first I thought it was a snake. Couldn't have been, though. It was too big.'

'Thing with a long neck?'

'Yeah.'

'You're right. That wasn't a snake. That was Pencil Neck. He doesn't live in here with us. He came out the worst.'

'You mean he's human?' said Jackson.

'Yeah. Mostly. He went feral months ago. Lives out there in the dark, hiding in holes, crawling about the place. God knows what he eats. He was always hard work. Never really fitted in. Can't talk, you see. Though some of us – like the

Queen and Betty Bubble, even TV Boy when he shuts up and listens – some of us can understand him. We tried to look after him, but . . .' Skinner trailed off, made a helpless, hopeless gesture.

'This is one seriously messed-up place,' said Achilleus.

'You said it.'

Blue appeared on the platform and called down to Achilleus.

'We need to talk.'

'What about?' Achilleus shouted back.

Blue came down the stairs.

'About what we're going to do,' he said, speaking as he walked. 'It's got way dark. Don't know how we're going to find what we need right now, to be honest, and then we got to get back to the church.'

'Can I show you something?' said Skinner.

Jackson watched Blue trying not to react to how Skinner looked. He did a good job.

'This is Skinner,' said Achilleus. 'Our new mate. He's like one of them dogs – a Sharpie.'

'Shar Pei,' said Jackson.

'Whatever.'

'You want to show us something?' said Blue.

'Yeah.'

'There's not going to be any singing, is there? Funny voices? Cheesy old jokes?'

'No. Come with me.'

69

Maxie stood up and stretched. It was boring sitting in the chair by the museum doors in the dark. Nothing to do except think. It was only her and Cameron and he'd just fallen asleep. The rest of the night watch, four of them in all, were off on patrol, looking for any signs of sickos trying to get in. They were also keeping an eye out for any signs of Paul.

Under the new system that Maxie had put in place they kept up a continual circuit of the blue and green zones, checking all the doors and windows. They were heavily armed and all carried torches. They also had whistles on string around their necks. As did Cameron. Any sign of trouble and they would start blowing.

They'd sealed off this part of the museum by closing all the connecting doors to the orange and red zones. So there was no way through to the Darwin Centre where Paul – assuming it *was* him – had attacked Samira. If he was hiding out over that way they were safe. Some of the kids had protested about patrolling all night. They reckoned they'd all be safer locked up in the minerals gallery. But Maxie had insisted on keeping the patrols going, all day and all night. If they could catch Paul they could stop him.

She was staying put here by the doors with Cameron,

waiting for Blue to return. They'd agreed to take it in turns to sleep, but Cameron had nodded off almost immediately. Even though the patrol came around every few minutes, Maxie wished he hadn't fallen asleep quite so quickly and left her staring at the tea light that she kept burning in a little glass jar at her feet.

She stretched her back. The seat wasn't too comfortable. She was beginning to wonder whether it wouldn't be better just to go to bed and get a good night's sleep. Leave Cameron to it. The long, dull hours of night-time stretched out ahead of her and she seriously doubted that Blue was going to stroll up any time before daybreak. She was jealous of Cameron. He looked very peaceful, and stupid, in that way that sleeping people do, his mouth hanging open, dribbling slightly, head lolling over on his neck. Vulnerable too. He looked much younger asleep than he did awake. She guessed he was about thirteen, maybe just fourteen. They'd all had to grow up bare quick, but like this, defences down, she was reminded that they were just children.

She heard a noise and glanced round quickly. It was only the patrol. Two boys and two girls, coming in from the right, where the museum shop was. They must have finished their circuit of the green zone.

'He asleep already?' said one of the girls. 'Cameron's so lazy. He's always asleep.'

'He's a useless guard,' said one of the boys. 'He should stick to the day watch. You OK with him?'

'No problem,' said Maxie. 'I think we've got everything covered down here.'

'OK. See you on the next circuit.'

She watched them walking off into the blue zone, their torch beams zigzagging on the floor, heard their chatter and a burst of laughter. It was a comforting sound. She supposed she ought to be more scared of Paul, but she had no real sense of him, couldn't picture him, didn't know how dangerous he might be. She understood sickos; she knew to be properly careful of them. She also knew their limitations. What they could and couldn't do.

A rogue kid was something different.

She got up and went over to Cameron. He'd started to snore. She kicked his leg and he came spluttering awake, looking confused and bleary, wide-eyed, like he'd been caught doing something wrong.

'What is it?' he said when he saw her. Relaxed a little.

'You're sleeping on the job, Cam.'

'Was I? Sorry. How long have I been asleep?'

'Not long. I was going to let you sleep a bit longer.'

'Yeah?' Cameron scratched his head and sniffed. 'Why didn't you?'

'I wanted to ask you something.'

'Go on then.' Even though he was in the wrong, Cameron had that grumpy, feeling-sorry-for-himself attitude of someone who'd just been woken up.

'It's about Paul,' said Maxie.

Cameron grunted.

'What was he like?' Maxie went on.

'Paul?' Cameron sniffed again, rolled his neck, which was obviously hurting him. 'Never really thought about him that much. He was quite quiet. Pretty smart, I think, always reading. He was well into all the stuff here, you know, the animals and the exhibits and that. I never had much to do with him, as it goes. And then he got sick. I don't know, I guess it was flu or something. You know when you get a fever and you start acting all weird? He was like that. Got quite edgy and aggressive. Lost it big time when his little sister got killed by a sicko. Went absolutely berserk. Started accusing us all of not caring. As if it was our fault somehow. It was quite funny really.'

'Funny? His sister had died.'

'Yeah.' Cameron looked down, gave an apologetic shrug. 'Not really *funny*, I suppose, as such. But you know what it's like when a quiet kid suddenly loses it? A wimpy kid? That was the first time anyone really noticed him, when he started trying to attack everyone.'

'Was it serious? Like a problem?'

'Not really.'

'So he's not that big? Not a fighter?'

'Paul? No way. I mean, he *was* big, but, you know, like, tall. Tall and skinny, not muscly. Never saw him fight. Must have done something early on, to survive long enough to get in here and stay safe. But most of us, once we got in here, we never had anything to do with sickos. Until the other night. When they got in.'

'So if he did pop up somewhere you guys could deal with him fairly easily?'

'Of course. I mean, no offence, but Samira was just a girl. Paul wouldn't never have stood a chance against one of us boys.'

'And me?' said Maxie. 'I'm a girl.'

'Yeah . . .' Cameron grinned at her. 'But don't worry. I'm here to protect you, babe.'

70

It was drizzling and thin clouds covered the moon, so that the area around the warehouse was washed with a thin, watery-grey light. Just enough to show that there were people down there. Grown-ups – too many to count. They were hard to see in the gloom, but definitely there. The warehouse was surrounded. Blue and Skinner were huddled together on the roof under an umbrella that Skinner had produced. It was green with a white Promithios logo on it. Achilleus was too cool to take shelter under a brolly. He stood out in the open. Getting wet.

'They come every night,' said Skinner. He was holding the cat inside his jacket. It peered out nervously at the rain. 'We go round every few days to repair the fences, but they always get back in again.'

'They ever get in the building?'

'Sometimes. One or two. We deal with them pretty quick.'

'How?'

'Oh, you know. We have our ways. It's always the cleverest get in, the least diseased.'

'Like Seamus and his mates?'

'Yeah. Like them.'

Blue wondered why it didn't feel stranger up here. On

the roof of a medical supplies warehouse, under this umbrella with a short, hunched-over kid whose skin was ten sizes too big for him, talking about an army of cannibal adults.

'Seamus and the others had been trying to get in for ages,' Skinner went on. 'Eventually we let them. TV Boy wanted them for his trap. His little game.'

'But what do they want?' Blue asked. 'Why do they come here night after night?'

'Same as you,' said Skinner. 'They want what we've got. But also, mainly I think, they want *us*. They're kind of attracted to us.'

'Is it worse after dark?' said Blue.

'Oh yeah. Much. There's only ever usually one or two during the day. They hide in the other buildings around here. Sleep while it's light. They'll come out and attack if they think it's worth it.'

'Was a whole load of them down there when we turned up,' said Blue, remembering the fight at the gates.

'They must have sensed you coming. There's twice as many tonight as usual. Lately they've been changing, getting more organized. The signal's different.'

'What signal? What do you mean?'

'You can't go out there now,' said Skinner, changing the subject. 'You'll have to wait till morning. They'll go back to their dens when the sun comes up. We can help you find what you need here and then you're clear.'

'We left some friends behind,' said Blue. 'Nearby. They'll be waiting for us.'

'Are they safe?'

'I hope so. They're in a church.'

'They should be fine then, so long as they stay inside.'

'Oh, they'll stay inside all right. Too scared to come out. We didn't bring much food, though. We were expecting to be back home by now.'

'They got water?'

'Yeah, plenty of water.'

'Then they'll be fine.'

'Hope so. This whole journey hasn't quite gone like I expected.'

'If the Warehouse Queen lets you take all you want it'll have been worth it, though, won't it?'

'Guess so. I don't know about drugs and chemicals and all that. That's Einstein's territory. Can I ask you something, though?'

'Yeah.'

'Is there a cure? For the disease? Is there a cure here?'

'If there was do you think all those creeps would be down there? Do you think we wouldn't have fixed them up?'

'I guess so.'

Skinner was silent for a while. They stared at the adults milling about, barely making a sound. Achilleus picked up something from the roof and threw it down. Laughed.

'I like it up here,' said Skinner after a while. 'I come up here all the time. Day and night. For me this is the whole world. Our parents never let us go out when we were growing up. Never in public. When the disease struck they brought us in here. This is all I've ever seen, the view from up here. I wonder all the time what it's like, the rest of the world.'

'It's pretty crap at the moment, to be honest with you,' said Blue.

'I want to see it, though.'

The cat shifted inside Skinner's jacket and Skinner soothed her. 'She doesn't like it out here.'

'Can't say as I'm enjoying it much either,' said Blue as the wind switched direction and directed a spray of rain down his neck. 'Come on. Let's go down. I've seen enough.'

As Blue went to move off, though, Skinner held him back with a hand on his sleeve.

'There might be a cure,' he said. 'There might be stuff here you could use. But we wouldn't know where to start. We're not scientists. Our parents were either scientists or doctors, but we were too young to learn anything and they all died before they could work anything out; they were trying, they were trying real hard. They felt guilty, you see.'

'Of spreading the disease, of bringing it here to England?'

'That would have happened anyway. As soon as the Inmathger came out of the forest and met other humans.'

'What then?'

'The thing is,' said Skinner, 'it was clear even before we were born that there was something wrong. That we weren't growing normally. But, like I said, they kept it secret, covered it up. They hid us away from the other people they worked with. Didn't tell anyone. All of them who had children. And when we were born we never mixed with other kids. Nobody knew about us at all.'

'But why?'

'Have you ever heard of toxoplasmosis?'

'What's that?'

Skinner tickled his cat under the chin and lifted its head slightly.

'You can tell us all about it, can't you, kitty?' he said.

'Inside,' said Blue. They called over to Achilleus and

headed for the door. Once they were safely back in the dry Skinner fastened the door shut and, as they walked along the metal walkway high above the warehouse floor, he explained.

'Toxoplasmosis,' he said, 'is a parasitic disease that used to kill thousands of people every year, and its main host is cats.'

'Never knew that,' said Blue. 'I ain't going nowhere near Mister Tiddles there.'

'It's *Mrs* actually,' said Skinner. 'Mrs Jones. But chances are you already have it.'

'What? Toxic Plodmosis?'

'Toxoplasmosis. Yeah. They used to reckon that up to half the human population was infected with it. Most people never know they've got it inside them, but if you're weak, with a bad immune system, or, like, a baby, it can kill you, or make you blind, or give you brain damage.'

'You saying I could have it and not know?'

'Yeah. Some people never have any symptoms, or they might just think they've got, like, flu, or something.'

They reached the stairway that led down to the ground.

'You trying to tell me that's what the disease is?' said Blue, starting down the stairs. 'It's a kind of toxoplasmosis?'

'Come on, we ain't got all night.' Achilleus pushed past the two of them, impatient with the slow progress that Skinner was making as he waddled along, limping slightly. Blue noticed that he was wearing no shoes and that his feet were covered in thick layers of leathery skin.

Skinner waited for Achilleus to get ahead and then carried on explaining things to Blue.

'Not toxoplasmosis,' he said. 'Something similar. We call it the Nightmare Bug. The way it works, though, is just like toxoplasmosis. So you can get infected without knowing it; you can carry it for years without any symptoms, and it can affect your brain, change you completely.'

'Can toxoplasmosis do that?' asked Blue, getting worried that there was one more thing in the world to stress about.

'You can catch toxoplasmosis from touching cat crap,' said Skinner. 'Or soil where a cat crapped, the parasite can live there. Then if you don't wash your hands it can get inside you, where it'll breed. The thing is, once it's in you, it can cause you to behave differently. If mice get it, for instance, they're not scared of cats any more.'

'You're joking me?'

'No. It's true. A mouse with toxoplasmosis will go looking for cats. They're attracted to their wee, I think, and they'll go up to them without any fear.'

'What? It makes mice become supermice and attack cats?'

'Kind of. The parasite controls their brains. So they go up to cats and . . . and, well, they get eaten. So the parasite gets into its main host. The cat.'

Blue stopped and Skinner turned to him.

'And people that have the toxo?' Blue said, looking suspiciously at Mrs Jones, who was still tucked up inside Skinner's jacket. 'Are they attracted to cats too?'

'Not as far as I know,' said Skinner. 'But it can cause depression, mental disorders, even suicide.'

'That is bad news,' said Blue. 'I wished you hadn't told me that.'

'Sorry. I was only trying to explain.'

Mrs Jones suddenly meowed and struggled free from Skinner. She jumped on to the handrail and then on to the steps. She was so skinny she looked more like a squirrel than a cat. Blue watched her slink down the stairs.

'But toxoplasmosis isn't what caused the sickness in grown-ups?' he said, carrying on down after the cat.

'No. It's a different parasite,' said Skinner. 'And once it got in people it altered their brains. So our mums and dads, they protected us, they protected the disease by not talking. They had the parasite growing inside them all the time.'

'They didn't know it, though,' said Blue.

'No. The parasite was making sure it wasn't found out, or it would have been wiped out before it had a chance to multiply. You see, we were the only signs that something was wrong. Otherwise the parasite was undetectable; it's very good at hiding. It meant our parents didn't behave rationally. We are a secret that has only now been told.'

They reached the bottom of the stairs and caught up with Achilleus, who had stopped to play with the cat. He was squatting down, scratching her behind her ear as she arched her back and rubbed against his knee. Finally he picked her up and held her under his chin. Blue winced, remembering what Skinner had just told him. It was weird seeing Achilleus like this. Blue didn't have him down as a cat person.

Blue smiled. Must have the toxo in him.

They walked over to where Jackson and Paddy were waiting for them.

'What's going on?' Jackson asked. 'What have you found out?'

'We've found out that we ain't going nowhere tonight,' said Achilleus. 'This place is, like, under siege.'

'And I found out that you need to keep away from cats,' said Blue.

71

Maxie was dreaming of pear drops. She always bought pear drops when they went to visit her nan in Wales. There was an old-fashioned sweet shop on the high street. It was always really busy, especially in the summer when all the holiday-makers were there. In the shop they had these shelves with every kind of sweet you could think of. Cough drops, sherbet bonbons, pineapple cubes, aniseed twists, Parma violets . . . and pear drops. The hard crystals of sugar on them dug into the top of your mouth, but if you sucked them long enough they became all smooth and slippery. Nothing else tasted like pear drops. Not even pears. She'd buy a little white paper bag, with a selection of sweets, carefully weighed. The smell of the pear drops was the strongest, always reminded her of Nan. Of being in Wales with the family.

And here she was. Up at the counter with her mum and her nan. The woman who ran the shop was struggling to open a jar, but it wouldn't budge. She was sweating, grunting. Maxie could see the pear drops inside, could smell them; the smell was so strong it was overpowering. They rattled and tumbled around in there, pink and yellow, frosted and glittering with sugar . . .

She wanted those pear drops so badly. Open it, open the jar, you silly old witch.

And then the top turned, spinning round really fast, and it came off and the shopkeeper held the jar out to her . . .

But there was something wrong. The sweets stank. Of something rotten. Maxie looked in the jar. There weren't any sweets in there, just a pile of rotting meat, bits of body, heart and lungs and intestines, mouldy and putrefying, and over it . . .

The smell of pear drops.

Nan. Wales. Sweets.

Only she wasn't in Wales, was she? She couldn't be. Nan was dead. Her mum was dead. Her whole family was dead. It was just a dream. *Sod it*. She'd been enjoying it. A nice trip to Wales. Her brain was teasing her, playing tricks. And that final nasty trick with the jar. Full of rotting meat. What was that all about?

And that smell . . .

It wasn't in her dream. She wasn't imagining it. It was too strong. Too real. Her sleeping mind was struggling to make sense of it. This foul mix of pear drops and rotten meat.

Only one thing smelt like that.

Grown-ups.

She had to wake up. There was danger. She had to be ready.

She forced her eyes open, gave a little shudder and for a moment sat there, suspended between awake and asleep, asleep and awake . . .

Now she couldn't tell if she was dreaming still. The great Gothic bulk of the museum rising above her, brick upon brick, falling away to shadows, a flickering light from the candle at her feet.

That was real.

Yeah . . .

Cameron sat there, slumped in his seat, dribbling, and someone was standing over him. Someone tall. Dressed in black. Shoulders hunched. Up around his ears. Elbows tucked into his sides. Holding himself as if he was in pain. Swaying slightly, moving his head with little jerky movements, like a lizard.

Long, spindly arms and legs. Very thin.

A spider. That's what Ella had said. A spider walking in the museum at night. He had a blade in his hand, its sharp edge glinting in the candlelight.

Maxie couldn't move, like she was still in the dream, frozen, couldn't speak, couldn't move, couldn't save Cameron.

Why did a boy smell of pear drops and rotting meat?

Her tongue felt too big for her mouth.

But she had to do something.

'Wait,' she said at last, the sound of her voice surprising her. The boy stopped still, tensed and then slowly, slowly turned. His face was a face drawn on a sheet of paper, so white, making his eyes look yellow, his teeth . . .

Yellow.

Spider.

Paul.

Maxie was fully awake now, no doubt about that, her throat dry, the blood throbbing in her temples, her legs shaking. All she could hear was her own breath, rasping through her nose. Cameron slept on in his chair. Either that or Paul had killed him already.

Paul had a look in his eyes that wasn't human. He seemed possessed by the spirit of some animal. He had the cold, pitiless eyes of a shark, or a snake.

Lizard, shark, snake, spider . . .

No. She had it now.

Dinosaur.

Maxie hated dinosaurs.

He looked like a raptor out of a Jurassic Park film. One of those nasty, clever, skinny ones. It was the museum that had possessed him.

'Wait,' she said again. He tilted his head to one side. Licked his lips and his tongue was shockingly pink. God, he stank.

Maxie tried to fix on her surroundings without taking her eyes off Paul. Her new samurai sword was propped against her chair, still in its scabbard. Cameron had his own weapon, a short sword, in his lap. He was supposed to be awake, it was his watch, but he'd fallen asleep again. Stupid bastard. And where was the patrol? Had Paul done something to them? He was a lot more dangerous-looking in the flesh than she'd imagined. Because he was no longer human. He was this dinosaur thing.

So had he dealt with the patrol or might they appear at any moment? She had no hope of getting to the whistle around Cameron's neck to alert them.

The only thing she could do was try to reason with him, to reach out to the boy who must still be in there somewhere.

'You're Paul, aren't you?' she said. He didn't reply, just licked his lips again. That pink tongue crawling over his dry skin.

'I'm Maxie. I'm new here.'

'I'm hungry,' said Paul, his voice dry and dusty.

So he could still talk then. That was a start. He moved closer to her and she saw that there was a film of sweat on his face and his skin was twitching, shivering, seeming to crawl on his face.

'We can find you something to eat,' she said.

'No, you can't.'

'I can,' said Maxie, sounding lame, even to herself.

Paul just made a dismissive noise. Moved his blade gently in the air.

'Why are you doing this?' Maxie said. 'Why did you kill that poor girl?'

'*Why did you kill that poor girl?*' Paul's mocking voice became harsh and grating, like he was channelling someone else. Someone older and fouler.

'Are you going to be a dick or are you going to talk to me?' she said.

Paul looked surprised by this. He peered at her again with that cold animal stare. She wondered whether to shout, to scream. It might bring the patrol running, but it might also shock him into action. She didn't want him to suddenly come at her. The knife looked horribly sharp. Even if it didn't kill her it could do a lot of damage. She thought of Brooke's face. Of Achilleus, mauled in the fight at the palace. And she was sitting down, couldn't move fast. He had the advantage of being on his feet, tensed and ready to strike. She pictured the knife lashing out, cutting cleanly through skin, through muscle, grinding on her bones . . .

The candle flickered as a draught from under the door passed over it. Even though Paul hadn't changed position the shifting shadows made it look like he was moving.

Maxie was aware of the tea light, right in front of her foot in its glass container. An idea came to her, but she couldn't risk looking down. Didn't want him to guess what she was thinking.

'Why don't you put the knife away?' she said, trying to make her voice sound calm and reassuring, soothing. Like she was *nice*.

'*Why don't you put the knife away . . . ?*' Paul wasn't trying to sound nice, more like something out of a rubbish horror film. He was swaying more noticeably from left to right, shifting his weight from one foot to the other, his hand, the one that held the knife, shaking. Maxie spotted a movement and glanced over at Cameron. He wasn't dead. He was waking up.

That was bad. Paul might get spooked. Do something rash.

It was now or never.

Maxie quickly jerked her foot forward as hard as she could, sending the candle skittering across the floor. At the same time she rolled sideways out of her chair, groping unsuccessfully for her sword, and hit the floor empty-handed . . .

The candle had gone out and the museum was instantly plunged into darkness. The sudden absence of light was dramatic. She was blind. Hoped Paul was too.

It wouldn't last, though. There would be enough light coming in through the windows for them to see each other soon, so Maxie kept moving, scrambling away on all fours, and now she was yelling.

'He's here! Paul is here!'

She prayed that Cameron was all right. Hoped that in the confusion, and with all the noise she was making, Paul would come after her and not try to attack Cameron where he sat.

She heard whistles, running feet, saw torch beams scratching at the darkness.

'Be careful!' she screamed. 'He's got a knife. Keep away from him.'

'Where is he?'

'I can't see him.'

'Where is he?'

Maxie looked to where she'd last seen Paul. No sign of him. He must have moved fast. She scuttled backwards, wanting to get against a wall. She was still unarmed. Paul might come at her, make a last desperate attack. But where was he?

'Cameron?' she called out. 'Are you OK?'

'Yeah. What's going on?'

'Paul was here. You fell asleep again.'

'Paul? Where?'

'I don't know. He's gone.'

The patrol finally ran over and Maxie felt a pathetic flood of relief. She got up and grabbed her sword, yanked it from its sheath, feeling much better now that she had a solid weapon in her hands. Her head was pounding, her knees weak, liable to give way at any minute. She was only glad she hadn't wet herself in her panic. The patrol was scouring the area, shining their torches into every corner, while trying to stay together in a tight bunch with Maxie and Cameron.

'You're sure?' said Cameron, staring accusingly at Maxie. 'You're sure it was him?'

'Who else could it be?'

'It's dark.'

'He fitted your description exactly.'

'I don't remember falling asleep,' said Cameron. 'You could have dreamt it.'

Could she? Could she have imagined the whole thing?

What if she'd been asleep the whole time and Cameron had been awake?

No. She was sure of it. The smell and everything. It still lingered in the air.

And then Cameron said something.

'I'm bleeding.'

One of the patrol shone a torch in his face. He looked as pale as Paul. He was shaking, about to pass out, his hand by his neck. He took it away and it was wet. Red. There was a smear of blood below his ear.

'He cut me . . .'

Maxie caught him as he fell.

72

Brandon wasn't sure what he was looking at. A head? But a head so swollen it looked unreal. With a face on it. Like a face drawn on a balloon. With huge eyes and a tiny mouth. That didn't make sense, though, did it?

So what was going on?

He was lying on the floor behind the counter in the reception area. He and Kamahl had moved there last night. Too exhausted and strung out to stay watching the doors and too scared to go into the bowels of the building to find Blue.

The counter acted like a wall and gave them a small sense of security. They'd ripped open the leather seats and torn out the stuffing to try to make some kind of a bed, but it had been a cold and uncomfortable night. They'd barely slept, being all too aware of the grown-ups outside, crowding up against the doors and windows. Every few minutes either he or Kamahl had woken with a start and jumped up to look over at them, convinced that they'd been disturbed by someone getting in.

No. It was only their dreams and their fears that had disturbed them, and they would slump back down, ragged and aching in their bones.

And now . . .

What was he looking at . . . ?

Maybe one of them *had* got in. It was only grown-ups who looked bloated like this, wasn't it? The disease could change the shape of their bodies. Make them swell and warp. But something about this face looked younger, the face of a girl, not a mother.

Brandon kicked Kamahl, who grunted and woke up. When he saw the face looming over the top of the counter he swore and scrambled clumsily to his feet, reaching for his spear. Brandon was immediately up and next to him . . .

And he saw, behind the girl, a boy with a face made out of folded sheets. He wanted to yell. And then all the air went out of him in a great sigh and his heart stopped racing as he spotted Blue, Jackson and the rest.

'Jesus Christ, Blue,' said Brandon, his voice wobbly. 'Where the hell have you been?'

'And who the hell are these two?' Kamahl added.

'That's Betty Bubble and Skinner,' said Blue matter-of-factly, as if it was the most normal thing in the world. 'They're with us.'

Brandon glanced quickly over at the doors. The rain had stopped. It was damp outside, but the sky was clear. Morning sunlight streamed in through the glass. There was no sign of any of the grown-ups. The only evidence that they'd even been there were the filthy streaks and smears on the windows.

Brandon felt sick and hungry and shaky. Angry with Blue that they'd been abandoned here and confused by the appearance of the two weird kids. One like an inflated balloon, the other like a burst one.

It was Blue who spoke first, though.

'Where's Mick and Jake?'

'They went out,' said Kamahl. 'And they never came back.'

'What do you mean?'

'Yesterday,' said Kamahl, pointing to the glass wall with a trembling hand. 'That was full of grown-ups. A whole mess of them.'

'And Mick went out there?'

'He was acting bare weird. He didn't look well. He went out to scare off some cats.'

'Cats?'

'Yeah. And he was ambushed by grown-ups. Then Jake went out to try and help him, and they got Jake too. There was so many of them.'

'Yeah. I saw them from the roof.' Blue walked over to the windows and looked out, as if he might see Mick and Jake out there somewhere.

'This was yesterday?' he said.

'Yeah. We didn't know what to do.'

Blue swore. A quick, vicious burst. Then he turned to look at Brandon and Kamahl, his face set hard.

'Mick should have known better than to go out there,' he said.

'We'd have helped him, but . . .'

'You did the right thing. Staying inside. I know how many there was out there. It was Mick's fault.'

'What's happening, Blue? Why've you been so long?'

'I'll tell you what's happening. We need to get round the back of the warehouse and bring the gear out through the loading doors.'

'But what have you been doing?'

'You reckon it's all quiet out there now?' said Blue, ignoring Brandon's question.

367

'I dunno. We only just woke up.'

'I'll go check.'

'We'll come with you.'

'No,' Blue snapped. 'You wait here. Nobody bloody move, OK? Can you manage that? I'm going outside. Alone. I'm not risking anyone else getting hurt.'

Jackson watched Blue walk over to the doors, unlock them and pull them open, and then he walked outside as if there was nothing to fear. Like he was leaving all the bad stuff behind, a boy storming off after an argument. He looked quickly left and right then went along the windows to the left. In a moment he was out of sight.

She wondered about Blue. There was something cold and hard about him. He'd barely reacted at all when the two boys told him his friends were dead. Just got on with business. Maybe you needed to be like that to be a leader. To not have any feelings. Maybe you had to just worry about the group. If the group was safe then the individuals in it didn't matter. That's why she never wanted to be a leader. She'd let someone else carry that load.

She just hoped she never got on the wrong side of Blue.

73

Blue walked away until he was sure he was out of sight of the others. There was a wide passage between the office block and the warehouse block. Several grown-ups lay dead and mangled on the ground. At least Mick had taken some with him.

Stupid sod. Stupid bloody stupid sod.

He kicked one of the bodies. A father. The body gurgled and split.

He kicked it again. He hadn't come out here to check on anything. It was obvious the grown-ups had left when the sun came up. Although part of him had been hoping there might be one or two still hanging about. Something for him to take his fury out on.

No. He just needed to be alone, away from the group. His throat was tight, as if someone had their hands around it. His eyes were stinging. It was taking all his effort not to start crying. He turned his face up to the sky and that seemed to help. OK. Good. He had it under control.

He sniffed. Who was he kidding?

Don't cry. Don't let yourself cry. Mick wouldn't want that.

Big Mick had been his best friend. By his side for the last year. They'd shared everything and had gone through so much together. Mick hadn't been very bright, or particularly funny, but he'd been loyal. Reliable. Someone Blue could always lean on. Blue had never been scared in a fight as long as Mick was with him, which he always had been.

And now he was gone.

That was hard to take. Blue kicked the dead father in the head. Gunk flew out and splattered across the ground. Grey jelly and bits of diseased flesh. Blue kicked him again, and again, and kept on kicking until the head came away from the neck and rolled against the wall.

Blue realized he was crying now. A fat tear rolled down one cheek and he swore and swiped it away with the back of his hand. That made him angrier. God, he wished there was a living grown-up here, walking around, so he could smash it to pieces. *The bastards.* Every time Blue thought they were getting ahead, getting on top of things, something like this would happen. He felt shaken and uncertain in a way he hadn't felt for ages. He had to get it all out of his system before he went back to the others.

He stared at the headless torso of the dead father. More grey jelly was oozing from its neck. He was about to kick the body again when it moved. The arms twitched and the fingers of one hand closed into a fist. The other hand seemed to almost be reaching out towards him.

He swore and stamped on the body. Crushed the closed hand beneath his boot.

The father didn't move any more. Maybe it never had. His vision was so blurred by tears he could easily have imagined it. Dead bodies didn't move. Unless it was a kind of post-death twitch, a muscular contraction or spasm of some kind? That was possible, wasn't it? One thing he knew for sure: the disease didn't turn people into zombies. They weren't the living dead.

But then meeting the Twisted Kids had shown him that there was more going on out there than he'd ever imagined. It was strange living in a world without TV, or school, or the Internet. Before the disease he'd been bombarded by information all day long, too much for him to ever take in. Now his world had shrunk to a tiny patch of London, and the day-to-day struggle to get food and survive.

Blue spat on the corpse. Cursed it. Looked around to check that none of the others were moving. And that was when he saw a dead mother's mouth gape open, as if she wanted to say something. He froze and a chill spread through his guts. He watched, unable to look away, as her tongue started to poke out and her cheeks bulged. Her eyes widened. She was definitely about to speak, he knew it. He had a feeling in his bones that she was going to say something that would flip the world on its head again.

But her tongue, purple with brown patches eaten into it, just kept on coming, sticking further and further out of her mouth, until it fell out completely and a moment later a small rat followed it. It picked up the tongue and glared at Blue as if to say, 'What are you looking at?' then quickly darted away holding the tongue in its teeth.

Blue laughed.

Zombies. What a dork he'd been. *Talking* zombies. Yeah, right.

He gave a mighty sniff, gobbed up a wad of green phlegm that he aimed at the mother's face, wiped his mouth with his sleeve and took a deep breath.

It was over. Big Mick was gone. Life went on. He had to saddle up, kick some arse. And God help anyone who got in his way. He knew his foul mood was not going to lift. He should be with Maxie right now. They should have been safely home at the museum yesterday. That was all he wanted. He missed her more than ever. Wanted with all his soul to get back to her, to hold on to her.

   Maxie.

74

'This is why we should never have come here, Maxie.' Maeve was pacing up and down anxiously, like an animal in a cage. She was in the sick-bay, where Maxie was sitting next to the unconscious body of Cameron. Cameron had a wad of cotton wool taped to his neck. He looked pale and feverish, his eyes twitching behind his closed lids. Every now and then he would moan and shift in the bed. And then he would become still again and Maxie would wipe his forehead and feel his pulse.

The only other occupant of the room was Robbie, who was still sleeping in there. He'd recovered from his exhaustion of the previous day and was looking healthy and cheerful. He'd offered to show Maxie his stitches. Said he looked like something out of a horror film. A monster crudely stitched together from spare body parts.

Maxie hadn't taken him up on his offer.

'We should have left London when we had the chance,' said Maeve. 'Not followed that liar Jester into the centre of town.'

'Maybe.' Maxie didn't really want to join in this conversation. She'd had it too many times before with Maeve and right now all she could think about was Cameron. Scared that it was her fault Paul had sliced his neck open.

The thing was she had no idea whether it had happened before or after she'd kicked the candle over.

'We should have gone to the countryside,' said Maeve. 'It's crazy living in the city. In the country we can grow food. We can defend ourselves from the grown-ups. There's nowhere for them to hide out there. Round here there are thousands and thousands of buildings. We can never search them all. Go to the country and we can build a fort or something. Find somewhere to live. We'll have to do it one day. The food the grown-ups left behind is going to run out sooner or later. Then what? We can't eat houses, we can't eat bricks.'

'It wasn't a grown-up who did this, though, was it?' said Maxie, feeling Cameron's forehead. He'd lost a lot of blood, though luckily the knife had missed his artery. 'It was a kid like us,' she went on. 'We don't always know who the enemy is. We all thought that as long as the grown-ups were the enemy we didn't have to worry about anything else. But think about it, Maeve. A bare lot of us have been killed by grown-ups, but just as many have been wiped out by disease. Arran was shot by an arrow fired by that posh girl Sophie. Freak died in the squatter camp. Josh and Joel were killed by diseased monkeys, for God's sake. And the last few deaths here. As far as we know, it was Paul. A boy.'

'Yeah, but he had a lot of help from the grown-ups he let out.'

'And what would have happened if we hadn't come here?' said Maxie. 'A lot more kids would have died.'

'Including me probably,' said Robbie from across the room.

'Exactly,' said Maxie. 'They need you here.'

'Oh, I can play at being a doctor,' said Maeve. 'But to be honest, I don't hardly know any more than anyone else.

Certainly no more than that geeky Einstein kid. Once he's back I won't be needed here at all.'

'*If* he comes back,' said Maxie gloomily.

'Are you worried about them, Maxie?' Maeve sat down finally, her rant over.

'What do *you* think?'

'They'll come back. And then what? Are you happy here?'

'Happy enough. I don't know when I've last really been happy. Maybe talking to Blue in the sick-bay back at the palace. It was quiet there. We could pretend that nothing existed outside those four walls. That we didn't have to worry about anything. That we didn't have to be scared.'

'You don't want to come with us then?'

'Us? What d'you mean?'

'I've been talking to some of the other kids here,' said Maeve. 'It's not just me feels this way. There's a few of us want to go. Some of the younger ones like Ella and Monkey-Boy are freaked out by this place and, let's face it, there's not enough food to go round. We'll be doing everyone else a favour.'

'You can't go, Maeve.'

'I can.' Maeve stood up. 'And I will.'

Cameron writhed in the bed, his legs thrashed under the sheets and he whimpered.

'Is he going to be all right?' said Maxie.

'I don't bloody know,' Maeve snapped, sounding very tired. 'As I say, Maxie, I'm not a doctor. I've had enough of this. Just keep checking his temperature. If you can get him to drink some water as well . . .' She paused, looking down at Cameron in his bed. 'He's got as much chance as the rest of us.'

75

'Something's not right,' said Blue and the group stopped.

The doors of the church were standing open.

Something was *definitely* not right.

Blue told everyone to quickly get under cover and they hurried off the path and into the trees. Ollie settled in next to Blue, crouching low behind a stump, Ebenezer with him.

'You've got good eyesight,' said Blue. 'Can you see anything?'

Ollie stared hard at the church, looking for any clues as to what might have happened. Of course there could always be a perfectly innocent explanation. The kids might have had to come out to do something, or . . .

Who was he kidding? Blue was right – something was off. They could all sense it, fine-tuned as they were to pick up any signs of danger. A crow flapped down from the tower and disappeared behind the church. Ollie looked up. There was nobody there. No look-out.

It wasn't as if anyone was running around screaming. It was spookily quiet. Ollie scanned the church again, then the churchyard. What was wrong?

'There,' he said at last, pointing.

'What?'

'Back over by those buildings, those shed things.'

'What am I looking for?'

'I can see it too,' said Ebenezer. 'A body, I think.'

'That's just made my day,' said Blue and he muttered something filthy under his breath.

'Can you see what sort of body?' he added. 'A kid? A grown-up?'

'All I can tell you is it's not moving.'

Now Einstein joined them.

'Why have we stopped? What's going on?'

'There's a body over there,' said Blue.

'Dead?'

'Well, I hardly think it's sunbathing, is it?' said Blue.

Ollie sat down with his back to the stump, started fishing steel shot out of his pouches. The morning had started so well. Too good to be true.

Blue had got them up at sunrise. The warehouse kids had made them some beds down among the shelves, piling up mattresses and sleeping-bags and duvets. They'd kept close to each other for security. It had been dry and quiet and warm, but few of them had slept well.

They'd negotiated with the Twisted Kids about what they could take. It hadn't taken long. The girl they called the Warehouse Queen had been in charge, but she never seemed to speak, just sat there, slumped in her wheelchair throne. The other kids hovered round her and seemed to know what she was thinking without her having to say anything.

The deal they'd struck was that Einstein would be allowed to take whatever they could carry as long as they also took some of the Twisted Kids back to the museum with them. They were supposed to find out what was going

377

on in the outside world. Check that it was safe at the museum, and then, when the time was right, report back to the warehouse so the Queen could decide on their next move.

The Twisted Kids were being cautious. Patient. They'd had fifteen years to think about it, after all.

Ollie slotted the steel shot into the leather pocket on his sling. Stretched the elastic cords back then relaxed them. Testing it. It was a nervous habit. As if somehow it could have stopped working or got broken since the last time he'd used it.

'I'll go and take a closer look,' he said.

'I'll come with you,' said Ebenezer and Ollie gave him a smile of thanks.

'Me too,' said Jackson, moving up from the group of kids who were hiding behind Blue.

'Yeah, all right,' said Blue. 'That's plenty. Everyone else watch their backs. And watch our backs. Until we know what's going on, this is a hot zone.' He turned to Einstein, suddenly angry. 'Why would they open the doors?' he hissed accusingly. 'Why would they come out? We told them to stay put. They were safe in there.'

'Don't ask me,' said Einstein. 'I was with you, remember?'

'They're your kids. If they've done something stupid they've put us all in danger.'

Ollie shook his head and moved off. What was the use of arguing about it now? The only thing to do was find out what had happened and get it sorted. He and Ebenezer and Jackson crept through the trees, sticking to the shadows. He was sniffing the air, searching for that distinctive sickly, sweet-and-sour perfume of rotten adult. All he could smell was greenery, earth, a fresh new world freed from the pollution of cars and planes . . . and people . . .

It had taken them about an hour to load what they needed back at Promithios. As much as they could carry, the Warehouse Queen had said. She'd also allowed them to take three trolleys to carry it on. The new trolleys were much better than the ones they'd lugged all the way from the museum and left here at the church. They had better steering and bigger wheels with solid rubber tyres on them so were much easier to manoeuvre.

Before they'd left, the warehouse kids had all come to see them off. The Pink Surfer, with his giant elongated foot, Betty Bubble, Flubberguts, Legs, Spider Boy and the Queen, whom Monstar had carried down from the plat-form as easily as if she'd been a little baby, before fetching her wheelchair throne. And TV Boy, chatting away still, puffed up from the show he'd put on the night before.

When Blue had asked which of them was coming and who was staying behind, it was Skinner who'd been the first to step forward. He was excited, nervous, jittery. Then Fish-Face, with her wide mouth and eyes round the sides of her skull. Like the Queen, she didn't seem to say a lot. In fact Ollie wondered whether she could speak at all. And finally Trinity. Ollie didn't know whether Trinity was tech-nically a he or a she, or something plural. He didn't like to think about that third shrivelled little body sticking out of their backs. It couldn't be dead. Ollie knew that much. If a part of you died, unless it was cut out, the rest of you followed.

They'd made a peculiar procession, tramping along the road, with the trolleys piled high with boxes. Skinner couldn't walk very fast and in the end they'd sat him on one of the trolleys with his cat in a box. Fish-Face was fine but quiet, and Trinity could move surprisingly quickly. Skinner was like a little kid, pointing things out, laughing and chatting away to Achilleus and Paddy, who were pulling his trolley.

Like a mad school trip. No sign of any grown-ups. Clear skies. An empty city.

And now this . . .

Two steps forward and three steps back.

They reached the edge of the treeline and halted. Ollie's eyes hadn't stopped darting about, scanning the whole area, alert for any signs of movement. Apart from the odd bird, though, there was nothing. And with every step they got closer to the thing lying on the grass among the gravestones. He prayed it was a grown-up. The body appeared to be wrapped in something that was a dirty white. He could see bloodstains.

'What do you reckon?' he asked Ebenezer.

'I reckon it's that girl who got killed on the way here.'

'Maybe they brought the body out because it was smelling too much or something.'

'So why did they not shut the doors?'

'Should we check in the church or carry on looking out here?' whispered Jackson. 'This is all new to me.'

'Outside first,' said Ollie. 'We need to recce the whole area. We don't want to get trapped in there. Come on.'

They left the safety of the trees and ran across open ground towards the body. They jumped a low wall and threw themselves flat.

'It's Gabby,' said Jackson. They were close enough now to see that the body was indeed hers. She'd been half unwrapped from the sheet and part of her face had been bitten off. Grown-ups had been here. The question was – where were they now? And what had happened to the rest of the kids?

'Over there,' said Ebenezer and he nodded towards something. Ollie looked. At the other end of the churchyard were four grown-ups, sitting as if having a picnic. They were spattered with blood and were chewing on lumps of raw meat, tearing off ragged chunks with yellow teeth. Ollie saw that one of them was eating a hand. A small hand. A child's hand. He felt his stomach lurch and fought off a gut-kick of sickness. And then he saw that another of them, a slack-jawed father, was picking at a wound in his own leg, digging out bits of rotten flesh, sniffing them and then popping them into his mouth.

The adults hadn't spotted Ollie, Ebenezer and Jackson yet. They were too busy eating. Ollie eased himself up on to his knees and got his sling ready. It was quite a distance to shoot from here, but he hoped he could still do enough damage. He took aim and loosed a steel ball. One of the grown-ups, a bald mother, jerked her head and toppled sideways. The others ignored her, just carried on eating. Ollie fitted another ball to his sling. The second shot got the father who'd been picking at his leg right in the neck. He put a hand to his throat and stood up, looking around. The next shot took his teeth out and knocked him down. The odds were balanced. It was time to go.

The kids charged. Ebenezer had three lightweight throwing spears. They may not have been very heavy but their points were sharp, and he hurled two of them as he ran, taking down the last two grown-ups, who had finally realized, too late, that they were in danger. Then Jackson was in among them and she finished them off with her spear.

381

It was over quickly and the three kids stood there, panting and gasping with rage. There were two dead children here. Too badly mauled to be able to tell who they were.

Ebenezer collected his spears and Ollie looked for his steel shot. Of the three balls he'd fired he only found one, but in his search he found another dead child in the long grass. A boy. The crow they'd seen earlier was pecking at his eyes. Ollie shooed it away.

'That's Reece,' said Jackson. There were tears on her cheeks. 'Oh Christ, what happened here?'

'They opened the doors for some reason,' said Ollie. 'We have to find out if any of them are still alive.'

'These grown-ups were too relaxed,' said Ebenezer. 'If there was anyone else alive . . .'

'We have to look,' said Ollie.

It was vital to act fast now. Careless of any other grown-ups that might be in the area, they hurried back to where the rest of their group were still hiding among the trees.

They quickly explained the situation to Blue, whose mood turned even blacker. He stood up, his muscular body tense.

'Hello?' he yelled, striding towards the church doors. 'Hello? Anybody in there . . . ?'

There was no reply.

He turned to the rest of his group.

'What are you waiting for?' he barked. 'We're going inside.'

76

Ollie ran to catch up with Blue. He wanted to be first in. Killing the grown-ups in the churchyard hadn't been enough; he was still all churned up inside. And he couldn't bear the thought of any more kids getting hurt. He had to get inside and do it fast. If some of the museum bunch were still alive in there he was going to save them. He never fought close up, hand-to-hand. He usually held back, letting his sling do all the work for him. That's what he was best at and that's where he was most use. Now, though, he couldn't wait. He had a knife in a sheath on his belt, but he hadn't used it for a long time. The way he felt right now he could take a grown-up apart with his bare hands. An alarm was sounding in the back of his head that he tried to ignore . . .

This is how you make mistakes. How you wind up dead. Don't let your emotions get hold of you. Don't take stupid risks . . .

But he wasn't listening. He wasn't listening to anything except the blood singing in his ears and his own tangled thoughts screaming at him. Blue shouted something, but he didn't register the meaning until it was too late and the next moment, as the words 'Look out!' formed in his brain, he collided in the doorway with a father who was coming out of the church. Ollie was sent spinning, the breath knocked out of him, and he went down heavily, crashing on to his arse on the hard, cold stone of the porch. The father was still standing, though he looked slightly stunned, not understanding what was going on.

Blue had got caught up in the collision as well, and was thrown off balance, his timing out. He was squaring up to whack the father, raising his club. *Too slow.* He hadn't spotted another father coming up fast behind the first one from out of the darkness. Ollie wanted to shout a warning, but was still gasping for air, his head spinning.

Blue was going to be taken down, and it was all his fault.

Blue swung at the first father, who was ready for him and batted the club away with his arm. And then Achilleus was with them. He barged Blue aside and let the charging father run on to the point of his spear. He turned with him as he came, and twisted sideways, letting the father slide off the spear and smack head first into the ground. Achilleus hadn't finished yet. He kept moving and punched his spear into the first father. In and out in one swift movement that killed him outright and sent him tumbling down on top of the other grown-up.

Achilleus paused long enough to pull Ollie to his feet and then carried on into the church. Ollie caught his breath. Waiting. The collision had knocked some sense into him and he'd calmed down. Achilleus was way better than him at this sort of thing. Ollie fitted a shot to his sling and went in much more cautiously after him and Blue.

The first thing he noticed when he got inside was that there were other people in here. It took him a couple of seconds to make sense of it in the gloom. A bright flame of hope burned briefly. *Was it the rest of the children?* The flame died as quickly as it had flared. The people were too big. They were adults. There was a large group to the right, down by the altar, and another smaller group to the left.

There were no signs of any children.

No. That was wrong. There *were* children in here. But they weren't moving. Ollie saw that there were bodies all over the floor. Mangled and trampled.

He had paused just inside the doorway and was now pushed aside by more of his gang coming in from behind. He grabbed Ebenezer as he went past.

'We've got to slow down,' he said. 'It's not good in here.'

Ebenezer muttered a prayer and kissed the crucifix that hung on a chain around his neck.

Blue and Achilleus had already piled into the group of adults to the right. Ollie switched his attention to the smaller group, fired off a shot too quickly, without really taking aim. Ebenezer was about to throw one of his javelins when the incoming kids got in the way. This was not the right terrain for ranged weapons. There was really nothing Ollie could do now except hang back and try to stop any grown-ups who tried to make a run for it. His eyes had at last grown used to the lower light levels and he watched as Jackson cut down a pair of emaciated mothers.

He moved to a better position in the aisle and stumbled on something. It was a young girl from the museum. He hadn't known her long enough to learn her name. She looked quite peaceful, almost as if she was asleep. There was another girl lying next to her, however, whose face was screwed up in fear and pain. He knelt down to check her pulse, just in case. Nothing. She was already cold, her flesh hard and solid.

He closed his eyes, wishing he was somewhere else. Fighting back tears.

'Look out, Ollie,' Ebenezer shouted.

Ollie looked up just as three fathers came hobbling down the aisle towards him. They had got away from Jackson and were moving fast. They were very close together, as if they had their arms round each other, and then Ollie realized that the father in the middle didn't have any arms at all, and the other two only had one each. They appeared to be working as a single unit. And they'd been busy. The lower half of the face of the father in the middle was painted thick with blood and his teeth were stained pink.

As Ollie struggled to pull his knife free, someone stepped in between him and the attacking fathers.

It was Trinity.

The three fathers stopped dead in their tracks and stared, mesmerized. A hideous, distorted mirror image of Trinity.

Trinity's arms were in the air, hands extended. The middle father began to whip his head from side to side as if trying to shake something loose. The other two hissed, but wouldn't attack. And then Jackson's war party stormed over and chopped them down from behind.

Ebenezer came over to Ollie.

'That's twice you nearly bought it, Ollie,' he said. 'Maybe we should get out of here. We're just in the way.'

'Yeah.'

The fight looked to be nearly over anyway. The grown-ups, bloated from feasting on the kids, had been surprised and quickly swamped.

Ollie felt breathless and dizzy. He'd been more scared than he'd known, and the shock of finding all the kids slaughtered was getting to him. There was a stink of blood in here, and human waste, rotting flesh and fresh meat all mingled in a foul stew.

Ebenezer was right – Ollie wanted nothing more than to get out into the fresh air before he was sick. First, though, he had to check there was nobody left alive. He forced himself to stand, willing his shaky knees not to buckle. He swallowed hard and walked towards the altar. Kids were strewn everywhere, too badly injured to possibly be alive. The grown-ups had pulled the small bodies to pieces, and now they lay dead among their victims.

Ollie caught Blue's eye. For once Blue didn't look like he was too cool to care. There was a haunted look about him. Ollie knew how he was feeling. He must look the same. They'd let these kids down. Should have been here for them. Should have come back sooner. Even Achilleus looked cut up. He was stalking the church, sticking his new spear into every grown-up body and twisting it with a foul curse.

'What we gonna do?' said Ollie.

'Bring the other bodies in from outside,' said Blue. 'All of them.'

'And then what?'

'Then we'll burn this stinking place down. It's all we *can* do. Burn their bodies.'

Ollie helped Blue organize a work party and they collected anything that would burn and piled it in the middle of the church: old prayer books, the little square cushions for kneeling on, the wooden pews, the cloth off the altar. They dragged the small broken bodies close to the pile and when it was ready Blue set light to it. It was slow to catch, but in a few minutes a flame had taken.

Ollie forced himself to stay a little longer and he and Ebenezer double-checked that there weren't any survivors. The last place they looked was the tower. There was an open door at the bottom; it had been splintered and broken in. They climbed to the top of the spiral staircase and out into the light. Ollie could see some of the children down below, the ones who hadn't come into the church with the war party, sitting or standing in silence.

And a big expanse of empty grey sky.

They went back down and walked outside where Ollie found Einstein and Emily sitting on a bench with their arms round each other. Einstein looked very pale.

'All of them?' he said.

Ollie said nothing. There was nothing *to* say. He left Ebenezer and walked away from Einstein into the trees. Managed a few paces before he sank to his knees, overcome with tears. He sobbed and wailed and beat his fists in the dirt till he had no strength left. And then it was over.

He crawled to a tree and sat with his back against it, hidden from the others by the shade. There didn't seem to be any more grown-ups around out here and he didn't have the energy to look. Let someone else be responsible. He'd had enough. He emptied his mind and let it become a blank. An empty shell of nothingness.

Smoke was drifting from the church. He watched it rise up and dissolve into the sky, like a cloud of angels escaping from the earth and returning to heaven. It was the souls of those poor dead children.

He had no idea how long he'd been sitting there when he became aware of a movement nearby. Before it had even properly registered he instinctively threw himself to the side.

A father was standing there. Tall and long-limbed. His arms were wet with blood up to the elbows. His face wasn't too badly affected by the disease. He had a few spots and had lost most of his hair, but otherwise looked fairly normal. He was wearing a long coat and Ollie saw that he had several small animals hanging from his belt, which was tight around their necks. Cats, a rabbit and a squirrel. Some were still alive and writhing. Most were dead. One cat was bent double, its back legs up and clawing at the belt, its eyes bulging from their sockets.

Three times. Three times in one day Ollie had been caught by surprise. It wasn't good.

The father smiled. He had something in his hand. He swung it at Ollie, who scrambled away on his back and then bumped into another tree. He used it to shuffle upright against. The father swung again and Ollie couldn't get out of the way in time. The blow took him in the side of the head, stunning him temporarily. The next thing he knew the father's arms were crushing him and he could feel his hot breath on his neck. Whatever happened he couldn't let the bastard bite him. He swung round, thumping the man into the tree and then kicked at his legs with his heel. It was enough to make the man loosen his grip and Ollie was able to duck down and out of the circle of his arms.

Ollie didn't let up. He had to go on the attack. He grabbed at the man's throat, locked his fingers into the skin and pressed hard, at the same time pushing forwards so that the man collapsed backwards with Ollie on top of him.

Ollie made sure he didn't let go. He could feel the animals on the man's belt struggling, trapped between their two bodies. The father was gurgling and scratching at Ollie's hands, but Ollie could feel him weakening. He had dropped whatever it was he'd been holding and Ollie saw it lying there. A large, leather-bound book, stained with bloody handprints.

He made a quick decision. Let go with one hand, picked

up the book and brought it crashing down on the man's forehead. The man gulped and jerked and went still. Now Ollie was finally able to get his knife out and he stabbed it upwards at his face, ramming it through the roof of his mouth and into his brain.

It was over.

Gasping and shaking, Ollie stood up and kicked the body, then untangled the cat. It hopped away, one of its legs broken. It probably wouldn't live much longer, but at least it was free.

Ollie left his knife where it was. He didn't want to look at the man again. Didn't want to touch him. He could get another knife. He also couldn't face the other kids yet. If he didn't have to talk about what he'd just done then it hadn't happened. He moved away and sat down again. This had been a private thing, between him and the man.

He looked at the book. Recognized it. It was the one that the little girl, Lettis, had been writing in. This book had been precious to her. She wouldn't have let it out of her sight unless . . .

Ollie looked over at the church. He could see flames at the windows now. Her body would be among all the others in there. By the end of the day it would be ashes. This book would be all that was left of her.

It was a journal, wasn't it? It struck him that it might contain some clues to what had happened here. He opened it and read the first line from the final entry . . .

This is the journal of Lettis Slingsbury.

He flipped through the pages and felt a tightening in his throat every time he saw her name, the way she kept repeating it, each time smaller and scratchier than the last. He worked back, found what she'd written about being left behind at the church, and then the discussions about burying the body. As he got to the part where the kids had got attacked outside, the writing became messier and more scrawled.

Finally he got back to where he'd started. The last entry in the book.

77

This is the journal of Lettis Slingsbury. I am writing my name in the hope that it sticks. That it is a mark of me and my existence. I think this might be the last thing I write, so I hope someone finds it and takes it back to <u>Chris Marker</u> at the museum. He will want it for the official records. And I hope it will explain everything that happened to us and why.

Maybe if my bones are still here with the book whoever finds this could bury me and say a prayer for my soul. Even though we used to go to church I've never really thought much about GOD before and praying and my SOUL, but I suppose being with some-one who really strongly believes in God (that is Jasmine) has made me think about that sort of thing properly for the first time. It was Jasmine that gave me the idea of asking someone to pray for me when I'm dead. She said that prayer is very powerful and as we were in a church she was praying a lot obviously. Which is something that I have written before.

I don't know. Maybe there is no God, but if there is one I would like to be with him when this is over. I know I shouldn't be writing so much about myself *and my thoughts and feelings, they are not important really. But there's no one else, to be honest. No one else to write about, that is. There is only me now. I wanted this to be a great adventure. Something to put in the history books to show how we survived after the disease. Chris says the history of our lives is important. Well, I suppose this is the history of my life. Even though it was just a short one.*

So this is what happened. I hope you will read it and remember me.

Hold tight to the book.

Some of it is written quickly so it might not be well written. I have looked at my last entry and it is just a scribble, not properly written at all. It was dark and I was on the top of the steeple and desperate so I didn't properly write about what had been happening. My last proper entry was when I was writing about the banging on the door and would we open it and was it our friends or was it sickos.

I wish now we had kept that door shut. When we opened it we let all the evil of the world into the church. But we couldn't leave it shut because our friends were out there and they were being attacked by sickos and we could hear their shouts and their screams. So you see we had no choice. Still, though, I wish we had kept it shut. I know it is a bad thing to say and maybe I won't get to heaven after all for thinking it and writing it. It is a selfish thing to have in your mind. I am only thinking of myself. Only it wasn't just me, was it? There were five of us still in the church then and four outside. Those five would all still be alive. The four outside would have been killed anyway, whatever happened. They were doomed as soon as they went outside. I wish I didn't have to write this. I have to tell the truth, though. Chris says we must always tell the truth and the truth is that I wish I wish I wish we had kept those doors closed.

It was Aiyshah who opened them. She said she had to, she said we couldn't leave our friends to die out there like dogs, and she opened the door and there was Jasmine and Reece on the doorstep in the porch all covered in red blood and unable to stand up. We went to pull them in and that was when there was a big thump, a loud bang as it were, and a rushing dark shape. Actually two dark shapes, the shapes of men. Two sickos came running over and barged the doors open, bashing into them as loud as anything. I screamed and someone else screamed and I was the first to run. I let go of Jasmine, who I had been holding up, and I ran back into the church towards the altar. I cannot fight. I am too scared to fight. I was almost too scared to run, my legs didn't seem to do what I was telling them to do. I was all wobbly and feeble and shaking. There were two of us running together and we got to the altar and there was nowhere else to go.

There were two sickos in the church, the two big fathers who had barged into the door. One of them had all animals tied to his belt. Cats and things. And it made me think, not then but after when I had time to think and there was nothing else to do except think. I thought it was interesting that sickos don't always only just eat us children. They eat other things as well. They will eat anything. Whatever they can get *their hands on. They do not eat us because they hate us, they eat us because we are food, the only fresh food they can catch. Except maybe cats and rats and small animals. In the same way that I didn't used to hate cows and chickens and, when I was smaller, I had a book about a farm and some farm animals I used to play with. I didn't hate them, I loved them, and I knew we ate animals, like the cows and chickens, and that's all we are to the sickos – cows and chickens.*

The big father with animals on him came down quickly, his arms swinging to the sides, and we ran this way and that, trying to get away. More sickos had come in through the door as well. Luckily the animal man got hold of Aiyshah instead of me. I say luckily: it was lucky for me not lucky for Aiyshah. I didn't look what he did to her and a bad part of me thought that it served her right for opening the door, although I knew I didn't really mean it. I liked Aiyshah and I was just relieved that I hadn't been caught. Now I feel ashamed to have thought that and wish the father had got me instead of her. I don't deserve to be alive. I feel sorry for Aiyshah and wish she was still alive, but that was the last I saw of her. I could hear her, though, moaning and wailing for a long time as the father did awful things to her.

While he was distracted I got away and ran to the other end of the church. I was not alone. Scott and Caspar were there and there were also three horrible sickos. They were sort of joined together as if they were one horrible creature. They only had two arms to share between them and the one in the middle had no arms at all and he just used his mouth to attack.

He would tilt his head back then bring it biting down forward with his top teeth sticking out. I saw him get Caspar this way. Caspar was too weak to defend himself. He couldn't run.

When things were normal and life was ordinary I used to like playing a zombie game on my dad's iPhone. It was called Plants vs. Zombies. It was good and fun and quite hard and quite funny as well. You had to put like special plants in the garden and they shot seeds or threw things at the advancing zombies and when you hit one a bit fell off, like their arms. And that's what the three sickos reminded me of. The middle father had already lost his arms and now he was all teeth and used his head in a bobbing forwards way.

As well as the normal zombies in the game, there was a zombie with a ladder who always had that same action when he had used up his ladder – bobbing forward and cutting down with his teeth. That was always the scariest zombie in the game cos he was quite fast as well. He looked like an old man and he bobbed down and down again with his teeth. That's what the real sicko did to Caspar, bobbed down so that his top set of teeth jabbed into the top of Caspar's head, while the other two held him still with one arm each, and every time he bit him, Caspar screamed. There was blood all down his face and his hair was sticking up where the man was biting it.

All around me now were screams and shouts and the sickos were going crazy, like foxes in a chicken run that I read about when I was interested in farms. Foxes are wicked and kill chickens for fun without wanting to eat them.

I was still running around like a mad thing and everywhere I turned there was a horror, another sicko attacking another child. I was sick with worry and fear and panic so that I didn't know what to do. In the end I saw a doorway. It was the doorway up to the tower. The steeple where Daryl had been. I didn't know where he was now, I hadn't seen him since the sickos had got in, or been let in I should say.

I ran to the door and hoped it wasn't locked. It wasn't and I got it open and I looked around to see if there was anyone else I could let in. There was only Scott that I could see. The others had all been taken.

I called out to him. 'Over here,' I called, and he saw me and a look of hope came into his face and I smiled with happiness and he started to run and I called, 'Come on!' and I thought I would have a friend with me behind the door. He didn't in the end get far because the three fathers got to him and the bad one brought his horrible teeth down, crack, on to his head, and he fell over and I didn't see him any more so I shut the door and found a key in it and I locked it fast as anything. Which meant I had locked out any of my friends who might still be alive. There was nothing else I could do, though, I hope you understand that.

It was dark in there, and there were winding stairs going up to the top of the steeple. I went up slowly and carefully and nearly jumped out of my skin when someone grabbed me. I gave a big scream, but it was only Daryl, though. He was panicked and crying and very relieved to see me, but disappointed that I was only one person and a girl and quite small. We both asked each other what we were going to do over and over, what are we going to do? I said the others must be back soon and they would save us, and he said yes, they would save us and we would be OK. I wish now that he had been right. The others have abandoned us, though. We don't matter to them and we didn't know it at the time, we still had some hope.

We went carefully to the top of the stairs and out on to the top of the steeple and looked down. There were several sickos outside. They had killed our friends and we didn't want to look at what they were doing. And it was getting dark now and I realized everything had taken longer than I had thought. Everything seemed very dark and bleak and there was no hope for us. That was when I wrote my last entry. On the top as the dark came on us. It was a sort of prayer for rescue. Praying that the others would come back.

Downstairs we could hear the sickos banging on the door. I could imagine the one with no arms banging his head on it and I knew nothing would stop him. He wouldn't ever stop until he had broken through.

And time passed slowly. So I was up on top of the steeple with Daryl, and the sickos were banging and banging and battering at the door, thump, thump, all night long, they wouldn't stop. And Daryl went down to see if it was all right, if the door was breaking, and I looked up at the stars in the sky and the way that they went on forever and it made me feel small and that my problems down here were small and to a starman I would hardly even exist. One moment this would make me feel not so scared and unhappy, because my problems didn't matter, and then I would feel bad because I thought I won't exist any more and nobody will know about me. I am still Lettis Slingsbury now, but when I am dead what will I be then? I won't still be me, I will be nothing.

Daryl came back and said the door was strong. He wanted to stay up on the top outside. It got cold at night, though, and we had to go inside. I didn't like to because the noise was louder in there. There was the banging and also a scratching and snuffling like animals trying to get in. Daryl remembered he had a small candle in his pocket and we lit it and it made it not so bad on the stairs, but still we couldn't sleep. We held on to each other for warmth and it was warm and not so bad, but we were crying. Sometimes it was me crying and sometimes it was Daryl and sometimes it was both of us.

In the deep and dark of the night, when all was lonely and lost, I slept a little bit I was so exhausted and also weak from hunger and thirst. We didn't have anything to eat or drink with us, but we did have the candle and a torch I used when the candle burned away, but I didn't leave it on to waste the batteries. When I woke up I was more wide awake than ever and Daryl was sleeping. That was when I had a lot of thoughts about me and my life and the sickos and my farm and praying and all the other stuff I have written down.

We had this RE teacher at school called Mister Pinker who was always trying to get us to think about things. He had a game he played where he would use what he called thinkazoids. These were things that were supposed to make us think. He'd say, 'OK, here's today's thinkazoid! Did Adam and Eve have belly buttons?' Or something like that. And there was one thinkazoid he did that I never really got at the time, but I've thought about it since and maybe I do get it now. He said if a tree fell down in a forest, and there was nobody there to hear it, would it make a sound? I think what he meant was that sounds only become sounds when we hear them, otherwise it's just waves that go through the air. So if there were no ears there to pick up the sound waves then is there any sound at all? Something like that. If things happen, and there's nobody there to see it, do they happen at all?

Well, I've been thinking about this book I'm writing and I have a thinkazoid of my own. If you write a book and nobody reads it, does the book exist? Stories in books, characters and things, you know, like places and monsters or whatever the writer has made up and written down, they only really come alive when we read them. Otherwise it's just a jumble of squiggles on bits of paper. So I'm writing this book now, but if nobody ever reads it does that mean it never really existed, and nobody will ever know my story? Does it mean that I never really existed? I think it's really sad to think about all the books there are in the world now, many millions and millions of them, that are sitting there in people's empty homes, and in bookshops and libraries and on miles and miles and miles of shelves, but nobody will ever read any of them again and all those people in the books won't exist any more. Like me.

In the end the only way I could forget about what

was happening and the shapes in the dark and the smell of the sickos at the door and the nasty little noises they made, sniffing and sniggering and scratching and moaning and whining like animals, was to read my journal and to write this all down using my torch to see. It gave me a little hope.

And now I have finished writing and there isn't anything else. Eventually the sickos will get through the door and nobody will come to rescue us. I am alone and I am going to die and I am scared. If I was braver I would throw myself off the tower, but I'm not brave enough. I am not brave at all, like I have said here before, so first I will hide the book so that the sickos do not get it and then I will sit and wait. I have finished writing and there isn't anything else.

78

The next page was blank. Ollie looked up from the book and over to the church, where poor Lettis had lived her last terrifying moments. The fire was bright inside and smoke was coming out of the door and between the tiles on the roof. He pictured the shattered door to the tower where Lettis had been hiding. Didn't want to think about exactly what might have happened to her. The pain and terror. Well, *he would* remember her. He would make sure of that. She had claimed not to be brave, but just to sit and write those words was the bravest thing he knew. He would keep the journal safe and return it to Chris Marker at the museum.

Blue was herding everyone together, getting ready to move out. Ollie would have to join them in a minute or risk being left behind. There was one thing he wanted to do first, though. He kept a pencil in his backpack along with various other useful items. He fished it out. He would write an entry in the book while the events of the day were still fresh in his mind. Something about Lettis and what they had found here. Why they were late turning up. It would mean a lot to Chris Marker.

He flicked to the last page of writing and turned it over. Looked at the two fresh blank pages . . . and then he spotted something. More writing, showing faintly through the paper. There was another entry. In her hurry Lettis had missed a page. He hadn't read to the end of the story. Ollie quickly flipped over and began to read.

79

This is the journal of Lettis Slingsbury. I don't know what day it is. Daryl is gone and I am in a tiny cupboard at the bottom of the stairs, scrumpled up and crammed in like a piece of old rubbish.

What happened was when it got light we realized that the sickos weren't banging on the door any more. We thought, or we hoped, that they had got bored and left us alone, gone back to their holes to sleep. Daryl and I went back up on to the top of the steeple. We peered out as light came over the land. The sickos had gone. All was quiet. Had they really left us all alone? Might we be able to escape? These were the questions we were asking.

We went down to the door and listened, too scared to open it. And we heard someone moving about, shuffling and stealthy. There was still someone there. It might be a child like us, but as I just said we were too scared to open the door and find out. I remembered what had happened when Aiyshah had opened the church door and let the sickos in. How the animal man had got hold of her and how she had screamed and screamed.

We talked about what to do and then Daryl said, 'We can't stay here. We'll starve to death or the sickos will wake up and start breaking the door down again.' We could see that the door was all cracked and broken and nearly broken in. 'I am going to climb down from the tower,' he said. 'And make a run for it.'

'It's too dangerous out there,' I explained, but Daryl wouldn't listen, he was wild-eyed. And I knew I couldn't stop him and part of me secretly wanted him to go anyway so that he might get help. I was being selfish again so maybe I didn't try very hard to really stop him. He had a map which showed the way to the place where the others had gone. It looked like it wasn't very far on the map. He would be all alone, though, out there, with no knowledge of if there were other sickos around. He was brave, but also a little crazy. He was desperate.

I watched him climb down the tower. Going carefully. There were sticking out stones and things to put his hands and feet on and it didn't take him long. He was a good climber. When he was at the bottom he looked around and then ran over to the gate. He looked back up at me and gave me a thumbs up and waved and I waved back and he took three more steps and a father came quickly out of the trees.

It was the animal man with the belt of cats, striding on long legs, and when Daryl tried to run the three sickos joined together came from the other way by a wall, spreading out their arms wide, and Daryl didn't have a chance and I didn't watch and I put my hands over my ears so that I wouldn't hear and I came inside and down the stairs and knew that all was lost and that I was truly alone now and I found this little cupboard, hidden under the stairs at the bottom, so I came in and I used my torch to write this. I will keep the book with me so that it is safe. I do not want the sickos to get their hands on it. They will find my skeleton with the book held in its bony hands for all time. And I will go to sleep and when I wake up it will all be over one way or the other way.

NEW ENTRY. I have been thinking, as I sit here, that if I stay hidden nobody will ever find the book and know what happened. It could be years and years and years. The church might crumble to dust around me. I want the rest of the children who went on ahead to find the book so that they can understand what happened. Chris Marker must know the truth.

What if they came to the church to rescue me and they didn't know I was here? I have come up with a new plan. Even though it is the most precious thing to me in the world I will take my journal to the top of the tower and throw it over the edge to somewhere that it will be seen so that when the others come back they will find it and they will know about me and more importantly what happened. Then I will come back to this cupboard and I will close the door and I will curl up again like this, like a kitten, and I will close my eyes and that will be that. Goodbye.

80

Ollie jumped to his feet. Blue was already moving the kids towards the pathway where the three trolleys stood waiting. Ollie ran over to him, shouting and waving his arms.

'We can't leave yet!'

Blue stopped and turned. 'Where you been, Ollie?' He looked angry.

'We have to go back in,' said Ollie, out of breath and gabbling.

'Back in where?'

'In the church. She's still there. She might still be alive.'

'Who you talking about?'

'Lettis, the girl, that girl from the museum, the one who was, like, writing that diary thing.' Ollie was falling over his words. 'She's hiding in there.'

Ollie shoved the book at Blue, who looked at it, confused and still angry. He wanted to be away.

'You can't go back in there,' he said. 'Look at the place. You'll be fried, man. We got to go.'

Ollie looked at the church. Blue was right. Smoke was pouring from the door now, thick and black. One of the windows had cracked and flames were stabbing out of it.

Ollie felt a terrible sick feeling of panic chewing at his guts. His head was pounding. *Was it too late?* He had to do something. *The tower?* What about the tower? If Daryl had managed to climb down it then maybe Ollie could climb up it.

'Wait,' he pleaded with Blue. 'Just *wait*, please. I can do it.'

'Ollie . . .'

Ollie ignored him, grabbed Ebenezer and pulled him away from the group back towards the church, frantically trying to explain to him what was going on, handing him first his backpack and then his jacket. Thank God Ebenezer got it and when they reached the tower he gave Ollie a leg-up so that he could get a grip on a run of stonework that stuck out about three metres off the ground. Ollie wasn't sure how he did it (he was running on adrenalin, his mind making choices before he was aware of it), but he pulled himself up and was soon scaling the wall, climbing by feel and instinct, his fingers and toes finding holds where none appeared to be, his fingernails tearing and his fingertips quickly cut and bleeding. At one point he slipped and nearly fell, found himself dangling by one hand, but somehow he located a foothold and carried on up. Luckily the tower wasn't very tall, only seven or eight metres in all, and he steadily worked his way to the top, Ebenezer shouting to him from below to be careful.

No. He wasn't being careful. He was in a mad rush again, acting too fast, fuelled by dread and fear. Not for himself. For the girl. In there somewhere. This was not in character for Ollie. He always held back, weighed things up, picked the enemy off from a distance. But not now, when the enemy was time itself. If there was any chance he could save Lettis, he would. Right now she was the most important thing in the world.

Just one . . . If he could save just one of them . . .

But three times today he'd nearly died from being careless.

Not a fourth. There wouldn't be a fourth time. He'd make it. He'd be OK. He'd save her.

And then his hands were scrabbling over the wall at the top of the tower, getting a grip and pulling his body up and over. He flopped down on to the flagstones, panting and gasping.

That was the easy part.

There was smoke drifting up through the doorway in the little circular turret at the corner of the tower. The steeple was acting like a chimney, sucking the smoke out of the church, even though they had lit the fire down at the other end by the altar. Ollie had read enough about fires to know that the smoke would kill you before the flames ever got to you. He tugged off his jumper and wrapped it round the lower half of his face, covering his nose and mouth. He had a knitted cap stuffed into the back pocket of his jeans and he jammed it on, leaving just a narrow strip for his eyes. He walked over to the doorway and peered inside. The smoke was making it very hard to see anything. He backed away then leant over the wall.

'Lob me up my torch,' he called down to Ebenezer. Ebenezer was a brilliant shot, and his throwing arm was strong. He threw the torch up so that it reached its apex right in front of Ollie, who simply had to pluck it out of the air. It was fully wound up and he snapped on the beam. Returned to the smoke-filled doorway.

He paused a moment and then filled his lungs with as much air as they would hold. If he could hold his breath all the way down and back he'd be safe. He plunged inside.

Smoke was climbing the stairs in a thick column. His eyes were already stinging. He forced himself down the spiral staircase, feeling his way, as, despite the torch, he couldn't see anything. Round and round he went, down and down, his lungs starting to burn. If he slipped and fell he doubted he'd ever get up again. And then he stumbled as he reached the bottom and there were no more steps. He crashed into the wall. Steadied himself. Chest tight. Eyes sore and watery.

Where was the cupboard Lettis had written about? Where was Lettis?

He groped around, feeling the brickwork, trying to get the layout into his head. It was under the stairs, she had said. Then he discovered a pocket of clear air that the circulating smoke was avoiding as it went into a swirling eddy before being sucked up the stairway.

Ollie moved into the clear patch, emptied his lungs with a groan and risked taking a breath. The air tasted sour and it clawed at his throat, but he held it in, hoping it would be enough to take him back up to the top.

And then he saw it. A small cupboard door, tucked under the stairs, too small for a person to fit through, surely. There was nothing else down here, though, and his air supply was rapidly running out. Already his lungs were filling with carbon dioxide again.

He yanked the door open and shone his torch inside. There *was* someone there – folded up in a bundle of skinny arms and legs. It was her. She stared at him with dead eyes . . . He was too late. She wasn't moving.

And then she blinked. Coughed as the smoke got to her.

Ollie took hold of her and dragged her out, scraping her knees on the edge of the door frame. He crushed her face to his chest to protect her from the smoke.

'Come on,' he croaked, letting the air out of his lungs. 'We're going up.'

And up they went, as the lack of oxygen squeezed his head and made it ache appallingly, his vision swimming, his legs weak, not sure if he could make it, Lettis a deadweight in his arms.

He tripped. Hit the wall again. Wanted to stop. Let go. Sleep. No. Not yet. Go up. Carry her up. Don't think about it. Keep moving . . .

And then there was fresh air, daylight. He let Lettis slip out of his arms and collapsed on to all fours, took in a great gulp of smoky air, coughed, retched, fell flat as a surge of dizziness shook him. He fought it off, spat the sick from his mouth and turned to Lettis, who was lying beside him, unmoving, her knees gripped tight to her chest, her face blank.

'Are you all right,' he wheezed, every word an agony as they scraped at his throat. 'Are you alive?'

Lettis still didn't move. She looked like she was staring at something a million miles away. But then Ollie felt a movement – something warm touching his hand – and her fingers twined round his and he broke down into tears of relief.

81

'You let them live? You useless piece of bogweed. You stinking snivel. You turdburger . . .'

'There were too many of them. The new ones. That girl.' Paul was curled up in a ball on the floor at the top of the tower, right up under the pointed wooden roof, where the pigeons lived.

'A girl?' Boney-M shrieked. 'A bloody girl? You let a girl beat you down? You are worse than I thought. You are the scrapings off the bottom of a sewage worker's boot.'

'Oh, shut up. I've got a headache. I can't handle this now.'

'You've always got a headache, because you're a *girl*. And girls always have headaches. Little Pauline heady-achey. Little Pauline pissypants. Little Pauline . . .'

'Shut up, I said! Shut up – shut up – shut up!'

He'd had to come up here to get away from the stench. Samira's body was liquefying, turning black and melting into the floorboards, covered in blossoms of green mould, crawling with flies and maggots. The decay had accelerated after he'd cut her stomach open. He should never have done that. Let all that foulness out. Released the bacteria that lived in there. He couldn't eat any more of her and he was getting hungrier and hungrier. He needed to eat again and

Boney-M wasn't helping. All the filthy bird did was screech into his ear, his voice drilling into Paul, burning through his eardrum like acid. Mashing and mangling his brain so that he couldn't think straight.

He itched all over, wanted to scratch his skin off, to let the heat out somehow, wanted to drive a spike into his brain and release the poison that was pooling inside his skull. The air pressed down on him; even the light seemed to want to get at him. It was drilling its way in through every window, every crack and gap. It hurt his eyes just thinking about it.

There was only one thought that eased the pain. The thought of fresh meat.

He had to go down there again. He had to find one he could catch, just a little one, even at the risk of being spotted. Because he had to eat and the only thing he could imagine eating was one of them. The thought was like a warm, safe spot deep in his heart. Deep in his guts.

He'd been so close last night. If that stupid girl hadn't stopped him he could have dragged Cameron up here. Fresh meat. That's all he wanted . . .

'Fresh meat.'

'What's that? Did little Pauline pickle-dickle say something?'

'I need fresh meat.'

'Well. What's stopping you, darling?'

'Nothing.'

Paul sat up and licked his dry lips. He could hear Boney-M still shouting, but couldn't see him, and it wasn't only him: there were other voices, distant and small, hundreds of them, thousands, yammering, buzzing like bees, humming bees, jabbering out their nonsense.

413

He wished they would all just go away and leave him alone.

'SHUT UP!'

He lifted his knife and slashed at the stale air, stabbing ghosts. He looked at the blade, flashing and shimmering. Held it close to his face. Sniffed it, taking in the sick smell of death. There was a faint red smear on the steel; he licked it off, tasting the harsh, metallic tang of the knife and the warm, electric jolt of iron in the blood sizzling through his tongue. Electric. Plugging him back in. Ready for action.

He moved slowly and carefully, out of the tower room, down the stairs and out across the roof. He crossed over the blue-grey expanse of tiles, loping along, stopping now and then to squint through the dirty windows, to catch sight of one of them – down there. Fresh meat.

He was a hunter. And if he didn't kill he wouldn't live.

82

'*We are the Twisted Kids. Twisted gits, the gifted twits!*
We are the screwed-up, twisted kids.
Our life's a joke, our legs are crap,
We try to walk but slip and slap.
You wouldn't want to ask us round for tea . . .'

Skinner was up on the trolley, singing at the top of his voice.

They'd sat Lettis next to him. She wouldn't walk, wouldn't talk, wouldn't react to anything. She just sat there, with that hopeless stare. Since she'd climbed down from the tower they'd had no other response out of her. She hadn't even blinked when she'd seen Skinner and his friends from the warehouse, Trinity and Fish-Face. And now Skinner was trying to cheer her up.

It didn't seem to be helping.

Skinner was enjoying himself, though. His voice rang out and was the only thing any of them could hear as they plodded along the wide expanse of the M4.

At first Ollie had wished he would be quiet. They needed to be able to listen for any signs of danger, to know if anything, or anyone, was nearby. And Skinner's out-of-tune singing would be heard by every living thing

415

for miles around. But he'd got used to it, and was quite enjoying it now. At least Skinner's singing meant they were still alive. Not beaten. Despite losing half their number.

God. What would the others say when they got back? Would they understand? It was worse for the museum crew, of course. They'd lost a lot of friends. Ollie had hardly known them really. And he hadn't really been that close to Big Mick and Jake either, when it came down to it. They were with Blue. They'd only all linked up a couple of weeks ago. And . . .

Ollie grunted. Told himself not to be such a jerk. He knew what he was doing: trying to distance himself from what had happened so that it didn't hurt so much.

He was walking along with Fish-Face and Trinity. Now and then Trinity mumbled a few words of the song and chuckled, but Fish-Face was as silent as Lettis. Ollie didn't know what to make of her. She seemed so distant; her peculiar face was like a mask. Ollie couldn't read her. Didn't know if she was sad or happy, bored or what. Trinity seemed chatty enough, though.

Ollie had found out that Trinity actually had several names. As a whole, 'they' were called Trinity, but the boy part called himself Trey and the girl part called herself Trio. Three names. That was fitting. Ollie didn't ask if the thing on their back had a name.

Trinity had four legs, two normal-sized ones and two short ones that they kept tucked up under their belly. The bodies were joined down the side, and as far as Ollie could tell they only had three arms. Trey and Trio bickered with each other the whole time and Ollie couldn't imagine what it must be like being permanently joined to someone like that. They worked efficiently enough, though.

Skinner was standing up now, the better to sing.

'He always this noisy?' Ollie asked as Skinner launched into a new verse.

'Yeah,' said the girl, Trio. 'He gets bursts of, like, happiness, and then he gets long periods of being, like, down. And when he's happy he sings. He's not being disrespectful.'

'We're not used to other people,' said the boy, Trey. 'We never mixed. Never met anyone outside of our group. So we . . . well, we probably don't feel about other people as deeply as we should. We're quite turned in on ourselves. Only care about each other.'

'Yeah,' said Trio. 'It's like we know it was a bummer what happened to your friends, but . . . well, we're free at least.'

'It's OK,' said Ollie. 'I hardly knew them, to be honest. Doesn't really make it any better, though.'

'Was it *bad* in there?' said Trio.

'Some of the worst I've seen,' said Ollie. 'We should have been there for them. Gonna have nightmares about this one long term. It was like falling. Out of control. I nearly lost it. Three times. I was attacked three times. Three times I nearly died. I was stupid.'

'You'll be safe now then,' said Trey.

'How do you mean?'

'It's the rule, haven't you heard? The rule of three. Everything happens in threes. That's how the universe rolls.'

'Yeah? Not sure I've heard that one.'

'He talks a lot of bollocks,' said Trio. 'He made the rule up. As a way of explaining how we got like this. Like we're important somehow. Part of God's plan. Yeah, right, good one. *Special*. Massive cock-up more like.'

Ollie glanced down at Trinity's legs, was impressed at how they worked together, not tripping over each other, in step. The two kids fitted round each other very well. If they even were an 'each other' and not one person . . .

'We're not a cock-up,' said Trey. 'We're part of a grand tradition. The three wise men, the three musketeers, three blind mice, the three bears, the three little pigs, and us – the holy Trinity.'

'Oh, stop there,' said Trio. 'You're getting embarrassing, my little appendage. We have never even *begun* to be holy. Don't ever say that, Trey. And don't say *that* either.'

'Say what?'

'What you were just thinking. That was a well stupid thing to think.'

'Fair enough.'

'Trey is full of it,' said Trio. 'But he's right in one thing. We've spent too long by ourselves. We've had too long to think about stuff and now he's making up mystical hogwash like it's his own stupid religion. The mighty *rule of three*.'

'I won't be the only one to make up a religion,' said Trey. 'You'll see. There'll be three of us. Always comes in threes.'

'He's just saying that, you know,' said Trio. 'He's got no actual proof.'

'Don't listen to her,' Trey protested. 'It's the God's own. I've observed it, and *you* will too. Everything works in threes. One-two-three O'Leary. So today is your lucky day. Three is your magic number. Three times you fell into the fire and three times you were rescued from the flames.

So, because you've nearly died three times, it can't happen again.'

'Yeah,' said Trio. 'Next time you'll actually die.'

'Cheers, that's a nice thought,' said Ollie.

'Oh my gosh. This is awkward. That came out all wrong. I am *blushing*,' said Trio. 'Didn't mean that. Sounded harsh.'

'It's OK,' said Ollie. 'We all do it. Make dark jokes. It's that or flip out.'

'Don't you flip out on us,' said Trey. 'You are supposed to be taking us to a better place.'

'I'll do my best. But I'm not looking forward to trying to go to sleep tonight. I know when I close my eyes . . .'

'We've all got bad films in our heads,' said Trio. 'Don't think about it.'

'I'm trying. So tell me, how does it work then?' Ollie asked Trey. 'Your rule of three?'

'There's three of everything in the world,' said Trey. 'Like the three of us.'

'If you don't mind me asking,' said Ollie, 'I was wondering. That thing on your back . . . is it alive?'

'Hey,' said Trio, with mock offence. 'That *thing* on our back is not a thing, it's a *person*. He's Mister Three. And he is very much alive.'

'Yeah, sorry.'

'It's all right,' said Trey. 'To tell you the truth, he's a pain in the arse. Literally.'

'He sleeps his life away,' said Trio. 'Wakes up every few days, looks around, has a moan and then nods off again. Most of the time he doesn't bother us, but sometimes, God give me strength and slap me down for thinking bad of the poor little deformed thing, I wish we could slice him off. He keeps us awake for days.'

'This is all too much for me to take in,' said Ollie. 'Too much has happened. Your rule of three thing, I'm not sure I get it.'

'Just look around you,' said Trey, excited. 'We're three of us in one, me and Trio and Mister Three. Yeah? And how many of us Twisted Kids came with you? If you count us as one, as three in one, there's us and Fish-Face and singing Skinner. Sitting on his trolley. Three. How many trolleys in all?'

'Three,' said Ollie.

'Three is right. The church? That was significant. So there will be three churches.'

'How do you mean? Where will they be?'

'*In your story*. It's like, where are we going?'

'To the Natural History Museum.'

'There's going to be three museums then. And where have we been?'

'Your warehouse.'

'So three warehouses as well. You'll see. There'll be three of them – three warehouses, three museums, three churches, three roads walked, three friends lost, three friends found, three little kids rescued. They'll all be important in your life.'

'I'll take your word for it.'

'I wouldn't if I were you,' said Trio. 'As I said, it's all crap.'

It may be crap, Ollie thought, but at least it was distracting crap. So that he didn't have to think too much about the long walk back to safety. All those miles stretching out ahead of them, with the chance of being attacked anywhere along the way. Down the motorway and on into London, over the broken bridge – the Hammersmith flyover, through the dead streets of town.

420

To bring back three trolleys of drugs and a huge load of bad news.

And then what?

83

Monkey-Boy was climbing. It was how he'd got his nick-name. He was always climbing things. He was small and so skinny he hardly weighed anything and he crawled up like a lizard, fingers spread, gripping with his knees.

He was scaling one of the stone supports at the side of the main hall to get to the gallery on the floor above. Ella was sitting cross-legged on the floor, watching him, gnaw-ing on a biscuit. The museum kids made them from flour and water; they were hard and dry and didn't taste of anything except salt, but they helped keep the hunger away. Ella had collected a small store of them that she kept in her pocket to chew on whenever the hunger chewed at her.

She'd offered Monkey-Boy one if he could get right to the top. He was doing well. It looked like she was going to have to give one of her biscuits up. Never mind. She liked Monkey-Boy. He was probably the best friend she had left of all the kids who'd come out of Holloway. He reminded her a little bit of her brother, Sam . . .

She gave a little shiver and sniffed. She tried not to think about Sam. It made her too sad. At first, after they'd left Waitrose, she'd hoped he might still be alive somehow, that he might escape from the grown-ups who'd captured him and come back to her. He'd always promised he'd look after her. And he always had – even though he was smaller than her. That was the thing about Sam: he was older by nearly two years, but he'd always been tiny. Dad had called him 'shrimp', which he hated. To Ella he hadn't been a shrimp, he'd been her hero. He'd been gone for days and days now, though, and she knew that she was never going to see him again.

He was gone forever.

She had to forget him or his memory would always make her sad. Like a ghost hanging around. When she pictured him he was trapped in the car park at Waitrose, stuck in a corner with grown-ups coming in at him from all around. What use was a memory like that? She roughly wiped away a tear with her sleeve. Bad thoughts didn't help anything.

'I'm up!' Monkey-Boy called down triumphantly, waving his hands and whooping, his long fair hair hanging down in his face.

'Well done.'

'So do I get my biscuit now?'

'Maybe.'

'But you said!'

'I'm joking you.'

'Not funny.'

'You're funny.'

'I'm the Monkey Man.' He was singing now, as if it was a nursery rhyme. 'No one else can climb as high as I can. Come up here.'

Ella wriggled to her feet and walked quickly over to the stairs where the statue of the granddad sitting in his chair watched over the hall. It was nice in the day, when they could run around in this part of the museum and explore and play. They didn't have to worry about any grown-ups, or the spider man, or the slenderman, or whatever it was.

It was different at night. At night they all came out, all the crawling fears, but then Ella and the others stayed safely locked behind the iron bars of the minerals gallery. She couldn't think of this place as home yet, not like Waitrose had been. Any more scares here at the museum and she wasn't sure she could cope. She would run away. Maybe back to Buckingham Palace. It had been safer there, even if David, the boy in charge, had been bossy and weird. The most important thing was to be *safe*. To have food and water and not be attacked by grown-ups. Nothing else really mattered.

When she got up to the next level she found Monkey-Boy looking at the human exhibits: models of cavemen and Neanderthals and old skeletons were all mixed up with stuffed apes. Ella didn't like the models. They were too realistic. They had clever, sneaky eyes and she feared they'd come alive. Monkey-Boy was making faces at one of them.

'I can climb higher than any of these losers,' he said.

'That's because they're dead,' said Ella. 'Dead and stuffed. They're creepy.'

'The dead can't hurt us,' said Monkey-Boy.

Ella looked at the figures standing there, waiting forever. The orange hairy face of an orang-utan, the friendly face of a chimp, the glass eyes of a caveman, and a pale face, with dark-rimmed eyes, white skin, black hair, at the back, behind the other exhibits, in the darkness.

That blinked.

Ella opened her mouth, wanting to scream, but could

make no sound come out. Her breath was tangled inside her. Frozen.

She grabbed Monkey-Boy's arm. So tight he yelped and pulled away sharply.

'Be careful,' he said, and then he saw her face. Panic came into his eyes. He searched around wildly, trying to see what it was that had spooked her. Finally Ella pointed, waving her arm . . . at nothing. Only shadows.

The face had gone.

She *had* seen it, though. She was *sure* she had seen it. Something alive. The slenderman. The spider. The thing. There was movement to their right, coming fast round the end of the cabinets, and finally she screamed, long and high and shrill, and Monkey-Boy saw it too. A person. A boy. Tall. Dressed all in black, his clothes shiny and filthy, with dark stains all over, and in his hands a knife, raised and ready.

Again Ella screamed. And she ran and Monkey-Boy ran and the black figure ran after them. And Ella got trapped among the cabinets. Could go no further. Monkey-Boy with her. Trembling. There had to be a way out, but in her panicked confusion the cabinets had made a wall around her, the apes and cavemen grinning at her.

And then she heard voices. People were coming out of the minerals gallery at the far end of the balcony, behind the slenderman.

'What is it? What's the matter?' It was Maeve, running ahead of the others, unarmed but unafraid.

'What is it?' she repeated. The only answer Ella could give was another scream.

The slenderman made a grab for Monkey-Boy, who somehow managed to duck and wriggle away from him. He slashed at thin air with his bright and shiny knife, but

Monkey-Boy jumped up on to the stone railing, then swung out and round and up on to one of the stone columns that supported the great arches above them. He scampered up, got clear and disappeared from sight.

That left only Ella. She crouched down, trying to make herself small.

At last Maeve had realized what was going on.

'You get away from her!' she screamed.

The slenderman turned to face the bigger kids, saw that there were too many and left Ella behind. Made a dash for the stairs. More people were coming up from below.

'Watch out!' Ella shouted as he got near to them. 'He's got a knife.'

'Who?'

'It's him! It's him!'

The slenderman reached the top of the stairs at the same time as the first of the kids. He barged into them, knocking two of them back down on top of their friends, and then he howled and carried on around towards the tree room at the back of the hall.

Maeve put out her arms and scooped up Ella, hugging her close to her body. Ella so wanted it to be over, but didn't know if the slenderman had got away or not. She could hear running, shouting, the sounds swallowed up and echoing away around the building. She looked into Maeve's face.

'Will they get him?' she asked.

'Yes,' said Maeve. 'They'll get him. You come with me. I'll take you back to the minerals gallery.'

'Don't ever let me go,' said Ella.

'I won't, darling,' said Maeve. 'You're safe now.'

Ella closed her eyes, enjoying for a moment the lies that

Maeve had told her. Dreaming that in another world they were true. The world that Sam lived in. She knew that they wouldn't catch the thing. She knew that she wasn't safe and that Maeve would let her go. Sometime. She'd have to. She couldn't hold on to her forever.

84

Maxie was ready for him this time. She stood in the centre of the hall, close to the diplodocus, her feet planted wide apart, tensed, knees slightly bent, katana held high, up behind her head. She would get him this time. Whatever his problem was – and right now she didn't really care – he wasn't going to do any more damage.

She'd watched him push past the other kids and go round the upper level into the tree room at the back, and out into the west gallery. And there he was, at the top of the flight of stairs that went up the left-hand side. Down he came, jumping three steps at a time, four, his long legs pumping away, arms flailing, knife waving in the air.

'Over here, dickhead,' she shouted as he reached the bottom. 'Come and get it.'

He skidded to a halt, hesitated, weighing up his chances, trembling. Close enough for Maxie to see the sweat pouring from his forehead. His red, feverish eyes. His teeth yellow against his bone-white skin.

He tilted his head back and howled like a trapped animal and Maxie ran at him, ready to swing, ready to take his bloody head off. Roaring.

He wasn't going to fight, though. Instead he turned and

bolted towards the green zone, Maxie hard behind him, calling to the other kids to come with her.

As she ran, she was aware of footsteps. Turned to see Boggle and the big-nosed boy who'd come with them from the palace. What was his name? He'd been guarding David's sick-bay.

Andy?

She was pretty sure he was called Andy.

Only three of them then. But they had the upper hand: Paul was on the run; Maxie had her sword. He was racing ahead of them, into the dark maze of galleries and passageways at the back of the green zone. Maxie didn't fully know her way around here yet, wasn't so confident away from the main hall. They ran round behind the insect and bird galleries and then Maxie realized she'd lost sight of him. She pulled out her torch and flicked it on. No sign of him.

'Stop!' she called out. The other two stuttered to a halt. 'What?' said Boggle.

'Be quiet . . . Listen . . . We've lost him. Can you hear him at all?'

'No.'

Nothing.

Just the sound of their own breathing. Voices behind them in the main hall. No hurrying footsteps. Maxie knew there was a way through here to the other section of the museum. The red zone. The doors were usually kept closed and locked, but Paul had keys.

And then there was an urgent shout and, from their right, running footsteps.

'Come on!'

They threaded their way through the bird gallery, past the weird dark shapes in the cabinets – parrots and eagles, an ostrich – and came out into a long, wide corridor with fossils of marine creatures mounted on the walls.

And there was Paul, up ahead. He'd done a big loop and doubled back towards the main hall. Kids were falling back, keeping out of his way. Maxie sped up, her sword held out to one side. She forced her legs to work harder, but unless he stopped she knew she wasn't going to catch up. There was a knot of kids in the hall up ahead and Paul barrelled straight towards them. They scattered as he approached and, in the confusion, Maxie again lost sight of him.

'Stop him!' she yelled as she burst out into the hall. 'Where is he?'

A terrified girl looked towards the main doors that stood partially open. A boy sat with his back to them. He'd been knocked down. Maxie couldn't tell if he'd been stabbed.

'Stay with me,' she bellowed at Boggle and Andy, and she squeezed through the gap in the doors, her katana held out in front of her. As she came out, blinded by the bright light, she saw a movement, swatted pathetically with the blade, aware that she was off balance and helpless. She slipped and slid down to the ground. Even more useless. She swiped desperately at the pair of legs she saw in front of her and they jumped back out of her way.

'Maxie! Stop it!'

She blinked, shielding her eyes, slowly getting used to the light. Aware that there was more than one person out here. And the person she had nearly hit was . . .

'Blue?'

She struggled to get up from her undignified position, sprawled on her arse half out of the door. Blue gave her a hand, pulled her up with his strong, muscled arm.

430

She looked around. Coming up the slope were several kids pushing trolleys. No sign of Paul.

'Did you see him?'

'Who?'

'A tall boy, dressed all in black, carrying a knife.'

'Nobody came out except you.'

Maxie looked at Blue now. Felt hot tears spring into her eyes. He was back.

'You OK, Max? What's going on?' He put his arms round her.

Paul must still be in the museum. He hadn't come out through the doors at all. They'd have to find him . . .

Later. Right now all she wanted was to hold on to Blue.

'It's a long story,' she said into his neck, her voice wobbly.

'I've got time.'

85

'Look, see, I can walk. It's not so bad.' Robbie was half hopping, half limping around the room. Maeve sat on one of the beds, watching him, unimpressed.

'You need to rest your leg, Robbie,' she said. 'It's too early to be walking around on it. You'll pull out all the stitches.'

'Nah, it's fine. Million times better. Hardly hurts at all any more. Well . . . It's still sore, obviously, but it don't burn at all. The stitches are holding up fine. The antibiotics have kicked in. You fixed me up. You're a genius.'

'Yeah, but if you open the wound then it'll *really* hurt some. Trust me, Robbie. Plus, you'll let infection back in. What's the big hurry anyway?'

'I want to come with you.'

'You what?' Maeve straightened up, looked hard at him, trying to work out if he was teasing her.

'I know you're planning to leave, Maeve,' said Robbie, and he sounded genuine. 'I know you've been asking around, seeing if anyone wants to go with you. Well, you never asked me.'

'That's because you couldn't come, Robbie, because of your wound. You know that. It's nothing personal.'

'Yeah, well, I'm going to come with you. Simple as that.'

'Well, you can't. Simple as that.' Maeve flopped back, leaning against the wall behind the bed. The only other person in the sick-bay was Cameron, who was fast asleep, as usual. The wound in his neck wasn't too bad, but he'd still lost a lot of blood, and without a proper diet it was going to take him a while to get strong again.

'Anyway,' said Maeve, 'I'm not sure I'm going any more.'

Robbie sat down next to her, sighing with relief. His leg was obviously hurting more than he was letting on.

'Why not?' he said, rubbing his thigh. 'What's the matter? What's changed?'

'It's what happened to Blue's lot,' said Maeve. 'It was awful. I couldn't bear it. All the crying. So many kids killed.'

'But how does that affect you? They weren't your friends.'

'There's still a lot of sickos out there, Robbie. It just reminded me, is all. It'd be too dangerous trying to get out of town. I couldn't ask anyone to go through that. They don't want to anyway. Every kid who said they wanted to come with me has backed down now, changed their mind. I need to wait now till I can convince them it's the right thing to do. Till I'm sure it'd be safe. Once we're out of London I know it'll be different, I just know, but it's getting there that's . . .'

'If you wait you'll never go,' Robbie interrupted her. 'You'll be stuck here.'

'Yeah . . . Maybe . . . I don't know.'

In truth, Maeve didn't know what she wanted to do any more. She was scared to go and scared to stay. It had been three days since Blue had got back. Three very dark, very bleak days, as the local kids learnt what had happened to their friends. And it had also been three very strange days as everyone got used to the newcomers, Skinner and Fish-Face and Trinity.

They'd seen nothing more of Paul. He'd disappeared into the depths of the museum somewhere. Blue had wanted to search the place from top to bottom straight away, but Maxie had persuaded him to rest up first. The trip had taken a lot out of them physically and emotionally and Maxie didn't want a load of kids to go running around the museum half-cocked. So they'd been talking to Justin and putting together a plan of action so that Paul could be safely flushed out.

'You don't have to ask me to come with you,' said Robbie. 'I'm volunteering. It's my choice.'

'It's sweet of you, Robbie,' said Maeve, 'but you can't. How can you walk anywhere like that?'

'Who said anything about walking?'

'What are you talking about?'

Robbie lay back on the bed, rested his head on the pillow and stared up at the ceiling.

'I want out, Maeve,' he said. 'I've always wanted to get away from here. I've never liked it and I never meant to stay. The thing is, not many of them here are fighters. When Justin and Brooke and the rest of them tipped up on that lorry of theirs I was amazed they'd made it this far. Just nerds and wimps and little kids. I only ever meant to stay here till I had a proper plan, enough food and water and that. But I stayed on because they needed me. I had no choice. I never wanted to be needed. Never wanted to be wanted. Never really wanted to be in charge of security neither. But there was no one else, see? Least I didn't think there was.

'I don't like it, Maeve. I don't like being responsible. In charge. Oh, it made me feel good, I guess. Made me feel big. And once I *was* in charge of security I didn't want no one else to do it. All along, all I've ever thought about, though, is getting out into the countryside, like you. It's what I dream about. I grew up in the country, only moved to London a couple of years back when my dad got a new job. I was out in Essex. I miss it. I never liked all these houses and buildings. It's cramped.'

He sat up suddenly. 'You and me, Maeve,' he said. 'We can do it. We can get away from here. I been lying here in bed and when I close my eyes I picture fields and sky and trees. We can grow things. My mum used to grow stuff. I helped her now and then. I know about that sort of thing. And your lot getting here – it's taken a load off of me. Blue and Maxie and Achilleus and the rest can look after this place better than I ever could. They're some well hard dudes. Way better than me. I think it can be safe here. Properly safe. And now Einstein's got all his medical supplies and stuff. Finally I can get out, Maeve. I can go free.'

'Yeah, Robbie, but that doesn't change how you are, does it? You wouldn't get a hundred metres like that.'

'It's getting better every day, Maeve. You fixed me. I owe you.'

'You don't owe me anything, stupid.' Maeve took hold of Robbie's hand.

'I was hoping you'd do that,' he said.

'Do what?'

'Hold my hand. Next thing I want is a snog.'

'Idiot.' Maeve shook her head, but didn't let go of his hand. He wasn't the best-looking boy. He was short and stocky, and put horrible gel in his hair, but she liked him. He was one of those boys who'd talk to you. She hadn't been expecting this, though.

'I like you, Maeve,' he said. 'I like you a lot.'

'Yeah, and I like you, Robbie, but this conversation is getting us nowhere. We're going round in circles and you're ignoring the main point. The fact of the matter is — *you can't walk anywhere.*'

Robbie struggled off the bed and eased himself into his wheelchair.

'Come with me, Maeve,' he said, scooting towards the door. 'I want to show you something . . .'

86

Kids were gathering in the Hall of Gods, taking their places on the seats between the two rows of statues. Maxie was sitting next to Blue. If she thought she could get away with it and not be laughed at by everyone she would have been holding his hand. Since Blue had got back from the expedition she hadn't left his side. The two of them showed a strong front to the other kids, accepting no criticism for either the deaths here at the museum or the ones at Heathrow. In private, however, when they were alone together, they shared their doubts and fears and pain. Blue told Maxie how shaken he was by Big Mick's death, and Maxie told Blue how terrified she'd been to wake up and find Paul about to kill Cameron. It helped to talk things through. It helped not being alone.

Justin had called this meeting, despite the fact that it was Maxie, Blue and Jackson who had worked out most of the plan to catch Paul. Justin was the guy in charge, though, and wanted to be the one to explain it.

He'd only told the fighters to come to the meeting. Those kids who could look after themselves. The rest of them were back in the minerals gallery with the doors securely locked.

Justin waited until he was sure that everyone was there and settled in their seats and then he raised his hand for silence. The local kids fell quiet pretty quickly, but some of the Holloway crew ignored him and carried on chatting. The loudest of them was Achilleus, who was telling a dirty joke to Paddy.

'Oi,' Blue shouted. 'Give the man some respect. Shut it, the lot of you. We got to get this crap sorted.'

In a few seconds they'd all stopped talking, though there had been some laughs and insults thrown around along the way.

'Thanks,' said Justin. 'This shouldn't take too long, I hope. Now you know the purpose of this meeting is to discuss the plan for finding Paul.'

'Yeah, we know, nerd,' Achilleus called out. 'Can we go now?'

'You don't know the exact plan,' said Justin. 'Listen, can't you?'

'I'm listening. Get on with it.'

'I would if you didn't keep interrupting.'

'Go on then.'

'Right. We have to work methodically through each part of the museum, starting in the green and blue zones. All the doors through to here and the orange zone will be locked, as well as the doors through to the offices, and library, and the lower level.'

Achilleus stuck his hand up and Justin looked irritated. 'What?'

'Does that mean I won't be able to use the library, sir? I wanted to read the *Twilight* books. I hear they're *awesome*.'

Paddy tittered and Blue looked at Maxie. Achilleus was one of her crew. Not his responsibility.

'Don't be a twat, Achilleus,' she said. 'The quicker we can get done here, the better.'

In reply Achilleus stretched out his arms and gave a big, theatrical yawn.

'Wake me up when it's over,' he said and slumped in his chair, to the delight of Paddy, who copied him.

Justin pressed on. 'Then we widen the search to the red and orange zones. If we still haven't found him we'll go up on to the roof and even check the gardens. Basically we're going to keep looking until we find where he's hiding.'

'Maybe he's disappeared up his own arse,' Achilleus whispered, loud enough for everyone to hear him. Justin didn't rise to the bait.

'Anybody not in a search party,' he said, 'will be locked in the minerals gallery for safety. As the museum is so big, there's a danger that Paul might be able to move from hiding place to hiding place, so you've been split up into six groups. That way you can spread out. All six search parties will work at the same time, and as each gallery is cleared it'll be locked down. Each search party will be controlled by a squad leader, and after this talk I want to keep the squad leaders here for a final briefing.'

'Roger wilco,' said Achilleus and Justin took a deep breath, trying not to lose his temper.

'The squad leaders are: Blue, team one; Achilleus, you're team two; Boggle, team three; Ollie is team four; and Jackson, team five. Lewis, you're team six.'

Justin went on to explain the plan in detail, but Maxie had stopped listening. She knew what the idea was after all. Justin had wanted her to lead a team, but she'd refused and quietly explained that from now on she and Blue were always going to stick together.

She wished it was over, that Paul was gone and the museum was safe. She wished she could sleep at night and not be poisoned with worry. It felt a lot better having Blue around, and sharing problems made them seem smaller, but she longed for life to be boring again.

It was never going to be over, though, was it? Not until every last grown-up was dead.

Justin droned on for a while until even he seemed fed up with the sound of his own voice and finally he stopped.

'OK,' he said. 'So I hope that's all clear. Blue, Achilleus, Jackson, Lewis and Ollie, stay behind, and you as well, Maxie, if you want. And Boggle . . . where's Boggle? He should be here. Bloody hell, when I call an important meeting I expect everyone to turn up. It's not good enough. The rest of you can go back to the minerals gallery and check the list I've left there explaining what teams you're all in. And remember – we're going to find him and stop him. Any questions?'

'Yeah, I've got a question actually, Justin,' said Achilleus.

'OK . . .'

'Have you ever kissed a girl?'

'It's not funny, Achilleus,' said Justin, going red in the face and losing his temper at last. 'Paul's already killed at least three kids that we know of. He's sick and he's dangerous. He has to be found. This isn't like hunting sickos, who are stupid. He's clever.'

'OK then, one more question.'

'Not if you're just arsing about.'

'No, is a serious question.' And Achilleus' whole manner changed. It was as if he'd got the reaction he wanted out of Justin and now he could get down to business. 'What do we do with him when we catch him?'

'Well, then . . . then we . . .' Justin looked flustered. 'You just catch him, basically, and we'll lock him up somewhere.'

'No,' said Blue, getting out of his chair. 'Too risky. When we find him we kill him.'

'No, no, no,' Justin protested. 'He's one of us, he's . . .'

'We kill him,' said Blue. 'End of.'

87

'I'm supposed to be in Justin's meeting,' said Boggle, who was pushing Robbie's wheelchair for him. 'But Jackson's gonna find out what it's all about and give me notes.'

'Christ,' said Robbie. 'It's like school, isn't it? Missing a lesson and getting your mates to fill you in. Justin's getting worse and worse.'

'You have to have someone like him,' said Maeve. 'Someone who's interested in the boring stuff. Someone to hold it all together. You put an ordinary kid in charge and it's all going to fall apart. People like Justin know what's important for survival. It's not all running around shooting guns and making rabbit traps.'

'That's just it,' said Robbie. 'That's what I want more of. I *want* to be setting rabbit traps. Hunting in the woods. I don't want to be stuck here, back at school, living in a bloody museum. We got the whole world out there.'

'Yeah, but you still haven't told me how you're going to get there in that wheelchair,' said Maeve. 'And where exactly we're going right now.'

'You'll see.'

They had left the museum grounds and gone out on to the Cromwell Road, then headed left past the Victoria and Albert Museum. The building next to it looked like a big church of some sort and they'd gone up the side of it towards the back.

It was quiet, and Robbie was confident that it would stay that way. He knew the area around the museum well. Had insisted that they wouldn't accidentally stumble across a gang of hungry grown-ups. But the three of them were still tensed and ready to bolt to safety if they sensed anything dodgy.

'You really thinking of leaving, Rob?' asked Boggle.

'Yeah, I've had enough, Boggo. You want to come with us?'

'No way. No way, man. It might not be paradise here, but it's safe. At least it will be when we get Paul. Oh Jesus. Let me tell you. I am *not* going out there. Not after what happened to Einstein's lot. That was cold, man. Bare harsh. I don't want none of that.'

'That's the way everyone thinks,' said Maeve. 'The only kids left who say they want to come with me are Ella and Monkey-Boy.'

'Them two little kids?' said Robbie and he laughed.

'Yeah. They've got it into their heads that I saved their lives. Though I really didn't do anything. They won't leave me alone.'

'Holy crap, you need me *bad*, Maeve.'

'Yeah, right, cos it's really going to help having a cripple along as well.'

'Oh, that wounds me,' said Robbie.

'I'm serious, Robbie. I can't go through with this.'

'But once we're out of London there'll be other kids,' Robbie insisted. 'We can find a community, you know, like farmers and that, real life, not this scavenging crap.'

'I'm not arguing with you on that,' said Maeve. 'You're probably right, but how the hell do we get out of London?'

443

'That's what I'm about to show you.'

'Well, go on then. Where? What am I supposed to be looking at?'

'Over there.' Robbie grinned at Maeve.

They had come to a small car park behind the church where four abandoned cars sat rotting beneath some trees, patiently waiting for their long-dead owners to return. Three of them had flat tyres and were covered in bird droppings and general dirt. Now that she looked Maeve saw that the fourth one was in slightly better condition. It was a black Range Rover with tinted windows. Boggle wheeled Robbie over to it. Robbie carried on grinning at Maeve.

'What do you reckon then?'

'What do I reckon to what?'

'The wheels.'

'Yeah, lovely . . . Wait a minute . . . You're not saying . . .?'

'I *am* saying. I've been saving this up for the right time. And now is that time.'

'I don't get it.'

'You don't have to get it. Just get in.'

Robbie dug a key fob out of his pocket, aimed it at the car and pressed a button with his thumb. The indicators flashed and there was a satisfying *thunk* as the doors unlocked. Maeve felt a little surge of excitement in her guts.

Robbie got up out of the wheelchair, opened the driver's door and climbed in with some difficulty. Maeve hurried round to the passenger side while Boggle stayed outside to keep watch.

Maeve settled in next to Robbie, who was sitting behind the steering wheel with a huge smile on his face, like a kid on Christmas morning with a new toy.

'Does it actually work?' Maeve asked.

By way of a reply, Robbie stuck the key in the ignition and turned it. The engine came to life with a deep rumble.

'Oh my God. Oh my God,' said Maeve, trying not to sound like an overexcited little kid herself. 'We can *drive* out of London. That is *brilliant*.'

'Well, yeah,' said Robbie. 'There's a slight problem, though.'

'You can't drive? You're just going to sit there revving the engine and hooting the horn?'

'I *can* drive. Least I can drive this baby. Not very well, to be honest, but I *can* do it. It's automatic so there's no gears, just two pedals, stop and go, and I can work them both with my good leg.'

'So what's the slight problem?'

'Petrol.'

'It's empty?'

'No. There's some. Remember the first thing that happened when the disease came down on us?'

'Yeah, the pumps dried up. All the petrol ran out.'

'Exactly, there was no more deliveries. The tankers stopped sailing, the lorries stopped driving, there was panic buying, petrol riots. You remember how everything just sort of . . . stopped?'

'Yeah,' said Maeve, remembering those scary times. 'We were all stuck.'

'Most of the cars you see just sit there reminding us of how useless they are, how useless *we* are. No gas in them. No keys to start them. But not this one. Not my Raymonda.'

'It's called Raymonda?'

'Why not? Gotta call it something. It was parked outside this house we was scavenging. And on my way out I've seen the keys, just sitting there on this shelf near the front door. I thought I'd give it a go and hey presto, hocus pocus, it started first time. So I drove it back here and parked it out of the way. It'll be our freedom bus.'

'So how much petrol is there then?'

'There was a bit left in the tank when I found it, enough to get it here with some left over. Since then I been collecting it from other cars when I can, but she's a big old tank really; she uses a bare lot of gas.'

'How far will it get us, do you think?'

'I don't know. See that?' Robbie pointed to an illuminated display. 'Forty-five miles till tank empty. That's what the computer says.'

'Forty-five miles? Forty-five miles, Robbie? That's further than Blue went, further than Heathrow. That's *out of London*. That's the countryside. That's all we need.'

Robbie looked unsure. Turned off the engine. Sat there in silence.

'Don't you believe it?' Maeve asked. 'Do you think the computer's broken or something?'

'No. But it'll change when we start actually driving. I used to watch it on my dad's car. It changed all the time, depending on how fast you were going. Or if you were going uphill.'

'But still, Robbie, even if it's only forty miles . . .'

Robbie brightened up, smiled at Maeve.

'I figure if we keep going slowly to save petrol we'll get far enough to find some other kids, and take it from there. Yeah?'

Maeve giggled and leant across to kiss Robbie. He blushed.

'*You're* the genius,' she said. 'You fixed it. Why didn't you say anything about this before?'

446

'Oh, you know, I kept it quiet. My little secret. Only a couple of my mates know about it, like Boggle. Didn't want Justin finding out, thinking he needed to keep it for himself. It wouldn't have been mine no more. He would have sent Einstein's lot off in it. And they'd have ruined it like they ruined everything else. I always knew that one day – you know, like today – the time would come. So, we on then?'

Maeve's mind was a blur, thoughts racing and falling over each other. This changed everything. 'We'll have to get ready,' she said. 'Pack what we need. Food, water, weapons . . .'

She stopped, overwhelmed by the reality of it all. She was going to get away. For the first time in a long while she was actually looking forward to the future.

She started to cry and Robbie put an arm round her.

This was their bus to freedom . . .

88

Blue was hacked off. They'd spent all morning searching and found nothing. Not even a trace of where Paul might have been hiding out. He'd been hoping they'd find him quickly and get it over with, but it was clear that wasn't going to happen. The tension of the first couple of hours had slowly drained away and changed to boredom as they trudged round the galleries, checking every cabinet, every cupboard, every door, every dark corner. And the more bored they got, the less care they took, until they were poking around aimlessly and half the kids were mucking about and playing stupid games.

The more they searched, the more Blue became aware of just how huge the museum was, how many places there were to hide. He remembered the first few days they'd been here, flushing the grown-ups out of the lower level. The time that had taken. And it wasn't just the galleries they had to search; there were all the areas that hadn't been open to the public – the offices and back rooms, the storage areas . . .

It was going to take them ages and, no matter how careful they were, Paul could easily just keep moving around and stay one jump ahead. He had keys and they could hardly change all the locks. They could be at it for days, weeks, months. All Blue really wanted was to sit on his arse and spend some time with Maxie, just jamming.

They'd taken a break in the middle of the day for some lunch – a thin, watery soup with tiny scraps of vegetable in it. And now, still hungry, *always* hungry, they were chilling in the minerals gallery before setting off to search the next section of the museum. Stretching the minutes out, making the most of it until Justin came in and told them it was time to get going again.

Blue was sitting on the floor with his back against the wall, Maxie slumped next to him, playing with the little puppy that used to belong to Joel. Joel. He'd almost forgotten the guy. Poor little kid. He'd been killed by diseased apes that had escaped from the zoo. Too many memories. They crept up on you when you were like this, your guard down. Maybe, after all, it was better to keep busy and not leave yourself too much time to think.

'I know it was our plan,' he said, 'but I don't reckon it's gonna work. I reckon we ought to just set some kind of trap for him. Stake the place out and wait for him to make his move.'

'What?' said Maxie. 'Tie some little kid to a pole and wait for him?'

'Yeah.' Blue gave a humourless little laugh. 'Something like that.'

'Seriously, Blue, what other way is there?' Maxie wasn't even looking at him. Too interested in the puppy.

'Can I talk to you?'

Blue looked up to see Skinner. He still hadn't got used to how the guy looked, all those folds of skin. Tried to hold his eye. Act cool.

'Whassup?'

449

Skinner shuffled about nervously.

'He's not here,' he said after a pause.

'Who's not here?'

'The one you're looking for.'

'Paul? How do you know? You seen him leave or something?'

'No. No. It's Fish-Face. She told us.'

Blue very much doubted it. In all the time since they'd left the warehouse he hadn't heard Fish-Face make a sound, let alone speak. Not to him, nor the museum kids, not to her own friends, not to anyone.

'She says he's not here,' Skinner went on, the words coming out in a muffled rush. 'He was here when we arrived, she could hear him, but soon after that he left. He's not here.'

'How can she know?'

'She knows.'

With a grunt Blue hoisted himself up.

'Let me talk to her.'

'Oh no. No, she wouldn't like that . . .'

Skinner backed away, even more uneasy now. 'No, she won't talk to you. She's shy. We all are. Being here, with all these boys and girls. We're not used to it. They look at us, and they don't look at us, I don't know which is worse. Fish-Face wished she'd stayed behind, but she had to come, The Warehouse Queen told her to.'

'If she knows something I want to speak to her.'

Skinner thought about this for a while and eventually he nodded.

'You can try.'

The warehouse kids had made their own little camp in a room at the end of the minerals gallery. There were no doors or windows in there, just glass cabinets with precious stones in them. There was a large door that used to slide shut like the door of a bank vault. Blue supposed these exhibits must have been pretty valuable and this had been a specially secure area. Well, they weren't valuable any more, were they? They were just shiny stones. No use to anyone.

Fish-Face was sitting on the floor with Trinity, playing cards. Blue thought that was pretty funny. Trinity was playing as two players, with two hands of cards. Blue wondered how that worked. If they shared any thoughts.

There was a bad smell in the vault. A rotting smell. Blue wondered if it was the Twisted Kids, then told himself not to be a jerk. Why should they smell any worse than anyone else? He hadn't noticed any kind of stink at the warehouse. He tried to put it out of his mind.

'Skinner says you want to tell me something,' he said to Fish-Face and she bowed her head on her long neck, embarrassed, and then looked at him sideways, out of one big eye. Like an emo peeping out from under a curtain of hair.

'Says you know something about this kid we're looking for.'

Fish-Face just gave a little shrug.

Maxie squatted down so that she was more on Fish-Face's level.

'If you know anything you should tell us,' she said. 'He's dangerous. Until we've found him we're all on lockdown.'

'She says she might be wrong,' said Skinner.

'What do you mean, "She says"?' Blue asked, trying not to get angry. Fish-Face hadn't said anything. Were they playing some kind of game with him?

'Just that,' said Skinner. 'She might be wrong about the boy. She doesn't want to cause any trouble.'

'When did she say this?'

'Just now, you know . . .'

'No, I don't know. It was you brought me over here. I don't know what this is all about.'

'I didn't bring you over,' Skinner protested. 'You wanted to come. I told you she'd be shy. And now you're upsetting her.'

'Not as much as you're upsetting me,' said Blue. 'Now she either said something to you or she didn't.'

'Leave it, Blue,' said Maxie. 'You'll frighten her.'

Blue checked himself. Wandered away. He knew he shouldn't get wound up, and if the morning hadn't been so frustrating maybe he'd have gone along with whatever the warehouse kids were up to. He had his back to them now, waiting to calm down, and realized that he was looking at a door that he hadn't noticed before. It looked almost like part of the wall.

'We should get going.' Justin was striding along the middle of the minerals gallery, down the passageway that the kids had left between all the sleeping cubicles they'd built.

'Where does this door go?' Blue asked Justin when he arrived. Justin looked at it and frowned.

'Don't know. Not sure. Don't think I've ever seen it before, to tell you the truth. Must have done, though. We don't use it anyway.'

'It's a door into where you sleep,' said Blue. 'This is supposed to be a secure area, sanctuary, and you're telling me there's a door and you don't know where it goes?'

Justin looked up at the ceiling, went over to peer out of the windows.

'I think it must lead up into the tower,' he said.

'What's up there?'

'No idea. As I say, I don't know anything about this door.'

'You never been up in the tower?'

'No.'

'Maybe we should look.'

Justin checked the door. 'It's locked.'

'Oh fine,' said Blue sarcastically. 'That's OK then. It's not like Paul has any keys or anything.'

Justin sighed. 'All right. I'll open it. I'll get my keys.' He went off muttering to himself and Blue banged on the door. It felt solid.

'You think he might be up there?' said Maxie, coming over to join him.

'He could be anywhere, Max. I've got a bad feeling we're going to spend the rest of our lives looking for him.'

Maxie slipped her fingers into his hand. He smiled at her.

'OTP,' he said.

'OTP,' said Maxie.

In a couple of minutes Justin returned with Wiki, who was carrying several huge bunches of keys. When Wiki saw the door he simply said, 'Hmm,' and then sat down cross-legged on the floor to sort through the keys, while Blue, Maxie, Justin and Skinner watched over him. Slowly a larger crowd formed. Without TV or the Internet or games consoles, this was about the only entertainment to be had right now. Watching a small boy sort keys.

At last Wiki said 'Hmm' again, selected a key and tried it in the lock.

It wasn't the right one.

Blue swore under his breath, wishing he'd never mentioned the bloody door. In the end it took Wiki at least half an hour to find the right key, and when finally the lock clicked open, he said 'Hmm' for the last time and stepped back. He'd opened the door, but he wasn't going through it. Blue looked around at the kids who'd gathered.

'Wiki's got the right idea,' he said. 'You lot stay back. We don't know what's behind there.' Now he turned to Maxie. 'Grab the rest of our team and we'll take a look . . .'

89

Blue was looking up a long, straight, narrow stairway, walls painted with shiny reflective paint, pipes and electric cables running along the sides. It went up and up and up and disappeared into a white-out of bright light at the top. Blue figured there must be some big windows up there.

The rotten stink was much stronger now. It hung in the still air and he swallowed hard, trying to get the taste of it out of his mouth. He wiped his forehead. Hadn't realized he was sweating so much, even though it wasn't that hot. They'd discovered an untidy jumble of tiny offices and storage areas immediately behind the door through from the gallery, all built into the great square tower that sat at the corner of the building. They were long ago deserted, filled with dust. It was the smell that had led Blue and Maxie and the rest of their search party to the stairs.

They would have to go up.

Blue was armed with a short club and had a knife in his belt for backup. Maxie had her katana, but it wouldn't be much use on the stairs, which were only wide enough for them to go up one at a time. It would be too dangerous to try to use it if they were attacked; she'd be more of a risk to her friends than to Paul. She held it down and to the side. Blue could feel her pressing him from behind to get moving.

He hesitated.

'After you,' said Maxie, trying to lighten the heavy mood. 'In your own time.'

'DBAP,' said Blue.

'DBAP?'

'Don't be a pain.'

'TOTKO,' said Maxie and Blue waited for an explanation.

'Takes one to know one,' she said. 'Now get moving, fat ass.'

Still Blue hesitated. 'If he comes at us – down these stairs,' he said, 'we ain't in a good position. We'll be crushed in and he'll be on top of us.'

'Who says he's up there?' Maxie asked.

'Well, there's something up there,' said Blue, 'and it stinks real bad.'

'Then we better go and check it out.'

'As far as you know he's only got a knife?' said Blue.

'Yes,' said Maxie impatiently. 'But you heard what Fish-Face said – he's gone.'

'I didn't hear nothing,' said Blue. 'She never even moved her lips. And anyway, do you believe them?'

'Blue,' said Maxie. 'Just go.'

'I'm going. I'm going. Don't hassle me. You want to go first?'

'I'm only a girl, you're a big, strong man.'

'Sexist,' said Blue and he felt her pinch his behind.

'Sex-y,' she said. Blue turned and Maxie made a face that said 'What? What?' Behind her the rest of the pack waited, even less keen than Blue to explore this unknown part of the museum.

Blue tutted, shook his head, turned round and started

up the stairs. They led right up inside the tower, and made a turn to the left at the top, disappearing into the white-out. Blue plodded on. Knew he had to act cool in front of the others and not show his fear in case it spread. It was amazing how quickly his boredom had switched back to nervousness. His eyes adjusted to the light as he climbed, so that details emerged from the brightness. Undisturbed dust on the stairs. A dead rat, dried up and leathery. Some broken glass. Nothing to show that Paul might have been up here, though. No footprints.

Yeah, he was a real Sherlock Holmes.

Where the stairs turned at the top they opened out into a large, square space with bare brick walls, exposed pipe-work and piles of discarded junk. A second, iron, staircase led on up to the next level. This part of the museum was nowhere near as grand as the public areas. It reminded Blue of the loft in his mum's flat. Where she'd piled everything out of the way.

His heart was pounding, but whether that was from climbing the long flight of stairs or from his nerves he didn't know. He paused to get his breath and let the rest of the group catch up. It was stupid, after all he'd been through, the horrors he'd had to face, to be this scared of a boy. But from what everyone had told him he needed to be scared. The guy had flipped out. Was running around cutting people up. Blue didn't want to finish this looking like Achilleus, his face rearranged, or Brooke . . . He hated to think what she was like under that bandage.

Stop it, man. Stop trying to freak yourself out.

Christ, there were six of them! Six against one. That *had* to be good odds.

Maxie came and stood next to him. She'd stopped

making jokes. Her eyes moved constantly, looking for any clues, her sword still down at her side, hand gripping it tightly. She grunted and put her other hand to her mouth. The smell was overpowering here. Something had definitely died.

'What do you think?' Blue asked. 'Could it be him?'

'What?' said Maxie, talking in a whisper, although if anyone *was* up there they'd have heard them all stomping up the stairs like a herd of elephants.

'*Paul*,' he said. 'Do you think that smell could be him? Maybe he died. Maybe that's what Fish-Face meant when she said he'd gone away.'

'Let's hope,' said Maxie. 'I'm not looking forward to having to deal with him.'

'You've seen him in action, Maxie. How bad is he?'

'Bad . . .'

Maxie stopped. They'd all heard it. Something moving. It wasn't loud, just a distant rattle and a thump, but the effect was as if someone had suddenly thrown a switch and passed an electric current through the group.

One of the museum kids swore and they all looked at each other for reassurance.

Blue took a deep breath.

'Come on.'

He led them up the other stairs and they found themselves in a maze of dusty rooms that had been built into the tower. They didn't fit perfectly so that some of the big, fancy windows had been cut in half by new walls and floors. Blue kept catching glimpses of London – rooftops, chimneys, the world outside. It reminded him of just how shut in they were. After the wide-open spaces of the galleries downstairs it felt claustrophobic up here; the low ceilings seemed to be pressing down on them and everywhere was clutter: shelves loaded with carefully labelled fossils, cabinets and drawers stuffed with rocks and crystals, boxes filled with junk. You could hardly move.

And there were a thousand places to hide.

Maxie was sticking so close to Blue that they were cramping each other. It irritated him and he was biting his tongue, anxious not to snap at her. He looked at the floor. *Now* there were footprints in the dust. Someone had been here recently. But there was a horrible stillness, and the air felt hot.

The smell was making him want to puke. His eyes were watering and he was breathing through his mouth in quick pants, like a dog.

They heard something moving again, deeper in the tangle of rooms. Maxie tightened in even closer to Blue and he felt trapped, wanted to shout out and smash the place up. He almost said something to her and just stopped himself in time. Moved quickly away from her. Looked out through a window that faced the museum roof. It stretched away, bigger than a football pitch, like the plateau on the top of a mountain range. A world above the world. There were all sorts of walkways and ladders out there. Easy for Paul to get around and into other bits of the building.

Blue's feet crunched on something and he glanced down to see the skeleton of a pigeon with some scraps of skin still attached.

Maxie's voice broke the stillness.

'Holy crap . . . Look.'

He turned round. She was pointing with her eyes to a pile of stuff on the floor. It looked like a nest of sorts. A bed. Made of feathers and old clothes and various other scrappy bits and pieces.

'We've found him,' Maxie whispered. 'This is where he's been hiding.'

'Is he here now?'

'I don't . . .'

Maxie suddenly jumped back as there was a blur of movement and something came at her with a whirring, rattling noise. She yelped and Blue froze in shock.

And then he saw that it was only a pigeon. It must have got in somewhere and was flapping in panic. It came at Maxie again and she instinctively swiped at it with her sword. There was a squawk and a shower of feathers and the pigeon spiralled into the wall.

Blue giggled with relief.

'Good shot,' he said and then went over to where the wounded pigeon was flopping about on the floor, one wing severed. He hit it with his club and it stopped moving.

'If that's the worst we got to deal with we're gonna be cool,' he said.

'It's not,' said Maxie, who had moved through to the next room.

There was a dark, glistening bundle lying against the wall. It looked like . . .

A person.

Blue clamped his hand over his mouth. One of the other kids was on his knees, throwing up.

'Samira.' Maxie was shaking. 'Oh God. This is too much. I want to get out of here. I can't stand this, Blue, I can't stand it. Where is he? We have to find him.'

Blue forced himself to look. The body was rotting and bits had been cut off it. The belly was ripped open and seething with maggots. He swore. Felt as if he might faint. It was like one of those old films where the walls start closing in on you. He hurried away, opened a window and gulped in fresh air.

'Bastard,' he said. Behind him he could hear the others moving about and Maxie shouting orders at them. Searching. He didn't care. He was going to leave them to it. The sky was darkening, and he heard a distant rumble of thunder. A storm was coming. He wanted to tear the roof off the tower and let the rain come in and wash out all the filth.

He stayed there for ages. Staring out across the grey tiles of the roof. Wishing that none of this had ever happened.

Finally Maxie put a hand on his arm. She was amazing. Stronger than him. She'd been disgusted and terrified, had wanted to run away, but she hadn't folded.

'Come on,' she said gently. 'He's not here. There's no one here. Only Samira.'

'He might be. He might be . . .'

'No.' She locked eyes with him. Telling him it was over.

Blue shook his head. 'I'm going to look properly.'

'We've looked.'

Blue brushed Maxie's arm off and stalked through the rooms, kicking boxes out of his way, screaming and yelling.

'Come on! Where are you, you bastard? Where are you?'

And then, as he completed his circuit and ended up back at the stairs, he saw someone . . . Their shadow on the wall. Creeping slowly.

He had him . . .

He tensed and got ready to swing his club. Felt acid flood his guts. His skull was tight, throbbing so hard he could hardly see straight. The shadow moved closer. And, at the last moment, it was as if something clicked in Blue's brain. Nothing conscious, but deep down. And he held back for an instant, his club hanging above his head.

It was Fish-Face. She looked at him shyly, her face turned to the side, and for the first time she spoke.

'He's gone,' she said, her voice sounding unexpectedly normal. 'He was here. He's left the museum. I'd know if he was still around.'

'That leaves two questions,' said Blue. 'One – if he's gone, where's he gone? And two – just how the hell d'you know?'

90

Rain was starting to fall on London. It spattered on to moss-covered roofs. It blew in through broken windows and splashed on the walls. It flattened the grass in overgrown gardens and flowed down the streets past blocked drains, creating rivers of rubbish. North, south, east and west, the huge cloud dropped its load.

To the south it fell on the blackened ruins of south London, destroyed in a huge fire. And it fell on Ed and Kyle, who were crossing Lambeth Bridge, heading back to St Paul's to look for Sam. To the east it fell on St Paul's and the City of London, where The Kid was trapped in a dark cellar with the Green Man, trying to stay alive, and where Sam was going crazy in the cathedral – desperate to know what had happened to his friend, desperate to get away from Mad Matt and his followers, desperate to find his sister Ella . . .

To the north it fell on the houses and streets of Kilburn where Shadowman was watching a group of kids he hardly knew get massacred as they blindly drove their cars into the centre of St George's army.

Paul was dimly aware of all this. Even though he could make no sense of it. It was as if his head had become a radio set and was receiving transmissions from all around the city. Voices murmuring, shouting, calling to him. Boney-M in there among them, screeching. And Paul realized that the bird thing had never been real. It had been created by his own brain, trying to make sense of the voices in his head.

They were all around him now, a flock of boneys, circling him like vultures . . . singing to him . . . some voices much stronger than others . . . Like the deep, deep song of the whales in the museum, travelling miles under the heavy water. A big voice in the north, roaring in battle. Another one in the east, cleverer, whispering, filled with the sound of the forest, the jungle, the big green. Clever, but still crazy. One calling to another and another, strung out around the city. Paul wanted to shut them out, but he could do nothing.

He was moving very slowly, from hiding place to hiding place, crawling through the rain-washed streets, half blind from pain, his head banging so hard it must surely split wide apart. It felt like there was a writhing mass of worms eating at his brain; he would claw them out if he had the strength.

It was growing dark and the sickos would be emerging soon. They may be singing to him, but he didn't want to risk answering. They were so hungry. So, so hungry . . .

And then he saw one. A mother. Standing right in the middle of the road, arms outstretched, face turned up to the sky so that rainwater ran into her mouth. Her long blonde hair hung down her back, glistening with water. She looked quite young, almost beautiful in the half-light. With the rain streaming over her you couldn't see her damaged skin.

There was a flash of lightning, and her face glowed for

a moment a ghostly white, as if she was an angel come down from heaven, and he heard her speaking to him. Not with words, but images and feelings. Buried deep down beneath the madness, down below her pain, were memories of better times, and a sort of crazy joy. She was burning up with it. As he listened to her, a thought came into Paul's mind, soft and gentle at first, not screeched like Boney-M, but growing, like a musical sound, a whole orchestra, building up in a wave . . .

'He's coming.'

It was Paul who said it, the words bursting from his mouth. And he felt again that great dark presence in the north, something powerful and overwhelming.

'God . . .'

There was a crash of thunder and it was like a door had been opened in Paul's mind and a million thoughts from a million different people flooded in, a punch so hard and hot and bright he fell to his knees and screamed.

A scream of joy and pain and terror . . .

He had no idea how long he stayed like that, face down in the road, arms reaching out to the sides, but after a long while he felt strong enough to get up, his whole body trembling. The mother was still there; she hadn't moved a muscle by the look of it. Her voice was soft and gentle again, like his own mother's had been. He remembered watching cookery programmes with her, talking about the recipes, laughing at the mad ones, the crazy chefs. Olivia at the table doing her homework. And helping his mum to make a cake. Flour everywhere. Mum patient, even when he dropped eggshell in the bowl. A birthday cake for Olivia. Paul had thought he might grow up to be a chef. Like Jamie Oliver.

'Mum . . .'

He went over to the mother, put his arms round her. She felt warm.

'Mum,' he said again. 'Look after me.'

91

'As far as I can work it out, it's like they can communicate with each other without talking. They don't even have to be in the same room. You know, a bit like using a mobile phone.' Blue paused, made a face. Laughed at himself. 'Not that I ever really understood how *they* worked. Like TV and Wi-Fi and that, messages through the air, waves and rays and particles and all stuff we did at school. I never really got my head round it. Probably because I wasn't listening.'

'But you *do* still have to actually *talk* into a phone,' said Einstein. 'It's not magic. Quite honestly it sounds ridiculous, what you're saying.'

'Yeah, don't it?' said Blue. 'I ain't no scientist. I don't know how they do it. It's not like talking, but they *can* send and receive messages somehow. It's something to do with the disease.'

'No,' said Einstein. 'It's impossible. Human beings can't suddenly develop telepathy.'

'Well, this lot have, so get used to it, science-boy. They developed it in the womb.'

'It's just not possible.'

'Well, maybe they're not human then.'

'They're disabled,' said Einstein. 'But they're still human.'

'I wouldn't call them disabled,' said Blue. 'They can do a whole mess of stuff that we can't. They're different. Not like any disabled kids I knew. It's the disease.'

The lab lit up and soon after there was a crash of thunder. The rain was noisy against the glass roof. Blue and Maxie were sitting with Einstein. It had still been light outside when they'd come over to the orange zone, but the storm had quickly brought on the dark. Einstein had had to find some candles as the generator had been turned off for the night. They were the last three here and soon they'd have to go back through to the main building and shut this area down.

Einstein got up and started pacing about. He was behaving like someone who'd been given some bad news that they didn't want to accept.

'Disease doesn't give us special powers,' he insisted. 'It's not like Spider-Man. Disease takes things away.'

'What about kids with autism?' said Maxie. 'You know, like the ones who can do amazing things – I don't know, maths and that. I saw this documentary about a kid who could just look at a building and then draw it exactly from memory.'

'That's just because some of the noise is taken out; some parts of their brains are wired, like, wrong, so other parts develop,' said Einstein. 'But doing hard sums is not a super-power, unless I missed that comic. Autistic kids may be different to us, but they're still human. Disease destroys us. Simple as that.'

'What about bacteria then?' said Maxie.

'What about it?'

'You know, like in our guts. That's not part of us, it's other living beings. But without it we'd get sick and

468

couldn't digest things properly. There are lots of parasites in the world that help the creatures they live on.'

'Here's the science part,' said Einstein sarcastically. 'Bacteria in our guts can't turn us into living mobile phones.'

'Not bacteria,' said Maxie, refusing to be fazed by Einstein. 'The *disease*. The disease, that you and everyone else know sod all about.'

'Are you saying the disease might be some sort of parasite?' said Einstein.

'It could be, couldn't it?' said Blue. 'It came out of the jungle with them Stone Age tribesmen, the Inmathger. You saw the show. They passed it on to the people who were studying them, the Promithios scientists, who brought it back here, only they didn't realize because it was a new disease they'd never come across before. Nobody knew they had it for ages. So what if it was some new sort of parasite, and it's the parasites that are talking to each other, you know, the way some insects can communicate with each other?'

'If it was a parasite it would have shown up,' said Einstein. 'We'd have seen it under the microscopes.'

Blue looked at the bench where Einstein had been working. He recognized the transparent plastic box that Einstein had used to pick up some of the grey stuff that had come out of Seamus when Ollie killed him. The stuff had stopped moving and looked just like grey sludge.

'You could be wrong,' said Blue. 'You're not the real Einstein after all, are you? Face it. You're just a kid, mate.'

'It's not possible,' Einstein protested. 'It can't be. I mean, it's a great story. You should sell it to Hollywood. Oh no, I forgot, Hollywood doesn't exist any more. That is *not* how the world works.'

469

'Well, the world has changed, geek-boy; it has jumped up and bitten us in the arse. You said it yourself, Hollywood don't exist no more. Who saw that one coming? Before all this, would you have said that every adult in the world was gonna get wiped out? No. Except the ones that fancied theirselves as cannibal zombies? No. Nothing's real until it happens. And this *has* happened and we've got to get on it. We've got to solve the problems it's given us before it's too late. So maybe you need to keep a more open mind.'

Before Einstein could respond to Blue they were interrupted by the arrival of Maeve, who had Ella and Monkey-Boy with her.

'Whassup?' said Blue. 'Everything all right?'

'Yeah.' Maeve sat at the workbench and the little kids climbed up on to stools on either side of her. 'Can I talk to you about something?'

'Sure. What?'

'Maxie knows about this.'

'I do?' Maxie looked intrigued.

'Yeah, about me leaving.'

'You're leaving?' said Blue.

'In the morning. Us three and Robbie.'

'You serious?' Blue stared into Maeve's eyes, trying to see if there was any trace of doubt there. He didn't know the girl well. She wasn't one of his Morrisons crew; none of the kids leaving were.

'Deadly serious,' said Maeve. 'We've been over and over it.'

'But where you gonna go?'

'We're getting out of town. Heading west. To the countryside. Out the way you went, past Heathrow. We'll keep going until we find somewhere safe.'

470

'You might keep going till you fall off the edge of the world, girl.'

Maeve smiled. 'If that's what it takes.'

Blue looked at Maxie, who shrugged.

'I can't stop them,' she said. 'But I wish you weren't going, Maeve.'

'Oh, come on!' said Blue. 'Four of you? Two little ones? Another kid who can hardly walk. You won't stand a chance.'

'It's a risk we're willing to take,' said Maeve quietly. 'We've had enough of London. All this . . .'

Blue turned his attention to Monkey-Boy.

'You sure about this?' he said.

Monkey-Boy looked very scared. He gripped on to Maeve's jumper.

'I'm not leaving Maeve,' he said. 'She looks after me.'

'And I'm sticking with Monkey-Boy,' said Ella. 'We're a team. There's nothing for me here.'

'What about your brother?' said Maxie. 'What about Sam?'

'He's dead,' said Ella quietly. 'I'm never going to see him again. And I don't want to stay here in London,' she went on. 'It just reminds me of him. We got so far, we did so well, and then . . .'

Blue didn't know what to say. He went round the bench and gave Ella and Maeve a quick hug. What he'd seen of Maeve he liked. She was quiet and serious and calm. A good kid to have around.

'It's your decision, doc,' he said. 'But we could do with you here. What with you knowing about medicine and all.'

'I don't know half as much as him,' Maeve said, throwing a look at Einstein. 'I think you'll do just fine without me.'

471

She stood up and gave Maxie a little kiss.

'I miss you already,' she said. 'But one day . . . I'm sure we'll all meet again. In better times, yeah?'

'I hope you're right,' said Maxie. 'I hope there's an amazing new life waiting for you out there. Send us a card, won't you?'

'I'll send flowers,' said Maeve. 'From the countryside. Freshly cut and smelling of . . . I don't know – life.'

'Good luck,' said Blue, and as he said it the whole lab was lit a brilliant white as lightning flashed in the sky overhead. 'Better times.'

92

David was stomping down the stairs from the royal bedroom at Buckingham Palace. In a *bad* mood. The storm had passed, but he still had a headache. Thunder *always* gave him a headache. So did problems, and this was a night of problems.

The last surviving members of the royal family, whom he kept in the room upstairs, had gone weird on him. They were standing there, frozen like dummies, holding their arms out as if they expected him to give them a tip. He'd been looking after them and keeping them alive in the hope that he could eventually use them to take over London. They were his mascots, the symbols of his authority. At least that was the plan. He was beginning to wonder if it was a huge waste of time and he shouldn't just use them for target practice instead. He'd been tearing into his quite frankly useless head of security, Pod, when they'd been interrupted by one of David's guards, who said he had a visitor. A visitor who wouldn't give his name.

Who the hell came visiting in the middle of the bloody night?

Some *idiot* probably.

Bringing more problems.

The world was full of idiots.

'It could be Nicola, or someone from the Houses of Parliament,' said Pod, plodding along behind, trying to keep up with David, who was walking angrily fast.

'Yes, and it could be Father Christmas,' said David.

'Wrong time of year,' said Pod, who had no sense of humour.

'Well, the Easter Bunny then,' said David.

Pod chuckled. *Idiot.*

David pulled open the door to his study and went in.

Oh. It was *him* then. The weird boy from the museum. Another born idiot. What was his name? Peter, or Richard or something. John?

'Yeah, hi, Paul,' said Pod as he came in. 'How goes it?'

Paul. That was it. He looked terrible. Thin and wasted. Soaking wet, black hair plastered to his white face. Shaking. Eyes red and bloodshot. Feverish. David hoped he wasn't going to infect them all with some boring disease.

'You're back then,' he said. 'What a lovely surprise.'

'Yes.'

'So what happened? The last we saw of you, you were going back to the museum to stir things up a little.'

'Did you let the strangers out of the cellar, dude?' said Pod. 'Did they, like, attack?'

'Yes.' Paul nodded. Didn't look like he was going to say anything more.

'Cool,' said Pod.

'So what happened?' said David impatiently.

'Some others turned up.'

'Other grown-ups?'

'No. Kids. A whole load of them. Good fighters. They killed my sickos.'

'Epic fail,' said Pod, and then he frowned. 'That was the

same night that Maxie and Blue and the north London guys left here,' he said to David. 'You don't reckon . . .'

David sat down at his desk. Oh, that would be a great joke, wouldn't it? If those bastards had double-screwed him. He was trying to help – why couldn't anyone see that? He was trying to unite all the kids in London under his rule so that they could be one single force. But as long as any of them held out, like Justin and his nerds at the museum, that was never going to happen, was it? He'd hoped to show them how vulnerable they were, how much they needed him, by getting Paul to set up an attack. And if the bloody Holloway kids had rescued them, then . . .

'I heard those names,' said Paul, who was dripping on to the carpet.

'Brilliant,' said David. 'Just brilliant. This night gets better and better. We should celebrate with a cup of cold sick. So what do you want now then? A medal? World's biggest screw-up?'

'I had to leave the museum,' said Paul. 'There were too many of them. They were too strong for me. They were going to kill me.'

They had the right idea, thought David. This guy was a total waste of space.

'Yeah?' he said. 'And what exactly do you want me to do about it? Quite frankly you look unwell. I'm not sure I want you here stinking the place up.'

'I can help you,' said Paul.

'*You?* I very much doubt it.'

'You have sickos upstairs.'

'That's no secret.'

'I can help you with them. I know sickos. I used to look

after them at the museum. Ones we kept in a cage. I can look after yours.'

'I already have people to do that. People who aren't crawling with germs.'

'I can help,' said Paul. He was pleading now, *pathetic* really.

'So you keep saying. But tell me in one short sentence exactly how you can help me.'

'I can talk to them.'

93

Lately everything had started to change. Brooke wondered if things were falling apart. It had all begun with the arrival of DogNut. Before that, for the last year, they'd been getting sorted, making the museum a safe place to live, finding food, growing food, learning what they could about their new world. It had felt like things had slowly been getting better. Tiny steps, sure, but going in the right direction at least.

And then DogNut had showed up out of nowhere and it had all started to come undone. First she'd tried to go back with him across London, and that had turned into a disaster. DogNut killed. Her oldest friend Courtney killed. Robbie wounded. Brooke herself wounded, cut across the face by a crazy mother. And then Paul had flipped out and let the sickos out of the lower level. And then Einstein going off to get supplies. Half the kids getting massacred . . .

All those kids not here any more. A small selfish part of her thought that there would be more food to go round. That's what happened to you. You grew hard and cold. All that mattered was survival.

She was sitting on the steps in front of the museum, making the most of the warmth from the sun. It was spring: leaves were opening on the trees. Summer soon.

Brooke sighed.

Things always seemed better in the summer. There was more to eat. It wasn't so cold and wet. Winter was one long nightmare. The images she had in her mind of the winter weren't great. Burning anything they could find to keep warm. Scraping the last bits of food out of cans. Breaking the ice on the water tanks in the roof. Dark most of the time.

No. Winter had nothing going for it.

She closed her eyes, felt the sun on her face. Her forehead ached beneath the bandage. She knew that sunlight was supposed to help you to heal, but she wasn't ready to show her scar to the world just yet. It was a mess under there, black and yellow and scabby, her skin all pulled and twisted out of shape.

How had it happened that she'd gone from being the golden girl to this? Miss Predator-face . . .

How had any of it happened? So fast. The world had turned and it had flipped into chaos.

She hated it when the darkness crept into her mind like this. She knew she should try to concentrate on the positive. And some good things had happened lately. She'd found Maxie and Blue and the others. They were good news. That wouldn't have happened without DogNut. The kids that had died recently had at least been replaced by new ones.

Good fighters.

Though not good enough to save the kids that had been attacked in the church . . .

Stop it.

She heard voices. Arguing. Down by the fence where the little gatehouse was. Where there were always at least two kids on duty.

Sounded like somebody was trying to get in.

Brooke opened her eyes. Squinted over, trying to see what was going on. No good. The gatehouse was in the way. She got up and stretched. Rubbed her aching behind. The stone steps were pretty cold, despite the sun on them. She walked on stiff legs down towards the gates.

There were four boys standing on the other side of the fence. Older ones. They weren't from around here. She didn't recognize them. Or did she . . .?

The boy in the middle . . .

As she got closer, Brooke felt her throat tighten.

It couldn't be. This wasn't real. It couldn't be *him*. She must be imagining it. She walked closer still. The boy turned to look at her. There was no flash of recognition from him.

But there was no doubt now because, as he'd turned, he'd shown the other side of his face. The ruined side.

'Ed . . .?'

He frowned at her now.

'Ed? Is it really you?'

He was still frowning, not recognizing her. Had she really changed that much? He was *still* Ed. Taller, bigger, older, thinner . . . but Ed all right.

'It's me,' she said, trying not to let her voice go pathetic. 'Brooke . . .'

His face opened up into a smile.

'Jesus, Brooke . . . what happened to you?'

'Shit happened to me.'

He looked her up and down. It was true she'd changed a lot, let the bleach grow out of her hair, cut it short, got rid of her tacky clothes and taken this old dress from the V&A . . . and the bandage.

479

Of course. The bandage. No wonder he hadn't recognized her.

'Open the gates,' she said to the two sentries. 'They're OK.'

The boys unlocked the gates and let Ed and his three friends in.

'This is Kyle, Will and Macca,' Ed said, and Brooke hugged him, crushing him against her chest.

'Bloody hell, Ed,' she said. 'I can't believe it.'

'Me neither.' Ed gently touched her back. 'You weren't who we were expecting to find here at all.'

Brooke pulled away from him and put her fingers to his scar, traced the line of it. It was both worse and better than she remembered it. Worse because in her imagination she had made it smaller and made him more handsome, and better because now it really didn't matter to her.

She could see him looking at her bandage. She had a million questions, and she was sure he did too, but for the moment neither of them could say anything. Ed's three friends were introducing themselves to the sentries and *they* were at least talking.

Brooke took Ed's hand and led him away from them. She kissed him lightly on the lips. He was awkward, stiff and embarrassed.

'I've missed you so much, Ed,' she said. Ed shrugged. Didn't know where to look.

'Really?' he said. 'It's been a long time.'

Brooke wondered what she could do to get him to relax. When they'd been split up during the big fire things hadn't been too good between them.

Because of his scar.

How disgusted she'd been by it.

480

Well, a lot had happened since then.

Without saying anything she unwound the bandage from her head. It was like she was undressing in front of him. As she removed it, she saw a look come into his eyes, the same look she must have given him when he was first wounded.

'That looks recent,' he said, and she nodded. 'The pain goes away eventually,' he added. 'Most of the time.'

Brooke began to cry. Started fumbling to put the bandage back on. Ed helped her. He seemed happier to be doing something. It was a distraction. She'd come on too strongly. Should have taken her time. He must be freaked out by all this.

'What are you doing here anyway, Ed?' she asked. 'Who were you looking for? Who were you expecting to find?'

She knew the answer. It was going to be DogNut. But she didn't know how she was going to tell him the bad news.

'We've got some other kids with us,' Ed explained. 'But they've stayed back where it's safe until we've checked everything out.'

'What kids?'

'We were helping them, well, helping one of them, to find his sister.'

'And you think she might be here? What's her name?'

'Ella.'

Brooke put a hand to her mouth, shook her head slowly.

'Not Sam,' she said. 'Please say it's not Sam.'

'Yeah, it's Sam. Why? Do you know Ella? Is she here then?'

'She *was* here. If you'd only come a day earlier. She left this morning.'

Ed looked confused, trying to take this all in.

'What do you mean, she left?' he asked.

One of Ed's friends came over, the one he'd introduced as Kyle, a big lump of a kid with a bony head and big ears.

'Come on, boss,' he said. 'You can get loved up later. Let's get inside, yeah?'

'In a minute,' Ed snapped, and Kyle raised his eyebrows, surprised at Ed's anger. 'Can't you see I'm talking here?'

'Yeah, sorry, boss.' Kyle backed away and returned to the gatehouse.

'I don't understand,' said Ed, his voice shaking. 'Where's she gone?'

Brooke told him. How Maeve had taken Ella and the others and headed for the countryside. Ed became more and more agitated the more he heard, looking off down the road as if he might see them.

'I need to go after them,' he said, gabbling, his mind racing. 'Sam's not going to take this. If you knew what he's been through. We need to get supplies. And I'll need to go back and tell Sam. Jesus, how long ago was this? What sort of start did they get? If we hurry . . .'

'Ed . . . Ed . . .' Brooke put her hand on his arm. 'Slow down. You can't just go charging off. You'll never catch them. They've been gone ages. You'll need to properly plan . . .'

Ed sagged, deflated, like someone had just punched him in the gut. For a moment he looked like a little boy, a very tired and miserable little boy. Broken. Then he shook it off. Sighed. Straightened up. Forced all emotion out of his twisted face.

'Story of my life,' he said flatly. 'I should have known this was never going to end.'

Brooke hugged him. Wanted to make it right for him.

And in that instant it struck her quite forcefully that she loved him.

But she had to tell him the worst.

'I've got more bad news, Ed,' she said. 'I'm sorry.'

She felt him tense.

'DogNut,' she said.

'DogNut?' Ed's voice was flat. 'He was here?'

'I thought that's who you were looking for, to be honest.'

'He found you then?'

'Yeah.' Brooke wondered how to tell him. In the end she knew there was only one way. 'He's dead,' she said. 'I'm so sorry, Ed.'

Ed's body began to shake. He sagged and buried his face in her shoulder.

'Him and Courtney,' said Brooke, stroking his back. 'They were trying to get back to the Tower. I was going with them. We were ambushed. It was during the day. We never expected it. They killed DogNut and Courtney. They did this to my face. Ella and Sam's friends rescued me. It's a long, long story, Ed, but I guess I'm going to have to tell you all of it.'

'Not now,' said Ed. 'I've had enough for now.'

They stood there like that, arms round each other, Ed's friends looking on awkwardly, and the darkness of their world seemed to settle all around them.

Finally Ed spoke.

'What am I going to tell Sam . . .?'

94

Maeve, Robbie, Ella and Monkey-Boy were in high spirits. They could not believe their luck. The car was running smoothly and they hadn't seen a single grown-up all morning.

It had taken them ages to get on to the M4. First they'd had to skirt all round the museum so that nobody saw or heard the car. Then, from what Blue had told them, they knew they couldn't actually join the motorway until after the roundabout where the bridge had collapsed. So Robbie had picked a route that kept close by. The only problem was that so many of the streets were blocked. There were buildings tumbled over by fire; there were fallen lamp posts and wrecked vehicles. Twice they'd got lost and ended up back where they started, but eventually they'd found their way on to the motorway out near Brentford.

Robbie wasn't the best driver in the world. The car was an automatic so he didn't have to worry about gears, but he still kept getting muddled between the brake and the accelerator, and they would jerk and lurch about in the road. The last thing he wanted was to crash their precious car so he went painfully slowly, and once they'd hit the motorway he hardly sped up at all. He was like an old man out for a Sunday drive. They crawled along, Robbie hunched over the steering wheel and squinting through the grubby windscreen. They'd cleaned it as best they could, but the washer was empty.

Ella kept leaning forward to check their speed and she'd never seen the dial show anything faster than ten miles an hour. It wasn't a difficult calculation. They'd started with enough petrol for fifty miles. That's what the display had said once they'd got going. Fifty miles at ten miles an hour would take them five hours, and that was without all the mucking about getting on to the motorway.

'We'll use less petrol if we go slow,' Robbie had explained when Ella questioned him about it.

Ella had been very nervous at first, as they'd nosed round the backstreets, trying a road, giving up, turning back, almost getting stuck. She'd been worried that at any moment they'd be attacked by grown-ups, but as the day had gone on and they hadn't seen any, not one, she'd relaxed. The others relaxed too. She'd watched Maeve and Robbie. How Maeve had started out with her shoulders up by her ears and her head tight on her neck, and slowly she'd loosened up. Like she was melting.

Robbie too. He'd hissed and groaned at first, his bad leg hurting him. Now, though, he seemed comfortable. And every so often he would touch Maeve's leg and she would smile at him.

He had a thing for Maeve. It was so obvious it was funny. Ella noticed these things. She hoped they weren't going to get all gooey and cut her and Monkey-Boy out. She didn't like it when people got girlfriends or boyfriends. They changed.

Seeing the two of them relax made her feel a whole lot

better, though. Maybe they were going to make it. Maybe they really *were* going to escape.

Ella looked out of the window as trees and buildings slipped past. It was over a year since she'd been in a car. She'd forgotten what it was like. She remembered long drives with her mum and dad and Sam, listening to a story CD. Harry Potter or Alex Rider . . . Jacqueline Wilson if she could get her way.

As they moved further along the motorway, it seemed that the whole world was empty. They passed the signs to Heathrow Airport and Maeve said how amazed she was that Blue and the others had walked this far.

Yeah, thought Ella, *they were probably walking faster than Robbie was driving*.

And then they passed under the M25 and Maeve cheered.

'What's the M25?' Monkey-Boy asked, seeing that it was important to Maeve.

'It's a motorway that goes all the way round London,' Maeve explained. 'A huge ring road. As far as I'm concerned, it's the boundary, where London stops and the rest of the world begins.'

Despite what Maeve said it wasn't proper countryside yet. There were still buildings here and there, but you could go further and further now without seeing any, and there were fields and woods and lakes.

'Are we there already?' said Monkey-Boy, staring out of the window on his side. 'Is this the countryside?'

'Kind of,' said Maeve, and she turned round to ruffle his hair.

'I'm getting car sick.'

'Yeah?' Maeve laughed. 'Well, if that's all we've got to worry about we're going to be OK.'

'We're gonna have to stop soon,' said Robbie. 'The petrol's saying we're nearly empty. Maybe we should find somewhere to camp down while it's still light.'

'It'll be hours before it gets dark,' said Maeve.

'Yeah. But we'll have run out of fuel long before then. I don't fancy sleeping in the car. We need to find somewhere safe while we can still drive and then figure out what we do next.'

'I guess we should turn off the next chance we get then,' said Maeve. 'It's a shame. Just when we were doing so well.'

'Yeah,' said Robbie. 'No sign of any settlements yet. I was hoping we'd have seen some other kids by now. There must *be* some out this way.'

'We may still find something,' said Maeve.

They came to a junction and turned off. Ella read the sign. Junction seven. The turn-off to somewhere called Slough. Ella made a face. She didn't like the sound of Slough. It was a horrible name to call a town.

'I really don't want to spend the night in Slough,' she said.

'Me either,' said Robbie, and he laughed. 'We'll avoid it. Find somewhere else. I want to steer clear of any towns.'

They took the slip road and looped round over the motorway. Maeve checked the map she'd brought along and directed Robbie away from Slough, going in a big circle and eventually back over the motorway again. They were quickly on narrow roads among trees and hedges. There was lots of water around, small rivers and lakes. Ella felt better now. This was what she'd been expecting.

'Here we go,' Maeve said. 'This looks perfect. There's an island in the middle of the river here, with a hotel on it. It'll be a perfect place to hole up for the night. I can tell from the name.'

'Why?' asked Robbie. 'What's it called?'

'Monkey Island,' she said, and turned to share the joke with Monkey-Boy and Ella. 'What do you think of that?'

'Sounds great,' said Monkey-Boy. 'Will there be real monkeys?'

'I doubt it.'

'I hope not,' said Ella, remembering the attack in Regent's Park, the diseased chimpanzees, poor little Joel . . .

She fingered her new gold necklace that she had picked up on her trip to the Victoria & Albert Museum. It comforted her, knowing she had this beautiful thing round her neck.

It took them a few minutes to find the hotel, Ella and Robbie both nervously checking the petrol gauge every few seconds. When they arrived Ella saw that you could only get to the island over a footbridge that led from the car park. They parked the Range Rover and sat there taking in the silence for a while, nobody wanting to be the first to leave the safe cocoon of the car. Staring at the river that was sparkling in the early afternoon light.

'What do you reckon?' said Maeve eventually. 'Shall we go check it out?'

'Let's do it,' said Robbie.

They all climbed out of the car. Sniffed the sharp air. There was the smell of the river and the nearby trees and grass. It smelt good. Clean. Ella knew what grown-ups smelt like, and it wasn't like this. It all seemed very peaceful. There were birds singing, but there was no sign of any human activity. No grown-ups. No children.

Robbie and Maeve both had swords, and Robbie had a crutch that he hopped along on. Maeve led the four of them over the metal footbridge to the island.

'I been thinking,' said Robbie, looking down at the

gurgling water. 'There might be a boat here. We could go upriver on it. Be safe from any sickos that way. What river is this anyway?'

'It's the Thames, I think,' said Maeve.

'The Thames? You're joking me. It don't look nothing like what it does in town.' He whooped up at the sky. 'Everything's better in the countryside!'

There was a wide lawn, completely overgrown, the grass up to their thighs, and past it there was a fancy old hotel, all white, with columns and arched windows. It was like something out of one of the BBC programmes that Ella's mum used to watch, where the women wore bonnets and the men wore top hats. It didn't look as if it had been vandalized at all, or broken into. There was still no sign of any human activity anywhere. They'd found a magic dream place. A summer island. They could live here as a family. With Maeve and Robbie as Mum and Dad and Ella and Monkey-Boy as their children.

'Let's go and check in,' said Maeve, and she broke away, running through the grass. One by one the others joined in. As she ran, the grass whipping at her, Ella felt suddenly wild and free.

They'd done it. They'd escaped London. She could forget all about everything that had gone before. As if none of it had ever happened, as if all those dead people – family and friends – had never existed. They were just characters in a story she'd been reading. That's all. And now she could close the book and start a new story.

No. Not just a story.

This was the beginning of a new life.

She was never going back.

95

'We should lock this new sicko in the lorry,' said Einstein. 'Where we kept the other ones.'

'No,' said Brooke. 'Ed says this one's different. We can't treat him like an animal.'

'We'll see.'

They'd been arguing ever since Ed had left to go and pick up the rest of his party and Brooke had announced that he was going to be bringing back some sort of grown-up with him.

There was a tense atmosphere in the central hall at the museum. Nobody knew quite what to expect. Most of the kids had been told to stay in the minerals gallery for their own safety, but waiting downstairs was a small welcome party – Brooke, Einstein, Boggle and Justin from the museum. Blue, Maxie, Achilleus and Paddy from the new arrivals, along with the three warehouse kids, Fish-Face, Skinner and Trinity. Justin had wanted to keep them out of the way as well, but they'd insisted on being there. They seemed agitated and excited. Kept mumbling among themselves. Fish-Face, in particular, was on edge, making little birdlike movements, holding her head as if listening, her long neck bent, her wide-set eyes staring into the distance.

Brooke wasn't sure about the Twisted Kids. They scared

her. Since finding out that they claimed to be able to communicate with each other without actually talking she was even more unsure of them. She wondered if they could read her mind and had to be careful to keep them out of her thoughts, in case they saw how she felt about them. She tried to think only about Ed . . . and the sicko he was bringing with him.

'How's he different?' said Achilleus, who had missed the first part of the argument.

'He's clever apparently,' said Brooke. 'He can talk.'

'Yeah,' said Achilleus. 'Just like Seamus and his dumb-arse losers out at the warehouse. Ollie had the right idea about them.' He spun his new spear in his hands. 'I'm keeping the Gay Bulge handy. You know what they say? The only good grown-up is a dead grown-up.'

Brooke didn't like Achilleus. Since she'd been attacked she'd lost her confidence when it came to boys. Before she could make them do whatever she wanted. Now . . . She was a freak like the Twisted Kids. And Achilleus, well, he was a bit of a mystery to her. She felt that even before he would have been somehow shielded from her powers. She wasn't going to let him get the upper hand, though.

'This grown-up's bare important,' she protested. 'He can help us.'

'How?'

'I don't know how. I don't know anything about him, do I? This is all new to me. But if Ed says he's important, and we mustn't hurt him, then . . .'

'Oh, Ed says this, Ed says that, Ed says kiss my arse,' said Achilleus dismissively. 'Who's this Ed anyway?'

'I know Ed,' said Justin. 'Ed's all right. If he says this one's important then . . .'

'Yeah, well, whatever *Ed* says,' Achilleus interrupted. 'If I have any doubts about this douche then the Gay Bulge is going to finish the argument, OK?' He lifted the spear to his face and kissed the blade.

'What you gonna do to him, Akkie?' said Paddy.

'What do you think, Paddywhack? I'm gonna rip his diseased belly open and wear his arse as a hat.'

'Yes, thank you, Sir Lancelot,' said Einstein sarcastically. 'I'm sure we all feel a lot safer knowing you're watching over us.'

Achilleus sneered at him, but said nothing.

'We'll give him the benefit of the doubt,' said Maxie, who seemed to be on Brooke's side. She and Blue had helped Brooke to make a bedroom of sorts for the sicko in the insect gallery, which was reasonably small and could be safely locked. They'd hauled in a bed and found a bucket and some food and water for him.

They had no idea what to expect, though. All Brooke knew was that she trusted Ed.

Ollie was standing on the balcony near the minerals gallery, looking down at the doors. Just like everyone else he was unsure about all this. And, as ever, he was ready for anything. His sling was stuck on his belt and he was crunching three steel balls against each other in his left hand, moving them around so that they rolled over his curled fingers. The cut on his face where the mother had scratched him was itching slightly and he resisted the urge to touch it. It was healing, thank God, and hadn't become infected.

He became aware of a movement and felt something touch his other hand where it rested on the stone top of the balustrade. He turned. It was Lettis, her face pale, dark rings round her eyes, which were wide and glistening. Her expression was serious, unchanging, and he wondered if she would ever smile again. He wondered if she would ever *speak* again as well. All she did was spend hours hunched over her journal, though she would never let anyone see what she was writing. Not even Chris Marker in the library.

She looked deep into Ollie's face and he held her hand tight. It felt small and dry and cold.

'It's all right,' he said. 'We'll be all right. I won't let you down again. There's no need to be scared any more.'

And then more kids appeared, a group of the smaller ones. He recognized them all – Blu-Tack Bill, Zohra and Froggie, Wiki, Jibber-jabber; the only ones missing were Ella and Monkey-Boy. They formed a ring round Lettis, as if they might protect her, though they were nearly all younger and smaller than her.

'Aren't you supposed to be waiting in the gallery?' he said.

'We wanted to see,' said Wiki.

Ollie was about to say that it might not be safe when he remembered what he'd just told Lettis.

'Well, keep still and keep quiet,' he said. 'I guess I'm responsible for all of you now.'

'We can look after ourselves,' said Jibber-jabber and Ollie smiled. Maybe they could. He felt Lettis squeeze his hand tighter and saw that she was staring intently at the doors.

They were opening and someone was coming in from outside.

'He's here,' said Skinner, who was pacing about nervously.

'Freak of the week,' Achilleus sang, just loudly enough for the rest of them to hear, and Paddy giggled.

But it was only Jackson who appeared in the doorway.

'They're coming through the gates now,' she said.

'What's he look like?' said Brooke.

'Can't see. He's under a blanket.'

'This is crazy,' said Achilleus. 'I tell you I'm gonna merk him.'

'You'll do nothing,' snapped Einstein. 'If this father is all that Ed claims he is, he might be a big help with our research.'

'*A big help with our research.*' Achilleus impersonated Einstein, making him sound lispy and wet, and then he spat on the floor. 'Stupid nerd.'

And then Ed walked in with Kyle, who was carrying an axe. Brooke felt a stab of longing for Ed. Her emotions had been so shredded she was a wreck; her moods had been pinging about all over the place like a kid who'd drunk too much Coke.

She heard Trinity say something that she didn't understand. Wondered if it was aimed at her.

'Two scarred faces. Rule of three. There'll be a third. You'll see.'

Behind Ed came a hunched figure, with Ed's friends from earlier walking on either side of him. He was shrouded in a blanket. She could see his skinny legs sticking out underneath. At first Brooke thought he was wearing green trousers, and then, with a little jolt, she realized that his legs were bare and his skin was covered in green mould.

Behind them came a little girl carrying a violin case and two small boys, one with fair hair, the other with a mad shock of dark hair. He was wearing what looked like a dress with a sleeveless leather jacket over it.

'Jesus Christ,' said Achilleus. 'Here come the clowns. The circus is in town.'

They came through and waited on the black and white tiled floor, looking round at the massive dinosaur fossils. Brooke went over to them. Smiled at Ed.

'We've got somewhere ready for him,' she said. 'But not everyone likes the idea. You have to promise he's not gonna be dangerous.'

'I can't promise anything.' Ed wasn't smiling back. 'But he's my problem. I'll watch him.'

The little fair-haired boy came over to her. He looked like he'd been crying. This must be Sam. Small Sam, Ella had called him, and Brooke could see why. She felt desperately sorry for him.

'Is it true that my sister was here?' he asked. 'She's called Ella.'

'Yeah,' said Brooke. 'I know. She *was* here, darling. She's all right. Don't worry about her. She's gone, though. She wanted to get out of London.'

'I told you, Sam.' Ed sounded tired.

Sam looked suddenly cross. He swiped at Ed's arm.

'We should have come last night,' he shouted. 'I wanted to come.'

'We couldn't, Sam, you know we couldn't. It was too dangerous and we were all too shattered. If I'd known we were going to miss her, of course I'd have tried to get here, but we didn't know. How could we have known? It's just bad timing. Bad luck.'

Sam sat down on the floor and his head dropped. 'What am I going to do?'

'We'll find her, Sam.' Ed tried to pull the little boy up. Sam wasn't having any of it, though. He struggled against Ed.

'Don't worry, we'll find her,' Ed went on. 'Not today. But when we're ready we'll go after her. We've got to get ourselves sorted first. Find out where she might have gone.'

There were tears running down Sam's face. This was too much for Brooke. She didn't want to think about it any longer. She turned her attention to the man, who was covered by the blanket.

'Does he have to stay under that?' she asked.

'He doesn't like the light.'

Kyle lifted up the side of the blanket.

'Oi, Wormy,' he said. 'You want to come out now and say hello to these nice people?'

The blanket shook. There were some muffled words from underneath it. He really could talk then.

'He don't want to show his face,' said Kyle, and then Achilleus came striding over. He gave Ed and Kyle a dirty look.

'If he's coming in here we want to see him,' he snarled, and snatched the blanket off.

Brooke winced and took a step back as the man was revealed. Apart from a green bowler hat he was naked and covered all over with more of the green mould, along with the familiar lumps and boils of the diseased. His long arms dangled at his sides and she saw that he had very long yellow fingernails. He looked shy, blinking, but also a little sly, peering out of the corners of his pale eyes as he took in his surroundings. Finally he looked at Brooke and licked his lips.

'Butters,' said Achilleus, lifting his spearhead towards the man.

Then there was a shout from across the hall and the sound of running feet. It was Fish-Face. She was tearing towards the man, her arms held out in front of her.

496

A look of recognition followed by great sadness came over the Green Man's face and he held his own arms out towards her.

Fish-Face was sobbing. She ran into his arms, crying, 'Daddy, my daddy.'

Achilleus gave a snort of laughter.

'Now that's something you don't see every day,' he said.

Ella was awake in the dark. The faint glow of the moon through the curtains did little more than fill the blackness with vague grey shapes. The larger blob was an armchair. The lumpy shape lying on some cushions on the floor was Robbie. The dark square against the wall must be the television.

Ella could hear breathing. She had gone to sleep sandwiched between Monkey-Boy and Maeve on a big double bed. It reassured her, knowing that Maeve was sleeping next to them. Like when Ella had bad dreams when she was little and would creep into Mum and Dad's bed in the middle of the night. If only it wasn't so dark. She didn't like the dark. She hoped that her eyes would adjust to the light and show her more of the room, but she soon figured out that this was as good as it was going to get. She had to try to get back to sleep.

Something had woken her, though. Something in her head had told her to fight off sleep and open her eyes. *What was it?* A sound maybe? She listened. Apart from the steady breathing at her side it was absolutely quiet. She concentrated, trying to remember what had come to her in her dreams. If not a sound, then what? A movement? Had Maeve stirred?

Ella looked at the grey bulk on the mattress. She could just make out the steady rise and fall of a sleeping body, but nothing more. *Go to sleep.* If there was anything wrong one of the bigger kids would have woken. She curled up a little and closed her eyes. Felt sleep creeping up on her. Went over the events of the day. Leaving the museum in the morning. Saying her goodbyes to her friends. All the crying. Even her new friends had cried, Wiki and Jibber-jabber. Soppy boys. Then the car journey, watching the buildings go by, and then the trees and the fields. The countryside. Finding the hotel on the little island. Smashing a window to get in. Exploring. How happy they'd been to find that nobody had been in here for months. No sign of any grown-ups. They'd even found some boxes stuffed with food hidden in the cellar. They'd taken this as a good sign and decided to definitely camp here for the night. All in the same bedroom. A *suite* Maeve had called it.

As they'd settled down to sleep, Maeve had said that she couldn't really believe it. 'I can't take it in,' she'd said. 'This morning we were stuck in the museum, and now look at us.'

'We shouldn't relax too much,' Robbie had said, trying to impress Maeve by sounding all adult and sensible. Honestly, he was *so* obvious. 'We should take it in turns to stand guard, just in case.'

That had made Ella feel very safe. Knowing that someone would be watching over her. She couldn't even remember going to sleep. It had happened so fast. She must have been tireder than she'd realized.

She would have slept all night until the sun came up if something hadn't woken her . . .

A smell . . .

A smell had woken her . . .

She could smell it now. Something thick and earthy and rotten. Something familiar. A smell that had haunted her nightmares for months.

Where was it coming from?

If there was any danger one of the bigger kids would have woken up . . .

Her stomach fluttered. They were supposed to be on guard. Robbie and Maeve. Keeping watch. But she'd seen Robbie asleep on the floor and Maeve was on the bed next to her.

Ella was wide awake now, her heart racing and her head buzzing.

'Maeve?' she whispered. 'I'm scared.'

The body next to her didn't stir.

'Maeve, please,' she said, louder this time, her fingers fiddling with her necklace. 'I can smell something.'

She could feel panic rising in her chest. She knew that smell too well. It was the smell of grown-ups. Grown-ups who no longer washed, or changed their clothes, or used the toilet properly, grown-ups whose bodies were a mess of sores and boils, leaking pus and blood and spit and worse.

But where was the smell coming from?

It seemed close.

She put out a hand to shake Maeve. Her body felt hot, and she was wearing some sort of heavy, scratchy material that Ella didn't remember.

And she was sticky and damp.

Now Ella knew where the smell was coming from. The body on the mattress. It stank. She shrank away from it, scuttling on her back. What had happened to Maeve? And where was Monkey-Boy? He was no longer in the bed. She flopped off the edge of the mattress and slithered across the room to Robbie and started to shake him.

'Robbie,' she whimpered. 'Wake up. Wake up! There's something in the room. Please wake up. I don't think it's Maeve. I don't know where she is. Robbie, please wake up. I'm scared . . .'

But Robbie was cold and still. Ella groped up his body, feeling for his face. She would have to force his eyes open. Scream in his ear . . .

But when her searching hands reached Robbie's neck there was no more of him.

His head was missing.

Ella screamed and, as she did so, the figure on the mattress slowly rose. It was too big, much too big to be Maeve. Too big to be a kid. It was a grown-up, a father, its eyes staring, its mouth a black hole. It put its feet over the side of the bed and stood up.

Fear snatched the voice from Ella's throat and she darted across the room and scrabbled in silence for the door. But where was it?

She hit the wall and felt along it. Where was the door? *Where was the door?*

She couldn't get out.

The father was lumbering closer.

No. Not like this. They should have stayed with the others. Not like this . . .

She was pressing herself against the wall. The door must be here somewhere. There had to be a way out. And then she was falling. The door had been open all along. She landed on something soft and cold and wet.

Another body.

She heard the sound of the father behind her. His feet

on the carpet, shuffling along, *sshwssh, sshwssh*. His heavy breathing. Wheezing and gurgling in his throat. Felt his hand on her ankle. Jerked her leg away.

Not like this . . .

She got up, slipping in a wet puddle. Skidded and hit the corridor wall. Carried on. It was even darker out here. All she could see was some dim light coming through a window at the far end of the corridor.

Ran towards it, the father behind her, moving faster now, moaning softly.

Not like this . . .

She came to the window; the corridor turned to the right. She went round the corner and there was a flash of light and now she screamed. A face seemed to hang in the darkness.

It was the worst face she had ever seen. Like it had been chewed up and spat out by something. The skin was torn and folded and shiny with scar tissue, the lips swollen, blistered. One eye a clouded, bloody mess, one ear missing.

And now she saw Monkey-Boy, his bloody, lifeless body held in the creature's right arm.

The creature raised its free hand and Ella felt her knees giving out, the blood draining from her head, light and sick and floating, slipping away from this world.

The hand came down.

Please . . . Not like this . . .

CHARLIE HIGSON Q&A

Charlie Higson photograph
© Andy Paradise

WHERE DID YOU GET THE IDEA FOR THE ENEMY?

I had two starting points for writing *The Enemy*. I wanted to write a book where all the adults disappear and kids have the run of the place — that's always been a great fantasy of mine. Wouldn't it be great to live in London if you could go wherever you wanted? You could live in Buckingham Palace, or go to the Tower of London and try on all the suits of armour. But I also wanted to write a scary book, different from the Young Bond series. My son is really into zombies — he's fascinated by them, but they also scare him a lot. After I'd written each chapter of the book I'd read it to him at night, in an attempt to scare him, and I kept on until I gave him nightmares!

DID YOU TAKE INSPIRATION FROM ANY OTHER BOOKS?

Yes. *I Am Legend* by Richard Matheson, which was written in the 1950s, is really the grandfather of this kind of story — about a man trying to survive when everyone else has become infected with a disease. There are also parallels with *Lord of the Flies* by William Golding, but in that book it's all about the things that would go horribly wrong if you leave kids alone by themselves. I wanted to show a world where the children had already been through that process and where they're now trying to put the world back together and establish a society without grown-ups.

DID THE STORY CHANGE MUCH FROM YOUR ORIGINAL IDEA WHILE YOU WERE WRITING IT?

It did actually. No matter how much you plan what's going to happen, when you start writing the book always takes on a life of its own. You might roughly know what's going to happen at the beginning and the end, but you don't know how you're going to get there. For instance, when I started, I didn't really know which of the kids were going to live or die. And I'd originally planned for there to be a lot more about the gang war between the two groups of children – the kids in Morrisons and the kids in Waitrose – but when I started writing I found that I wanted to move the book past that point and focus on their battle with the adults instead.

DO YOU FIND IT EASY TO KILL OFF CHARACTERS?

Yes and no. If you've decided early on that a certain character has got to go, you start to distance yourself from them. But there were other characters that I'd thought I was going to kill off, and then realized I'd become too attached and couldn't do it. But even when you've decided that you're going to get rid of someone halfway through and you manage to go through with it, you need to look back and make sure they've been given enough of a presence before that point to really make their death hit home. And that can sometimes be a bit painful. When I was doing events for Young Bond, kids would often say they really enjoyed the books but that they always knew that James was going to be all right, because he grows up to be James Bond. So with *The Enemy*, I wanted to make it clear from the start that no one was safe.

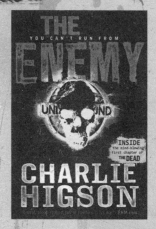